THE MAN WHO LOVED TOO MUCH

Book 2: Entendre

by John Rachel

Published by
Literary Vagabond Books
Los Angeles • Osaka
literaryvagabond.com

Table of Contents

3

Acknowledgements

Special appreciation goes out to Justin Beardsell for helping me bridge enormous generation gaps and connecting me with contemporary youth culture. Also to Ryan Paul Burke and Max Coldham Brewer for bringing me up to speed on currently popular traditional and designer recreational drugs.

As has become my heartfelt custom, I want to thank my best friend and wife, Masumi Nishida, for her encouragement and faith in me, and her magnificent ongoing role as my teacher and guide in discovering the wonders of Japan and Japanese culture, despite my resistance to achieving even a rudimentary grasp of the Japanese language.

For their inestimable, seminal contributions to my literary and intellectual development, and my tentative, fleeting grasp on reality, I also wish to express my appreciation and awe shucks to: Tom Robbins, Kurt Vonnegut, John Irving, Stanislaw Lem, Studs Terkel, E. L. Doctorow, Jerzy Kosinski, Ken Kesey, Sinclair Lewis, Ralph Ellison, Bertrand Russell, Ludwig Wittgenstein, Ralph Nader, Noam Chomsky, Naomi Klein, Chris Hedges, Howard Zinn, Bill Moyers, Malcolm X, Martin Luther King, Buddha, Jesus of Nazareth, the Dalai Lama, Nelson Mandela, Mahatma Gandhi, George Carlin, Cornell West, Thomas Kuhn, Aldous Huxley, Neil Postman, and Jared Diamond.

Inspiration ... Masumi Nishida, Rebecca Jones, Randy Calligan, Julia Isabel, Nic Pendrake, Gerald Everett Jones, Henry Martin, and Lance Collins.

Perspiration ... Gary Cambra, Alexa Wiley, Megan Stonic, Sabrina Nagel, Chelsea Nouvelle, Kamaria Wilson, Chad and Rachel Hamar, Kate Mann, Shannon McAllister, Keary Kase, my adopted mother and father (may they rest in peace), my natural mother (may she be reincarnated as a sane human being for another go at it).

Conversation ... Travis Rood, Mickey Finn, Mansur and Neelofar Langoo, Sigismund and Ursula Hadelich, Ron Ruiz, George Polley, Oliver Lamm, Russell Swider, Gary Clark, Judy Rachel, Kristi Cobb, Gilly Adkins, and Alex Malherbe.

Very special recognition is in order for the original and very tasteful cover art by my graphic artist, Archimedes Delusio III. It is a vast understatement for me to say how impressed I am with what you do, Archie, lacking optic nerves in both of your eyes. And let me also add, you sure do make a mean tofu loukaniko! Yum yum! You're going to make me fat.

Lastly, for their belief in me and their unwavering enthusiasm, thanks and butterfly kisses go out to my unapologetic publisher Literary Vagabond Books, specifically the svelte and droll head of that organization, Sybil Fairbanks, and my new editor there, Constanza Bonita Antoinette. Both of you are studies in and witness to the irrepressible power of the human imagination.

Chapter One

THE HABITS OF CREATURES
GREAT AND SMALL
2003 – 2004

Dear Ann Landers

Billy had a quirky professor Spring Term for his PSYCH 2800 - Introduction to Social Psychology class. Her name was Dr. Phyllis Hargus and in spite of the fact that her physical appearance placed her somewhere around 110 years old, she had the enthusiasm and energy of high school cheerleader.

Billy found her classes, if not informative, at least entertaining. For her often risqué lectures, Professor Hargus had a good sense of humor, a sharp tongue — which she routinely turned on herself in hilarious bouts of self-mockery referencing her dwindling sex appeal and 100% failure rate with the opposite sex — plus a seemingly infinite number of personal anecdotes to draw from. It was clear that Professor Hargus thought that the psychology of social interactions 99.9% of the time revolved around sex, but never bothered to identify what that other .1% might be. No one seemed to care.

She also had a nearly pathological obsession with the personal advice columns that typically appeared in daily newspapers and had over the years increasingly become a staple in popular magazines as well, especially men's and women's monthlies — such as Playboy and Cosmopolitan — or targeted niche publications — like Seventeen and Ebony.

She had apparently grown up reading the advice columns of Ann Landers and Dear Abby. They were twin sisters who competed fiercely for popularity and syndication in newspapers all across America during the last half of the 20th Century, and made no secret how much they hated one another.

These two legends had spawned a whole industry, so that now there was a vast number of personal help pundits, each with a following and distinctive style. Dr. Hargus had enormous respect for the whole range — Dr. Ruth, Miss Manners, Dr. Tracy, Dr. Joyce Brothers, Carolyn Hax.

But Professor Hargus also enthusiastically embraced the new breed of irreverent, caustic, outrageous columnists who delivered advice and abuse in equal proportions. Whereas Abby and Ann were gentle and genteel, Dan Savage, The Love Doctor, Dog, and a host of new print and web-based counselors were more pop pugilists than pop psychologists.

Of course, Billy thought all advice columns were crap. What little exposure he had to them, browsing through the occasional pop zines and now going online as part of his class assignments for Hargus, only made him wonder what was so special about these editorial psychologists that they were now in a position to be telling others what to do. Plus he had the suspicion that they themselves were probably pretty screwed up, prompting him to conclude that they should deal with their own issues before tackling those of everyone else.

But Dr. Hargus was convinced that advice columns were insightful portholes into the psyches of the public, and if that's what the professor had decided, Billy would suspend judgment and go through the required motions, buoyed by a blind faith that something valuable might come out of it.

One thing Billy couldn't deny. Hargus's classes were a lot of fun and never predictable. The most comical, sometimes heated discussions would arise out of some silly, seemingly innocuous question, and the advice offered by the columnist.

"Okay, class. We have an interesting one today. I'll hand these out. Please pass them along. We can read this together." Dr. Hargus took a couple big handfuls of the printed questions and responses and gave them to students in the front row to distribute. "Now do not, I repeat, *do not* turn these over to look at the columnist's advice until we come to that. Okay. Everybody's got it? Let's go over the question and see what we think."

Professor Hargus read aloud.

Dear ————— :

My girlfriend acts like a dude. It didn't bother me when we first started dating but it's getting to me, more and more, lately.

How can I get my girlfriend to act more feminine?

- Guy Who Wants A Real Lady

"Alright. I see a number of hands already in the air." Pointing at a hard-looking blond with tattoos and a leather jacket. "Yes? You there. Courtney Love."

"This guy's the problem. Who is he to tell her how to act?"

Groans from some of the guys.

"Yes. The guy with the Hard Rock Café shirt."

"If the guy wanted to date Tom Cruise, he'd be a homo, right? So he wants a girl who acts like a girl. But Lizzy Borden over there might be right. He's probably a wussie boy who would be better off with some cuddly kewpie doll instead of the dyke he's with right now."

That brought a lot of laughs.

"Okay, class. What's the advice we give him?"

Courtney Love again.

"The guy needs to get a clue. He should cancel his subscription to the Disney Channel and start going to strip clubs."

"Hard Rock Café?"

"He should sign up to become a pen pal with a bunch of Japanese high school girls."

A girl a few seats over shouted. "Is that how you got started?"

"Anyone else want to venture advice to our poor femininity-starved boy?"

Billy stood up.

"Masculine and feminine are artificial categories, solely made up by human beings with a lot of time on their hands and too many products to sell. Either the guy finds his current girlfriend attractive or he doesn't. If he doesn't, it's time to move on. Unless she looks like Marlon Brando, some other guy will think she's a dish and she won't have to waste the time and energy trying to match up to this guy's comic book idea of femininity. The guy should have no problem finding someone. He should just start hanging out in the cosmetics and perfume department at Macy's or Walmart."

There seem to be unanimous approval from the girls in the class. The guys offered polite nods of assent. There were a lot of why-didn't-I-think-of-that expressions, probably at having lost a great opportunity to impress the girls, who now thought Billy had it pretty much together.

Dr. Hargus loved it when the boys got slapped in the face by one their own. She always stressed in her lectures that male competitiveness was one of the primal forces driving civilization building, matched only by female competitiveness, both of them trumped by the ongoing age-old battle between the sexes.

"Nice work, young man. That pretty much agrees with the columnist's reply. Flip over your sheets and check out the response given by the advice professional."

GWWARL:

How does she act like a dude? Spitting, cursing, scratching her balls in public? And she pees standing up? What? Don't tell me she's finally beating you in Guitar Hero and your ego is being bruised?

She is who she is and your asking her to act more feminine around you will result in you playing Guitar Hero on your own.

If the attraction isn't there anymore ... well, then it just isn't there ... She prancing around, following a script (if she went there), would only work for so long.

"Let me ask you this. With a show of hands, please. Is this columnist male or female?"

The class decided almost unanimously it was a male. Only two dissenting votes.

To the raucous laughter of the rest of the class, she pulled two dunce hats out of a large bag she always brought to class with her, then had them passed up to the two students — one male and one female — who had guessed wrong. They had to wear the hats for the rest of the class period.

"Yes, class. He's pretty gnarly. But he knows the subject matter. It was probably himself he was describing there. Spitting. Scratching his crotch. But I love the guy. He really nails it. Besides, I don't know any girls who play Guitar Hero. Okay. Hopefully you didn't peek at the reply to the next one. Let's go back to the front of the page. This is a broken-heart letter. This young man got dumped. I can't imagine that happening to any of the handsome, well-mannered, highly intelligent lads in this room."

The girls got a big hurrah out of that one. Choruses of *'Oh no, never'* and *'Not them'* went up all around. The guys were good sports and took it in stride, having often been the butt of Professor Hargus' taunting.

"Here we go." She read aloud.

Dear ———— :

In October, my college girlfriend ended our relationship by email within a week of our year anniversary, my longest relationship to date. She said a lot of stuff about us living too far away (30-minute drive) and that she needed time to be alone.

Not three weeks later, I found out she was dating some other guy.

I never contacted her after the first month of being broken up. When I got the email, I called her and told her how much she meant to me, but she insisted that the distance wasn't working, and that she needed to be alone. A week or two later, I called to just say hello because I was feeling pretty low (I didn't tell her that) and she got off the phone pretty quick. I never contacted her since, because I knew that would only be bad for me.

I've been doing everything to get over it; taking her number out of my phone, getting rid of anything she gave me, all mementos of the relationship.

But yet I'm having a hard time forgetting her. I've gotten to a point where I know that if she wanted me back, I'd even say no to her, because I see now that it wasn't like the relationship was working so great by the time we broke up. So it's not like I feel like she was the only one for me. But I can't forget the good times, and I can't forget the way she just left me like that. I've been on a few dates since the breakup, but I didn't enjoy it.

I've done everything to start living my own life and forget about her (I've been good enough to not even try to get in contact with her since the break-up), so why am I still dwelling on it? It's been almost eight months!

I feel like I need some sort of closure; I want so badly to tell her how she hurt me by dumping me so coldly and lying to me. But I feel like it would be a bad idea to call her up just to say that.

- How Can I Get Some Closure?

"Alright. Once you've all pulled yourself together and stopped crying, I'd like your thoughts on both the letter and whether any of you have ever had this much trouble getting over a relationship."

There wasn't much crying going on but there sure were a lot of strong opinions. The class took on aspects of a bedlam-based TV talk show.

"Why is it some girls get in your head and lodge there like
an intestinal parasite?"

"That should only be a problem for guys with their
intestines in their heads."

"Or their heads up their butts."

"This guy's a drama queen. He's wallowing in his self-pity.
He's like twenty years old and he thinks his life is over.
Why doesn't he just go out and get laid?

"God, I hope I never go out with someone like you."

"You won't have to worry about that."

"What is it with you guys? Is it that you don't have
feelings? Or is it that you're just way too cool to admit
you have feelings? Here's a guy who actually loved a
girl and misses her. Tell me. What's wrong with that?
You have to make fun of him for caring."

"He thinks she was so special because she got out first. If he
had been smart enough to dump the bitch first, she'd be
writing this pathetic letter."

"It's a question of sensitivity. Or I should say,
insensitivity. There are too many people in the world.
An individual has no worth. So he or she gets no respect.
This girl took the coward's way out. The guy got
majorly dumped on. It's that simple."

"The guy's a pussy-whipped idiot. He should
have seen it coming."

"It's not that simple. You don't know anything about him."

"And you don't know anything about her either.
Maybe she's a slut."

"Regardless. The truth is that nowadays, for both sexes, it's all just fast food. There's no loyalty anymore. No one is in it for the long haul. We change partners like we change our underwear."

"Maybe that's why she left. Because he never changed his underwear."

"The issue is not that she broke up with him. It's the callous way she handled it. You don't have to mess the other person up. There's a right way and a wrong way."

"Well, as a really sensitive guy, I agree with you there. By the way, what are you doing Saturday night?"

"I'm weightlifting with my three lesbian girlfriends."

"Anyway. Like I was saying. The email thing was not happening. Very bad form. When I broke up with my last girlfriend, I used a much more delicate touch."

"And that was?"

"She had this cat that used to attack me every time we were in bed together. I still have the scars on my back if you want to see them. Anyway, I attached a note to the cat after I strangled it with a guitar string from my ex's Martin D-40. Her guitar playing sucked anyway. Not the cat's. My ex's. The girl played guitar like Stephen Hawking plays rugby. Maybe not even that good."

Professor Hargus couldn't let this one go by.
"Excuse me. If you're not making this up, what did the note say?"

"I'm not making it up. The note was direct and to the point. It said, 'Hey, you know the Paul Simon song, 50 Ways To Leave Your Lover? Well ... here's number 51 ... I ain't gettin' hitched, bitch.' She definitely got the message."

"Your mom must be proud of you."

"My mom's dead."

"Strangled with a guitar string?"

"Fuck you! I didn't really kill the cat.
It died of natural causes."

"Like rat poison?"

Before all hell broke loose, Professor Hargus jumped in.

"Okay. Let's cool it down here a bit. I like a spirited discussion, students. But let's stay away from personal attacks. Alright. Let's look at what the professional has to say to this jilted guy, who does not want the girl back, mind you, but says he wants 'closure'. Does anyone want to tell me what closure is in this context?"

Most students seemed to be slipping lower in their seats. A few looked thoughtful, while two others popped open laptops, presumably to look for the dictionary program. So far there was a conspicuous lack of hands.

"Anyone? Not all at once now. Okay ... you young lady. The only one with her hand up."

"He wants to clear the air of any bad feelings. Just feel like they understand one another and are able to end their relationship with no resentment or bitterness. Maybe come clean as to what exactly happened and be completely honest about it."

"Excellent. Excellent answer. Okay, let's see what advice-giver says."

> *HCIGSC:*
>
> *Let me count the ways in which you are better off without this girl ...*
>
> 1. *Timing the break-up to an anniversary is just incredible weak. She had ample time to end the relationship. (She is inconsiderate and selfish).*
>
> 2. *A 30-minute drive is not a long-distance relationship. That is almost like being neighbors, in any metropolitan area. (She is lazy and dumb).*
>
> 3. *She told you that she needs "time to be alone" ... This in reality, translates to "please don't bug me; I'm already working on this other guy". (She is a cheat and a slut).*
>
> 4. *Email break-ups are laughable. (She is cowardly and pathetic).*
>
> *The fact is: She was already working on that other dude before even breaking up with you ... Sooner or later, the other dude will also get to experience her weak-arse excuses and blame games.*
>
> *You'll get closure when you have a new and much hotter girlfriend's legs wrapped around your head and she can't get through a single day without fucking your brains out.*

Give it time. Go out with your friends and meet some new people. You will be hard-pressed to find someone "weaker" than this ex-girlfriend. When you stop moping around the house and start meeting people, you will also start remembering the times when she bugged the hell of you ...

Really ... your old girlfriend laying naked, sweaty and panting in your bed, was not your whole relationship. It wasn't ... really.

Good luck!

"I feel like I should fire a starting gun. In any case, it's off to the races."

"This columnist is the same as for the last letter, right? Only a male would trash a girl like that. What a pig! He called her a slut."

"You're right about that. If the tables were turned and it was the guy who started banging another girl and left his ex stranded, this writer would be whapping the guy on the back, telling him how incredibly cool he was."

"That's not fair. You can't second guess what he'd say."

"How can he go second guessing the girl? When he says that her saying she needs time alone has to mean that she is already with another guy. How can he claim to know that? Maybe the girl was thinking about it but hadn't done anything yet. Maybe she wanted a clean break before she got into the new relationship. Meaning time alone."

"Maybe Mary Magdalene was a virgin."

"Is that the best you can do? Maybe she was a virgin. That was 2000 years ago. Maybe Monica Lewinski was a virgin. Who cares?"

"Maybe Bill Clinton is a virgin!"

"I love the ending where he says, 'your girlfriend laying naked, sweaty and panting in your bed, was not your whole relationship.' I don't know. I could go for some of the naked, sweaty and panting."

"Join a nudist colony and take up jogging."

"This writer makes some sense. And gives some good advice. The girl was lying. She said the same stupid things everyone says when they want to break it off but don't have the guts to just say it. And Mr. Feel Sorry does need to just get out there and stop moping."

"But the way he goes out of his way to demean her. Look at this. She's inconsiderate and selfish. Lazy and dumb. A cheat and a slut. Cowardly and pathetic."

"He's got a problem with women. He is definitely a misogynist."

"How do you even like know he's married?"

"What's that got to do with it?"

"Duh! Misogynist? Someone with like more than one wife."

"That's bigamist. B-I-G-A-M-I-S-T."

"No matter how you dice it, for someone who is in the public eye telling others how to behave and conduct their lives, he may be funny, but he has no sensitivity."

"Fuck sensitivity. I eat sensitivity for breakfast and spit it out on the way to class. It's Darwin, baby. SOTF. That's what it's all about."

"SOTF? What's SOTF?"

"Survival of the fittest. If you can't compete, it's in the street. Next to the garbage."

"I envy the lucky girl who marries you."

"I ain't ever getting married. But thanks for asking."

"I'd rather have my tongue pulled out through my ass by a monster truck."

*"What about the whole legal aspect? He should be able
to sue the bitch for damages. For all the mental grief.
And for lying. That's fraud. She should have to pay!"*

*"Then she should be able to sue him for being such a
boring wimp-ass and a crybaby. Think of all her mental
grief listening to his girly-boy eunuch whining."*

*"If the guy's a eunuch, it's because she's a castrating
bitch. Look what she did to him. And how he ended up."*

*"I love the way everyone can read so much into this.
The letter is from the guy. What if she had written the
letter? You'd get a whole other story."*

*"Men are such pigs. Take away their beer and call
them on how inconsiderate they are, and suddenly
we're all running around with axes and machetes.
Think about how stupid that is."*

*"Besides. Guys don't need us to castrate them. They do
it to themselves. It's happening all of the time."*

"I don't think so!"

"No way!"

*"Just look at the way you act. Jealousy.
Possessiveness. You think if you sleep with a girl,
you own it. The thought of another guy putting his
willy in there drives you nuts. The big strong stud
bull becomes a whiny little mouse. This guy that
wrote the letter so much as admits it."*

*"That right. It's been eight months and the guy says he
still can't enjoy going out. What else can you take from
that? Snip snip. He's his own worst enemy."*

A boy speaks out in a very high-pitched voice.

"Alright. Who put the helium in my asthma inhaler?"

And so it went. In every class Dr. Hargus continued acting like a
supercharged hybrid of Jerry Springer and Oprah Winfrey. Billy cruised along,
never even once tempted to change the channel. It was a hoot!

14

Spring Term galloped into April. Billy and the rest of the class continued unsuccessfully trying to second guess what the core substance of PSYCH 2800 was — in other words, what the material was they were expected to master and would ultimately be tested on. There seemed to be no formal lesson plan. It was impossible to figure out in terms of coherent subject matter, where they had been, much less divine where the course was ultimately heading.

The question of tests and grading was solved the third Tuesday of the month. Professor Hargus marched into class precisely at 10:00 am and launched into her carefully prepared speech.

"Okay, class. We've only got three weeks of regular class to go, and I have a very important announcement. First, the good news. I will not be giving you a final exam in this class."

Whoops and cheers filled the room. It felt momentarily more like a pep rally than a bonafide psychology class.

As the ovation subsided, one male student yelled out from the back of the room.

"What's the bad news? Am I going to have to have sex with you?"

Dr. Hargus laughed along with the class.

"You could wish. I'll say this. If you did, I guarantee you'd never look at your grandmother the same way. No. The bad news is … I'm pregnant and I don't know which one of you is the father."

A chorus of groans from the boys competed with tittering and laughter from the girls. One girl then yelled out.

"It would be bad news if any of these guys were the father, that's for sure."

Boos and catcalls from the males collided head-on with hisses and catcalls from the girls.

Professor Hargus decided to get down to the business at hand.

"Okay. Okay. Enough fun. Let me explain how you will earn your grade. As I said, no formal exam. So don't even show up exam week at the designated time. I won't be here. Neither should you. Now let me explain. This is the first time I've tried this. But I think it's going to really pull everything together. Let's see." She picked up the enrollment form listing the members of class. "We started out with forty-two. Six drops. And from what I can tell, three of you have never been to class ever. That leaves thirty-three. What I want each of you to do is write a short letter, just like the ones we have been looking at all term. Address it to Dear Hargee — that's me. In this letter, you will describe some real or invented problem. 'Dear Hargee. I caught my new boyfriend trying on my panties the other day. He claims it was an honest mistake. But he was also wearing lipstick at the time. What should I do?' Okay? That's just an example. But that's the idea. Whatever problem you want answered. But listen, class. Part of your grade will be based on the originality of your letter. So don't just regurgitate the same old predictable stuff. Really think about some problem we haven't discussed here in class. Or maybe you have some really unique situation in your life. Your originality, that's part of your grade. The other part comes from advice you give to others. This is how it works. Each letter turned in — there should be thirty-three total — will be given to the other members of this class. They will each write their own advice. You should get thirty-two replies. Since every reply will be signed, I will know what each and every one of you have said and will grade you accordingly. Let me summarize this and make it completely clear how this will work. Your overall grade for this entire class will be based first, on what question you come up with, and second what advice you give to the thirty-two questions you receive from other members of this class."

The groans were back. And they weren't fun groans.

"Now now. I know this sounds like a lot of work. But it's not. Not really. The problems and the replies should be short and sweet. Direct and to the point. Just like what we've been reading all along. The key is common sense. You can be weird and wacky and try too hard or think you want to be clever. But that's not going to cut it. Because being weird does not reflect the majority of the people out there. People have real problems and the want sensible answers. This is not a class in science fiction or creative writing. This is about the dynamic psychological elements — the unwritten rules of behavior, if you will — which are the sum and substance of our social interactions. Human interactions. So let's keep it real. Have fun with it but *please*, keep it on planet Earth, year 2003 C.E. Any questions?"

One mock-whiny voice from off to the side filled the silence.

"Is it too late to drop this class?"

Dr. Hargus looked at him over the top of her glasses.

"Will an F hurt your grade point average?"

Another student replied.

"An F would raise his grade point average."

Professor Hargus laid out the timetable. Letters were due at the beginning of the next class. She would have them copied for distribution by the end of the 90-minute lecture period. That would give everyone just under three weeks to come up with their replies. All replies were due in her office no later than Monday of Study Period week.

"Go to it, lads and lasses. See you day after tomorrow. Same time. Same station."

It was a very somber group of students that lumbered out of the lecture hall.

Billy walked out of class and sat down under a tree. He finished his letter less than twenty minutes.

Dear Hargee,

I am deeply in love with a girl I've been dating for about a year.

She has a lousy family. She can't stand them, and has minimum contact with them.

There are only two people in her life, people she is truly close to.

I, of course, am one of them. Her best friend, a girl who she has known from all the way back in elementary school, is the other.

This friend occasionally comes to visit my girlfriend here at Cornell, and I have slowly grown to like her. They are obviously very good for one another and I can see their friendship is a very positive thing.

This friend visited very recently and we all went out to dinner.

We had a great time but then at the end of the evening a very strange thing happened.

My girl's best friend first told us that she thinks we are a really great couple and believes we should get married. That was cool. Then she said she knew I couldn't afford to buy an engagement ring right now. So she had gone ahead and bought one for us.

Yes. It's true. She pulled out a 1½ carat diamond engagement ring, gave it to my girlfriend and said it was hers to keep, so that if we wanted to get engaged, we could make it official.

I have been thinking a lot over the last few months about someday asking my girlfriend to get married. But obviously I assumed it was something I would do sometime well off in the future. The ring really caught me off guard.

I don't know what to think. Or how I should feel.

On one hand, it was such a kind and generous gesture.

On the other, it seems kind of weird having someone else just take the ball on this and run, without even checking with either of us.

Maybe whatever hangups I have about not buying the ring myself are silly and it's a gift I should accept. But I am really having trouble convincing myself. Something just doesn't seem right.

Am I off base here? Is this too weird? What should I do?

Broke and in love,
Billy Green

Billy's was one of three letters Professor Hargus singled out for uniqueness, relevance and creativity. Having identified it as such, she added as an aside, that we could safely assume this was not a problem actually confronting Mr. Green at this time, making it an even more noteworthy triumph of his imagination.

There was greater agreement in the responses given to Billy than for any of the other letters.

(29) recommended that if he and his girlfriend finalized their engagement, they accept the ring, and moreover make special mention of the friend's generosity at their wedding. The 29 judged it as an act of extreme unselfishness, demonstrating the value of true friendship. 23 went on to say that for Billy to be threatened by the gift of the ring was just his male ego clinging on to outdated ideas about the rigid roles of men and women. 17 used the phrase "that's what friends are for", and 9 said "don't look a gift horse in the mouth", or words to that effect.

(1) said in no uncertain terms that the best friend was way out of line and being pushy. She obviously was threatened by Billy and was trying to regain top billing for herself in his girlfriend's eyes, even if it meant giving her friend up to marriage. This person surmised she would always hold it over them that she was the one who pushed them into it, exerting some sort of weird control over them. They should give the ring back and tell her to mind her own business.

(1) suggested Billy grab the ring for himself, dump his girlfriend, and either pawn the ring or ask the best friend to marry him. The best friend was obviously loaded with bucks and loose with her wallet, two qualities which a discerning man should always look for in a prospective wife.

(1) told Billy to bail immediately, because there was something funny going on. The girls had probably planned the whole thing together. In all likelihood, they are man-haters or lesbians playing a sick joke on a poor unsuspecting male.

Billy got the only A for the class.
Everyone else got B or below.
Two schmucks got an F.

Back in March while Billy and Natalie were holed up in the Motel California huddled in each other's embrace, there were thousands of people in another part of the world holed up and huddled as well.

Shock and awe.

That was what they called the raining down on Baghdad of tens of thousands of pounds of explosives as punishment for Sadam Hussein's refusal to cede his iron-fist rule over Iraq, as demanded by President and Commander-In-Chief, George W. Bush, and the cobbled-together Coalition of the Willing.

The message was unequivocal.

Do as we say or we kill you.

So the innocent citizens of Iraq — young and old, men, women, children — already struggling to survive the aftermath of the Iraq-Iran war, the punishing defeat of Operation Desert Storm, and cruel sanctions imposed on their country because of the tyrannical rule of a ruthless and sinister Sadam Hussein, were now holed up below the ground, huddled against one another, trembling and afraid as explosion after explosion wreaked unfathomable terror and destruction on their cities, homes, temples, schools, hospitals, museums, and mosques.

People were holed up and huddled.

Billy and Natalie.

The citizens of Iraq.

The same three days.

Let's do some war math.

In the first 72 hours of the air assault on the relatively defenseless country, over 1000 cruise and other sophisticated missiles leveled building after building, vaporized or dismembered thousands of civilians, and sent tens of thousands of screaming citizens scrambling from one burning building to another. Smart and dumb bombs alike, launched by technological miracles like the F-117A Stealth Fighter, and dropped in random carpet bombing by behemoth cargo airships of death like the stalwart B-52, also ran into the thousands. Some of these bombs were so massive they had destructive capabilities which rivaled nuclear devices.

The air assault impersonally and efficiently almost completely destroyed the infrastructure required to support the millions of people crammed into Baghdad and other urban centers, dotting the vast uninhabitable sea of hot sand which comprises 98% of the country of Iraq. The people who survived the initial shock and awe faced a long difficult battle. They would be holed up and huddled for some time to come.

Now let's do some love math.

In that same 72 hours, Billy and Natalie made love 11 times. Billy's orgasm count was 14. Natalie's was 27.

Let's take this a step further.

There are over 7 billion people in the world.

For arguments sake, let's safely assume that about half of them are coital capable-and-ready.

That's 3½ billion.

19

Let's say that half of those are in some sort of relationship or have within their immediate range of options someone to make love to.

Now we're at 1¾ billion.

Let's conservatively say that each of the 1¾ billion has sex once a week, resulting in a happy ending, meaning an orgasm.

That would suggest that during the three day shock and awe bombardment of Baghdad, 3 out of 7 of the 1¾ billion coital capable-ready-and-accessible had happy-ending sex.

Click click click equal sign.

So while thousands of bombs were being dropped on thousands of people in Baghdad, there were over 750,000,000 people having orgasms.

Let's see.

Drop bombs kill people.

Or.

Make love happy ending.

Hmmm.

Tough call.

While Billy and Natalie followed a make-love-happy-ending scenario along with 750 million others, no one died, no one had their arms or legs shot off, no one was blinded or crippled for life. Both Billy and Natalie emerged from their experience with blissful smiles and hopeful dreams for the future.

Probably a good number of the other 750 million did as well.

They at least were in a decent mood.

President Ronald Reagan, one of the most popular presidents in recent history, probably because he articulated an easily-grasped vision of the world, unencumbered by logic and uncomplicated by fact or historical perspective, had a favorite phase he used to completely baffle and disarm his critics. It was one of those perfect combinations of words, for which American English seems particularly adapted, which said absolutely nothing but managed to bring to a complete halt any further equivocation, or for that matter any further intelligent communication. The phrase was ...

"There you go again."

Yup.

There we go again.

It does kind of sum it all up.

The repetition. The familiar patterns. The cyclical nature of things.

Birth. Life. Death. Birth. Life. Death.

The good and the bad. All the glory and tedium that defines us.

The dreams. The despair. The optimism and pessimism. Triumphs and tragedies. Boldness and cowardice. Daring and fear. Celebrity and anonymity. Order and chaos.

There we go again.

Yup.

2003 was the Chinese Year of the Sheep.

People in the U. S. generally lived up to the characterization. They flocked to the malls, flocked to the stadiums, flocked to the movie theater, flocked wherever the powerless and unthinking flock to when they can't look at the mess the world is in, or own up to the tiny bit of responsibility and blame which falls on them for the catastrophic shape of things.

Beyond the initiation of war in Iraq, many notable things happened in 2003.

In January: The last signal is received from NASA's Pioneer 10 spacecraft, some 7.5 billion miles from Earth. The 108th United States Congress is sworn in. In Phnom Penh, Cambodia, the Thai Embassy is burned and commercial properties of Thai businesses are vandalized. Super Bowl XXXVII, the Tampa Bay Buccaneers defeat the Oakland Raiders 48-21. The Space Shuttle Columbia is launched on what turns out to be its last flight because …

On February 1st, at the conclusion of its mission, the Space Shuttle Columbia disintegrates during reentry over Texas, killing all seven astronauts onboard.

That same day, in Northern Ireland, Protestant Ulster Defence Association Belfast leader John Gregg is killed by a loyalist faction.

Also in February: An arsonist destroys a train in Daegu, South Korea, killing more than 190. The Station nightclub fire in West Warwick, Rhode Island claims the lives of 100 people, when the stage incendiaries of the feature band, Great White, turn the facility into an inferno. The kids-show TV star Mr. Rogers and country-western singer Johnny Paycheck die.

In March: In two separate opinions, the Supreme Court of the United States, by 5-4 margins, upholds California's 'three strikes and you're out' law. Serbian Prime Minister Zoran Đinđić is assassinated in Belgrade. The UN's World Health Organization issues a global alert on SARS. The scientific journal Nature reports that 350,000-year-old upright-walking human footprints had been found in Italy. FBI agents raid the corporate headquarters of HealthSouth Corporation in Birmingham, Alabama, on suspicion of massive corporate fraud led by the company's top executives. The 75th Academy Awards ceremony, hosted by Steve Martin, is held at the Kodak Theatre in Hollywood. Chicago wins Best Picture. WHO doctor Carlo Urbani, who first identified SARS, dies of the disease.

In April: A passenger bus is destroyed by a remote-controlled land mine in the Chechen capital, killing at least eight innocent people. Syracuse wins the college basketball National Championship. The Human Genome Project is completed, with 99% of the human genome sequenced to 99.99% accuracy. Nina Simone dies.

In May: A major severe weather outbreak spawns more tornadoes than any week in U. S. history, as 393 tornadoes are reported in 19 states. A female suicide bomber blows up explosives strapped to her waist in a crowd of thousands of Muslim pilgrims, killing at least eighteen people in Chechnya. May 15th is the date predicted by Pana-Wave Laboratory, a Japanese cult, for a close encounter with an unknown planet which would result in the extinction of most of humankind. Dewey, the first deer cloned by scientists at Texas A&M University, is born. Top Thrill Dragster opens in Cedar Point in Sandusky, Ohio as the world's tallest, fastest roller coaster. Prometea, the first horse ever cloned, is born.

In June: The 29th G8 summit opens in Évian-les-Bains, France, to tight security and tens of thousands of protesters. Martha Stewart and her broker are indicted for using privileged investment information and then obstructing a federal investigation. A female suicide bomber detonates a bomb near a bus carrying soldiers and civilians to a military airfield in Mozdok, a major staging point for Russian troops in Chechnya, killing at least sixteen. Sodomy laws are declared unconstitutional in Lawrence v. Texas by the U. S. Supreme Court. The largest hailstone ever recorded, the size of a volleyball, falls in Aurora, Nebraska. Gregory Peck and Katherine Hepburn die, as do author Leon Uris and television journalist David Brinkley.

In July: SARS is declared to be contained by the WHO. The 70-meter Eupatoria Planetary Radar sends the METI message, Cosmic Call 2, to five stars: Hip 4872, HD 245409, 55 Cancri, HD 10307 and 47 Ursae Majoris, that will arrive at these stars in 2036, 2040, 2044, 2044 and 2049 respectively. Canon Jeffrey John, the first would-be gay bishop in the Church of England, withdraws his acceptance of the post of The Bishop of Reading after discussions with church leaders. The last Volkswagen Type 1 rolls off its production line in Puebla, Mexico. A Russian security agent dies in Moscow, while trying to defuse a bomb a woman had tried to carry into a café on central Moscow's main street. Bob Hope dies.

In August: A suicide bomber rams a truck filled with explosives into a military hospital near Chechnya, killing 50 people, including Russian troops wounded in Chechnya itself. The highest temperature ever is recorded in the UK at Brogdale near Faversham in Kent, a scorching — scorching by British standards — 38.5°C (101.3°F). Two bomb blasts in Mumbai, India kill 52 people. A rocket explosion kills 21 at the Brazilian rocket complex in Alcântara, Brazil, due to the premature ignition of a solid rocket booster. A heat wave in Paris results in temperatures of 44°C (112°F). A widespread power outage affects the northeastern United States and south-central Canada.

In September: Europe's busiest shopping centre, the Bullring in Birmingham, Great Britain, is officially opened by Sir Albert Bore. Swedish foreign minister Anna Lindh is stabbed in a Stockholm department store and dies the next day. Two suicide bombers drive an explosive-filled truck into a government security services building near Chechnya, killing three and injuring 25. A power failure affects all of Italy except Sardinia, cutting service to more than 56 million people. Johnny Cash dies.

In October: California voters recall Governor Gray Davis from office and elect actor Arnold Schwarzenegger to succeed him. The Peoples Republic of China launches Shenzhou 5, their first manned space mission. The Concorde makes its last commercial flight, bringing the era of supersonic airliner travel to a close, at least for the time being. The Florida Marlins defeat the New York Yankees to win their second World Series title. Mahathir Mohamad resigns as Prime Minister of Malaysia after 22 years in power. Neil Postman, American educator, media theorist, and cultural critic dies.

In November: Gary Ridgway, The 'Green River Killer', confesses to murdering 48 women. Two car bombs explode simultaneously in Istanbul, Turkey, targeting two synagogues, killing at least 25 people and wounding more than three hundred. Anti-same-sex marriage laws are ruled unconstitutional by the Massachusetts Supreme Judicial Court in Goodridge v. Department of Public Health. Several more bombs explode in Istanbul, Turkey, destroying the Turkish head office of HSBC and the British consulate.

In December: A suicide bombing on a commuter train in southern Russia kills 44 people, an attack which President Vladimir Putin condemns as a bid to destabilize the country two days before parliamentary elections. Saddam Hussein, former President of Iraq, is captured in Tikrit by the U.S. 4th Infantry Division. A female suicide bomber blows herself up outside Moscow's National Hotel, across from the Kremlin and Red Square, killing five innocent bystanders. A mad cow disease outbreak in Washington State is announced, prompting several countries including Brazil, Australia and Taiwan to ban the import of beef from the United States. An earthquake in California kills two. Libya admits to building a nuclear bomb. Beagle 2 is scheduled to land on Mars, but nothing is heard from the lander. Keiko the whale dies.

It all had a familiar ring. History was going into reruns before it happened.

There seemed to be one incremental change. As each year passed, mankind seemed to grow increasingly impatient with the slow pace of natural disasters. So from all appearances, it was taking up the slack with disasters of its own making.

There we go again.

Who could make sense of any of this? Chaos and violence, destruction and disorder, mixed in with some isolated, random happy thoughts and amusing curios, commanded the airwaves and dominated the hearts and minds of most Americans. Many people would be hard pressed to find China on the map, and most could care less if it was the Year of the Sheep or the Year of the Pitbull.

For Billy and Natalie, the year plodded along at a breakneck crawl. At least until the end of August. Then big changes got underway.

Natalie had graduated right on schedule and in the blink of an eye had moved off campus, still in upstate New York but almost 200 miles away, where she started a new job.

They kept in regular touch by telephone but Billy saw her only three times during the new academic term which started only eighteen days after she left. The third time he saw her, she had a new more "professional" hairdo, and he noticed that she was wearing the engagement ring Pam had bought for them. He also noticed that she had gotten a tattoo. It was a tiny symbol centered high on her back at the base of her neck.

"Nice tattoo, Natalie. Is it the Chinese character for the Year of the Sheep?"

"How did you know?"

"Just a lucky guess."

Darkness Before Dawn

10 - 9 - 8 - 7 - 6 - 5 - 4 - 3 - 2 - 1 - HAPPY NEW YEAR!!

The party was being held at Natalie's apartment in Newburgh, NY to ring in the new year. Of course, Billy and Pam were there. Plus an odd and mismatched assortment of people unfamiliar to either of them. A few were neighbors, people who also lived in the building — that they had nothing else going on for one of the most important celebrations of the year, spoke volumes as to the extent of their social networks. Others scattered here and there at the tables full of snack food and the kitchen counter where the hard liquor and drink mixes were lined up, were Natalie's colleagues from her new workplace. They were professionals in the Newburgh sense of the word. As could be immediately ascertained from the casual to ragged state of their attire, all of them were pretty laid-back upcountry types, whose fashion sense wouldn't cut it in a soup line in the Big Apple.

Natalie had graduated on schedule in August. It took her three days to find her new job. Actually, it found her. The Clinton administration — in particular Al Gore — had conferred anything to do with ecology and the environment, a high degree of prestige and popularity. Moreover, the best efforts of the Bush administration had not entirely eradicated that meritorious gesture or trashed all of the programs which grew out of their initiatives.

Toward the end of both Spring Term and Summer Session, numerous eco-companies from various parts of the country visited Cornell with the intention of recruiting the best newly available talent. Natalie's B. S. degree was in Human Ecology and Sustainable Development. She graduated Summa Cum Laude, third in her class, so was at the top of the list for several of the personnel reps interviewing the new grads.

Seminole Environmental Consultants had everything she was looking for. In terms of money it was not the best offer, but with a total of fifteen employees, including the management, they were a small firm, as much an extended family as a business enterprise. Six of their current employees were women, including the number one and two executives in charge of the operation. They were set up as an employee-owned corporation, meaning that after a year of employment, Natalie would be eligible to participate in the success of the firm with gifted shares of stock ownership, which presumably would increase in both quantity and value over time. From what Natalie had gathered, the work at Seminole was interesting and made important contributions to society at large, most profoundly in terms of the ecological integrity of the surrounding region.

Nearly as important for Natalie as any of the purely professional aspects of the company, was the fact that they were located Upstate New York, in the Hudson River Valley. Of itself this was a pleasant and bucolic place to live, but even more to her liking, it was less than two hours by train from New York City.

Billy had never been to the Big Apple. He naively assumed that all big cities were created equal and Detroit had from his earliest memories seeded in him a deep distaste for urban life. On the other hand, it was apparent that Natalie loved New York. She and Pam had on several occasions used it as an escape hatch from the mundane and predictable. Billy never knew what they did there. But he figured it was just a matter of time before he and Natalie together would make a visit, and he might then begin his education as to what was so special about this renowned city, such that people all over the world regarded it as the center of the *homo sapiens* universe.

Newburgh worked for Natalie from the get-go. Only days after her last final exam at Cornell, she made an exploratory trip to the town, visited the offices of Seminole, met the entire staff, and definitely liked what she saw. With the help of one of her future co-workers, she then found a decent two-bedroom flat right near the center of town. This put it a stone's throw from the Hudson River and the bridge to the train station. Perfect. Within a week, she moved her meager possessions from Ithaca and was ready to report for her new job, which officially started the day after Labor Day.

Billy helped her move her stuff in a small rental truck, and spent a few days with her, before his return to Ithaca for the beginning of Fall Term. It was for both of them, of course, sad and traumatic to confront their coming separation. But their time together during the short transition was full of both the pleasant domesticities of setting up her new apartment, and the hot carnalities of test driving her new bed. It proved quite worthy as a recreational vehicle for their erotic exploration.

Despite the 190 miles separating them, things remained excellent between Billy and Natalie.

Really good.

"Happy New Year, my big hunk of guy!"

Natalie was all over him. She was obviously a little tipsy. He could smell the champagne on her breath as she covered his face with kisses and licked his lips with her tongue.

"I'll give you two hours to stop this or else."

He never got tired of her attention, the feel of her body against his, the taste of her lips, the warmth of her skin, her smell, the delicate touch of her hands.

"I'm going to play hostess and make the rounds. I'll be right back for the other hour and fifty nine minutes."

He stepped into the tiny kitchen, freshened his gin and tonic, then stepped into the foyer and looked out the front door at the fresh snow, still coming down in slow-motion flurries, as the whoops and hollers, hugs and kisses, and general revelry of the party went on behind him.

Billy stood there thinking about the year that had just passed. After all, it was New Years Eve and if you weren't too drunk, it's often-as-not what you did. That and make foolish resolutions for the coming year which, after coming to your senses the following few days, you accepted you had no intention of keeping.

This past year: What a journey!

First of all. He really had to hand it to Natalie. She was only a year older than him and here she was, already graduated from college, with highest honors no less, now with a nice paying, challenging, professional job. He could easily see, even through the bubbly mirthful glaze of New Years Eve, that she was well-regarded and enthusiastically accepted by the people she worked with. There was a definite hint of awe in the eyes of those with whom she exchanged small talk and shop talk, as she made the rounds this evening.

They should be awed: Just the last stretch of her final academic year was monumental and would have broken most mere mortals.

After completing a single three-week class during Winter Session, she took on five classes. Five real *monsters*, including PAM 4060, Politics and Policy: Theory, Research, and Practice, taught by Dr. E. M. Castle, reputed to be the most ornery, most formidable, most punishing professor on campus.

For Summer Session, she took three classes, one more than necessary to graduate, but she judged that ECON 7640, International Trade and Foreign Investment, would be an enormous asset to her in whatever job she accepted.

Through it all, she was a rock.

It was Billy who sometimes succumbed to nerves. Apprehensions about Natalie's graduating and moving on. Anxieties about doing his best in school. Worries about money.

Billy had decided to stay in Ithaca for that last summer. He would just have to find a job locally and make do. While he could make more money working in a factory in Detroit, as far as he was concerned that was not an option this year. Frankly, he wasn't even sure his dad would try to arrange it for him, considering their never-abating hostilities.

But more importantly, he wanted to be with Natalie. He wanted to be right there with her every available opportunity until she packed up and left.

Beyond that?

That was another source of anxiety.

They never really talked about what was going to happen next.

Was there any way to know? To plan? There were too many variables.

Standing here now on New Years looking out from the foyer of Natalie's new apartment at the hypnotic cascade of weightless snowflakes, it suddenly struck Billy how grateful he should be. Maybe he and Natalie weren't together every day. But they were still together!

Like Sister Mary Felicia had said way back when, always count your blessings.

He knocked back another mouthful of gin and tonic. His thoughts drifted.

It suddenly occurred to him what a lousy son he had become lately. Over the past year, he had not been home once. Last time Billy had been with his mom was Christmas vacation over a year ago, while his father played in Las Vegas. They celebrated a quiet New Years Eve together. Two days later he was back to campus. That was the last time he had actually seen her.

Of course, they had talked. She got off of the chemo and radiative treatments in February. The good news — the really *great* news — was that her cancer was in complete remission. She had gained weight and her hair grew back. Much to Billy's relief, the last few times she had called him, she sounded like she was pretty much back to normal, and life was back on track again. She was going to live, anyway. As long as people typically live.

That's what the doctors assured her.

But through it all, through her whole painful ordeal of recovery, he had not been there for her. Not in body or even in spirit. So concerned about school, Natalie, the future, what to do, how to do it, how to pay for it. Time slipped away. He had become too busy for his mom.

He felt guilty.

She didn't deserve that.

Maybe that should be his New Year's resolution. One that he would actually keep. To not let the drama of his own life come between them. Make time for her. *Be a good boy.*

Billy felt someone walk up behind him and slowly turned around from the quiet winter scene he had been viewing, an agreeable backdrop for his thoughts about the past year. Holding a tumbler of Zinfandel in her long fingers was Pam. Her eyes were as dreamy as Billy's private ruminations had been. A pleasant if somewhat vacant smile was plastered on her face. She came so close, the glass bumped against Billy's chest.

"Well, Pam. It's just you and me."

"Not quite."

Billy nodded toward the Zinfandel as Pam took another sip.

"How many of those have you had?"

"Just enough."

Billy felt trapped in the foyer with her alone.

"Let's go back in. I hear there's a party going on."

Offering no resistance, Pam turned and they stepped through the kitchen into the living area. They both were watching Natalie talk to one of her new colleagues and his wife. Billy leaned toward Pam so that she could hear him over the din.

"Whaddya think?"

"She seems pretty happy here, eh? Is that what you're getting?"

"Same thing I'm sure she tells you. Loves the job. The community is what it is. Growing up in Indianapolis turned out to be good training for Rubeville here. The place is not in any hurry to enter the 21st Century. In some ways, it's still adjusting to the 20th Century."

"Growing up in Indianapolis doesn't prepare you for anything but death. Believe me. I speak from experience. She needs you here, Billy. Well... maybe *needs* is the wrong word. But that would fill in the blanks. Lacking that ..."

Pam paused to look at Billy. She seemed to be studying him. Or playing his anticipation.

"Yes. You were saying. Lacking that?"

"Lacking that ... there's me."

"You?"

"This just happened. I haven't told her yet."

"What? What's the big secret?"

"No secret. I'm just a little amazed. Actually, a lot amazed. The way things just happen sometimes. It looks like I have a job waiting here for me, if I want it. See that man over there with the red and brown plaid shirt. Jesus fuck! Who dresses these people?"

"Yeh. I see him. He probably calls the local square dances."

"Close. He manages the biggest radio station here in the Hudson Valley. Soft Rock 104 FM. They dish up high-energy elevator music plus a lot of community jabber. Anyway, his name is Bollis Shattuck and he owns the station. He just offered me a job."

"You're kidding?"

"What? Don't you think I'm qualified?"

"I ... I didn't ... that's not quite—"

"Well, I'm not. But based on my good looks, charm, slightly visible nipples,

27

blond hair ..."

"I get the picture. What will you be doing? Beside looking good?"

"Not what he thinks I will be doing." Pam laughed loudly at her own joke. "Promotions and sales. You know. The annual 4H tractor pull. The apple butter festival. Then selling ad time whenever they're overstocked on harvesters and chain saws over in Red Hook."

"Wow."

"I can see why Natalie raves about your vocabulary."

"I ... I just ... it's kind of sudden."

"I haven't decided yet. Wait. I just decided. I'm going to take it. So if the next word out of your mouth isn't 'congratulations', you might want to sleep with a shotgun under your pillow tonight."

"Congratulations, Pam. This is *great* news!"

"I hope Natalie feels that way."

"I can't imagine otherwise. You're her best friend. Her best *female* friend anyway."

Pam gave him an enigmatic smile. Bordering on snide.

"I'm her best friend."

Whether it was the alcohol, the sheer force of the surprise, or the pure stuff of true friendship, Natalie's reaction was, to put it mildly, over the top.

"I can't believe it! Ohmigod! This is fantastic! What a great way to ring in the new! When, Pam? How soon? Can you believe this, Billy?"

Actually, he couldn't. He was wondering if by some miracle of academics he could finish his degree in the next thirty seconds and make a similar surprise announcement about himself, if Natalie would be anywhere as consumed by heart-pounding elation and hysteria.

Just when he thought it was safe ...

She's back!

Billy went to the kitchen and threw a few more ice cubes in his glass. He made a death row mix of gin and tonic, five parts gin to one part tonic. After pouring that into his gullet and swallowing it in one gulp, he mixed another equally as potent anesthetic gut bomb.

The almost instantaneous numbing of his brain mitigated some of the anxiety that had just been smothering him. Billy by nature was a mellow drunk, rather than an aggressive drunk. Therefore, he started thinking nice thoughts and making a lot of room for gratuitous optimism and arbitrary cheer.

He started to reevaluate — and rationalize — the unexpected turn of events.

Maybe this *is* a really good thing.

Natalie may not "need" someone right now — she was as self-contained and autonomous as practically anyone he had ever met, male or female — but that didn't mean she would not benefit from and appreciate the companionship and support of someone who really cared about her. If it couldn't be him — the ideal situation, if it were possible — then it *should be* Pam.

Thus his alcohol-lubricated brain now reasoned.

Billy realized, to be entirely fair, he needed to square himself away about Pam. Granted, things had started out pretty rocky. He had misjudged her right off.

But the truth was, at that particular time, he had no truly clear, adequately formed impression of Natalie herself. How could he have gotten any perspective on her best friend?

The surprise birthday party Pam threw for Natalie was when he really started to get a more rounded picture of Pam as a person, and the quality of the friendship she had with Natalie. Truly how much they meant to one another.

To be fair, from that time on he and Pam had gotten on pretty well.

Realistically, right until the very moment she just announced moving here to Newburgh, all of his anxieties about her had pretty much subsided. Even the engagement ring — whether it was appropriate or not — did not detract from what Billy perceived overall as her good intentions. Why should he be threatened by her? Pam meant well. He had no reason to think otherwise.

And no matter how you cut it, they had one hugely important thing in common. They both cared deeply about Natalie and wanted the best for her.

Maybe he should grow up a little. Stop perceiving every little unexpected twist in the road as a threat. Stop being so paranoid. From this point forward, Natalie wouldn't only have Pam in her life. She was going to be developing a whole new set of friends and professional relationships. It was inevitable.

Did that mean that what he had with her was any less?

Less important?

Less powerful?

Less ... period?

"Natalie, I think this is fantastic news. I know you'll be in good hands."

"You're right about that."

He gave Pam a big brother hug.

Natalie gave Pam a big sister hug.

There were smiles all around as he and Natalie wrapped their arms around one another in a lover's embrace.

Did she notice his fierce erection begging for her tender mercies?

Seeds of Deception

Pam moved in with Natalie on January 31st.

Billy had been back in Ithaca for almost a whole month, straight off in the throes of another cram Winter Session. Now a week of classes had already passed for the new Spring Term, as he made his regular weekly call to Natalie. He always called her on Saturday evening.

Pam picked up the phone.

"Hello."

"Pam?"

"Wow! You recognized my voice? I guess we have become buds, eh?"

"How long have you been there?"

"Just arrived today. Gave four weeks notice on my old job and here I am."

So the time had come, Pam's moving in with Natalie. It made sense. Save money on rent. Make the transition into the new community easy for Pam. Give

Natalie someone she knew well and cared deeply about to spend time with. Keep them both out of trouble.

Absolutely. It made total sense.

The only awkwardness might be when he came for his weekend visits. But they could work with that. They were adults. Pam had her own room. He would stay with Natalie in hers.

The logistics of that were still a few weeks off. For now he had to deal with the day-to-day challenges of keeping up with an intense five-class load, and the other sundry details of campus life.

Billy had yet another new roommate.

Maybe he was a jinx. He remained in the same townhouse he had been living in since his sophomore year. But for everyone else, it had been a revolving door.

He had certainly seen an interesting cross-section of humanity.

There was Skid aka Beavis, the highly forgettable, easily dismissed, whack loser from Florida. That was the first semester living in the North Campus suite.

He got to live alone Spring Term. But at the beginning of Summer Session — when Natalie was completing her studies — a mutant ninja turtle from Japan showed up. He spoke no English, giving rise to the mystery as to how he could possibly finish a single class, much less get all the way through a degree program. He was always asking Billy how to spell words. Such daunting formulations as 'equals' and 'sorry' and 'milk'. The spelling bee apprenticeship ended abruptly after three weeks. One afternoon, Yuji — that was his real name — went into convulsions and was carted off to the campus hospital. They suspected a viral meningitis but Billy never found out the final diagnosis. Nor did he ever see him again.

The following Fall Term he shared his apartment with a bull ox from Nebraska, who was there on a football scholarship. Obviously, he couldn't be that great of a player or he would have gone to one of the Big Ten or PAC 10 teams. Billy couldn't remember ever seeing him with anything but food in his hands, certainly not anything as intimidating or foreign to his early-hominid skull as a book. He called Billy 'brain boy' and was always asking him to start buying his share of the beer. Of course, Billy didn't ever drink beer, so he had by default already bought his share of the beer. This reasoning was lost on Bluto or whatever his name was — Billy never found out — and the benign but annoying harassment continued. One day Bluto, about the middle of the term, packed up and left. The empty beer cases proved handy.

Four hours later, the person bull ox had conned into trading residential space with, showed up. This was a very effeminate, light-skinned AfricAm, who had an obsession with the singer Prince. While he somewhat toned down his look-alike dress and make-up for class, it was obvious that this guy had probably seen *Purple Rain* at least a thousand times. On the week ends, it was full out masquerade. Billy discovered he was making ends meet as a Prince impersonator in various venues off-campus, at frat and sorority parties and the like. For Prince Wannabe, like Bluto, studying was a distant option. Most of the time in the apartment itself, he spent either in front of the mirror making fine adjustments to his hair or make-up, or perfecting Prince dance moves in their common living area. Because Billy loved Prince's music, it would have been impossible for him to study with it blasting all of the time. Mercifully, the qua Prince man wore headphones so that he could totally immerse himself in the music while gyrating, playing air-guitar and feigning erotic sex with imaginary stage dance partners.

Like the others, he also evaporated into air without so much as a good-bye. So concluded the end of Fall Term.

After the holiday break, when Billy returned from Newburgh and opened his apartment door, he stumbled on the latest in the lineup of unusual suspects. This guy had taken over most of the living area. There were four desktop computers arrayed in front of him. Two were in some auto-function mode and their monitors were scrolling, re-drawing, bouncing between different screens and programs as they performed some calculation or analysis. A third monitor displayed a screen saver of piranha fish eating each other.

The person Billy presumed was his new roommate — if he wasn't a cyber cult leader, or a in-transit operative for a terrorist cell which had appropriated the work space for the day — was typing away. He was wearing headphones with an attached microphone, although it wasn't apparent why. A cigarette dangled from his chapped lips and the entire room reeked of tobacco smoke. He took a long drag, then put the cigarette out in an already overflowing ashtray.

Finally, he noticed Billy and gave him a broad, stained-tooth smile.

"Hi! I'm Garth. Garth Francot. From Wright Patterson Air Force Base. You're Billy Green. They gave me that name at housing. Billy Green."

"I am. Yes. That's me. What's up?"

"Just crunching some numbers. Writing a compiler. I'm only here for Winter Session. Just blasting my way through two courses — Comp Sci 6322 and 6830. Hope you don't mind if I smoke a little. I try to be considerate of others."

"Not at all. I encourage people to smoke. Helps thin out the population. But I don't approve of smoking inside the apartment. I only have one lung and I have a severe allergy to nicotine and tar. Even light contact causes my brain to swell, then I go into cardiac arrest."

"Right. No problem."

Garth lit up another cigarette and looked back at the computer monitors.

It was obvious that he was now again totally oblivious to Billy's presence in the room. He typed away, inputting code and running consistency tests on whatever it was he was creating.

Billy only had to put up with Garth for nine days. On Tuesday of the second week of Winter Session, Billy came in huffing from the cold and stamping the snow off his feet from a heavy winter storm. All evidence of the computer whiz's existence had vanished. Except for two items: There was a cheap electrically-activated air freshener plugged into the wall next to the kitchen sink, emitting a lemon-pine odor, which apparently was supposed to mask the malodor of several days of chain smoking. And there was a five-dollar bill and a note in the center of the coffee table with a large heavy rock holding them down. Better safe than sorry. You never know when hurricane conditions are going to suddenly develop inside a townhouse apartment.

The computer-printed note simply said . . .

31

What cookies?

Browser cookies?

Now it was Spring Term and it certainly appeared that Billy's luck with roommates was about to change.

This time it was someone familiar — in one sense as familiar as a person could be — and it had come about in a very unexpected way.

His roommate for the current Spring Term was none other than Julianne. Yes. *That* Julianne. The Julianne of the Fast and Foxy Five. Julianne, the surprise birthday gift Billy's freshman year.

He had run into her at the beginning of Winter Session, only a few days after the New Years Eve bash in Newburgh. It was late afternoon and he was walking at a fast clip back to his room after a grueling day. He was trying to decide whether to grab a bite on the way or fix something himself back at the apartment.

"Billy Green! I am so glad to see you. How is Natalie?"

"Great! Fantastic! Just got back from Newburgh, NY where she now has a new job and apartment, new friends. It's all good."

"Listen. This is way off the wall. But maybe you could help me out. Maybe not. I'm in a bit of a bind."

"This has a very familiar ring to it."

Julianne laughed and then almost looked embarrassed.

"No. Not that. I've grown up. Can't you tell?"

She looked the same to him. Beautiful. Delicious. Intense. Enigmatic.

"I'll take your word for it."

"Have you got a roommate? I know you're living in the townhouses."

"They never tell me. I think they just open the doors of a mental institution and whoever makes it to my place first, voilà! There's my new roommate. But to answer your question. As far as I know, my current roommate is going back to his planetary system in the Pleiades when winter cram session is over. Then, it's anyone's guess. Are you homeless?"

"Homeless would be an improvement. I'm in a rut. Still at Mary Conlon. I just can't do that anymore. It's like pre-school. I've got four more semesters and I've got to stay focused. The party bunnies have dropped out or moved on, which sure is a relief. But I'm still getting paired up with either the congenitally compromised or the intellectually impaired. You'd think that Cornell would attract a higher percentage of students whose lives weren't lived within the confines of a 29" television screen. I can't even understand what they're saying much less reply. I feel like I've been exiled to 6th Century Constantinople."

"You're rambling a bit. But I gather you're looking for a quiet, studious atmosphere. Okay. Let's see. You're still a girl, right?"

"Yes, I was a few minutes ago when I looked."

"I mean, despite my worldly playboy image and reputation, I've never roomed with a girl."

"Billy. We pretty much do the same things. Breathe, eat, sleep, bathe, other body functions. We do sit down when we pee."

"So do I."

"Congratulations! Good for you. Anyway. Give it some thought."

He recalled his conversation with Pam at the New Years Eve party.

"Yes. I really need to think about this. There. I've thought about it. The answer is yes."

Julianne went to Student Housing early the next morning. No assignment had yet been made for Billy's living unit. She only needed Billy to sign a simple request form and it was done.

Since by the time the approval came through, computer whiz had already left, Julianne was able to bring a few things over right away. When Spring Term started, she was fully moved in and ready to hit the ground running. Like Billy, she had a very demanding schedule. They discovered they even had one class together — HD 3470 Human Growth and Development: Biological and Behavioral Interactions — which might prove to be valuable in terms of studying. They could share notes, as well as discuss anything which was problematic or difficult.

Both were soon into the rhythm of the academic machine. They didn't really see much of one another — Julianne was doing some volunteer work related to her specific degree program and Billy was back to working part-time to try to keep his financial house in order — plus they were both very private people, and correspondingly respectful of one another's privacy.

She was the ideal roommate.

Of course, so far — more than two weeks into the new term — he hadn't mentioned any of this to Natalie. He wasn't sure if it would be an issue, and frankly didn't know how to broach the topic. It was awkward, so he avoided it. But this hedging naturally made him feel guilty. Like he was hiding something. He *was* hiding something. Without knowing why or whether he should.

But how could he casually bring up the fact that his new roommate is a devastatingly beautiful girl, who by the way is someone Natalie not only knew, but caught Billy in bed with the first time he had sex? And oh yes. There's nothing going on now. Really. We just sleep with a thin wall between us and it has never occurred to either of us to do what comes naturally between a man and a woman. Even though we already did that. But that was a long time ago.

Either saying or not saying what needed to be said seemed fraught with peril and suspicion. What a totally lose-lose situation he found himself in.

The lesser of two evils seemed to be to take the cowardly approach and just not mention it. Then blindly hope for the best.

That's just what Billy did. And then did his best to stop thinking about it.

Billy belatedly did make good on his New Year's resolution. It was the 3rd of February, a Tuesday night, and the moment felt right. He called his mom.

"Surprise. Happy New Year!"

"I was just thinking about you, Billy. We have a psychic connection."

"Then I won't have to pay for this phone call?"

"I think the phone company charges double. How are you, my favorite son? How's the new girl?"

"Not so very new, mom. We've been going out for a while now."

"Natalie? Is that the one? When do I get to meet this girlfriend? At least send me a photo."

"Now that's a great idea. She's in a town in the Hudson Valley, north of New York City. Next time I visit, we'll take some pics and I'll send them along. How are you feeling?"

"Like a songbird on the 5th of May. Everything's fine, Billy. Clean bill of health. Have I got some news for you, though! You won't believe this."

"Okay. I'm sitting. My seat belt is fastened."

"Your dad bought a motorcycle. A Harley Davidson."

"What! Has he flipped? This isn't exactly great weather for motorcycling. Or has global warming turned Detroit into a desert town?"

"Nope. Still snow on the ground. But he rides it anyway. I keep expecting him to come back with frostbite. But he's got the leathers, the whole shebang. He looks like a Hell's Angel."

Now that Billy had no problem picturing. He had seen photos of Hell's Angels. They didn't exactly age well. They were fat and grizzly. His father could fit in well with that scene, that was for certain.

"So what brought this about?"

"He says it's a wonderful way to see the world. He claims we're going to ride to Mount Rushmore this summer. There's a place near there called Sturgis. Every year, thousands of bikers from all over get together. A lot of beer drinking."

"What's new? He drinks beer at home. Let's see. Last year it was Vegas. Now he wants to ride a Harley across the country. What's happening with the old guy?"

"I think it's a mid-life crisis. From what I read in the magazines."

"And what about you? Any signs of a mid-life crisis? Thinking about joining a roller derby team? Or living on a commune in Sedona, Arizona?"

"I re-scheduled mine. I moved it to my 65th birthday."

Birthday. Billy suddenly had a very rude awakening. Like a knee to the groin. He suddenly realized he didn't have a clue when his mom's birthday was. He was sure they had never celebrated it. Home life had always been about hiding and dodging bullets from his father, so it had never come up. The old man certainly had never brought a gift or anything home. Never acknowledged or mentioned it once. What a screwed-up family!

"Moving your mid-life crisis to 65. That is brilliant! That means you'll live to be 130."

"You didn't know how clever I was, is that it? Listen, I just heard the rumble. He's here. Wanna talk to your father?"

"I think I better go. But thanks. Just tell him I said 'hi'. And to never downshift in sand."

"I will. Whatever that means. What was that again?"

"Never downshift in sand. Or on ice for that matter. He'll get it."

"Be a good boy, Billy. I'm expecting some pictures of you and the lucky lady."

Damn it. He should have asked her. But it was embarrassing. To not know your own mother's birthday. Of course, he didn't know his father's birthday either. But he probably wasn't even born. He probably grew from a pile of old rags, rat shit and tossed garbage. What did they call that? Spontaneous generation. That's it! A Harley Davidson? Wonders never cease. Maybe he could find out his mother's birthday from public records. They must have files for all of that. Did he know where she was born? Was it beautiful sunny Detroit? Her maiden name was Jovovich. That's was a start.

It was only a little after 10 pm but Billy's head was still spinning from the phone call and the lingering guilt, his feeling of neglect for his mom. He lay down on his bed, rolled on his side, as his thoughts continued scattershot — ricocheting from place to place, from the distant past, to the recent past, to the present, and around again.

Billy's back was turned but as soon as Julianne's knee touched his bed, he rolled toward her. In the same instant, her lips were against his ear.

"Let make love. I'm horny."

"I—"

Whatever objection he might have made was smothered as her lips covered his in a dreamy, passionate kiss, immediately leaving romantic foreplay in the wake of urgent tongues and hot heavy breathing.

His mind said no. But his body said yes. His body shouted it loudly and insistently, as Julianne caressed his member to rigid rocky heights of astonishing pleasure. Between lips and tongues, the tangle of their limbs pulled desperately at one another's clothes and within the minute they were both naked.

Julianne liked to be on top. Billy liked it any way he could get it. She just kept saying over and over, "Oh Billy. This feels so good." He had to concur.

They climaxed almost simultaneously and kept going. After a few minutes, she came again and relaxed the grip of her legs enough to permit a long slow penetration. As she moved up and down, in and out, Billy's pleasure built and built. He thought if he came again the Earth would rip apart. The planet somehow survived his time-and-space-shattering climax.

When the hot clouds of euphoria cleared from his mind and reconnected him with the starkness of the moment, he felt his body floating in the mundane reality of his campus room. Julianne gracefully dismounted and now lay next to him, curled up in his arms with her head tucked against his neck. It was like paragliding from one dream into another.

She kissed her way up his neck to his ear. After playing his earlobe with her tongue, she softly and breathily whispered.

"We don't have to do this if you don't want to."

"I think we already have."

"In the future. It could happen again. It should happen again, as far as I'm concerned."

"You have a boyfriend."

"Yes. Aaron. And you have Natalie. But for the past few days, late at night I've thought about this. I was laying there in bed picturing you over here by yourself. There I was by myself. Wanting to be with you. And I thought, what a waste. There's no excuse for wanting something and not taking it. If no one gets hurt, why not?"

She took his hand and pulled it across her stomach, then looked up and gave him a soft gentle peck on his cheek. She nestled her head on his shoulder and whispered.

"This will make life just a little better. Don't you think?"

He ran his fingertips across her nipples, up the center of her chest, her throat, then opened his hand and placed it against the side of her face. He tipped her head toward his and kissed her. It was short and sweet, all of his erotic energy for the time spent and diffused.

"I'd say life is definitely better right now. Right this minute. I just hope I can ... I don't know whether I can handle this. I mean can ... you know, with Natalie. We'll see."

"Sleep tight. Thanks for the love."

She went to her room and he could hear the sheets rustle as she got in bed. Seconds later her light went out.

And that was that.

One week later to the day, as Billy lay on his bed plodding through Howard Zinn's *A People's History of the United States* for his Religion and Politics in American History class, Julianne appeared at his door. She was wrapped in a blanket, looking like either the Virgin Mary or Mary Magdalene, smiling calmly and invitingly. She said nothing. She didn't have to. Her beautiful smile and presumed nakedness wordlessly and seductively spoke with blunt and evocative clarity.

Billy put down the book.

"I think I've had enough religion and politics."

There was a little less urgency this time. But no less passion. They made love efficiently. Yet an objective observer would assume they were both in love and deeply committed to one another. They were certainly deeply committed to giving one another as much pleasure as possible within the 45 minutes or so that they shared Billy's bed. Neither one a stranger to oral sex, they took turns sending one another into singular rapture, then consummated the entire process with missionary zeal, shaking the entire north campus with the perfection of simultaneous orgasms in the classic man-on-top coital position.

If no one gets hurt, why not?

And so it went. Like clockwork. Or more accurately, like calendarwork. Once a week on Tuesday night.

Life was definitely better.

They never spent the entire night in bed, which was difficult, to say the least. After the final rush and collapse, it was all Julianne could do to make herself get up and return to her room. But that seemed to be the understood terms of the bargain. Along the same vein, they never shared anything resembling romantic exchanges — not even glances or nods or knowing looks — between their buddy fucking sessions. While they certainly cared for one another, at the very least as good friends, this arrangement was not about romance. It was purely about sex. They were not having an affair, not even considering becoming boyfriend-girlfriend, not tempting fate or threatening the status quo of their respective relationships, Julianne's with Aaron and Billy's with Natalie.

If no one gets hurt, why not?

Billy was still having trouble with it. Maybe it was the inertial guilt which traditionally plagued Catholics. Maybe it was his relative youth and naiveté. Maybe it was his lack of sophistication and appreciation of the countless number of possible acceptable arrangements which could be fashioned between a male and a female.

So while it felt good, it still didn't feel right.

Not that this contradictory mix stopped him.

One thing that puzzled him was how quickly his resistance went down that first night, and how completely it disappeared afterwards. He spent way too much time pondering what the significance of that was. Did it mean he really didn't love Natalie as much as he thought? Did it mean that he was incapable of attaching himself to one woman at a time? Did it mean that he had been deluding himself in thinking he was somehow superior to, or at least more in control of himself than the typical fuck-anything-with-panties guys his age?

One salient point played an important role in his rationalizations. That was that he had had a relationship — if you could call it that — with Julianne in the past. He had a history with her anyway. In fact, she had played a singularly unique and vital role in the stage play of his short life. It was a small part, but as any male or female will probable agree, one which is never forgotten. She was the first girl he had ever had sex with. Didn't this confer on her some special status, some special privilege, some unique ranking?

This practically made her family.

Right.

After wasting much too much time wrestling with the ethics, psychology and sociology of his hot little arrangement, Billy did the only thing which a rational person with proper survivalist instincts could do. He put the whole thing — meaning all of the issues surrounding the erotic covenant with Julianne — in a little grey-matter box, and tucked the thing deep inside his brain behind the wall of conscience and consciousness, somewhere between his cerebellum and his brain stem, and went on with life. Life, of course, now included approximately one hour of the most mind-boggling, beautiful, briefly-satisfying but breathtaking sex imaginable, every Tuesday night, with certainly one of the most intelligent and stunning girls ever to ever attend Cornell.

Sex was sex. Good sex was good sex.

If no one gets hurt, why not?

As a bonus, Billy was spared the pointless, time-consuming, hormone-driven wandering about, checking out girls, fantasizing about the improbable but still entertaining it as possible, that many guys seem possessed by — at all ages, but particularly in their late teens and twenties. He had the perfect release.

A truly great thing about the arrangement was that it did nothing to interfere with school. Perhaps the temporary relief from sexual hunger in certain respects actually optimized the performance of his academic work. Billy continued to plug away and in spite of his working 25 to 30 hours a week at his part-time job, never fell behind on his studies, and in fact had time to supplement his class work with additional relevant reading and research.

As February was coming to a close, Billy knew it was high time to visit Natalie.

He was very excited. With Natalie in Newburgh, he felt her absence as tangibly as he felt her presence when they were together. His arms could feel, like a dark sticky lump of unfulfilled expectation, the void which held in reserve the Natalie-shaped space where she should have been.

Julianne — for all of her overwhelming beauty, for her staggering intelligence, for all her virtuosity in bed — wasn't Natalie. And an hour once a week was not forever.

It just wasn't at all the same. The Tuesday night sessions were no temporary or permanent substitute for building a life together. In every respect, that was what Natalie was all about. Consequently, Billy's not being with her every minute, not taking each step, not being there putting each little building block in place, left a gigantic gaping hole in his life, no matter what was going on at Cornell. He knew he had to finish school, but being away from her now, especially after all the time they had had together last year, was truly driving him crazy. He had to see her. It had been almost two months.

At the same time, he was very nervous.

As the weekend approached, the quandary about this new thing with Julianne — harmless and unthreatening as he had finally convinced himself it was — came back to haunt him.

He and Natalie talked fairly regularly but he still had not even mentioned Julianne was his new roommate. Now that he had the sex arrangement, there was a lot more not to mention. Unfortunately, he was lousy at lying. He suspected his face was its own lie detector read-out. He could imagine a record of his recent infidelity would be written in huge block letters across his forehead, even if not specifically queried. Plus he had always suspected that women were gifted with mysterious mind-reading powers — especially when it came to men.

Yeah. He was nervous. The bird cage empty and feathers sticking out of the cat's mouth.

"Julianne. What should I say? What should I do?"

"Go and love her like there is no other. Because, you know in your heart, there is no one else like her, Billy. She's one of a kind. I love our Tuesday nights. But put it in perspective. We're just having fun. Natalie loves you. She's not against you having a little fun. Trust me."

Billy arrived late Friday afternoon. This was his first trip since the Christmas holiday break. He had had the luxury of chauffeur service back then. Natalie had come to pick him up in her new used car and even brought him back to campus on New Years Day. This time he took a bus directly from North Campus to the Short Line bus terminal in Newburgh.

Natalie was waiting there as the bus pulled up, big smile on her face. Unfortunately Pam was at her side.

"Look, Pam. Our son is home from college. How wonderful!"

"Isn't he cute!"

"Hi, mom and dad. It's so good to be home! Where's the dog?"

They exchanged hugs all around and made the short ride through the snowy streets. To Pam's credit, after they arrived at the apartment, she made herself extremely scarce for the entire rest of the weekend. Billy and Natalie spent a lot of time in bed, both doing the obvious and just being together. It was relaxed and fun and even productive. Billy brought a couple of textbooks with him as well as class notes, and Natalie had piles of work to do for a rush proposal assignment she had just been handed at work.

It was very remindful of their time together on campus, when he would spend an evening and the night in Natalie's room at Mary Conlon. Particularly when they were both under the gun with heavy study loads, or needed to prepare for an upcoming examination.

On Saturday, they got up late, then right after having a delicious lunch at a local Mediterranean deli, took a nice if very cold walk along the river and through the rustic town.

"So, Billy. Whaddya think? Could you live here?"

"This is great. From what I can tell. You're happy! That says a lot."

"It's kind of sleepy. Compared to the City. But it's a great place to raise a family."

"Are you hinting at something here?"

"No. Yes. No. I mean, family-oriented communities have a whole different atmosphere. That's all. People are going about doing different things than in bigger communities. This is almost suburban without being a suburb. But it's not soulless like a suburb. There's so much history here. It's almost like living in a museum."

"You should be chairman of the welcoming committee."

"I am. The Welcome-To-Newburgh-Billy-Green-Welcoming-Committee."

"Okay. I'm sold! And do I get the keys to the city?"

She stopped walking, and as they turned to face one another, pressed herself against him. Discreetly she slid her hand down and lightly touched the front of his pants.

"It's right here. Just make sure you put it in the right lock and all the doors will open."

She was smiling at her own modest cleverness. Billy felt a rush of guilt, suspecting for no particular reason other than his paranoia, that this was a veiled reference to his "key's" recent wandering. It must have registered on his face, because then Natalie's expression changed. She gave him a 'what's-going-on? I-was-only-kidding' look. She pinched his cheeks like you would a pouting child.

"Come on. Smile! We've got some celebrating to do. My Billy's come to visit. I tried to hire a brass band but I guess my Walkman will just have to do."

They returned to her apartment. Pam was there but her door was closed. Natalie got a bottle of champagne out of the refrigerator, grabbed two tall-stem glasses and Billy followed her back into her bedroom.

"Hey. Where's your computer?"

"I have it in Pam's room. That's kind of the office."

"Seems inconvenient to have it in there."

"Very convenient. Broad-band internet connection paid for by my company. In fact, they bought the whole thing. Computer, printer, scanner. The works. They treat me very well."

They made love, fell asleep in one another's arms, woke up in time for dinner, but were both too lazy to make anything. They had pizza delivered from Stella's Pizzeria, reputed to be the best between Lake Erie and the Italian Alps. Then they went back to bed and spent the entire evening pretending to get something done. Actually, after they made love again, they both did get a lot done, laying side by side, then across from one another, then her head on his lap, then his head on her thighs, then laying opposite one another legs tangled like pretzels. Neither seemed much in the mood to sleep until almost five in the morning, when they finally collapsed.

They staggered out of bed just after 10 am and reached a groggy agreement that they should go to Sunday brunch and stuff their faces like it was their last meal. The Yellow Pages gave a wide selection of options but they settled on Anna's, a fancy but family-friendly restaurant downtown.

Pam's door opened and she made her way to the bathroom.

"Hi guys. Top of the morning to you."

While she was in the bathroom, Billy and Natalie got ready to leave.

"Hey, Nat. Should we invite her?"

"It's up to you. She told me she wanted to make sure she stayed out of our way. She knows how important this time is to you."

That caught Billy off guard. It had always seemed previously that Pam was bent on staking her territorial claim of friendship whenever he was around.

"It's fine with me."

Pam started to head back into her room and Billy spoke up.

"Pam. We're going to Sunday brunch at Anna's. Interested in joining us?"

"That's so sweet, Billy. But I look a fright and I've got some things to do. But thanks."

In addition to getting dressed for the restaurant, Billy packed and had everything ready to go for his return to Ithaca. His bus wasn't leaving until 6:35 pm but he didn't want to have to scramble when they got back to the apartment.

After brunch they stopped at a coffee house for Billy's first experience with designer drinks for the caffeine addicted. He had a caramel latte with whip cream heaped on top, and as they walked out he was still licking his lips like a cat after a can of albacore tuna. Then they went to Natalie's office. He had never been there, as Natalie wasn't comfortable during Billy's initial holiday visit with bringing an "outsider" into her place of work. She was too new at the time. In two short months, her comfort level had substantially increased. She had quickly established herself as a solid member of the Seminole family-workforce.

Billy was surprised at the lengths the owners of the company had gone to create a pleasant, as well as functional, work environment. None of the typical boilerplate office furniture. Instead there was a mixture of antique and modern, all wood, classical motif desks and tables. Large extremely comfortable chairs, even a couple couches and luxurious coffee tables, strewn with a wide selection of currently popular fashion and trade magazines. Beautiful healthy plants grew everywhere, in pots on the elegantly carpeted floor, hanging from the ceiling, and in the spacious windows. The best, most modern computing equipment and accessories were situated throughout the expansive working area.

What was ultimately most striking was the graceful use of floor space. The room could have easily accommodated over 25 employees, had they been crammed together the way most businesses configure an office. But Seminole only had 15 people working there, including management. Moreover, the three individuals who ran the operation were not sequestered in private offices but had their executive desks right in the general work area shared by everyone. Apparently, privacy during phone calls and meetings was not an issue. There were no secrets. This was an employee-owned company, so everyone was privy the workings of the company, the deals made, and those in progress.

"This is incredible, Nat. You have done very well for yourself."

"I guess I got lucky. I couldn't ask for a better situation. They're already giving me some serious assignments. I don't at all feel like an apprentice here."

As they walked casually through, they stopped at the desk of one of Natalie's co-workers, who was spending her Sunday off at the office. She looked up from her work, an open welcoming smile greeting the two of them.

"Cassie, this is my boyfriend Billy."

"Hello, boyfriend Billy. Is this your first visit?"

"I was here during Christmas but spent the whole time in a bathtub full of champagne."

"I can still smell it. It was pink champagne, if my nose serves me correctly."

Billy spotted a digital camera on her desk. Suddenly, he remembered.

"Ohmigod! I promised my mom."

Cassie could see through her wire-rim glasses the object which prompted Billy's epiphany.

"It belongs to the office. Ah! You want me to photograph the two of you?"

"Are you the office mind reader? *That's* what you call a marketable skill. I promised my mom a picture of us and almost forgot. This is perfect."

Natalie picked up the camera and the three moved to the other end of the room where a large stuffed couch was backed up against a window arrayed with various flowering plants on the sill. Through the window was an excellent view of the Hudson River.

"How's this?"

Cassie snapped a number of photos. They downloaded them to her computer, chose two — they were both great, Billy preferred one and Natalie the other — then printed them out, photo quality on the high-end networked Epson printer Seminole used for their best graphics.

"That's $1000 per photo. Do you want to put that on your Visa card?"

"Can you bill it against my student loan? Thanks so much for your help, Cassie. Mind reader. Photographer. You're the whole package."

Natalie gave her a co-worker hug.

"See you tomorrow, Cass. Don't work too hard."

A brutal wind had come up in the last hour and surly grey clouds threatened a punishing winter storm. Billy and Natalie opted for the comfort and shelter of her apartment, until she had to take him to the bus station. They sprinted and made it to Natalie's car without freezer burn.

"I can't believe it, Nat."

"You can't believe what."

"Everything. Your job. This apartment. Everything just falls into place. Then I get this photo thing taken care of. I would have really hated myself if I'd forgotten. But that's what I mean. It just took care of itself. If life at Cornell could be so ... so smooth."

They arrived at home and dashed from the car through the buffeting gale. Their noses were red and eyes watery as they dropped their coats and gloves on the chair next to the fireplace, and luxuriated in the 70° coziness of the apartment.

It was closing in on 5 pm. Pam finally came out of her room.

"Looks like trouble brewing out there, eh? What time's your bus?"

"6:35 and counting."

"Take survival gear. Ice picks. Snow shoes. Flares."

Natalie warmed up some cider and set out some crackers, onion dip, celery sticks and sliced carrots, for them to munch on.

"Billy. Do you really have a student loan?"

"Yes. I'm desperate. I can't keep up. And I don't want to lean on my parents any more than I have to."

"I hear that."

"So right after you left last August, I took the plunge. It was either that or cut back on class load and work full-time."

"You do what you have to do."

"I do."

There was an awkward silence. Billy knew that Natalie had every right to know what was going on with his finances. After all, they shared a common stake. But to Billy, it felt a little weird discussing matters which would affect only him and Natalie and their future in front of Pam, even if it wasn't something particularly intimate, but just financial odds and ends. For several moments, all three stared at the same invisible object somewhere in the center of the room. Billy finally broke the conversational logjam.

"How do you like your new job, Pam?"

"It's great. The first thing I did right after starting was to insist on meeting my boss's wife and kids. I'm good buddies with the wifey now. I bring her cakes, fresh flowers, recipes I cut out of women's magazines. Even hang out with his two teenage daughters. That puts a real damper on his roaming hands. Anyway, the work is easy and I get to rub shoulders with everyone in town. From the town board, police chief and mayor, to the owner of the feed store. I'm hoping to be the Grand Mistress in the annual Memorial Day parade. Or at least captain of the baton twirling team."

"You know how to twirl a baton?"

"As well as you know gandy dancing."

"Natalie! You told him about my job at the Ride My Rail Club? That was our secret."

And so the cleverness went for the next hour. Nothing personal. Not very funny. Pleasant. No one wanted to mention the obvious. The obvious announced itself in the form of an alarm clock in Natalie's room.

"I wanted to make sure we didn't lose track of the time. Time to go."

Billy grabbed his duffel bag, he and Natalie bundled up for the short drive, Pam shifted in her seat, then finally stood up for the final farewell.

"See you soon, Billy. Don't work too hard. Guess we'll see you in what, three weeks? Spring break?"

"Am I invited?"

"You're always welcome here, Billy. Like a bull in Barcelona."

Isn't that where they have the bullfights? Billy struggled to get the joke.

Pam followed them to the door. She watched them as they went down the steps. It was already starting to snow heavily. But the real avalanche came from Pam. Just as he was getting into the car, she delivered a parting shot.

"Hey, Billy. Say 'hi' to Julianne for me."

Billy tried to contain his reaction. He glanced over. Natalie was pre-occupied with cleaning off the windshield, then getting into the driver's side, and wasn't looking his way.

Pam knew about Julianne? *They* knew about Julianne? Julianne knew Pam? Whatever. They must have been talking about it in any case. Natalie knew about Julianne. Holy shit. What did she know? She couldn't know ... maybe ... what? Women! What now?

His mind was definitely not performing at its best. He was in panic mode.

As they rode to the bus station, the radio playing some generic pop love song with Natalie, to Billy's surprise, humming along, Billy started to calm down a bit. His brain functions started to assume acceptable parameters — more like a programmable VCR than a nuclear power plant that had just been hit by lightning.

"This has been great. I'm going to miss you. I guess that's obvious."

"Hmmm ... mmmm ... mmmm."

"I see you like this song."

"Hmmm ... mmmm ... mmmm."

"It's nice."

"It's stupid. But catchy. Ultimately forgettable. Like most guys."

Since he wasn't driving, he had the luxury of being able to study her face. Was that remark directed at him? She seemed intent, but was still humming along, smiling faintly.

They stopped at a traffic light.

She looked over. There was that 'what's-going-on? I-was-only-kidding' look again.

"Hey you! Thank god you're not like that. You're pretty catchy. But definitely not stupid. Or forgettable." She leaned over and kissed him. "Billy Boy. I love you!"

The five-hour bus ride back to Cornell was tedious. But the bus wasn't full and Billy had two seats to stretch out. He spent the entire time studying the text books for his art history class, taking detailed notes and listing the questions he knew were key to making sense of the subject matter they were covering at the time. He had missed the lecture this past Friday afternoon — something he rarely allowed himself to do — to catch the last bus to Newburgh.

When he got back to the townhouse, it was approaching midnight. Julianne appeared to already be asleep. Billy had some cereal and an apple, then hit the sack himself. Monday was a very busy day. Three classes, then shifts at both of his part-time jobs. There were gaps between them. But he didn't even return to the apartment, choosing just to find a place to study, sometimes a empty classroom or the corner of a café along the way, rather than waste time making trips back home. When he finally did return to the townhouse, it was after ten and he found Julianne sitting in the dinette reading a textbook over a cup of herb tea.

"Hey guy. How was the break? How is Natalie doing?"

"Great on both counts. And you?"

"Eh … so so. My family — what's left of it — is moribund. I can't say I enjoyed myself."

"Sorry about that. But now you have the bright optimistic environment of Cornell and your always-laughing-never-dull roommate."

"I think I can go along with that general assessment. Tea?"

"Naw. Time to take the laughing show to bed."

Billy didn't see Julianne the entire next day. Tuesday mornings and afternoons were hectic.

Then Tuesday night came. Billy would have assumed, considering how much lovemaking he and Natalie had done over the brief but sexually intensive weekend, he might be a little more lukewarm to the prospect of some quick-release fucking. But as soon as she walked into his bedroom and sat on the bed, it was all over except for the heavy breathing. They both sighed deeply and collapsed into one another's arms after their second set of orgasms.

So that was the plot line now.

Billy often pondered over the next several weeks why he found it so effortless to go against his own firm belief that what he was doing was terribly wrong. The easy answer was that he was just a typical guy under extraordinary circumstances.

But that wasn't entirely the reality of the situation. He didn't believe nor was he in fact a typical guy by any stretch. Nor were the circumstances extraordinary. Probably on any given night, thousands if not millions of men and women — and Julianne had to be included here because she was after all doing the same thing behind the back of her boyfriend — were cheating on their significant others. The ones to whom they had some paramount commitment.

An atypical guy in a far-too-ordinary circumstance? That was both frivolous and a dead end.

He continued to think about it. In fact he was haunted by it and for some time continued to be plagued by guilt. Still he came up with no answers. He made absolutely no sense to himself.

Eventually, he decided that he was asking the wrong questions to the wrong person. He stopped asking and just went with it.

Just because.

There!

That would have to do.

Normally he and Natalie talked a couple times a week. They had recently agreed — at her insistence — that to save him money, she would call him. She had become more protective of Billy's money than he was. He was slipping so far behind financially, he had pretty much given up budgeting. He figured he would just make up his shortfalls by arranging a student loan to cover the deficit at the end of each semester. But Natalie decided that since she had a full-time job, she should carry a little bit extra of the burden, at least for now. She had pretty much paid for all of the food and entertainment both during Billy's Christmas holiday break and for the recent weekend visit. She even offered to pay for his bus ticket.

Her calling him had its downside, however. He never quite knew when she was going to call. Though she officially had regular hours at her job, the 9 to 5 regimen was more the exception than the rule. While she pretty much knew Billy's schedule, she often could not call him at an opportune time or even when they had agreed.

Billy missed both of her calls the week after his visit. She left short and very sweet messages on voice mail but that just heightened his frustration. He broke the rule and tried to call her on Saturday, but there was no answer.

Then on Tuesday night, fairly late, right after he and Julianne had just finished making love, the phone rang. He and Julianne looked at each other, probably thinking the same guilty thoughts referencing the same people — her Aaron and his Natalie. He got up and answered.

"I finally caught you."

Not the best choice of words.

"You did. How are you, Nat?"

"Did I wake you?"

"No. No. I ... I was just lying down. Some quiet time."

Technically true. He was lying down, and he and Julianne had finished and were listening to one another's quiet breathing.

"I'm so glad you called. I was beginning to think I was jinxed."

"Jinxed?"

This was not going well. They sounded like strangers to him.

"You know. I keep missing your calls. So. Everything okay?"

"Great. Really good. Say. I've been thinking. Next week is your break, right? And I'm really wondering if you should be coming here. I mean, of course I want you here. But maybe you should be earning money. Is it too late to get a job?"

Billy felt like she had just handed him a live hand grenade.

"Well ... I could. The grounds department—"

45

"Billy. The thing is, I'm going to be working all day, sometimes into the evening. What are you going to do? We just got this big project. Four of us are going to be working day and night. The deadline is the end of the month."

"Maybe I could get something there."

"You'd spend the whole week looking, then have to leave. Listen, I can't make your decisions for you. But ... why don't you just come the last weekend? If you're not working, that is. Maybe I'll have some time that Saturday or Sunday. Think about it. Okay?"

"You're way too sensible. You're probably right. But I was so looking forward to spending some time with you."

"I guess that's the point. If you're just sitting in this apartment alone, it kind of defeats the purpose of coming. Hey, Billy. Not to change the subject, but is Julianne there? I need to talk to her. Just a quick one."

How long before a hand grenade explodes? It should be getting close.

"I'll see if she's around."

White lie #1.

Like he didn't know.

Billy waited a few seconds, then went to his room and got her. She was wide awake and calmly staring at him as he approached, then got up and picked up the receiver in the living room.

"Natalie! How are you? . . . . Things are going well. Can't complain . . . . Sure. I understand . . . . Okay. I promise. . . . . Right. So. When are you thinking? . . . . Perfect. Did you want to talk to Billy? . . . . . . Can't wait. See ya."

She handed the phone back to Billy.

"She sounds in good spirits. What are you doing there? Giving her foot massages?"

Natalie had a teasing chuckle in her voice.

"Nothing really. I hardly ever see her. Maybe that's it."

White lie #2.

He saw her enough. Enough to be her lover.

"I'm sure you have studying to do. I've still got a project action item breakdown to do tonight. Then some cost spreadsheets. It never ends."

"What were you two talking about?"

"Just your basic girl talk. Are you worried?"

Again the taunting laugh.

"No. Of course not."

White lie #3.

He was as white as the bed sheet Julianne was still laying on. His stomach was in a knot. Acid was dissolving the back of his throat.

"Do you like Stephen Stills? Pamela turned me on to him the other night."

"Never heard of him. Is he a movie star? Football player? What?"

"As in Crosby, Stills and Nash?"

"Who?"

"Billy. We've got to educate you. Anyway, check out his solo album."

"Oh. He's a musician."

"You got it. 70s and 80s guy. Big time. The album is just called Stephen Stills. Just listen to the first track. Great philosophy of life there. I think you'll appreciate it. Good night, love. Sleep tight. I'm thinking about you."

"Good night, Nat. I miss you."

What was with the games? Billy was sure that this rated as the strangest conversation he had ever had with her. They went from being strangers, through Natalie's basically putting the brakes on for spring break, to him listening to one half of a puzzling conversation with his once-a-week-lover who he had just had sex with, to Natalie embedding some bit of philosophical wisdom inside of an upgrade of his musical tastes.

Maybe the grenade hadn't gone off but Billy was left with the uncomfortable job of pulling pieces of shrapnel out of himself anyway. He definitely felt wounded.

Julianne had gone into her room. Billy knew it would be bad form to bother her. Her door was closed. But he was going crazy. What had they talked about? She and Natalie.

He knocked so softly he was afraid Julianne didn't hear it. But after a few seconds, just as he reached his hand up to knock again, she opened the door the width of her head and peered out quizzically at Billy, who looked like the next door neighbor wanting to borrow an egg at three in the morning.

"Have you ever heard of Stephen Stills?"

"Yes. Anyone who has owned a stereo system in the last thirty years knows who Crosby, Stills and Nash are. Do I win something?"

"I ... I ... this can wait. Sorry to bother you. Good night."

"Good night, sweetheart. I shall be counting the minutes until I know you are squatting in the bathroom like a girl. It just tickles me pink to think about it."

Paradoxically, her little bit of midnight mockery put him completely at ease. Suddenly, he felt that whatever it was that was bothering him was ridiculous. Julianne was a good friend to have, at whatever hour. He laughed like she had just given him a shot of nitrous oxide.

"That's beautiful. Because I know it comes from here."

He was tap tap tapping his heart as she closed the door.

And that's what friends are for.

Billy never bothered to track down the first track of the eponymous Stephen Stills album, as Natalie had suggested. That was too bad. It might have put some things in perspective. Then again, it might have confused the shit out of him.

The song she referred to was Mr. Stills' biggest hit, called "Love The One You're With."

It was famous and popular for giving license to a whole new level of promiscuity. The final words to the chorus became a mantra for the generation which kept true to its message until running smack up against the AIDS epidemic . . .

*If you can't be with the one you love
Then love the one you're with*

Billy really needed to start paying attention.

At some point the latter part of Spring Term, Billy fell in love with Julianne.

A couple weeks into April they had already upped the ante. It was Tuesdays *and* Thursdays.

Then she was gone. Summer came and she moved out. It was time.

That short, turbulent period of several weeks was — at least so far in his twenty years — easily the most confusing time of his entire life.

Of course, in years to come, life would be so messy that it would make this little dramatic episode seem like a cellophane-wrapped store-bought shirt from Van Heusen.

But a person has to start somewhere. Confusion is not something anyone masters overnight. It requires years of practice and rigorous application of one's worst judgment. Start small and build the dead-ends, detours, burnt bridges, cul-de-sacs, sink holes and road closures slowly and methodically over time. That is, if you want to really get confused, and make life a string of maybes, what-ifs, whatevers, could-have-beens, should-have-beens, what-was-I-thinkings, what-to-dos, and what-nows.

And who doesn't? At least that's how it seems.

Judging from the way most people muck up their lives.

As is most common, Billy just stumbled into his confusion. Blindly, cluelessly, unwittingly — with the naive and furtive optimism of relative youth and the addled brains of wide-ranging inexperience.

He had never been in love even once. Now he was in love twice. At the same time. Was he twice lucky or twice cursed?

They say absence makes the heart grow fonder.

How true. It sure did in Billy's case. Natalie was absent. So he grew fonder of Julianne. Ultimately, it was Julianne's absence which made him fonder of Natalie.

And for a good stretch he loved them both equally.

One did not subtract from the other. If anything, they seemed to build off of one another. His feelings for Natalie colluded with and augmented his love for Julianne. And as the intensity built for Julianne, it synergized and magnified his love for Natalie.

This in turn synergized and magnified the pain and the guilt he felt for what he was doing. Though that ironically seemed only to inspire him to further seek solace in the hot inferno of his affections for Julianne. He genuinely feared that this superheated infatuation was plunging him headlong toward a total meltdown.

He had no idea how to begin sorting it out.

He wasn't even sure he wanted to.

Maybe he was just in love with love. Maybe he was just out of his mind.

Against his better judgment and with reluctance on her part, he occasionally got Julianne to talk about it. Usually, it was as his semen was slowly oozing out of her vagina. Her impatience with him could be cut like a chunk of warm taffy.

"You can't be serious, Billy."

"Of course, I'm serious."

"I love you, Billy. But it's not the same. It's a biological love."

"Like between two frogs? Or lily pads? Or a frog and a lily pad?"

"You weren't a complete idiot three minutes ago."

"I just know how I feel."

"Good for you. I think I better go."

"You're saying you don't feel the same way about me as I feel about you."

"I'm saying you don't feel the same way about me as you think you do. I know what you and Natalie have. Consider yourself lucky and leave it at that."

"I am lucky to have both of you."

"You have me on Tuesday and Thursday nights. For a while. You'll have Natalie for the rest of your life. If you don't blow it."

"It feels exactly the same."

"But it's world's apart. It's a distinction it seems most guys don't make, much less understand. Figure it out. Good night."

He tried. He really tried.

Sometimes he tried to drop all pretense and delusion and just view the whole thing entirely superficially.

Hedonistically might be the better word.

He hardly had to remind himself, that within each world, the Julianne world and the Natalie world — completely separate and isolated from one another in space and time — he was definitely having a phenomenal shot of good fortune.

At the same time, Billy was no stranger to his fatalistic side — perhaps some semi-latent self-sabotaging component of his personality — which pointed its reprimanding finger and reminded him not to expect the current course to have anything but a tragic ending. Think of his father. Was Billy a chip off the old block? Think of Detroit. You can take the boy out of Detroit but can you take the Detroit out of the boy?

He felt cheap. White trash cheap. Typical guy cheap. Mutant strain cheap. Garbage-in garbage-out cheap. No-escaping-what-you-are cheap.

Of course, this was pure, self-deprecating hyperbole. The tricks and torture the mind resorts to in order to goad itself into risk-averse retreat.

The inescapable truth was that Billy had no real perspective on himself or the situation. He was flying blind and for now had no idea where he would land.

Despite his best efforts and his spectacular failure at understanding, explaining, or at least coming up with a plausible rationalization for his duplicitous, if sexually entertaining behavior, Billy did accomplish one notable thing. It would not find him a place in the intellectual history of the West, or even garner him a footnote in a grad student's unpublished philosophy paper. But it would put his own mind to rest and give him a certain amount of satisfaction.

Out of all of the analysis, merciless self-examination, cold chills, cold sweats, teeth-grinding, guilt, frenzy, frustration, empty epiphanies, and rare moments of calm contemplation, Billy came to know one thing for sure ...

Love is real.

He could now with the absolute cocksure confidence of pure enlightenment, scoff at the naysayers and spit in the face of the purveyors of romantic nihilism, the cynics who say that love is an illusion.

Billy knew the real score.

Love is the light that never dims.

Love is a wine that flows in our hearts.

Love is a wonder that has no beginning or end.

Love is a master key that opens the gates of perfection.

Love is the language our souls use to speak to one another.

Love is the trafficking of fantasies and transcending of mortality.

Love is an energy that can neither be created or destroyed.

Love is God Allah Yahweh Shiva Qat Aphrodite.

Love is touch smell feel taste listen pray.

Love is the poetry of the senses.

Love is metaphysical gravity.

Love is the gift of oneself.

Love is sweet tyranny.

All you need is love.

Descartes. You almost got it right.

Je aime, donc je suis.

Yes. That's how it should go.

I love, therefore I am.

Valentines Day solipsism.

It should have come as no surprise that Billy fell so deeply — or at least was convinced he was so deeply — in love with Julianne. Regardless of how matter-of-fact and calculating their arrangement was, at least on paper. Regardless of what prior commitments were on the table when Billy and Julianne struck their self-serving, mutually convenient arrangement. Regardless. The music at the closing curtain played the same recognizable universal melody.

By the end of Spring Term, Billy was deeply, madly, passionately crazy about her.

And realistically ... how could it be otherwise? Given the circumstances? They had been living and regularly sleeping together for five months. Tuesday followed Tuesday followed Tuesday. Then they threw in Thursdays for dessert. How could he not fall in love with her? After he felt the urgent needy rhythms of her body and the tight cool convulsions of her climax. After he tasted the sweet salty suppleness of her breasts and the milky lubrication between her legs. How could he not fall in love with her? Every girl has a unique taste. Julianne was uniquely delicious. Honey-lemon mixed with the spicy sweet of nutmeg. Toward the end of their lovemaking sessions as he entered her, he would wet his lips and the luscious smell of her sex would enter his nostrils. They had gotten so familiar with one another, they could sustain their coital ballet for the longest time, savoring the promise and all of their pre-orgasmic sensations with miserly joy, until the volcanic roar of their climaxes — after their months together more often than not simultaneous — collapsed them in a perfect erotic embracing fusion. They never rushed anything anymore. Until she got up and went to her room, she would wrap her long lithe arms around him and the barriers between their bodies and souls dissolved. Their shared warmth would permeate everything they could feel, touch, smell, hear. His fingertips would light on her face and hair, as he brushed her lips with his. Her hands would delicately caress his back and buttocks. Finally their breathing would slow and synchronize, as they became one.

How could he not fall in love with her?

Unfortunately, this raised another profoundly troubling question. One which would never be answered and continued to add to his torment and bewilderment for years to come.

The great mystery, the thing that left him stumbling punch-drunk, wobbling and reeling in a black hole of confusion when Spring Term came to a close and they had parted ways, was how Julianne had seemed so completely unaffected by their love trysts. Sure. She had always been affectionate, kind and considerate, and generous as a lover. But love? She had kept that locked away in some private chamber which Billy had never seen, much less approached or broached.

For better or worse — probably worse — he would never forget her parting words the final day of exams. Her bags were packed and stuffed in the trunk of a waiting taxi. They shook hands like they had just settled a bet. Julianne spoke with the cold authority of Galileo addressing the Pope.

"Thanks for the great sex, Billy. You've got a beautiful body and you know how to use it."

Billy Green.

Gigolo. Stud boy. Fuck buddy.

He boarded the very next bus to Newburgh and spent the weekend alternating between sulking and sobbing.

He never gave Natalie a straight answer why. He couldn't.

"What's wrong, Billy. Talk to me."

"Life. Pollution. TV. Twinkies. Iraq. Mad cow disease. Nuclear weapons. Paris Hilton."

"You're in love with Paris Hilton?"

"I love you, Natalie. You. Don't you forget it."

Who was he reminding? She certainly already knew.

His dramatic declaration of the obvious seemed to calm him down some, leaving him for the remainder of his visit, closer to catatonic than agitated.

Natalie drove him late Sunday afternoon to catch the last bus to Ithaca. She waited with him in the departure lobby. The bus was delayed due to some unspecified mechanical problems. They sat in the midst of a small but increasingly impatient crowd, saying nothing, both bored and jumpy. Almost an hour passed. Finally the announcement came.

> *The Short Line bus bound for points west including*
> *Middleton, Monticello, Binghamton, Ithaca, Geneva,*
> *and Rochester is now ready for departure. Passengers*
> *should immediately proceed to Boarding Area 5.*

They stepped out of the terminal to the boarding area. It was the most unromantic of all possible settings for any exchange of sweet nothings, big or small. The gunning of the diesel engine pumped brown-black smoke into the hangar-size bay. The croaking rumble almost made any exchange of words inaudible. Just before stepping up into the behemoth steel box which would ferry him back to campus, Billy turned to Natalie and made a huge push from the back of his throat, which was partially paralyzed from speaking so little over the past few days, partially in the grip of a trepidation he had never felt before. In his effort to speak, he almost seemed to be choking.

Four halting words with a grimace.

"Will you marry me?"

Her response was calm and without hesitation.

Two lilting words with a smile.

"Of course!"

Chapter Two

LIFE IN THE O.C.
2004 – 2006

Of Course!

It was the first day of summer and it had splendidly delivered on the buoyant promises of spring.

Gardens and window boxes were overflowing with azaleas, honeysuckles, hollyhocks, tulips, pansies, petunias, impatiens, hyacinths, and columbines — a stunning fractal rainbow. Lawns were infused with the lively green ink of April and May showers. The Hudson River moved the spring deluge with energetic efficiency, between banks thick with towering old maples and oaks, and a vibrant undergrowth of saplings and flowering bushes.

Billy had graduated from Cornell with a B.A. degree in Sociology and Ecological Systems, exactly three years and nine months from the first time he stepped on the highly-respected and acclaimed university campus in Ithaca.

He now stood next to Natalie at the County Courthouse before a magistrate, exactly three years, six months and seven days from the first time he saw her in a third floor dorm room in Mary Conlon Hall on that same campus.

"Do you take Natalia Diamond to be your lawfully wedded wife?"

"I do."

"And do you take William Green to be your lawfully wedded husband?"

"Of course."

"Then by the powers vested in me by the State of New York ..."

And that was that.

He kissed the bride. She kissed back. Pam hugged the bride. Billy shook hands with his "best man", Chuck Everest, one of Natalie's co-workers who he barely knew. Billy hugged Pam. Natalie hugged Chuck. Chuck hugged Pam. Billy handed a check to the magistrate. Then they went to the grand connubial lunch. They had a window table at Pamela's On The Hudson.

Since it was a Wednesday — Natalie had taken the day off while Chuck had merely extended his lunch hour to accommodate the ceremony — Natalie had to be at work next morning. Mercifully, she put off pressing matters related to her job, and she and Billy spent their honeymoon night cuddled up watching a movie, the Hugh Grant comedy *Love, Actually*.

Billy and Natalie had decided to keep the wedding small. It couldn't have been any smaller. While Billy would have loved to have his mom there, too many anxieties and issues surrounded the potential presence of his father. Similar concerns and antipathies haunted Natalie with respect to her family.

They took the easy way out. Bride and groom, two witnesses, a simple civil ceremony which cloaked the marriage in the appropriate legal garb. The spiritual aspects of their union would be in the private venues of their own hearts.

So much had happened over the long course of their engagement, most of it if not uneventful, certainly not supercharged with high drama. As they preferred.

Billy had, of course, finished his degree. He graduated Magna Cum Laude, a small miracle in itself, considering he had continued to work 25 to 30 hours a week almost the entire time he was taking classes. He got a straight 4.0 grade point average in all of the courses related to his major areas of study, sociology and ecological systems. The only courses which gave him problems were the "touchy-feely" ones — FGSS 3590 Consuming Passions: Media, Space, and the Body, and FGSS 3690 Fast-Talking Dames and Sad Ladies, both offered by the Department of Feminist, Gender, & Sexuality Studies — and modern philosophy courses which concentrated on technical aspects of contemporary philosophy like ordinary language analysis and syntactical deconstruction of philosophical issues, exercises which seemed to cut off actual philosophical discussion at the knees. He certainly grasped the subject matter both in the feminism and philosophy courses, but had trouble translating that into optimal performance at exam time, probably because he simply could not relate to the conceptual terrain.

Billy had been encouraged by his academic advisor and several of his professors, who had taken a liking to him and respected his brilliance, to continue on to grad school in pursuit of advanced degrees. But the thought of any more time away from Natalie was inconceivable to him, so he decided to postpone any post-graduate work for sometime in the distant future.

Natalie, as expected, had done really well at Seminole. In under two years, she was already a project manager and only answered to the three people who headed up the company. Seminole had grown in this short time to 27 employees and still had more work than they could possibly handle. Everyone worked extremely hard, both out of dedication to building the company into a serious and effective player in the field of sustainable human systems engineering, and because they all believed they were making an important contribution to their local community and the world at large. Green technology was not just a future. It was the only future for a planet if it were to survive a population expected to exceed 15 billion within a few decades. Now Seminole Environmental Consultants had a new shining star in their constellation of highly qualified and able employees. They treated her well and Natalie reciprocated by giving them her best. It was a solid and mutually-gratifying arrangement.

Pam likewise was doing well in her job. Her new job, that is. The position she originally had at the radio station fell apart after six months. The basic problem was that she did her job way too well. The owner of the station had long prided himself with "getting his hands dirty", doing a lot of the promotional work himself. So in addition to running the station as manager/owner, he spent a lot of time glad-handing. Unfortunately, Pam had quickly supplanted him even with his most longstanding customers, in large part because of her feminine charm and luscious good looks, but even more so because she had fresh and innovative ideas. His rejection by his old buddies and her continued rejection of his ham-handed sexual advances, quickly combined to spell 'pink slip' and she was dismissed. By then, she had developed excellent relationships with a number of local businesses and had her pick of job offers. She went to work for a small but very successful public relations and advertising firm, with the unfortunate name of You Win I Win Everybody Wins, Incorporated.

Natalie and Pam continued to be close, but with their demanding jobs they had much less leisure time than ever before. They both still loved going into New York City. When they had the same couple days open on their calendars — occasional weekends and extended national holidays — they took the train into the city and did what they did. Though Billy was never exactly clear what it was they did, apparently they had some favorite restaurants and evening haunts, as well as seemingly endless places they liked to shop for clothes. He never remembered seeing the same store logo twice on any of the shopping bags they brought back.

Of course, in anticipation of Billy's return and the wedding, Pam had found her own place. Her new job and much more generous salary allowed her to buy a new luxury condo. Her move timed perfectly with Billy's arrival.

Billy certainly now no longer felt the unstated but real competition from Pam that he had felt when he was back on campus and she was there in Newburgh with Natalie. Back then, whether he needed to be or not, he was very threatened by Pam and was often haunted by an envy which bordered on desperation. Because of his need to earn money and try to be frugal, he had only managed to get to Newburgh twice each school term these last couple years. Even though Pam was usually considerate enough to make herself nearly invisible on those rushed and frantic visits, he still felt he was at an unfair advantage and was being cheated out of his due with Natalie, whereas Pam theoretically had 24/7 access.

Running a respectable second to Billy's desire to see Natalie, was his desire to visit his mom.

Fortunately, her health had continued to improve. She got tested regularly and there was no sign of cancer in her body. She had returned to her original weight and level of activity less than a year after the chemo and radiation treatments had ended. With all she had gone through, she had decided to forego reconstructive surgery on her breasts. While it never specifically came up in conversation, Billy sensed that she was okay with her body now, despite the surgical pruning which had originally left her feeling like a monstrous freak. She laughed easily, and no longer slouched or crossed her arms in front of her. She was back to being the mom he always knew and loved.

Despite his preoccupation with school and of course with Natalie, he found himself thinking about his mom more and more, as graduation approached.

He did manage to talk to her with moderate regularity. But he rarely visited. In the last three years, he had gone back to Detroit only three times. Once was for Christmas, the first time his dad went to Las Vegas. Another time he dropped by for a three-day July 4th weekend. That time, Billy and his mom watched the fireworks on Belle Isle in the middle of the Detroit River with a picnic basket and a blanket — his father again was MIA, coincidentally out of town with "the boys" on some excursion. His most recent visit occurred when Natalie told him she was going to be completely slammed for the Christmas holidays with a work assignment, prompting him to spend the nine-day break in Detroit. For that visit, his father was again back in Vegas, presumably chasing showgirls, losing wads of cash, and generally making a nuisance of himself.

Billy's father had kept good to his promise and rode to Sturgis, South Dakota for the annual Harley Davison road rally and beer orgy, Billy's mom hanging on for dear life on the back. That was the first and last time she would ever do that.

"My butt is just too bony to sit on a motorcycle for more than 15 minutes, much less two weeks. Besides, the way your father drives my whole life passes before me every time I get on that damn thing. But your dad loves it. More power to him. He can have it!"

His dad's crush on the metal monster on the other hand, had blossomed into a full-blown romance. Whenever weather permitted, every available opportunity he now took to riding. He had become what is known as a weekend road warrior. Now instead of a worthless, immobile couch potato, he was a worthless, highly-mobile big daddy biker, with a bulky black helmet sporting a built-in CB radio. He wore pointy mod rocker boots, and leathers from head to ankle. These included a jacket with the dragon logo of *King Komodo of Detroit (Demons of the Highway)*, a semi-geriatric motorcycle club based in nearby Warren, which he had joined right after returning from his summer road trip to Sturgis.

Quietly and without fanfare, his mom tripled the size of his dad's life insurance policy.

The more immediate benefit to her was that the old man was rarely at home. Had they had anything resembling a healthy relationship, this would have caused her concern and loneliness. But their relationship was at best boring and at worst abysmal, which meant that his absence was a liberating and empowering turn of good fortune, in a marriage too-long plagued by spousal sufferance and indignity.

"I'm having the time of my life, Billy. I joined an astronomy club. I'm on a bowling team. Believe it or not I rolled a 104 the other night, first time to break 100."

"Wait! Back up. An astronomy club?"

"Have you ever seen the rings of Saturn? Or the gaseous nebulas of Pegasus?"

"I missed out on that. You know how busy I was in high school. Captain of the badminton team. Exchange student in Sweden."

"I'm telling you, Billy. The world is full of wonders."

"You're right about that mom." He was looking across the room at Natalie as she labored away at some proposal or concept paper on the computer. His mom read his mind.

"And how is the little lady, my big grown-up-living-with-his girlfriend son?"

He still hadn't told her they were married. Not very smart.

"Fantastic, mom. Just fantastic."

"I'm glad you're happy, Billy. Happiness is a good thing."

"Hey mom. Congratulations on that 104 game."

"Congratulate me when I get through a game without at least five gutter balls."

"Hang in there. It's just a matter of time."

"But do I have that much time? I'm becoming an old lady."

Whew! How old was she now? 50? 52? Not an old lady. Not yet anyway. But the years were piling on.

Despite his heartfelt desire to the contrary, he could feel the closeness with his mom — in fact with both of his parents — diminishing. It was a closeness he had always taken for granted. It had less to do with not caring than not sharing. He certainly cared about his mother deeply, and even had some feeling for his father embedded in him from the inertia of spending eighteen years of his life under the same roof. But now they no longer shared the day-to-day of living. They no longer had the experience of life in common. They thought about and did very different things. It was inevitable that a distance would grow between them. In some ways Billy regretted this, in others he was grateful.

At least he and Natalie would have no in-law issues. It went beyond the nearly thousand miles of geography which separated them from their next of kin.

Natalie had severed all ties with her family, conveniently forgetting to give them either her forwarding address or phone number when she moved to Newburgh. And Billy had for a long time been vaguely promising his mom he would bring Natalie to Detroit to meet her. His demanding study and work schedules had provided proper cover until now. His mom graciously never pressed the matter. Sweet lady.

But since he and Natalie were now married, he knew it was just a matter of time before he would just swallow hard and make himself actually arrange it. However that turned out, the physical distance between Newburgh and Detroit and the immutable hostility between Billy and his father would provide sufficient barriers to any pretenses of chumminess between the two Green families.

He decided he had to break the news. The longer he waited, the harder it became. He should have told her up front. Hindsight is a beautiful thing.

July 4th weekend was coming up in less than two weeks. Chances were his father would be out riding his metal hog somewhere, so they would be safe dropping in on mom's home turf. On the other hand, it might be nice for his mom to get out of the torment and torpor of Detroit for a few days.

"Hey Nat. Can you spare a couple days around the fourth to meet my mom?"

"That would be fantastic! We're family now. I'd say it's about time."

"Here or there in Detroit? Whaddya think?"

"Your descriptions of the lavish lifestyle you had in Detroit and all of the cultural offerings of the place are really tempting. I've had it up there on my list with St. Petersburg, Rome and Paris. But I suppose I could postpone one of my dream vacations for now. Detroit will have to wait. Let's bring her here and show her how we party in Newburgh. I'll go and buy the sparklers right now."

And so it was. Not surprisingly, Billy's mom had no urgent commitments. Bowling team was on summer hiatus. Her plants could handle not being watered for four days. Harold probably wouldn't even know she had been gone. He was heading up north on his Harley with his riding buddies to Greyling, Michigan for the annual 4th of July Independence Day Rodeo Round Up, the official name for three days of belly-busting beer drinking, with some square dancing, horse riding and cattle wrestling thrown in for good measure.

She would arrive late Friday afternoon on the 1st and fly back on the 5th.

Natalie left work early and they greeted her at Stewart International Airport, just outside of town, holding a big sign.

Billy and Natalie welcome
Irene to Newburgh.
Hi, mom!!

The four days couldn't have gone better.

They let her relax and rest Friday evening, while she got comfortable with her surroundings and got acquainted with Natalie. They ordered a huge take-out feast from YOBO Oriental. When Billy returned with the three giant bags of food, they all dug in like they hadn't eaten for days. Chinese was a rare treat for his mom, since his dad refused to even try it, insisting that all of the meat in Asian dishes was either dogs or cats.

After the great meal, the next hour was devoted to digesting the food and just getting comfortable with one another. His mom seemed at ease, which put to rest any anxieties which Billy and Natalie had about her being there.

Natalie noticed Irene looking at her left hand and smiling.

"You two make a wonderful couple. I'm very happy for you, Mr. and Mrs. Green."

Billy looked at his mom both amazed and relieved.

"Thanks, mom. I ... um ..."

"Good-night, you love birds. I'm exhausted. See you in the morning."

Later that evening, after waiting until they were sure that Irene was fast asleep, in sharp contrast to their usual wild abandon in bed, they made love as quietly as they possibly could. As they lay in one another's arms, Natalie whispered softly in Billy's ear just before they both drifted off for the night.

"Your mom is so cool."

Saturday, they took her on a driving and walking tour of Newburgh. Later they boarded the train for New York, stood in line at the TKTS discount ticket booth near Times Square, and managed to get front-row center seats for *The Lion King*. After so many years as a mainstay of the Broadway musical scene, it was past its prime and not the best production. But since Billy's mom had never seen a Broadway play, she was thrilled beyond their most optimistic expectations and couldn't stop talking about it through dinner and on the train ride home. They thought they were going to have to call in professional help to get her calmed down. But only minutes after returning to the apartment, she was in the guest room and out like a kitten that had been playing all day in the sun.

Sunday, Pam joined them at what was becoming their favorite brunch venue, Anna's Restaurant, right downtown. They all then went to the Newburgh Historical Society Museum, for a little town history. Afterwards, they picked up a picnic basket at Villa Italia and spent the afternoon lolling at Downing Park, the main park in town. The sky was full of majestic billowing white cumulus clouds, a fresh breeze kept them cool in the 78 degree sunshine, and conversation was light and lively as they feasted on antipasto, garlic bread, Italian sausage sandwiches, bowls of sliced fruit, and a flamboyant 1997 Chianti Classico. It was a perfect day.

Sunday evening, they rented and watched two fun Hugh Grant movies — *Mickey Blue Eyes* and *The Englishman Who Went Up a Hill and Came Down a Mountain*. Irene thought she had died and gone to Heaven. Despite the rest of the country's infatuation with Brad Pitt, Johnny Depp and George Clooney, her love affair with Hugh Grant continued unabated.

"He reminds me so much of your dad when he was a young man, Billy."

That was way too much of a stretch for Billy, even under the influence of too much Italian wine and the buoying spirits of a great day.

"They wear the same size shoe?"

"Billy! You are such a funny boy. I meant the length of their penises."

That brought down the house. Pam and Natalie couldn't stop laughing, while Billy just sat there grinning sheepishly.

Monday was the big day. For a city the size of Newburgh, barely large enough to host a wheelchair race and a hog calling contest, it was a really big deal. All of the surrounding communities for twenty miles were participating. The City Council and Independence Day Events Planning Committee pulled out all the stops — well, all of the stops at their disposal.

The big annual parade started at 11:30 am. It seemed like there were more people in the parade than lining the street watching it. Everybody who had an organization or business got their 20 minutes in the Newburgh spotlight. The Kiwanis, Boy Scouts, Girl Scouts, the Rotary, Kneedles For Knewburgh Knitting Klub, the Volunteer Firefighters Association, several 4H chapters, the Library Trust Builders, American Legion, Organic Farmers of Orange County, the Municipal Police Motorcycle Drill Team, MADD (Mothers Against Drunk Driving), an independent group of marchers dressed in red, white and blue carrying 'Support Our Troops' banners, the First Church of Crawford Square Dancing For Jesus dancers, several wide-eyed youths dressed in track suits carrying a banner that said 'Special Olympics 2005', two VFW marching troupes, three all-girl dance teams doing pumped-up hip hop routines, four tractors pulling hay wagons full of sunburned teenagers, five baton twirling squads, six high school marching bands, seven monocyclists, eight mounted policeman, countless clowns squirting the crowd with Super Pumper water guns or giving out balloon animals to the children in the front row, the Hudson River Rowing Club, Cloggers Without Borders, and last but not least the Senior Citizens Hula Hoopers.

To bring up the rear was Wayne Brinks, the Mayor himself, sporting a tux and suede cowboy hat, beside the Grand Mistress of Independence Day her fourth year running, Annie Roberts. They rode standing up in a 1958 pink and white Edsel convertible driven by the Police Chief, all three waving and smiling at the crowd, who cheered and waved back, their enthusiasm more out of gratitude that the two-hour plus parade had finally come to an end, than for any special affection they held for Mr. Brinks or Ms. Roberts, both of whom were way-too-familiar fixtures in the community.

The parade terminated at Downing Park, where a stage was set up and more entertainment was provided to wile away the day. This included a couple local rock bands, a blue grass group, a mini-concert by a string quintet, the Civic Pride Men's Chorus, a poetry reading by several ladies from the local Battered Women's Shelter and Help Hotline, tap dancing by dozens of pre-teens from Lilly's School of Ballet and Tap, an Elvis impersonator, a ten year old boy ventriloquist who amazed the audience — the eight or nine people who sat down to give their legs a rest — by singing duets from the 30s and 40s with his dummy Jeez Louise, and finally, chainsaw juggling by two retired lumberjacks from Vermont. The jugglers drew the biggest crowd, curious gawkers who apparently savored the possibility that they would see a few fingers or limbs chopped off.

After the parade finally ended, there were several hours before the climactic riverfront pyrotechnic display, scheduled to close the day's festivities. Rather than go indoors — it was such a perfect summer day, not too hot, with the pristine air still charged with excitement and community pride — Natalie, Billy and his mom opted to just hang around downtown, watch the town folk, and snack from the numerous food booths set up in and around the park. Conversation was intermittent and light. Often they were just content saying nothing and just being together. They saw Pam off and on. She was semi-working, since many of her clients had participated in the official festivities. She constantly came and went. Early evening she finally settled in with them, and the four of them had a leisure dinner at Capri Restaurant on Broadway, in the center of the business district.

Fireworks started around 9:30 pm and went on for a full half-hour, capped by a spectacular finale that left babies crying, dogs howling, and the crowd oohing and aahing in a Gregorian croon of appreciation.

They made the short walk back to the apartment in the cooling but pleasant evening air, stopping to look at the shop window displays. The scattered billows of cottony clouds from earlier in the day had completely cleared, and despite the lingering smoke from the fireworks, a myriad of stars sprinkled the heavenly canopy overhead.

The long day in the sun and their lolling on the banks of the river took its toll. Natalie, Billy and his mom were exhausted and went right to bed. Irene had an early flight and a long awkward schedule of connections to get her back home, so it was just as well.

No one had to feign sadness at the airport. They all genuinely appreciated the time they had spent together and sincerely regretted having to say good-bye.

Natalie held Irene in an extended farewell embrace.

"Once I had a mom. She was no way as great as you but I loved her. And I miss her. But I feel like I have a mom again. Thank you so much for coming here. This has been the best 4th of July of my life!"

When they parted, Billy did the final honors and gave his mom the biggest hug ever. He felt the wetness of her tears on his cheeks, the frail but firm length of her arms around him.

"I love you, mom."

"You're a good boy, Billy ... the best."

And then she was gone. Back to whatever it was that held her captive in Detroit.

Newburgh — the Newburgh where they worked and spent most of their time — was the largest city in Orange County, New York.

But to call it a city was a bit of an exaggeration. The year Billy moved there, it only had slightly over 24,000 people. To make things confusing, the adjacent Newburgh Town, which abutted the City of Newburgh on its northern and western borders, had a larger population, approaching 28,000 that same year.

Billy asked everyone why it was called Orange County. It wasn't orange. It was green. Except in the autumn, when some of the large maple leaves, the ones hovering indecisively between yellow and red, sat precariously in the orange band of the color palette, orange was definitely not a significant player here. They certainly didn't grow oranges. So that was a non-starter. He even noticed when going by the outdoor basketball courts in town, that the basketballs weren't orange anymore, as they had been not that long ago when he was growing up. They were designer colors now — yellow, green, tawny, puce.

Orange was not Billy's favorite color. In fact, it was his least favorite color. From his way of thinking, Halloween was the only excuse for breaking out orange, and that was a poor one at best. Thank goodness for the balancing act of black for this scary holiday. Otherwise, he would have cloistered himself in a closet every year at the end of October.

As it was, Billy did not become a hermit his first Halloween in Newburgh. In fact he became a Kermit.

Kermit the Frog.

Natalie was the Good Witch from *Wizard of Oz*.

Pam came as Billy Idol. No one seemed to know who that was and she spent much of the evening explaining. Each time she took another swig of Jim Beam directly out of the bottle, snarled like Elvis, and rolled her eyes.

"I should have come as a pickle. They even had a costume for me at work. I mean, I say Billy Idol and I get this total blank look. Then if I say "White Wedding", "Cradle of Love" or "Flesh for Fantasy", the lights come on. Christ, the guy was a huge star. He's a legend! At least as much as Johnny Rotten or Sid Vicious."

Sid Vicious? Pam was eclectic, to put it mildly.

They were at the Seminole Environmental Consultants annual employees and significant others costume party, this year being held in a small events rental room at the Holiday Inn.

In attendance were King Arthur, Darth Vader, Tina Turner, George W. Bush, Cinderella, an anonymous ghost, Spiderman, Britney Spears, a huge stalk of celery, Smoky the Bear, Salvador Dali, the Dalai Lama, a molar holding a tooth brush, a rapper bearing an uncanny resemblance to Biggie Smalls, a hockey player with the number 9, and an assortment of farm animals and house pets.

Billy had the option of attending a similar affair with his own employer, but that wouldn't have been as much fun. They tended to be a bit less frivolous.

Right after his mom's 4th of July visit, Billy had landed a position with Habitat For Humanity.

Despite the presence of a lot of old wealth in the Hudson Valley, its proximity to New York City — a guarantee that property values would keep climbing — and the gentrification of many now upscale communities in the area, there were still a lot of poor people in Orange County. This was not surprising, considering that the median income was under $30,000 per annum. But many of the 36% of the city's residents who were Hispanic/Latino and of the 34% who were Black/African American, earned far below this. In 2005 the unemployment rate overall was higher than the national average. And people kept moving to the area, so the population was increasing at a steady 2% per year, the number of people without jobs right along with it. The pace of employment opportunities was just not keeping up, so in real numbers more and more people ended up at or slipping below the national poverty line.

These were individuals who had been left out of the American Dream, who had no hope of home ownership beyond some miracle. Habitat For Humanity, as it was doing all across the country, provided that miracle. Using donated materials and labor, and land either ceded or bought at discount rates using charitable contributions, the organization — inspired and established by former President Jimmy Carter — built houses, then turned the front door keys over to the impoverished residents of Newburgh, and the other communities which hosted their admirable work.

The local Habitat For Humanity, which Billy worked for, took this one step further, believing that any newly constructed homes should meet standards of sustainability within the immediate environment. This took into account the ecological properties of the surrounding land and water, the social dynamics of the neighborhoods where the houses were located, projected growth in the area, and of course, the energy efficiency of the house itself. The idea was to make the contribution of living spaces not merely socio-economic, but one which would lead to a greener future for the world.

Billy was to hired provide the technical expertise and brainpower in meeting these new higher standards. Quite frankly, the job didn't pay all that well. Habitat didn't have the money to hire a full-on certified environmental specialist. Instead they did the next best thing. They hired a brilliant new graduate with all of the academic qualifications to become one within a reasonable amount of time.

For Billy, this was ideal. Every day brought new and interesting challenges. He was being paid to turn his book learning into real-world learning, midwifing theoretical knowledge into practical results. He was doing what he loved to do and deeply believed made an important contribution. That the ownership of the houses was in the end granted to disadvantaged people — people who looked a lot like many of those he grew up with in Detroit, people of color, the working poor — was rewarding in itself. That these homes were engineered to be friendly to the environment was doubly gratifying.

There was a lot of overlap between Billy's work and Natalie's. Of course, most of the jobs that Seminole did were at a higher level, dealing with issues of community planning, land and resource use. Their contracts were both with local government agencies and private development firms. Billy's work was restricted entirely to projects that Habitat had initiated and were implementing. But the goals of Seminole and Habitat in the global sense were identical. Often the specific technical issues were even the same.

This led to some intense, often heated, but always constructive discussions over the dinner table, sometimes on into the evening. As if they needed something else to rivet their attention to one another, they found themselves more and more discussing work-related matters. Only a few months into Billy's new job, they took to calling time-outs. One or the other finally reaching saturation level, would give the T hand signal popularized by televised professional football. That was the signal for *"time out"* on the immediate topic and required an immediate switch to something completely unrelated to work.

Despite the intense pressures of their professional lives, Billy's and Natalie's personal lives and marriage could not have been better. They were making new friends faster than they could keep track of. There was now a steady stream of invitations — usually resulting from connections they initially made at their respective jobs — for intimate dinners and gala parties alike. Increasingly there were invites for them to attend community functions, or just to hang out dining and drinking at one of the many restaurants and bars in Newburgh or the surrounding communities of New Windsor, Glenwood Park, Cronomer Valley, Cornwall on the Hudson, and even occasionally across the river in Beacon. Though they had no personal stake in the outcomes, Billy and Natalie even found themselves sitting now and again in the bleachers at a soccer tournament or a Little League baseball game.

In August of that year, almost immediately after he had started his new job at Habitat For Humanity, something unexpected came to Billy's attention which would dramatically impact their personal fortunes for years to come.

Billy paced the apartment waiting for Natalie to come home from a late night staff meeting. As soon as she came through the door, somewhat later than he had expected, he dispensed with the formalities and burst out with the news.

"Nat, I found out something really interesting today."

"You discovered you are actually left-handed."

"More interesting than that. Habitat tried to buy some land off the 9W over by Balmville but the owner wouldn't budge. He's some sort of right-wing fanatic who is suspicious of any charitable work. It's a long story. Basically the guy is nuts. Anyway, rumor has it that the land is being looked at for development by Warner. It's a nice chunk. Twelve acres. It has a decent little home on it already. But there would be plenty of room to put up an apartment building and some multi-family housing units."

"I could find out if Warner's been testing the waters with the zoning board."

"You read my mind."

Warner Residential and Commercial Development, Ltd. was normally very on top of things. Which is why they were the largest, most successful property development organization in the area. But they somehow dropped the ball on this one. Their original long-term plan was to buy contiguous property totaling more than ninety acres, all of which was farm land. Being on the growing edge of town, it was ripe for turning into multi-family dwellings. Perhaps they were distracted by other more pressing concerns. Maybe they were frustrated having to deal with the crazy old coot who owned the twelve acres which was the spearhead property for the development.

Whatever the case, Billy and Natalie got there first.

The old man was a character, no doubt about that. His name was Harvey Feathers. Billy found out that the old man had at one time worked for Ford Motor Company, their Electrical Systems Division in Fort Wayne, Indiana. He had retired and moved back to farm the land that had been in his family for three generations there in Newburgh. As would be expected of someone who had spent 35 years in a automotive industry factory, the only thing he could abundantly grow was weeds.

But apparently, he had not yet completely abandoned his far-fetched dream of raising edible crops — though the neglect of his small field would suggest otherwise — and had not given any serious thought to selling the property until Warner came sniffing around. His ears were now perked and he was listening, as much as the wary and wizened old coot would allow himself to.

Billy used their common ground in the automotive trades to his advantage. After all, his father was a "lifer" and Billy himself had worked in a Chrysler factory for all of three months. So what if he and the old codger were separated in age by more than 40 years. Maybe they could be buddies long enough to make a deal on the property.

On instinct, Billy wore his blue jeans and worst looking shirt and late one Saturday afternoon, strolled up the dirt drive leading to the dilapidated front porch of the Feather family farmhouse. Harvey was leaning back on a wooden chair with his feet propped up on the porch railing. He eyed Billy suspiciously but held his tongue. When Billy finally reached the steps to the porch, he turned sideways, looked at the horizon, stopped humming, waited a country minute, then spoke.

"You Ford guys used to kick our ass."

"Whadder you talkin' 'bout, boy?"

"Ignitions. Generators. Alternators. The whole works. Chrysler products used to start when they felt like it. Not in the mood? You couldn't go anywhere. But Fords!"

"I don't knowin' zactly how some young punk like you'd know it. But yur damn right!"

And so it went. After two more Saturdays and a Sunday on the porch, chucking and jiving, and letting Feathers' dumb old dog lick the hair off the back of Billy's hand, they got down to business. The old man's main problem was that he resented on sight anyone who wore some "fancy bidness suit with dem fancy ties and all." That was reinforced with a surreal assumption that any corporate entity or even charitable organization was an arm of the Communist Party, bent on destroying the "good ol' U S of A" by taking over all of the land and giving it to a bunch of "undeservin' niggers and spics." He must not have been paying very close attention in high school civics class, if he ever went to school at all.

Billy allayed all his suspicions. Since Billy was a family man, true to the Constitution, loyal to the flag, Christian to the core, and had a hard-working father still doing his patriotic duty building cars in Detroit for this great nation —

even if it was for that "damn Chrysler bunch of fools" — they could do business.

Obviously, Billy had stretched the truth a little.

Finally, he brought Natalie out to meet the old guy. Feathers' eyes almost fell out of his head as she and Billy walked up the drive. By the time she stepped on the porch, the old boy was beside himself with 'gosh darns' and 'aw shucks' pouring out of his sheepishly twisted leathery lips. The three agreed on a price so far below market value it was embarrassing. But the property was paid-off and Feathers would walk away with more money than he could possibly spend, even if he lived to be a hundred.

Natalie talked to the owners of Seminole and they co-signed on a $20,000 loan for the down payment, then she and Billy went to the bank for a mortgage on the rest. Property values were skyrocketing nationally and the America was awash in foreign loan money. The only way you could be declined for a secured loan in 2005 was if you were on death row with no work history or an alien from another planetary system. The approval was pro forma.

They moved into the modest farmhouse two weeks before the Halloween Party.

"How is the new place?"

They were talking to Darth Vader who was the Force at Seminole.

"Quaint." Answered Kermit.

"Dusty." Answered the Good Witch.

"Thanks for your help, Darth." Added Kermit.

"My pleasure." Darth Vader smiled inside his helmet as he sipped his beer through a straw.

"It's only temporary." Mentioned the Good Witch with a wink.

Temporary it was. Over the next few months, Warner had been busy buying up the other eighty acres of surrounding property. In February, two executives and an attorney showed up on the rotting doorstep of Billy's and Natalie's quaint and dusty little farm house. In hand was a letter of intent to buy the house and the twelve acres. It was a very generous offer, at least $45,000 more than they had paid for the place.

Natalie knew hunger when she saw it.

Billy sensed desperation and vulnerability.

They went into their bedroom. The three Armani-suited gentlemen shifted uncomfortably in their seats and tried unsuccessfully to hear the details of the whispered discussion coming from the other room.

Billy and Natalie came back in and gave it to them straight.

"Not enough." Billy said.

"Put $80,000 on top of that and we have a deal." Natalie said pointing at the letter of intent.

"Non-negotiable." Billy said.

"We love it here." Natalie lied.

The attorney swelled up like an inflating clown, his face reddened, and after a few harrumphs and other phlegmy guttural sounds of indignity, started to object.

"That's absolutely out of the question. Why just look—"

The executive with a Caribbean tan and final-say interrupted.

"Done. We'll be back to you in 48 hours. Let's close by the beginning of next week."

They shook hands. The attorney, obviously not happy with the way things had gone, tried to crush Billy's hand. Billy just smiled and squeezed back.

"You've got a powerful handshake ... for a girl."

"Fuck you."

Both of the executives were more diplomatic as they stepped back out into the February cold.

"Thanks, Mr. and Mrs. Green."

"Have a nice day."

After the three men were snugly back in their Mercedes Coupe and couldn't hear them, Natalie and Billy whooped and laughed and danced around the living room like a couple of Christmas elves high on crack.

"We're rich!"

"We did great!"

"I thought we'd be lucky if they threw another $10,000 at us. $80,000! Holy moley!"

"Kick-ass job, Billy. I saw smoke rising from that lawyer's toupée."

"Should we start packing now?"

"Tomorrow. Tonight calls for some serious celebrating."

They drove down to the local 7-Eleven, bought some microwaveable popcorn, two bottles of the cheapest champagne, two pints of Ben & Jerry's ice cream — Cherry Garcia and Chunky Monkey — and two kielbasas, which looked like they had only been in the rotisserie for a few days and conceivably were still edible. After gorging themselves on the junk food and drinking the champagne like it was Kool-Aid, they made love and passed out.

Moving was easy. They didn't have that much.

Finding a new house was not so easy.

But having over $100,000 in hand sure helped.

Fortunately, Natalie had no urgent projects in the pipeline during February. Billy, of course, always had his evenings free. They had agreed to vacate the premises by March 1st, so they spent every available evening and two weekends in February looking for a new home.

Again, work connections came into play. The other Natalie at Seminole — her name was actually Natalia — an administrative assistant from Queens with parents who had emigrated from Russia fifteen years ago, had been renting a room from a retired couple. They had announced their intention to sell their place and move to a sunnier climate, either Biloxi, Mississippi or Sarasota, Florida. They had not even put the place on the market yet, but said they were serious about selling it as soon as possible. Natalia had already found a new room and was about to move. Knowing that Natalie and Billy were desperately looking for a house to buy, she thought that they might want to take a look at the place.

It was perfect. At least Natalie thought so when she breezed through on her lunch hour with Natalia giving the guided tour.

She made an appointment with the owners to return that evening sometime after dinner with Billy in tow.

It wasn't love at first sight for Billy, but he warmed up quickly.

"Not quite what I pictured for us."

Fireplace. Wood floors. Nice big living room.

"Not too shabby."

Big kitchen. Den. Finished basement with a workshop.

"It's got some nice features."

Four bedrooms. Refurbished master bath with a huge jacuzzi-style tub.

"This could work. I can picture some good things happening here."

Balcony overlooking a huge back yard with majestic maples and pines.

"Jesus H. Christ! I love this place!"

The immediate advantage was how kind and accommodating the old couple — Mr. and Mrs. Peacock, who were very proud to point out more than once that in April they were celebrating their Golden Wedding Anniversary — turned out to be. Billy and Natalie had less than two weeks to move from their farm residence and were thinking they were going to end up in a motel on State Highway 9W. The Peacocks basically said that if they were interested in the place, regardless of when the transfer of ownership was completed, they could store their belongings in the basement, and stay in the room Natalia was soon vacating. Small-town hospitality was still alive and well in isolated pockets across America — in Newburgh, NY for sure.

It was an old barn-style house originally built in 1910 but which had seen some dramatic improvements and modernizations over nearly a century. The front yard consisted of large boulders and an English-style garden which seem to be growing every bush and flowering plant the climate would allow. The house was recessed from the street — a residential street which saw only local traffic — on a half-acre lot. It was three minutes from the banks of the Hudson River and maybe fifteen minutes at a granny-strolling pace from the main business district of town. This meant Natalie could walk to work and Billy ride a bicycle, weather permitting. Habitat's office was three miles directly south, in the Town of New Windsor, a pleasant spin and good exercise. Picnics and outdoor ambling would be convenient as well. They were two blocks from the beautiful Mount St. Mary's Campus and five minutes from Downing Park, with its 35 acres of hills, valleys, ponds and streams, rich vegetation and flowers, through which serpentine paths wound under the shade of magnificent old trees.

It was as close to perfect as a new old home could be.

Over the next few days, they went back and forth on the price. Only a few thousand dollars separated them, so negotiations were cordial, bordering on humorous. They were essentially on the same team — the Greens wanted the house and the Peacocks wanted them to have it. The Peacocks felt that the stewardship and love Billy and Natalie would bring to the home would be proper homage to the fifty years they had spent there, surviving the early struggling years of their marriage, their raising three children, and more recently entertaining their eight grandchildren. It was a proper renewal of the cycle of life, passing the baton to a deserving young couple at the beginning of their marital journey.

It only took a couple of days to arrange bank financing — the $100,000 and change they had coming from the farm house deal more than relieved any anxieties about the fact that Billy and Natalie were so young and so new to their jobs and the community — and a local attorney put together the paperwork for the sale faster than it took the Mayor's wife to get her hair and nails done at her beauty salon of choice, the Corinthian House of Beauty.

It moved along so quickly that both couples were almost caught off guard, despite their both wanting the transfer of ownership done and over. The Peacocks in particular had a huge task ahead of them, sorting and packing the accumulation of fifty years worth of stuff. Billy and Natalie, returning the consideration the old couple had extended, volunteered to let them use the basement as a way station for the month of March, as the old couple prepared for the big move to the deep South. Because of the size of the house — ten rooms plus a finished basement — it was no problem for both parties involved to load and unload without getting in one another's way.

At 7 pm on Wednesday March 1st in the cab of an 18-foot U-Haul rental truck only half-full with their meager belongings, Billy and Natalie drove up to their new home, got out and were handed the keys by two charming old people in their early seventies.

The Peacocks drove away in an old Studebaker coupe. Billy and Natalie brought in two suitcases, a mattress and some blankets, ate some Chinese take-out they had picked up on the way, made love, then fell asleep in the center of the living room with the drapes wide open. No one could see them anyway.

The rest of the stuff in the truck could wait till tomorrow.

Home Is Where the Heart Is

Blissful marriages — even those charged with high levels of drama and excitement — tend usually to look pretty placid, if not somnolent, from the outside.

The public face of Billy and Natalie as a couple broke conspicuously from this commonplace stereotype.

"My my! Look at those two."
"The way they look at each other!"
"Are they the perfect couple or what?"
"To be in love like that again. In my dreams."
"Maybe there's hope for this corrupt and ugly world."

The running commentary, particularly from the older citizens, was constant and consistent. Oohs-and-aahs, sighs and dreamy observations, radiated from withered faces, which for a few brief moments shone again with the shimmering joy of remembered courtships and innocent youthful flirtations.

Even younger singles and couples took notice. Some were secretly envious. Others were openly resentful that these two mid-westerners had managed to capture and hold on to something spitefully lacking in their own loveless lives.

Billy and Natalie put love and its potential for spectacular rewards back into the much-maligned, statistically discredited institution of marriage. While more than 50% of American couples were getting a divorce, often within only a few years of taking their wedding vows, these two had 'forever' written all across their beaming faces.

To give substance to these romanticized views of them as a couple, and remove them from the suspicion that they were merely the stuff of fairy tales, wishful thinking, naive fantasies, or incurable delusions, it would have to be said that this is exactly how Billy viewed their relationship as well.

It never failed to surprise, amaze, and ultimately to please him, that in terms of his feelings for Natalie, the passion, the "edge", never went away for him. Whenever they had to be apart for whatever reason — on a daily basis it was just them going to two different workplaces — he always felt a gnawing anticipation and tangible excitement about seeing her again. Even if they had only been apart for a few hours, the exact moment he set eyes on her again was a kindly jolt of electricity and a whiff of euphoria. It was never just Natalie. It was *Natalie!!*

He knew this was a rare, if not a completely unique and singular experience. All around him, he either heard the monotone drone of those who had fallen into a passive, inertial acceptance of their significant others, or the mumbling grumbling of those who had forgotten — or were now blind to — what initially attracted them to their spouses. They now could only find fault.

Billy listened amused, as he would to a bad sitcom. What these other pathetic losers in the game of love had to say, and what lousy TV typically offered, had no resemblance to his reality. Rather than try to counter with his alternate reality, or switch the channel, he would just nod and smile and uh-huh and yep, and laugh along where the laugh track demanded his complicity. Through all the background noise of other people's woeful tales of married life, the soundtrack he was hearing was the music he shared with Natalie. What kept him going each day were those previews of coming attractions he could and often would pull up in his mind, of when they would again be together. It could just be seeing her come through the door. Standing in the kitchen making dinner. Retouching her makeup in a mirror. The never-exhausted list of things they did together. Everything felt special.

A drive in the country.

A dinner and a movie in the evening.

A shared lunch on the fly in the middle of the day.

The hike and picnic they had planned for the coming weekend.

Getting ready and hand-in-hand going to a restaurant with office colleagues.

Sitting around their new house, each in their own little head space doing job-related work.

Laying in bed on a Sunday morning each reading a novel or popular magazine.

Just being at home together with no special plan or fixed agenda.

Just being at home both doing the household chores.

Just being at home talking or relaxing.

Just being together at home.

Together at home.

Home!

Yes! For the first time in his life, Billy could say he had a place called *home*. A place that felt like a home should feel.

Granted, there had been this building — actually consecutive buildings in three different Detroit suburbs — where he coexisted with his parents while growing up. Then there was the hotel-like dorm and the time-share apartment at Cornell. And Natalie's apartment which he had moved into after his graduation. Finally the brief stop at the farm house investment property, which had a lot of privacy and admittedly even some primitive charm.

But while none of these seemed especially lacking at the time — each providing a functional setting, shelter, and a central base of operations — after settling in and experiencing the house here at 372 Grand Street, the amorphous and relatively abstract idea of *home* gradually began to flesh out, and become anthropomorphic and 3-dimensional.

Obviously, the first thing that made it a home was having Natalie there to share it with him.

But building on that, their home was what they could and would now create, to house and nurture their individual but increasingly commingled lives.

A cocoon within which those events and moments and feelings, their shared confessions and confidentialities, their unfolding triumphs and disappointments, their private jokes and judgments, fantasies and fears, euphoria and pessimism, laughter and tears, bravado and diffidence, drama, comedy, certainty, uncertainty, hysteria, calm, melancholy, malaise and mania … yes, *here* … all of the stuff of life as a couple, would play out, moment by moment, day by day, month by month, year after year.

A home.

Now that he had it, he realized what he had been missing all these years.

A home … a real home.

The house that Billy and Natalie bought was quite spacious. And they kept it spacious.

Neither were accumulators. Unlike the majority of Americans, especially others their age, buying for the sake of buying held no special appeal, purpose or place in their lives. In sharp contrast to many of their new friends, shopping was not their main recreational activity. Stuff simply was not important to them. So cluttering up the 2459 square feet of floor space was not now, nor would it probably ever be, in the cards.

Over time they might outfit some of the extra rooms, maybe turn one of the bedrooms into a guest room, the other into a sewing or hobby room. Kids room? But for now, they just needed a few more chairs and a love seat for the living room — Natalie already had a sofa — some bookcases, lamps, perhaps another desk for their shared office, now that they had room for it. To address these modest needs, they went to yard sales and a couple antique shops — for the most part glorified second-hand stores — and bought just what they needed, pleased that they had opted for more traditional furnishings, rather than the modern assembly line stuff that they both felt had little character and looked tacky.

If they splurged on anything — and it would have barely qualified as a splurge by most people's consumerist standards — it was on their bed. They were young, their marriage was young, their sex drives were young, so the bed was still where a lot of the action was.

They did some window shopping. When it was obvious that what they wanted was not available from the stores in the immediate area, they went online and ordered a deluxe framed Mekong waterbed, shipped all the way from Santa Ana, California. It had a polished black lacquer finish, and came with a matching bedroom set. This gave the entire room a sleek but simple Asian ambience. They had new white silk drapes and cushy, soft wool carpeting installed. The result was an elegant asceticism which would frame their athletic eroticism perfectly. Nothing would pull focus from the main act.

By middle of spring, the house looked and felt great. Comfortable, tasteful, open, inviting. The garden in the front started coming to life. Thus added to the many activities they shared and enjoyed, would be gardening. Billy surprised both himself and Natalie by coming home one day with a bag full of seeds and seedlings to start a vegetable garden in the one corner of the back yard which got healthy amounts of sunlight. It was not very large but considering the only thing Billy had previously grown from scratch was mildew on his sweat shirt one especially rainy autumn in Detroit, this was a major undertaking. It didn't seem like it was all that long before they were introducing their own home-grown cucumbers, green peppers, tomatoes, eggplants, carrots and scallions, into their evening meals. By the end of summer, they even had some squash and a handful of tiny but tasty potatoes to add to his agricultural achievements.

The front yard took care of itself. The Peacocks had long ago set in motion and perfected over the years, a dynamic combination of perennials which thrived in flawless counterpoint. It was like watching a ballet, with the entrance and exit of various dancers, as bushes and bulbs and shrubbery flowered, then made way for the next set of performers. It seemed like something was always foaming in nascent green, exploding like a rainbow across the floral spectrum, or glowing in the warm flames of autumnal retirement, during the six months starting in April and winding down end of September. The front yard was time-lapse fireworks.

Best of all in terms of the property — front, back, sides — there was no lawn.

Billy hated lawns.

"Natalie. I have something to tell you. I hate lawns."

"Ohmigod! How does this happen, Billy?"

"How does what happen?"

"I hate lawns too."

"I always picture some nerdy guy with a buzz cut standing out in front of his house, after spending weeks pouring bag after bag of seed, fertilizer, herbicide, pesticide, and God knows what else, looking out over this billiard table green felt lawn, and smiling like he had just solved the Unified Field Theory equations."

"Or riding one of those little tractor style lawn mowers, wearing golf shoes and a polyester alligator polo shirt, with his wife standing on the porch holding a tray of lemonade."

"What a waste of time."

"I love you, Billy Green ... for hating lawns."

And so it was. Heartfelt emotions.

Billy and Natalie loved their new home.

Especially because it had no lawn.

The Crush

It was a game. People in their neighborhood would stop Billy and ask him.

"How long have you and Natalie been married?"

"Seven months and two weeks and five days."

The women loved him for it and the men hated him. After all, a lot of men not only forgot their anniversaries but had to sit down with a calendar and a calculator just to figure out how many years they had been married. Forget the months, weeks and days.

"How long have you been married?"

"Nine months and three weeks and two days."

"My my. Still counting. How sweet!"

Yes. Sweet. Exhilarating. Amazing.

Not even a whole year had passed, yet so much had happened so quickly.

But people were always saying: If it's meant to be, then it's effortless.

Billy wasn't so sure of the metaphysics of the situation, but it did seem that things for him and Natalie had fallen beautifully into place. Their jobs, the house, the community. Maybe not effortless but the best of all possible real worlds. Simple and straightforward. No games. No disappointments. No broken promises. No egos. No jockeying or bullying. Uncomplicated and fulfilling. Hopeful. Promising.

"How long have you been married?"

"Three hundred and sixty-five days."

"Is tomorrow your—"

Billy smiled from ear to ear.

"Yes it is. June 22nd. One year to the day."

"Congratulations!"

Their anniversary fell on a Thursday. Both Billy and Natalie had informed their bosses that they would be leaving work no later than 6:00 pm. They planned on spending the entire evening celebrating, starting with dinner at Pamela's On The Hudson — a reprise of their wedding celebration dinner — and then sipping Grand Marnier and making love in their beautiful, still relatively new waterbed.

For Billy, June 22nd was also the day Habitat For Humanity was marching through and introducing three new summer interns.

Just after 9 am, they filed into Billy's office.

"This is Billy Green. He is our Regulatory and Systems Compliance Analyst, which is a long way of just saying he's the guy with the brains around here. Billy, this is Davey Zjaborski — I hope I said that right — from New York University at Plattsburgh, Mike Spaneau from University of Pittsburgh, and Katie Burke from University of North Carolina."

Davey looked fourteen. Tall and fair-haired. Pimples. Probably a computer game geek.

Mike was self-assured. Cocky. Mr. know-it-all. Fancied himself a ladies man. Checking out Katie.

Katie. Stunning. Tall and graceful. Perky but intelligent. Probably a Christian. Virgin?

Billy shook hands with the boys.

"Pleased to meet you. If you ever have any questions or need help, that's why I'm here. Just write your request on a $20 bill and slip it under my door. Even better, all of your questions are entered in our annual eco-prize drawing. The winner walks away with a life-size cardboard cut-out of Al Gore in a Speedo bathing suit holding up the World."

"What's a Speedo bathing suit, sir?" The geek. Obviously not gay if he didn't know Speedo.

"Are you making a formal request for me to answer that? Where's my twenty bucks?"

They all laughed, following an awkward pause, when they simultaneously came to the conclusion that they could — laugh, that is. Billy had charmed them.

Maybe a little more than he intended. One of them, most definitely.

While the two boys were making excited, feeble attempts at their own little jokes, and as Henry Blackledge, the director of the office who had introduced them to Billy, added his own dweebie lead balloons, Billy noticed that Katie was quietly staring at him and smiling.

What a lovely smile.

While Blackledge and the boys bantered randomly, Billy's curiosity got the best of him.

"Is it Katherine?"

"No. It's Katrina. Don't ask me why? No one seems to know. My family's always been out of control."

"You won't have that problem here. We've all been lobotomized."

That broke her up. She had this infectious but flirtatious giggle. Something between a Disney cartoon princess and a porn-queen playing a college cheerleader.

"Have you ever been a cheerleader?"

"I really wanted to. It was a lifelong fantasy. But my legs were too short to reach the ground. I kept blowing away at the tryouts. One time the fire department took three hours to get me down from some power lines. There were tennis shoes on both sides of me."

Whew! Drugs? Schizophrenia? Funny girl!

"You'll be relieved to know that we don't test interns here for drugs."

This really cracked her up. When she finally calmed down and managed to tame her giggles to an amused purr, she came closer to Billy and extended her hand. He started an all-business handshake but hers was slack and lay in his hand like a kitten curling up to go to sleep. He stood there holding the delicate hand of this quirky adolescent creature, hugely disarmed by how personal she had made the physical contact. Then she suddenly adopted a playful, wholly ironic stiff propriety, as it to mock the idea they were anything but just-introduced business associates.

"I am most certainly looking forward to working with you, Mr. Green."

Billy popped out of the tight bubble of deliberation that had channeled in on Katie, as if waking from a dream. It quickly registered that the other three had stopped talking and were staring at him. He self-consciously let go of her hand.

How much had they heard? Did they pick up on her obvious flirtatiousness? His curious fascination. He hoped not.

Director Blackledge offered no clue. He always looked a little confused, which presently he masked with a bureaucratically-tempered grin.

"Well, let's let Billy get back to whatever it is that he does in here." He laughed at his own lame tongue-in-cheek and guided the three interns out of Billy's cluttered office. Whether out of coyness or shyness, Katie did not look back but stared straight ahead as if she had been programmed to do so by her inventors.

Strange but fascinating girl.

Just before five, Billy shut down his computer and headed for home — to celebrate his first wedding anniversary!

It fully lived up to his and Natalie's expectations.

Both put all of the workday's trials and tribulations completely out of mind — there was not a hint of shoptalk, which had become a staple at the dinner table most evenings — and they each simply enjoyed the straightforward company of the person who had become number one in each of their lives. Over fillet mignon, Caesar salad, kale and asparagus in a vinaigrette sauce, French bread with garlic butter, and a peppery 1992 French Margot wine, they laughed over recollections of college days, teased and coaxed from one another hitherto unrevealed anxieties and doubts during their courtship, and sweetly melted into a shared awareness of how special and enviable their relationship was.

Lightheaded and still tumbling in the rolling rapids of giggling at everything and nothing, they stumbled through their front door, looking more inebriated than they were, and made their way forthwith to their luxurious mail-order water bed. Their clothes were gone before they were half-way across the bedroom, and they fell onto the thick soft duvet like two desperate teenagers, alone now that the parents had just left for an evening out.

They stopped mashing long enough for Billy to pour into two elegant stemmed shot glasses, the aperitif sitting on the bed stand. Natalie proposed the toast.

"To those who get what they deserve."

Neither were shy about their favorite pre-sex beverage and both downed the sweet sticky syrup with little hesitation or fanfare. Their faces flushed as the drink quickly suffused them with a warm incandescence.

Billy poured the last few drops of his bracer onto Natalie's nipples and licked it off, savoring both the liqueur and her skin. He looked up and smiled.

"I am very lucky to have you."

"Did you win me in a raffle?"

"I know what I mean."

"Me too! But do I mean what I say?"

"It's a difficult question. This requires scientific testing."

He slid down her body, his lips leaving a tingling trail of delicate kisses. Down down down. Natalie purred with pleasure as the anticipation built. Then she let out a soft but urgent moan as his tongue parted her labia and brushed across her clitoris.

One year is plenty long enough to figure out what your partner likes. But since their courtship and engagement was intensely sexual as well, Billy had long ago perfected his oral technique with Natalie. Within a minute, she was writhing ecstatically, within two minutes, she was thrashing wildly, within three minutes, she had lost any semblance of control and filled the entire house with her piercing yelps and squeals. Seconds later, she climaxed convulsively, her body tensing and arching with the strength of three men twice her size. Billy backed off but did not stop, now just barely caressing her vaginal lips with his tongue and ever-so-lightly coursing his hands like feathery wings over her breasts and torso. Natalie continued to moan in gently decreasing rounds. After a few minutes she finally calmed and Billy adopted the pseudo-scientific tone of voice one associates with researchers.

"The results are in and are conclusive. Yes. You do."

"I do? I forgot the question."

"You sure gave the right answer."

"I did, didn't I? So we're good for another year?"

"I'd say so. Let's go for it."

To kick their second year of marriage off right, they immediately proceeded to make love again, this time with her providing the oral overture, then conducting the symphony of their mutual pleasure from on top of him, with special attention to the nipple section and the slow building passage of a testicle solo. After an explosive climax to the perfectly orchestrated concerto, they drifted off in one another's arms, in a dreamless unconsciousness, then slept through their alarm clock next morning. They were both an hour late for work.

This was such an anomaly for Natalie, and since Seminole's office was so uncluttered and open, she got a lot of winks and smiles as she made her way to her desk. It was the opposite for Billy. Comings and goings were not easily observed. Habitat's office operation was spread throughout a hundred-year-old English Tudor-style house which had been re-zoned commercial a number of years ago. But more to the point, nobody kept track of him. Billy's tasks always got done on time, if not early, his work was thorough and free of errors, and he always did more than was required of him. So the two supervisors above him in the chain of command let him do his thing at his own bidding, and just sat back calmly waiting for him to deliver the excellent results of his analysis and research. They had yet to give him an assignment which he hadn't completed satisfactorily. The upshot was that after less than a year on the job, he had more independence than anyone else on staff.

One person did comment on his strolling in at 9:30 the day after his wedding anniversary. That was the young intern Katie, who he had met only the day before.

"Look who has banker's hours around here. Or are you working a second job, the evening shift at McDonalds?"

75

"Busted. Would you like fries with that McSpam sandwich, miss?"

"Yes. And ..." She started reciting. "... *hold the pickles, hold the lettuce.*"

"No offense, but if I'm not mistaken, that was the Burger King advert. Long before you were born, at that."

"I studied contemporary American poetry my junior year ... *special orders don't upset us.*"

"And they say American education is in decline."

There was that seductive giggle again as she strolled back to her work table. She made Billy feel like he was a real charmer. He had to remind himself ...

Be careful with that one.

The following week — in fact, first thing Monday morning — Director of Operations Blackledge marched into Billy's office, sans his usual maître d' smile, and sat down heavily in the one chair across from Billy's desk.

"We just got a really big assignment, one that might take you through the end of summer. There's some funding to be had from the Tessler Foundation out of San Francisco but they want us to write a book. Five years of data. It's a lot of boilerplate stuff. Compiling, cross referential tables, pretty standard number crunching. Unfortunately, it's not going to require much creativity, but it is important work. I can't think of anyone else who could handle it, Billy. This just came up. It was on the FAX machine when I arrived, and I just got off the phone with the grant administrator."

"No problem. When do I start?"

"If you're not putting out a five-alarm fire, immediately. Leslie is printing out a summary of what we need right now."

"I'll clear my desk before lunch. I'll get right on it."

"Listen Billy, I suspect the interns can do a lot of the grunt work for you. Piles of files to go through to get what you need. So they're at your disposal. Everyone else just has them sharpening pencils anyway."

That afternoon, Billy dug in his heels on the new assignment. He decided to use only two of the interns and called in the two boys, Davey and Mike. For reasons hopefully obvious to only him, he didn't want to set up a situation which encouraged contact with the lovely Katie.

Not that he didn't talk to her. He had left his door open to all three of them at the time they were introduced. All of them were studying environmental science or something related to ecological systems at their respective universities, and he was after all the office expert in such matters.

As the June slid into July, it seemed that Katie sure had a lot of questions. These went way beyond the projects he had been working on for Habitat, embracing broad kinds of policy concerns. Billy had to hand it to her. They for the most part were intelligent questions, showing a keen appreciation for environmental issues, their social and political implications. Often they focused on the particular the kinds of obstacles which both private enterprise and government agencies themselves constructed to protect the status quo. Occasionally they were even quite technically intensive, which made Billy wonder if she was doing research on her own, or just tuning in to the constant banter which took place around Habitat, then putting her own spin on them, so that she wouldn't sound like she was merely parroting.

Katie had this other habit which was becoming all too obvious. She always left something behind when she came in with one of her questions for Billy, or as part of the routine errands she was given as an intern.

"Did you see my cell phone? Oh here it is. Thanks, Mr. Green."

Mr. Green. Then that delightful smile. What a little flirt.

It was obvious where this was going. Billy knew better. He wasn't going along with it, regardless of how cute she was. He was a happily married man. He knew a schoolgirl crush when he saw one. There was no future in it. Particularly for this innocent young lady. Innocent? As innocent as young ladies were these days, he surmised. Cleverly innocent beyond their years. Calculatingly innocent. Artfully innocent. Seductively innocent.

Whether Katie voiced it to others in the office, which Billy doubted — covert lover seemed more her style than overt stalker — it became painfully obvious to everyone that by the end of summer, this young intern was massively in love with him. It was the tittering talk of the office and he took his share of ribbing about it. Whenever she wasn't around, of course.

When she was there, Billy's coworkers looked on with knowing smiles, as some contrived interaction would unfold. Seething with electric undercurrents, both romantic and sexual, pheromones plumed from her like a thick spicy heart-pumping bouquet of youthful craving. She would shift from one foot to the other as her longing for Billy descended from her chest, and concentrated itself in the space between those long legs that she claimed didn't reach the ground during her cheerleader tryouts. Billy tried his best to ignore all of this, but lapses became more common, and he found himself thinking more than he preferred, about where those legs started and what physiological splendor had been summoned to form her incredibly lovely ass and coyly sloping pelvis.

And yes, she noticed.

She could sense his interest was building.

She could surmise what he against his better judgment was thinking.

Katie fully well knew Billy was married, in fact had met Natalie a number of times, at least twice coming to the house. Once it was for a Saturday barbecue and another time for a birthday party Billy threw for the Assistant Director of Habitat, a barrel of a woman turning sixty-three, who had devoted most of her professional life to service organizations.

The first time Katie walked through the door, with the sixth sense that women seem born with, it took Natalie about three seconds to determine what was going on with the young girl.

She couldn't resist teasing Billy about it a few minutes later as he was tossing chicken parts and hamburgers on the grill for the hungry party guests.

"I see you have an admirer."

"Is it that obvious?"

"I can smell her wetness."

Billy couldn't conceal his shock over Natalie's bluntness and her graphic characterization of the young girl's feelings for him, normally the crude province of overheated males. But he tried to hide behind understatement.

"Interesting way to put it."

Billy spent the summer backing away, while Katie became bolder in her attempts to close the physical distance between them at every given opportunity, against the unstated but clearly understood rules of office decorum. Billy was constantly dodging her not-so-subtle invitations to "get together and do something", Katie never being at all specific about what that something was.

He actually started to feel guilty about being such a showstopper. He wasn't so much older, in fact only four years, that he couldn't appreciate how it felt to be fond of someone and be forced to endure their constant rejections. Crushes come and go like head colds and fashion fads in the early years of puberty, and often continued with only slightly diminished frequency into later adolescence and adulthood. Billy certainly had had his share of "the hots".

And while he could say with complete and total honesty that he had no serious interest or designs on Katie — not even a primitive in-and-out urge to exploit her amazing physical assets — as the summer was coming to a close, he started to relent a bit in his relentless spurning.

The first time, with only a couple weeks left in her internship, he went to lunch with her.

They were rescued from the intense awkwardness of being alone together after fifteen minutes, when three of their associates at Habitat stumbled in to the same pizzeria and joined them for the duration of the meal.

It was, however, a very long fifteen minutes. Katie was usually given to non-stop talking when she came into his office, armed with some technical issue or set of work-related problems to discuss. But in the cold, naked environment of the restaurant, where the only purpose of the time they were spending together was starkly personal, she clammed up like a turtle under a shark attack.

"Did you grow up in North Carolina?"

"Yes."

"Have any brothers and sisters?"

"Yes."

"Pets?"

"Two."

"Dogs? Cats? A giraffe?"

"Two cats."

"What do you think of Newburgh?"

"It's fine."

"Can I borrow $10,000?"

"Sure."

"I think I'll set my hair on fire."

"Okay."

She just stared at him the whole time. Not looking particularly happy.

He could feel her pain.

The moment of high empathy was interrupted by the raucous arrival of their office buds. Free-flowing chatter and uninhibited consumption of vast quantities of pizza and Coke filled the rest of the lunch break. Billy and Katie walked back to the office side by side, both very aware of the several inches that separated them, while the others carried on like high school students playing hooky, until they walked into the office and got back down to business.

The next week presented another opportunity, not by any means planned. It just happened.

It also demonstrated the depth of Billy's occasional bad judgment.

For the first time in their marriage, Natalie was going to be away for three days. The three founders and chief executives of Seminole were attending a conference in Washington DC, and decided to take along Natalie and one of their other associates, to present a concept paper on sustainable mid-sized community planning, specifically designing and integrating sub-villages into existing city configurations, to reduce the dehumanizing effects of urban sprawl and the destruction of community spirit by unregulated development. It was a dicey problem both logistically and politically but Natalie had become, in her very short career, Seminole's resident expert. She and her colleague — a semi-retired consultant named Marv Catlin — had just recently presented the same paper to the Orange County Community Planning Council, and it had been warmly received. A published version drew national attention and acclaim from many experts in the field. Thus arose the invitation to present it at a new conference, *Emerging Concepts In Sustainable Community Planning and Development*, organized and funded by the Department of the Interior.

Billy drove Natalie to the airport early Friday morning, where she and the other Seminole conference attendees boarded the plane bound for DC. She would be back late Sunday evening.

After work on Friday, four of Habitat's younger regular employees and the three interns invited Billy to go bowling. It had been quite a while since he had bowled. Faced with the prospect of a Natalieless home, he couldn't resist the opportunity to have a few laughs and make a fool of himself.

Billy's luck was with him that night. For reasons which defied logic or statistical probability — both would have the odds tenaciously hugging the threshold of impossibility — Billy rolled like he had been born with a bowling ball in his bassinet. Three games over 200 blew everyone else's combined scores away. His performance frankly took a lot of the fun out of the game, since with an activity as completely frivolous as knocking over big chunks of wood with an unwieldy round ball made of plastic, the laughs are born in the relative levels of ineptitude. Billy's high-flying performance spoiled the joke. He was partially forgiven when he bought three large pepperoni pizzas for them to share, right after they finished the last game, even if it wasn't exactly the best pizza in town.

"This crust is something else."

"Now I know what they use to resole the bowling shoes."

As they were leaving, Billy trying to suppress his victor's self-satisfied smile, offered lame apologies for doing so well. As the others did their best to ignore him and change the subject, Katie discreetly pulled him aside.

"I don't want to go home yet. It's too boring. Let's go to your place."

"What for?"

"I don't know. I'm leaving next week. We could talk maybe. Please?"

Talk. Like they never talked. Well ... actually they didn't. Not *talk* talk.

"Listen, Katie—"

"Billy." That was the first time he could remember her not calling him Mr. Green, despite his repeatedly asking her to use his first name. "I know you're a married man. And I'm smart enough to have figured things out. Talk. That's it. Just talk. I just don't want to be alone."

He believed her.

But did he believe himself? He had been saying over and over that he had no interest in her. No designs. No short term agenda. Certainly no long terms plans.

So what harm could come of this? Talk. A nice talk on a hot summer night.

Right.

A nice talk on a hot summer night with a beautiful sexy young girl who had the hots for him.

But rationalization is the evil step-brother of rationality.

"Okay. But no funny stuff."

"We can't laugh? That would seem to take the fun out it, wouldn't it?"

Her comeback certainly wasn't very funny. But they still both laughed eagerly at her pseudo-cleverness. She could be irresistibly cute at times. Actually, most of the time.

He drove them home to his empty old house on Grand Street with its English garden, four bedrooms and a jacuzzi. Neither spoke for the short ride. The radio provided the perfect musical bed for his inner dialogue. Negotiations within himself, which neither benefited from common sense or good faith.

Why was he doing this?

Was he being a Good Samaritan or a fool?

Was this going where it obviously could be going?

No. He wouldn't let it. Absolutely not! Just ... talk.

But really ... why was he doing this?

Ego gratification? Thrills? To see how close he could hold his hand to the fire?

Even as a kid he wasn't one for double dares. Then as an adolescent, typical macho just-to-prove-he-could stunts had no appeal for him. It wasn't that he was chicken. Billy just thought daring-do was frivolous, pointless, and more a sign of insecurity than courage.

So back to the question: Why was he doing this?

Maybe it was the company he was keeping. Especially in this very moment. Peer pressure is a powerful and persuasive promoter of virtue and folly alike. He was twenty-two, Katie was barely nineteen. She was mature for her age. Apparently he was not. That put them at parity.

They pulled into his drive. The moment of truth accompanied them up the steps and through the front door.

"Grandma, I'm home. I have a friend with me. Hmm. She's not home. She's probably out on military maneuvers. Finally got promoted to a lieutenant-colonel in the National Guard."

"Sounds like my grandfather. Only he's a Grand Wizard in the KKK."

"Really?"

She immediately showed a sparkle in her eye and assumed a mocking tone.

"*Really?* I see Mr. Green can dish it out but can't see it coming when he's on the receiving end. Of course not, silly man! The only time my little southern family ties rope to a tree is when they want to hang some laundry."

She continued to giggle, clearly enjoying a little one-upmanship. Very cute.

Okay. This could be fun after all. She definitely had a good sense of humor. Quick. Quirky. Plenty of sunshine. But not afraid of the dark.

Just as they plopped down on the couch, a safe arm's length of distance between them, Katie decided she was thirsty. She made it clear that she meant something harder than Fanta or fruit juice.

"Have you got anything to drink? I mean a *drink* drink."

"Are you old enough?"

"I know how to use a glass. I left my Tommy Tippy at home when I started college."

Billy had to think. Recently they hadn't kept much in the way of alcohol around the house. There was a bottle of Jack Daniels but that was probably too strong.

"I have some Grand Marnier."

"I don't know what that is but I'll try it."

He poured two thumbs in each of their small glasses and handed one to her.

"Now just sip and savor. This stuff is stronger than you think. It goes down very smoothly."

She proposed the toast.

"To a man who is everything a man should be."

Billy might have blushed or been put off by such a serious jolt of flattery. Or a come-on. But Katie had a slightly sardonic gleam in her eye and her voice was chipper and somewhat mocking, with only the vaguest hint of seductiveness to it. What complexity in such a youthful and unassuming little package.

He withheld a reaction and gave her a non-committal once-over, before turning his gaze to his still-unsipped drink, to search the deep vermillion liquid for some appropriate comeback.

Billy proposed a counter-toast.

"To a young lady who should be home in bed counting sheep."

"I'm happy here counting my blessings."

They clinked glasses.

They chit-chatted and sipped. Billy poured another round. They exchanged banter about the people at the office and some unfounded rumors that were being bandied about. Katie really liked it at Habitat but wished she had been given more serious work to do. Most of the time she felt she was a glorified gofer. But she had had a great summer. She stood up.

"The bathroom? Upstairs. Right?"

"Yep. U-turn at the top. Second door on the left."

She went up. Billy kicked off his shoes and slouched low into the sofa. He was just starting to feel the effects of the Grand Marnier. A nice little glow. He reached over, picked up a Time Magazine and started to read the cover story about Fidel Castro. The old autocrat was undergoing surgery and had temporarily ceded power to his brother Raúl, who political analysts had speculated would succeed Fidel in office either should something happen to him, or should he decide to retire.

Christ, she was taking a long time.

Billy waited a few more minutes and skimmed an article and an editorial on the Lebanon War. Then he stood up and went to the foot of the stairs.

"Katie! Are you alright?"

No reply. He went up and called her name again.

"Hello! Katie?"

When he got to the landing, he noticed that the bathroom door was open. He made the U-turn, walked over the open door and stepped in.

She was completely naked, stretched the entire length of the tub. Her skin was angel food white — she must have never been in the sun — and smooth as glazed porcelain.

"Should we run some water and take a bath?"

Billy was speechless. He knew with absolute certainty that he should not look but his eyes had a different idea. He had stopped moving. He had stopped breathing. She was perfection. God Himself could not improve on the alluring length of her neck, her kissable collarbones, the curve of her breasts, the color of her nipples, her perfectly flat stomach, her lickable belly button, the delicate shape of her mons veneris and short shadow of wispy pubic hair, the thin pink line of the entrance to her vagina.

Then he noticed her glance at the front of his pants and realized he was hard. Very hard.

Instantly he went into action.

Billy frantically reached for the towel rack and the shelf above it. Piece by piece he threw everything at her in an attempt to cover her up. Towels, hand cloths, washrags, even a camisole which Natalie had hand washed and left hanging there to dry.

It was such a ridiculous display, that Katie started ducking and laughing at the same time.

"You missed. You can still see me. You're crazy, Billy Green." There was that girlish seductive giggle, somehow still as innocent as if she were eight years old and playing with a friend after school.

"Get dressed."

Billy hastily turned and bolted out of the bathroom.

He sat downstairs staring straight ahead, damning his own stupidity over a crystal tumbler of whiskey, twice refilled. It so far had had no effect on him. The full impact of his foolishness and guilt was unblunted by alcohol. He was kicking himself real hard.

Idiot. Idiot. Idiot.

Katie came down the stairs fully clothed again, looking almost refreshed, casually smiling as if nothing had happened, like she was thinking of something entirely unrelated to the incident upstairs. Then she caught Billy's expression.

"Hey. Don't be so mad at the world. It was no big deal."

"That was a really stupid stunt."

"Nothing ventured nothing gained."

"Katie. Life isn't some game."

"Oh! Believe me I know. Except I should have started sooner."

"Sooner? What are you talking about?"

"I had the whole summer. I shouldn't have waited till now. Really really stupid. Can I sit next to you?"

"No." Billy pointed at an armchair across from him. "Sit there." She did.

After a few moments of silence, while Billy studied her and she gazed out the window into the darkness lost in her own thoughts, she suddenly looked very sad.

"Okay. I give up."

"You never should've started in the first place."

"It would have been great. I wish you could see that."

"Katie. You are a very attractive young lady. Beautiful beyond words. I'm sure you must get that all the time. But—"

"Guys will say anything."

"Well, it's me that's saying it. Not just some guy. But you have to understand. I have never been available to you. In case you hadn't noticed, I'm a married man. I love my wife. I truly, deeply, passionately love Natalie."

"And tonight? Why am I here?"

"To talk?"

"You are so clueless. Either that or you are kidding yourself. You don't even know what goes on in your own head."

"I thought you wanted company. You said you were lonely."

"I said I didn't want to be alone. God! I hope other men aren't so stupid."

She looked at Billy with eyes that could melt an iceberg. Sad puddles of unfulfilled fantasy. Warm inviting pools that promised the splendors of honest, innocent, unfettered love.

"I wanted to be with *you*, Billy. I wanted *you*. You would have been my first."

That took Billy by surprise. Truly shook him to the core. Over the course of the summer, he had come to the unvarnished conclusion that no way was Katie a virgin. She was a wild card. Certainly selective and not very experienced. But no less a wild card.

"Sorry, Katie. Wrong man."

With that she abruptly stood up and headed to the door. She opened it, then turned to confront him. He was instantly on his feet as well and on his way over to her. She was obviously struggling to control her anger. She managed to speak evenly, sympathetically, with an understatement that multiplied the malignancy of her condolences.

"If you want to spend your life married to a lesbian, I wish you luck, Billy Green."

What?

"Let me give you a ride. You can't—"

"I'm fine. I'll walk. It'll give me time to cool down. And think."

"No. Really. It's no—"

"I really need to think. See you tomorrow, Mr. Green."

And she was gone.

Billy felt like a real chump. What had he been thinking? He never NEVER should have brought her back here. Especially with Natalie gone. Stupid. Stupid. Stupid.

The following Friday at the end of the work day, Habitat held an informal farewell party for the interns. Soft drinks and snacks.

It was on these occasions that the Director, Henry Blackledge, always eager to be liked and viewed as "just one of the guys", obviously thrived, and didn't appear to be trying so hard. He stood in the spacious first floor reception area, in front of the door of his private office. Beside him were Davey, Mike and Katie. They could have been his nephews and niece visiting from Tulsa. He signaled for everybody's attention.

"We have been so fortunate this summer to have such hard-working, talented young people. We're going to miss all of you. As a token of our appreciation and so that you will remember us, we have a little something for you." He nodded to his secretary and she handed him framed certificates of service, which he then passed to each of the interns. They were individually inscribed with each of their names and signed by Henry himself.

"I think I speak for everyone here, when I wish the three of you success and happiness in all of your personal and professional endeavors."

Everyone in the office applauded enthusiastically, sprinkling in some over-the-top hoots and hollers for effect.

Henry then shook hands with them, and the four of them posed for the photographs which would be posted on the local Habitat website. But before they dispersed, Mike spoke up.

"We have a special announcement as well. Actually, it's a special award. Mr. Billy Green? Please come up, Mr. Green."

Against his better judgment, fearing some completely humiliating prank, Billy went up and stood next to the cocky young intern.

"After much careful consideration, we would like to present you with an award which recognizes your enormous talent and unique gifts. Katie?"

She reached into her duffel bag and pulled out a trophy. A bowling trophy! A funky old beat-up bowling trophy, which they must have picked up at the local Goodwill Industries or other second-hand store. The bronze plate had been papered over with a white mailing label.

Mike held the trophy up for everyone to see. He read the inscription, as he handed it to Billy.

> MR. BILLY GREEN, NEWBURGH *ECOLOGICAL BOWLER OF THE YEAR* - SUMMER 2006
>
> IN RECOGNITION OF HIS EXTRAORDINARY TALENT AS AN ENVIRONMENTAL ENGINEER AND AS AN OVERACHIEVER IN THE GAME OF BOWLING.

Everybody loved it. Billy pulled out a handkerchief and feigned big weepy tears, then thanked them for the unforgettable honor. There were hugs all around.

Katie was last.

"This was your idea, wasn't it?"

"Of course! I'm going to miss you. Even if you threw me out with the trash."

"I hope I don't regret it."

"You will."

"I'll always remember you, Katie. Now go and find yourself a real boyfriend. If there is anyone out there who deserves someone as special as you, that is."

"Thanks, Billy Green, overachiever."

Everyone went home for the weekend.

Billy never saw her again.

He would regret it.

Kind of.

Polythene Pam

New Years Eve. Again. In less than two hours they would be ringing in 2007. Another year older. Another brick in the wall.

Billy was feeling an uneasiness he couldn't pinpoint.

He hadn't seen much of Pam for a while. How long had it been? Maybe the last seven months? She had been around. She and Natalie had gotten together a number of times. They had even spent the weekend in New York City twice — once in September and again just before Thanksgiving. But for whatever reason, he just hadn't run into her. Schedules?

Well, here she was now. She seemed different. A lot different.

What was with the clothes? The new hair style? Her make-up as well was something new. Something else. She looked like she was on a movie set getting ready to shoot a love scene for Franco Zeffirelli. No. Scratch that. She looked like she had already shot the movie and was on her way to make her acceptance speech at the Academy Awards.

Pam had just come in and was doing the rising starlet greeting thing with those who knew her — which seemed to be everyone — big surprises and hugs like they hadn't seen each other for years, even if it was only yesterday, or at most last week. Now she was talking to that mysterious Annie Roberts lady, another one who seemed to know everyone and treated Newburgh like it was her own private fiefdom.

Billy worked his way over. Finally, Pam noticed him and closed the distance between them, nearly spilling her champagne as she reached to wrap her arms around her dear old friend, Billy Green. Were those acrylic nails?

"Hello stranger! It's been ages."

"You're right. It seems like we keep missing one another. You look ... great! Different! Amazing!"

"That *is* your favorite word, isn't it? But I agree. I do look amazing."

She laughed at her own conceit. Then she turned and indicating Annie Roberts, inched the two of them her way.

"Do you know *this* amazing lady, Billy? Hmm?"

"I know *of* her. You couldn't live anywhere in this town other than the cemetery and not know *of* her. She's everywhere. Does she have six clones?"

They were now directly in front of Annie Roberts, who smiled warmly at Pam, then gave Billy the once-twice-three-times-over, as might a pickpocket or a CIA agent looking for signs of a concealed weapon.

"Annie. This is Billy Green. Natalie's husband. He works for Habitat For Humanity."

"A handsome man. And a saint. Giving his time and talent to the world for McDonald's wages. Pleased to finally meet you, Billy."

"Likewise, I'm sure. Well, not sure. But leaning that way. I'll let you know."

"Ha! Funny man. Nice party. Beautiful house. Great place to raise children. Any on the drawing board?"

"Interesting that you would mention that. Because we haven't. But I guess it's a predictable step for a young couple. The ideal world of perfect bliss shattered by wailing babies and the clatter of toys and kitchen utensils being bounced off the walls. I'll definitely bring it up at our next family board meeting."

"My my. You had a less than happy childhood."

"I love my mom. My dad recently became a Hell's Angel. Sort of. You know, a spin off."

"Do they kill people?"

"Only with their looks."

"Nice chatting with you, Billy Green. Happy New Year."

She abruptly turned and started talking again to the 30-something lady she had put on hold for the introduction to Billy. The lady was Billy's neighbor from down the street, a divorcee both overweight and unkempt, with two teenage children, a boy 13 and a girl 15, who Billy saw coming and going or playing in the neighborhood. He didn't know their names. Their mom was Phyllis, if he remembered correctly. She had been waiting patiently as Billy and Annie conducted their exchange of TV generation wittiness, but now lit up like the arc lamp of heavenly grace had been pointed at her, as Annie gave her full attention. What could they be talking about that inspired such rapture?

Natalie came up behind Billy and slipped her hands under his arms and brought them up on his chest.

"Billy Bob Thornton! You got such big strong hands." Billy turned around to face her. "Natalie! It's you."

"Billy Bob Thornton is here? And you're having an affair with him? Billy, you never fail to surprise me."

"And you never fail to get me excited. Let's go up to our room and usher the new year in right. What do you say?"

"I say you're crazy and I love you. But I need to put out another tray of finger foods."

With that she headed to the kitchen.

Hmm. Not quite a brush-off. She probably did need to put out more of the buffalo wings, whitefish dumplings, wheat crackers and Brie, chili and lime pretzels, mini-quiches, Rhineland sausages, pickled eggplant, white chocolate crêpes, and various soy-based crunchies, now that soy was the new wheatgrass. People were eating like there was no tomorrow. Typical. They were already fat. They stuff more and more in their face hole and wonder why they're overweight. Join a gym and never go. Keep scratching their heads over the baffling phenomenon of an expanding waistline, going up the size ladder in their clothes, exclaiming 'I can't believe I'm wearing a size 14' or 'This must be a mistake, this label says 38 inches' or 'My metabolism just isn't what it was when I was growing up'. Then comes New Years and the predictable resolutions to lose weight, give up fast food, quit eating chocolate before going to bed, stop drinking beer, start jogging every morning, give up dairy products, no more dessert, join Jenny Craig, become a vegetarian, fast for forty days and forty nights. Who were they kidding? Well, that was obvious. First of all themselves. Second, anyone with whom they had the bad judgment share their soon-to-be-abandoned commitment to discipline and self-improvement. In some unwritten but universally accepted pact, however, nobody called out anyone else on their humiliating failure, because everyone was complicit in the pandemic of self-delusions, and suffering from television-induced attention deficit disorder.

So …

Keep those greasy-sugary-hydrogenated gut bombs coming, sweet Natalie. Everybody will love you for it and hopefully not implicate you in the quadruple bypass they're going to be getting when they're forty-three.

I need to put out another tray of finger foods.

That rankled him. But why should it? Seriously. Billy wanted to dismiss it as his own stock contrariness. He typically was somewhat agitated at these social gatherings.

Sure. He liked people. He liked interaction with people. But he much preferred real interaction, substantial interaction. Is it too much to ask to have a actual conversation, something beyond the typical polite exchanges which never venture beyond the first month of an ESL class? Parties were so superficial. He really would have preferred to have all of these people gone and to take Natalie upstairs like he had only half-kiddingly suggested. Instead, here she was flitting around trying to make the best of what he perceived was an intrinsically flawed arrangement. Everybody getting stuffed and shit-faced for what? To ring in the New Year. What was *that* all about anyway? Whoopee. Whoop-dee-fucking-do.

He continued to smile and conceal his deeper discomfort and distraction, the gnawing sense that something was getting away from him. That something he desperately needed to hang onto if life was going to have real meaning, was escaping, was dispersing, dissipating, disappearing.

What was it?

Was it lost opportunity?

Was it youthful, exuberant confidence?

Was it the elation and hopefulness, the vast stretches of optimism he felt a year-and-a-half ago when he got to Newburgh, got married, got settled, finally had Natalie in his life for real?

I need to put out another tray of finger foods.

Something besides the gastronomical implications of it bothered him.

Not quite a brush-off. But the type of remark which he was getting more and more of lately. Like ... *I can't eat dinner with you tonight because of the riverfront project*. Or ... *I'm just so exhausted, give me a couple days*. Or ... *I think I'll take the evening off and go over to Pam's*. Or ... *Just go do your own thing and don't worry about me*.

It seemed like he was doing his own thing more and more these days.

The thing that was bothering Billy was both subtle and fleeting. Sometimes he thought he was just imagining it. Maybe it *was* just in his head. He loved her so much and that kind of love typically came with over-inflated expectations. Probably unfair expectations.

Wasn't some degree of independence a healthy thing? Wasn't it a sign that their relationship was so solid and enduring that they could each wander a little further and linger a little longer away from the nest, in the secure knowledge that the real essential core of their lives, the true meaning of life lay in their union, as husband and wife, friends, lovers? Eternity is a long time.

Even so, at times there definitely seemed to be some uninvited seed taking root, some tiny green shoot, some unwanted weed breaking ground, threatening the unspoiled beauty of the garden.

Natalie was still attentive and affectionate. Up to a point. Then?

Then there seemed to be this territorial barrier. This gateway guarding an enclave he was allowed to enter less and less frequently. Some protected, sealed personal space around her.

Things definitely weren't quite the same as they had been for so long.

Right up to maybe two or three months ago.

Something had changed.

Some changes are good. Some are not.

Billy didn't feel good about this change. He had an uneasy feeling. Almost menacing. He had misgivings.

And he didn't know why but somehow it all seemed to have something to do with Pam.

He felt someone behind him and turned around.

"Speaking of."

Pam had made her way over again, champagne glass refilled to the rim and poised against her chin ready to be sipped.

"Were you talking about me?"

"Just the voices in my head."

"So my suspicions are true after all."

"Those are?"

"That you are stark raving mad. A complete nutcase."

"Anything else?"

"A full-tilt loony. A rabid dog. The Foul Wizard of Bezoar. The Mad Hatter of Orange County. Shall I go on?"

"Then you'll sleep with me now?"

"See. Right there. Absolute proof you have lost your mind. Who do you think you've been fucking for the last four nights, Billy?"

"Her passport said Maria Sharapova. That was you?"

"Speaking of passports."

"Yes? Speaking of passports?"

"Did Nat mention to you what we talked about maybe two minutes ago?"

"If it was two minutes ago, I have to admit she hasn't gotten around to it yet. So you tell me. What's the blindside this time?"

"Okay. Admittedly. It's kind of a recent pattern. I didn't used to be this way. But freedom. It's like a narcotic. Only not a downer. A super upper upper! We are going to London, Billy! Fucking London, England!"

London? Billy couldn't remember in all of their hundreds of hours of conversations, casual and intimate, Natalie ever even once mentioning London, much less expressing a desire to actually go there. What was going on? This had to be Pam's doing. Was the competition for Natalie up and running again?

He couldn't let on what a cosmic blow this was, that Natalie apparently found it so easy to make such a dramatic decision without even a word with him. Whether it was something she had been discussing with Pam for some time or it was an impulse arrived at in the floating menagerie of tonight's party, he was on the outside looking in.

"Recent pattern? You've always been this way."

"What way? What are you talking about?"

"Never mind. London, eh? Jolly good. Pip pip. That's phenomenal, Pam. Your first time, right?"

"Billy. I've never been anywhere. 99% of the idiots in Indianapolis have never been outside of Indiana."

"So you'll be in the 1% of idiots. Hey! You already are. Illinois. New York. Now London."

She evidently didn't appreciate what was a not-very-cleverly-masked dose of sarcasm.

"Don't underestimate me, Billy."

"I never have. And I never will. Anyway, I was just joking."

"Like they say about last laughs ..."

"What *do* they say? Whoever *they* are."

"Google it."

She turned and walked away.

For a good ten months from the day Billy and Natalie got married, Pam had been pretty much an afterthought or a diversion in the Green household. And for good reason. Pam had been extremely busy with her job, and for a whole variety of considerations, appeared to be developing her own group of friends and acquaintances, independent of Billy and Natalie and their social circle.

So infrequent were the times the three of them got together to do something, Billy quite enjoyed seeing her when they did. It was with genuine enthusiasm for his wife's best friend that he used such occasions to catch up with what was happening in her life, and share any details on the events of his own life which might be of interest to her. But these were rare, certainly sporadic get-togethers.

Billy rightly assumed that Natalie kept in touch with Pam by phone, though the calls rarely occurred at home. Every so often, Natalie would mention that she and Pam had had lunch, had briefly encountered one another at the store, or spent a few minutes window shopping in the downtown business district.

Then the last seven months, leading up to the Christmas holidays, Pam was so pre-occupied with yet another new job — this past July she had resigned from You Win I Win We All Win, to become Public Relations Director for the Orange County Tourism Council — and Billy was likewise buried under multiple rapid deadline assignments at Habitat, she had fallen completely off the radar screen for him. No visits, lunches, dinners, parties, nights out, or afternoons around town, nothing put them in proximity. If he didn't bring Pam up — and he didn't — Natalie never talked about her. It was a Pam blackout, punctuated only by Natalie's surprise announcements that she and Pam would be going into New York City for the weekend. That had happened only twice. Other than that, it was as if Pam had disappeared or died.

Until tonight. Now she was back. With a vengeance. Maybe that was putting it a bit strongly.

Maybe not.

After nearly forgetting about her, to now find out that she and Natalie were going to be gallivanting off to London, well … it felt like some sort of doomsday cloud had suddenly descended on him and was threatening to destroy all that was near and dear to him. It wasn't so much that he worried about or didn't trust Natalie. It was that it was so easy for him to worry about and mistrust Pam. She was most certainly the joker in the deck. Long dormant anxiety and suspicion now poisoned his world view, a sudden jolting, total paradigm shift. He was once again on high alert, wondering how soon he would be fielding yet more of Pam's stealthy assaults on the quiet stability and calm predictability of his life.

London. Holy shit! When? How long?

It suddenly occurred to Billy that he needed to check on something. He had … a feeling.

Without drawing attention to himself, he slipped away from his guests — easy enough since they were either still stuffing their faces or chattering away like a bunch of magpies on crystal meth, sometimes both simultaneously, creating a horizontal blizzard of syllables and crumbs — and went upstairs to the office.

He knew exactly where to find what he was looking for. Indeed, Natalie's passport was in a small documents box at the back of a file cabinet drawer, where they kept their important papers.

Folded inside her passport was an e-ticket. Yes, she was going to London alright. And then on to Ibiza, Spain. The airline ticket had been bought online on November 15th. Billy looked through the passport. Everything was current. Good until May 6, 2015. She had apparently gotten it just before they got married.

At least he knew the details now. Natalie was leaving Saturday February 3rd, spending at least three days in London, going on to Ibiza for a week and returning February 14th.

Valentines Day.

How romantic.

And what was in Ibiza? He frankly had never heard of it. Then again, he wasn't exactly a world traveler.

Why hadn't she told him? This wasn't like taking the train into the City for a Broadway show and pastrami sandwiches at a Jewish deli. This was a major adventure — one that he had to confess, out of some immediate galling envy, he would have loved to share with her.

As Billy slipped back downstairs, doing his best to don his best party smile and appear unruffled by what he had discovered, the clock was ticking its final 2006 clicks toward the midnight hour, that imaginary threshold in the continuum of the 4th dimension when humans across America — for now those in the Eastern Time Zone — would by their own act of free will embrace temporary insanity.

The magic moment arrived just as Billy's right foot touched the dining room floor.

Happy New Year! Whoo-hoo! Happy New Year!!

Cheers and toasts and even a few bubbly drinks poured over giddy heads. Hearty back slaps. Fists pumping skyward. High fives, hugs and party kisses all around. A few copped feels.

Should auld acquaintance be forgot and ...

Auld acquaintance be forgot? What does that mean? Who or what are they singing about? Drunks! A bunch of drunks. But ...

If you can't lick 'em, join 'em.

Billy reached for a bottle on the table, picked up an empty tumbler — maybe abandoned by someone else, who cares? — and poured himself some amber whiskey or brandy or scotch. He didn't bother to turn the label toward himself to see what he had grabbed, but just downed whatever it was in one smooth motion. It burned his throat and twisted his face momentarily into something like a English pug being subjected to high voltage.

Pam suddenly came over and embraced Billy like they had just won the big prize on a shared lottery ticket. The tension from their last exchange seemed to be gone. At least for her. After seeing Natalie's ticket and passport, and knowing full well that Pam was a co-conspirator, if not a singular instigator, Billy couldn't exactly bring himself to feel warm fuzzies toward her right now. She didn't seem to notice. Her eyes were glazed and pupils dilated like galactic black holes.

"Pam. You have purple eyes! Is that possible?"

"Designer contacts. I almost wore green snowflakes tonight but that freaks people out."

"You wouldn't want to do that."

"Of course not, Billy. I'm a kind and gentle person."

She laughed hysterically, then moved on to someone else to spread the love, a pretty blond girl, maybe in her mid-20s, that Billy hadn't noticed before. He had no idea who she was. Maybe she had just arrived. Pam sure seemed to know her.

Billy spotted Natalie among several people who were dancing in the living room. They were trying to do the Macarena but either no one could remember it, or no one was coordinated enough to pull it off in their advanced state of alcohol-induced palsy.

He jumped into the center directly in front of Natalie. The drink he had just taken had submerged his cerebral cortex in a whirlpool of euphoria, dulling the bashfulness receptors. He was such a total lightweight when it came to drinking.

"Hey everybody! This is how it goes."

Billy started jumping around and doing a variety of hand motions and butt choreography.

"That's amazing! Where did you learn that?"

"I studied with the Bolshoi Ballet."

"I think what you're doing is either the hokey pokey or the chicken dance. It's definitely not the Macarena."

Everybody laughed and Billy kept on dancing unfazed, in the center of the circle that had formed around him. Natalie seemed particularly amused.

"Justin Timberlake has nothing on you, Billy. Go! Go! Go!"

When the song finished, he and Natalie headed toward the kitchen. She was glistening with perspiration and thirsty.

"Whew! I've been dancing for over an hour. I need something quick. Do we have any more vodka and orange juice?" She poked him in the ribs. "Hey you! Where've you been? I was looking for you."

"Upstairs. Making arrangements."

"Making arrangements? On New Years Eve? What kind of arrangements?"

Billy poured her a stiff drink — heavy on the vodka — plopped in some ice cubes, and handed it to her.

"Pam tells me you're going to London. So I was upstairs putting it all together for you."

Natalie stopped mid-swallow and stared at him guiltily.

"And you know, Nat. I was thinking, why stop there? Maybe it would be a good idea to take a few extra days and keep going. You know, maybe head to Ibiza. What do you think? Does February 3rd work for you? It's a Saturday."

Natalie put down her drink and wrapped her arms around him. Then she went up on her tiptoes and planted a long, deep, passionate, vodka-flavored French kiss on him.

"I love you, Billy. Because I know you trust me."

Her trip with Pam never came up again.

Not even when she left for the airport.

She packed, took a shower, then kissed Billy goodbye.

He watched the taxi pull away from a bay window on the second floor.

Then he ate a slice of cold leftover pizza and a bowl of cornflakes for breakfast.

How long have you been married?

One year, seven months, twelve days.

Still counting the days. How romantic!

She loves me because she knows I trust her.

Trust is very important.

And I love her because … well, I just do.

She's very special.

Very special.

She's everything?

Everything.

Chapter Three

PICKET FENCES AND BARB WIRE
Winter Spring Summer 2007

The Slow Lane

They were gone. Natalie and Pam. London. Ibiza, Spain. Without him.

Billy wasn't going to play the self-pity card.

On the contrary. If it makes her happy, why should he object? Look what it says about their relationship. They were strong in their love, could totally depend on one another, but each could still enjoy independence, autonomy, individual dignity. They actually chose to not rely on one another unnecessarily, avoiding the kind of co-dependence so typical of marriages these days. That's exactly what was going on here. Extremely healthy.

How many couples could say that?

It was a noble arrangement and he would put aside his own selfishness and pettiness. He would rise to the occasion and be a real man. Not some pathetic, clingy, possessive, jealous type. But the kind of man who supports and trusts his wife. In fact, _admires_ and _respects_ her for her strength and audacity, her honesty and self-determination, her unpredictability and sense of adventure, her...

He picked up the phone and dialed. It rang twice.

"Hi mom."

"Billy! This is an unexpected surprise."

He had just talked to her a couple weeks ago.

"I think my marriage is going down the tubes."

"Oh no! Why, Billy? Why?"

"Natalie's gone. And I—"

"She's left you? What happened?"

"No no. I didn't mean gone, as in _gone_. She's in Spain with her friend Pam."

"Well ... that doesn't sound so bad. Pam is a girl, right?"

"But she didn't actually tell me she was going. And ..."

Billy was beginning to sound stupid to himself.

"... I mean, she planned this whole thing last ... maybe last October."

"She probably was going to tell you. I don't tell your dad everything right away, you know. Sometimes I just wait until the right time. Timing is important."

Now his and Natalie's relationship was being set side-by-side with his mom's and dad's for a little product comparison. If that wasn't a slap in the face! What was he thinking? Why did he even bring it up to his mom?

"How you feeling? Everything okay?"

"Fine. Fine. But what about Natalie? Are you—"

"It was nothing, mom. Forget I mentioned it. I guess I'm just lonely. I miss her. That's it."

"If you say so. But remember, my favorite son. You can always talk to me. Anytime."

"I know. Thanks, mom. You sound good. Still doing the astronomy thing?"

"Only once a month. The weather hasn't been good and a lot of times, I'm too tired after my Tai Chi class."

"Whoa whoa whoa! What's this? You're taking Tai Chi now?"

"I just started last month. But I love it. It's like meditation, I guess. I mean, I feel so good doing it. And my body feels so strong and relaxed afterwards."

"Tai chi."

"See, there is this women's empowerment group that meets at the church now. Once a week. It's not women's liberation or anything. Well, it kind of is actually. It's called AWOL — A World of Liliths."

"AWOL."

"It's like women should go on strike. You know, AWOL, until men shape up. Lilith was this really strong biblical woman. But because she was so strong, a lot of powerful men hated her. So she was pretty much written out of the Bible. That's how I understand it."

"My mother, a feminist revolutionary."

"Let's not to overboard, Billy. I'm not about to join an Amazon army. Although, we did read about the legend of the Amazon women. It's not easy, especially for women my age, who have always accepted the traditional ideas of what a woman should look like, how she should act, how she should serve the men of the world, the same men who have screwed up this world so badly."

"Have you stopped shaving your armpits?"

"No. But I got your father to start shaving his."

"Do you make him lay down so you can run the lawnmower over him?"

"What a great idea! Maybe I'll bring that up at the next AWOL meeting. The other women will love it. We're always looking for new things. You make me so proud."

"You're getting more sarcastic than me."

"Anyway, these meetings are really interesting. It gives me perspective. It really helps knowing that it's not just me. It's not just the way Harold treats me that's the problem. It's society."

"Dad makes the rest of the society look like the Garden of Paradise bound up with a utopian dream of eternal perfection."

"You know, Billy, your father has his good points."

"And what would those be, mom?"

"Billy. I know what you're saying. Just take my word for it. He really does. But what I was about to say was, whatever few good points he might have had when we first got married, even now, when he's not plastered to the floor or in his usual foul mood, whatever the man has going for him, he's basically a butthead. And that's that."

Billy had trouble believing his mom was really saying this. She was finally facing up to what he had always known about his father. Even if he had been waiting all his life for this particular moment, it made him uncomfortable. Was she saying she had wasted her life? Was she thinking there was some solution? Divorce? Rehabilitation? What?

"Have you talked to him about this?"

"Very funny, young man. You know there's no talking to him about anything. Besides, it's too late. Just too darn late."

"Mom. If there were a magic wand and I could make all the bad things go away, I would wave it and wave it until you were happy."

She laughed. Not in a mean or unappreciative way. Just a mom laugh. The kind he would get when Billy was just a boy and would do something incredibly cute.

"Billy! Come on! I'm fine. I'm pretty happy. I've accepted things the way they are. That's not the point."

"What is the point, mom? I don't understand."

"The point is I want you to respect me. I've always been afraid because you're so smart and all, that you would think your old mom was just some damn fool. Some pathetic dingbat who didn't know up from down. The truth is, Billy, I made my bed and now I have to sleep in it."

"But why? You deserve better."

"Maybe I do. Maybe I don't. Life goes on. When you're young, it's so easy to fall in love. The thing is, you don't always know what you're getting. You have no idea how things will turn out. That's all."

"That's all?"

"Yes, Billy. I got married so young. You got married so young. Things happen. All sorts of things. People change. Just remember that."

"But ... Natalie—"

"I'm not saying anything about Natalie. She's a good one, Billy. I think that you did real good there. But ..."

"But what?"

"The what is this, my Billy Boy. I know you think you're grown up. But you're still very young. You've got a long way to go. People change. You're going to change a lot. I'm sure for the better. Natalie's going to change. Everyone gets it backwards. They put on blinders and can't see the writing on the wall when they can still make a difference. Then they take the blinders off when it's too late. When there's no going back. That's what I did, Billy. I married Prince Charming, the man of my dreams. I put on the blinders and couldn't see the changes. Then one day I took off the blinders and here I am married to a butthead."

"It's never too late, mom."

"I have no idea what that means. It's too late. And I'm fine with it. Besides, your dad has become a real character lately. I have to say, now that he's actually out of the rut he was in for the last twenty years, Vegas and the motorcycle gang he's in—"

"I thought it was a motorcycle club."

"Call it what you like, those bunch of burnt-out losers should be locked up on general principle. Anyway, your old man is getting eccentric in his old age. Did I tell you he grew a beard? And he hasn't gotten a haircut in over four months. He looks like Moses in leather whenever he leaves the house."

"A beard? Long hair? He hates hippie types. This is too much to process. Way too much!"

"And I have to say, I like it. Not that we're Romeo and Juliet or anything. But *the guy has got some sex appeal these days."*

"No offense but 'sex appeal' and the dad I know don't inhabit the same universe much less belong in the same sentence."

"So why did you call? Something about your marriage coming out of a tube?"

"Going down the tubes. The expression is 'going down the tubes'. But never mind. I was just having a brain fart."

"Brain fart? What causes that? Eating beans and onions while reading a book?"

Billy burst out laughing.

"Mom. You crack me up! You are one of a kind."

"I am. And so are you. We all are."

"I wish I could believe that. 99% of the people look the same to me."

"That's because you're not looking. In some ways, when you get older your vision actually gets better."

"Then why do you wear glasses?"

"Because when my brain farts, it fogs my eyes."

Billy almost dropped the phone. He finally stopped laughing.

"Mom, I miss you. Sometimes I wish I were a kid again. We had some good times."

"And we'll have more. When are you ...? Uh-oh. Time to go. I think Jerry Garcia just came in the door. Give my love to Natalie when she gets back. Tell her I want to see the pictures."

"You and me both."

It was only 7:42 when Billy got off the phone with his mom. As was happening more and more often after their conversations, his head was spinning.

He went upstairs and lay down. There was so much to think about.

Let's see. It was Tuesday. February 6th. Natalie was still in London. But tomorrow she and Pam would be flying to Ibiza, Spain. He still hadn't bothered to look that up, to figure out what Ibiza was all about, why they might have chosen to spend a whole week there.

His dad had a beard. His mom thought his dad was a butthead. But a sexy butthead.

She was right about one thing. He shouldn't try to fool himself. He was still very young. Sometimes it seemed like he knew so much, and at others, that he didn't know a damn thing. Not about life anyway.

People change. That's for sure.

You don't always know what you're getting. You have no idea how things will turn out.

But Natalie? What about Natalie?

She's a good one, Billy.

She is. She sure is.

Married so young ... blinders ... Prince Charming ... women's empowerment ... Moses in leather ... brain farts ... Tai Chi ... she's a good one ...

Billy had no idea what time he fell asleep. He hadn't moved and woke up the next morning in the same clothes he had been wearing the night before.

He got up, took a shower, put on some fresh attire, and made himself some breakfast. Cheerios, orange juice, coffee. Then it was off to work.

In the seven remaining days of Natalie's vacation in Ibiza, Billy read three books and saw five movies he had been curious about. He went to the theater and saw *Blood Diamond* and *Firewall*. Then he rented three DVDs and watched them at home — *Flags of Our Fathers*, *American Psycho*, and *V For Vendetta*. He seriously doubted Natalie would have liked any of the films. Guy flicks. Actually, he didn't particularly like them either. But it was something to do and nicely filled the void of the evening hours without her.

On Saturday afternoon, he went ice skating at the Mid-Hudson Civic Center rink, losing track of how many times he fell on his butt somewhere around twenty.

Sunday, it was off to wander among the 500 acres of sculptures at the Storm King State Park and Art Center. Though it was a pretty cold hike, he had bundled up and brought extra clothes and was able to spend almost the entire afternoon there.

Even if he would have preferred to have Natalie at his side for the leisure hours of the weekend — and he obviously did — he had to admit that he had a pretty decent time.

As for the more mundane domestic aspects of his life, it was a breeze. He kept the house orderly, something he tried to do when Natalie was there as well. He even managed to feed himself, though usually he let her do the cooking, since she was much better behind the stove and in front of the cutting board than he could ever be. But he got by without any occurrences of food poisoning or losing his fingers to cutlery.

The first three evenings he microwaved various frozen Stouffer's and Sara Lee pre-fab dinners and desserts he had picked up at the local Food Barn supermarket. But after reading the ingredients, Billy decided the boxes they came in were probably more nutritious. So the next four nights, he delved into a cookbook and laboriously prepared Italian, French, German and Greek dishes. Blinded by both pride and the anticipation which built over a couple hours in the smoke-filled kitchen, he declared the results entirely fit for Europe's most discriminating and elite tastes. After a couple glasses of wine, he decided that if the human ecology thing didn't continue to pan out, he definitely had a future as a great chef.

Wine. A very empowering thing.

It was both strange and liberating to live in the house for eleven days without Natalie. There understandably was a familiarity about being alone. He had after all spent more than 80% of his life as a bachelor. Nothing new there. Still it most certainly was not how he preferred things. He wished she were right there with him, and missed her sorely, especially late in the evening at bedtime. But he told himself — and he was positive he was being objective about this — it was probably a healthy thing. To have a break from one another helped keep things fresh and prevented them from taking one another for granted, probably the most common affliction of long term relationships.

Then it hit him. Maybe that's why Natalie took off. Just for a little break, a little change of scenery, something to shatter the routine. He should be grateful for a wife who understood the value in that, who was willing to prod and tease and nudge, even test their relationship, so that it didn't become mundane and predictable. So that they didn't fall into a rut and lose the amazing vital edge they had had so far.

Looking at it that way, he could accept the value of her little adventure. He shouldn't be angry about it. It was a good thing, both for her individually and them as a couple.

The one thing that still puzzled and irked him, however, was why she didn't tell him about it. Why he had to find out on his own.

He wasn't upset. But that one thing did gnaw at him. After all, he kept nothing from her. Well ... alright. That wasn't entirely true. There was that incident with the intern — the nude bathtub scene with Katie. And ... oh yes. Before they were married, the physical relationship he had had with Julianne for several months. That was intense! He suspected Natalie somehow had found out about it, or at least suspected it. But he himself had never had the courage or the decency to tell her, that was for sure.

Hmm. Secrets. He didn't exactly have a spotless record.

Maybe she was going to tell him eventually. Just like mom said on the phone.

But didn't he have every right to know? Didn't he have a right to some explanation?

That would be it. When she came back, he would ask her. Plain and simple.

They shouldn't have secrets from one another.

Even if they already did.

Baby Fever

When Natalie got back, she looked great. Really great! She had a fantastic tan.

But no tan lines.

"Don't even think about it, Billy. There were no men there. We found this really private beach and went for it."

"Does Pam have tan lines?"

"I can have her come over and you can look for yourself."

"Let me think about that."

"Better yet, check this out."

She went over to her computer, plugged her camera in, and pulled up some photos of a magnificent shore, lapped by foamy whitecaps emerging gracefully from a turquoise sea. Sure enough, there were no men. There was one amazing shot of Natalie and Pam laying side by side on a beach blanket wearing only sunglasses and tanning lotion. His imagination had fallen far short of how beautiful Pam's body was.

Natalie caught him staring, mouth agape, eyebrows arched in wonder.

"The sand is so white."

"Right. Like you were looking at the sand. Hey! I just got an excellent idea."

She stood him up, got around behind him and playfully pushed him into the bedroom, not that he offered much resistance.

She proved for the next several days to be insatiable.

"Good grief, Natalie. What did they feed you there on Ibiza?"

"Dreams, Billy. Dreams."

Of course, they both had their work schedules. But it seemed at least for those first few days after her return, Natalie managed to avoid any professional commitments in the evening and was there for him, ready and able to make love as often as was physically possible.

She had to catch up at work Saturday during the day but they had a phenomenal evening. Sunday they actually had slept in a bit, the consequence of being up half of the previous night in pursuit of carnal bliss.

Natalie woke first and looked at him. Eventually his eyes opened and she cuddled up to him, placing her lips teasingly against his ear and whispered.

"Happy Valentines Day."

"Hmm. That's right. I forgot. You got back on Valentines Day."

"There's something else, Billy."

"What's that?"

"I want a baby."

"I think the stores are open today. We can go after breakfast."

"I'm not kidding."

She wasn't.

They talked about it over brunch at Anna's, then as they walked through town afterwards, continuing on the drive along the Hudson River and through Hudson Highlands State Park, and finally that evening over a blackened dish which Billy claimed was genuine Livorno-style lasagna, complemented with a circular cardboard-like object which was supposed to be Sicilian pizza.

There was no doubt that they both wanted to have children. The whole question was timing. That they didn't seem to agree on.

"I'm too young to be a father, Natalie."

"No you're not."

"I'm only twenty-three."

"A perfect age. You're young, energetic, yet mature, established."

"Like I'm going to be some burnt out shell of a human being at 25 or 28, a moneyless bum sleeping in a dumpster behind Home Depot."

"If it's a boy, you can name him. If it's a girl, I want to call her Lilith."

That had a familiar ring. Wasn't Lilith some Amazon queen his mom was telling him about? Or was she a biblical terrorist that had all of the kings in a tizzy?

"Lilith. Lovely name. If it's a boy, I want to call him Chairman Mao."

Natalie laughed and jumped on top of him and proceeded to nearly cause heart failure by tickling him so relentlessly. It was obvious she was not going to stop without a commitment.

"So are we on, papa Billy? Are we going to make a baby? Are we? Are we?"

"Ha ha ha ha … if you don't stop tickling me … ha ha ha … I'll be dead … yes dead … ha ha ha … and that'll be … ha ha … please … ha ha ha … I'll do anything … ha ha ha ha … just stop … ha ha ha …"

"So that's a yes?"

"Yes … ha ha ha … yes, Natalie."

And they went to work.

At making a baby from scratch, that is.

It should have been simple. But in the end it turned out to be hard work. Very hard work.

It has confounded some of the best medical minds of the 21st Century why fertility rates have been gradually declining over the past fifty years. Those from three generations back claim — obviously exaggerating, of course — that back in those days, post-World War II, and on into the featureless 50s, getting pregnant was supposedly easier than catching a head cold. Teens were especially at risk. Schoolgirls were cautioned about sitting too close to boys for fear that sperm would somehow leap out, magically pass through clothing and skin, then home in like some precision-guided weapon on the cowering uterus, resulting in unwanted pregnancies.

Then came the 60s. A measurable decrease in fertility rates among both males and females started around the same time that the Beatles and the British invasion of pop musicians took over the radio airwaves, and has continued to this day. Egg production in women is still off, miscarriages continue to increase, sperm counts are down.

No connection could be established between the music of John Lennon and Paul McCartney, the Kinks, the Rolling Stones, Herman's Hermits and the other British bands, and the inability of couples to make babies back then or now.

So what precipitated the subtle but steady decline in fertility rates? Was it the cancellation of the Ed Sullivan Show? The unrequited romancing of the apparently still virginal Annette Funicello by any number of viable suitors on the Mickey Mouse Club? Chubby Checker and the twist? Lingering physiological effects from the Hula Hoop craze of the 50s? Radiation from the spaceships landing in Nebraska and Indiana abducting illiterate corn farmers and road-weary truck drivers?

The most plausible connection turned out to be the enormous numbers of chemicals, artificial substances, plastics, and man-made pollutants which were gradually introduced starting in the 50s, but were dramatically increased in both quantity and variety during the 60s, and are being increasingly used today. These include food additives and preservatives, pesticides and herbicides, fertilizers, cosmetic chemicals, over-the-counter and prescription drugs, household cleaners, detergents and dry cleaning fluids, auto exhaust and factory pollution, industrial solvents such as acetone and trichlorethylene, the new generation of paints and varnishes, carpet and furniture fire and stain retardants, synthetic fabrics and clothing treatments, dioxyn, PVCs, plastic food and beverage containers, even monosodium glutamate. On and on the list goes.

This man-made inhibition of the natural reproductive process has spawned a fertility industry — both specialists within the ranks of the conventional

AMA-approved health service providers and those working in naturopathic and other alternative treatment environments — raking in far in excess of a billion dollars a year.

Of course, Billy and Natalie weren't aware of any of this when they decided they would try to get her pregnant. She stopped taking birth control pills, and they just did what they normally did, with a little more focused effort the five or six days that were midway between her periods.

Away they went doing what came naturally for three months or so. Understandably they were both rather surprised when their energetic efforts produced no results in the embryo manufacturing department.

At first, their lack of success was taken with a lightheartedness, both of them assuming it was an anomaly which would soon pass.

"Maybe you're firing blanks, Billy."

"I'm definitely firing something."

"You're definitely hitting the target."

"Practice makes perfect."

As the weeks and months passed, however, the whole subject became charged, more and more the trigger for arguments or catalyst for tears.

"You don't want a baby. That's it, isn't it Billy?"

"Natalie. Of course I do. I said I did. But whether I do or not, it's not like I'm holding back. You can see for yourself that I'm doing my job."

"Then how come I'm not pregnant?"

"How should I know? Maybe you fried your uterus in Ibiza. Maybe you got sand in the works. Don't point the finger at me."

"Billy. Please stop bringing up my trip like it was some negative thing. It wasn't. It was a very good thing. It got me to a good place. It got me to where I am now."

"Frustrated. Angry with me. Yeh, that's just great."

Natalie's eyes turned red and started to pool, as her lower lip noticeably started to quiver.

"Billy. I'm sorry. I'm not mad at you. I know it's not your fault."

Actually, it didn't appear that either of them were at fault. The doctors couldn't find anything awry. At least none of the five fertility specialists they had eventually consulted, stretching from the Hudson Valley to New York City.

Billy's sperm count appeared normal, in fact, better than normal. The quality of the sperm appeared fine. No two-headed mutants, none with tails missing, none suffering from lethargy or lack of swimming skills, no union organizers urging a sperm walkout or sit down strike.

Likewise, Natalie checked out. She was ovulating like clockwork, producing the approved and recommended number of eggs, there were no blocked Fallopian tubes, no cross winds, no feminist demonstrations or marches going on in there.

The experts were stumped.

Of course, they had a solution. A very expensive solution indeed. With no guarantees.

This was a multi-phased program of hormone doping, fertility drugs, taking his sperm and concentrating it to increase its strategic effectiveness, and further closing the statistical hit-miss gap by either inserting the sperm into her fallopian tubes or removing one of her eggs and performing *in vitro* insemination then replanting the fertilized egg in her uterus.

It was all so scientific and calculating but unscientifically unpredictable. They could end up with twins, octuplets, or a swaddling bundle of air. Who was to say. The doctors couldn't.

Billy and Natalie could see the five-figure bill for services coming from miles away.

Monetary issues aside, they couldn't imagine turning over what should be the natural unfolding of the miracle of life, to a bunch of lab coats surrounded by stainless steel tables, test tubes, oscilloscopes, pipettes, ultrasound scans, Petri dishes, electronic imaging equipment, electrophoresis separators, and whatever else the medicine men would drag out of their expensive bag of tricks. It was about as romantic as changing the motherboard or putting more RAM in a computer.

They decided at least for now, to continue their reproductive Olympiad, which despite the growing anxiety and tension introduced by their absorption and obsession with getting her pregnant, they both still thoroughly enjoyed. At the same time, they would try to increase the prospects of babymaking in their lovemaking by introducing some less-expensive, hopefully effective alternative assistance.

Their bedroom stand now included a vaginal thermometer, homeopathic medicine, and a small glass dish of opaque pink fertility stones. Both Billy and Natalie were taking specially formulated vitamin/mineral/herb supplements, specifically designed to fortify the male and female reproductive systems — his was called Inseminator Rejuvenator and hers Motherhood In A Bottle.

One day Billy pulled up on their computer the page of a website trumpeting the efficacy of various crystals, and showed it to Natalie.

> The Shiva Lingham Stone is from the sacred Narmada River in Onkar Mandhata, one of India's seven holy sites. Villagers gather this unique Crypto-crystalline quartz from shallow river beds. In Tantra, the shape embodies masculine energy, dynamic expression and knowledge. The markings named Yoni (sacred sanskrit word for vulva), depicts the feminine energy, wisdom and intuition. Together, the female energy arouses the masculine urge to create. As such, the Tantric Lingham unifies the dualistic (male female) world into harmonious balance. Place a Shiva Lingham in the Relationships/Marriage area of your home to increase fertility and to bring you closer to your partner.

"Well, there's the solution to our problem if I ever saw it."

Though they laughed about it, the true extent of their desperation was evident when they immediately ordered one. When it arrived Air Express, it was given a guest-of-honor place in the center of the headboard shelf of their bed, next to a faux-ancient scroll containing a Sanskrit fertility mantra they obtained from a local store. The emporium's name was printed in gold leaf on the front window, a moniker which only a few months ago they used to make fun of ...

Things New Age: Your One-Stop Enlightenment Shop

They also went out of their way to eat healthy. More salads. Less fat. More fish. Less meat. They eliminated wine with their meals and never ordered cocktails when they went out with their friends. Five times a day, Natalie was drinking an unpleasant-tasting herbal tea consisting of Chasteberry, Red Raspberry Leaf, and Nettle. Billy had virtually eliminated coffee from his diet since he read that there were studies suggesting that coffee compromised sperm production. He switched to vitamin C-enhanced peppermint tea.

Unfortunately, none of this seemed to work. The only ones who seemed to benefit were the manufacturers and outlets who pocketed exorbitant profits for a lot of worthless crap, which they then used to generate and hawk new, promising, pricier, but at the end of the day, equally worthless crap.

By August, they were exhausted. It wasn't the sex but rather the anticipation, disappointment, the regimen and monotony of the "fertility rites" they had signed on to, the evident futility of their efforts, and last but not least, the heat.

Whether it was global warming or just an anomalous seasonal shift, the end of the summer was turning out to be a scorcher. They would lay in bed, sweating and sweltering, panting like dogs in the desert, after pleasurable but nonetheless incredibly draining sessions of lovemaking — during which they thought more about whether his sperm and her egg were going to end their Cold War standoff and finally get together, than to abandoning themselves to the carnal ecstasy of their union.

When the end of Natalie's most recent menstrual cycle again declared that she was not pregnant — an announcement signed in blood — Billy tried to make light of it.

"Maybe we should just get a dog."

"I'm not having sex with a dog."

"I meant for me."

"You want to have sex with a dog? I feel a little threatened."

"Dogs are man's best friend. No one ever said that about babies."

"Wait! We'll get two dogs. A male and a female. Then watch them. Maybe we're doing something wrong."

"I don't think my ego could handle it. What if they got it right the first time?"

"Ohmigod! You're right. I'd have to kill the bitch."

"I'd have the vet chop off his balls. That'd show him!"

They laughed but their laughter was hollow. Hollow to the point of melancholy.

And though neither of them said anything, each invisibly was waving the tearful white flag of resignation. An impregnable sense of hopelessness had slowly but surely sunk in. This was the first failure of their relationship, the first tangible setback of any importance.

They never officially gave up. Thus, they never discussed a next step, either adoption or designing their lives together around childlessness. They never acknowledged they might be entering the next phase. A phase without a baby of their own making.

They clung to some thin, frail thread of optimism. After all, there were countless stories of couples trying and trying again over years, even decades, then finally producing the long-desired child. Billy and Natalie had many years ahead of them. The waiting and trying and trying again theoretically could define them as a couple, as it had many other couples.

If it did, would that be a good thing? In truth, it was a moot point.

They both somehow knew this wasn't going to happen.

Something had changed. Billy could sense it.

The baby thing was over and done.

A Pink Cadillac

Annie Roberts was the one lady in Newburgh you could never miss. Nor would you want to. If you did, she'd let you know. Or somebody else would.

She was the most unavailable available bachelorette of Orange County, New York with its nearly 350,000 residents living in three cities, nineteen villages, twenty towns, countless hamlets and other unincorporated farming communities.

What made her so unavailable?

That was certainly the question.

That was the frequent, lingering, oft-repeated, never-answered question on the lips of all of the citizens of Newburgh, some who were so dissimilar to one another, the only thing they had in common was that particular question.

The more obvious, more relevant question that never *ever* came up — and certainly would have in a larger, more urbane, or more suburbanized community than Newburgh — was: 'Who cares?'

But this was Newburgh, loosely centralized, not small-town gossipy but obsessive about its local celebrities.

Frankly, everybody cared. Everybody wondered. Everybody speculated.

Women wondered how it was that she had not succumbed to some beautiful, seductive hunk — some devastatingly good-looking, stylish, rich, well-connected, studly Harvard or Yale-educated guy, with a pedigree past and a brilliant future. She certainly rated someone like that.

Or if she was into plain, she certainly had plenty to choose from in this town.

The simple truth: it wasn't quite that simple.

No doubt. She was a real dish. Stunning. Sophisticated. Elegant. Charming. Engaging yet mysterious. Unpredictable. Quirky. Funny in a severe big-city way. Charming in a coy small-town-homecoming-queen way. Demure at times. Bigger than life at others.

Annie Roberts stood an even six feet tall. When she wore high heels — and she more often than not did— she towered over most everyone around her. She was elegantly thin but deceptively strong. She had coquettish but fiercely intelligent, big blue eyes. Her naturally Nordic blond hair was usually combed back from her flawless face, which was always airbrushed to pristine porcelain perfection with evening-at-the-theater make-up.

Strangers were inclined to ask why someone like her would apply such a thick coating of cosmetics to such a perfect face. But everyone in Newburgh already knew the answer to that question.

Annie Roberts was the makeup queen, an empire builder of the largest single franchise in America for Mary Kay Cosmetics. Thus, she was a walking advertisement for the miraculous possibilities of her line of beauty-enhancing, allure-creating and youth-preserving products. A finer advertisement could not have been devised by the best creative minds of the fashion and cosmetic industry.

She always dressed with impeccable style, spoke with authority and grace, flirted relentlessly, created smiles and laughter at will, filled every room with a musical and optimistic light, inspired her friends, terrified her enemies, fascinated all.

Annie carried herself with absolute certainty and confidence, basking in the attention of acquaintances and strangers alike. At the same time, she could be self-effacing enough to create the opportunity for others to grandstand and make fools of themselves. This was something she thoroughly enjoyed, the timing of which she had honed to a science.

While on principle she never let anyone else makes jokes at her expense, she was cleverly disposed to making well-crafted, perfectly-timed, self-deprecating comments, which not only amused everyone, but temporarily put them at ease. She frequently employed her irony to diffuse the tension that overwhelmed people when they first met her, or more balefully to cut detractors off at the legs before they lobbed their own cheap and ultimately ineffective shots.

To one highly educated man — who really should have known better — commenting on her natural assets: "There's a good reason for all this makeup. I'm hoping that no one as distinguished as yourself will notice how completely vapid and dull I am. But damn you! You're so perceptive. I really don't deserve you, you *wonderfully* clever man!"

To a elderly high-society lady who seemed affronted by Annie's revealing evening dress at a fundraiser: "I believe in never disappointing people. That's why I'm so crassly superficial. What you see is what you get. Only less. But still more than you can handle, eh?"

There were a few women in greater Newburgh who had somehow avoided being captivated by Annie's hypnotic siren song, but heard and were haunted instead by the shrill catcalls of envy. These she dispatched with a surreal potion of charm and sarcasm. Almost too easy.

To a society woman who, upon meeting Annie, feigned indifference: "We all know beauty is skin-deep. But skin can't begin to hide the emptiness inside. I am a glamorous void you'd be better off to avoid. A quality you're undoubtedly intimately familiar with."

To the wife of a prominent area obstetrician who was indiscreetly flirting with Annie at a dinner party: "If you have a medical degree, people expect you to help others become healthy. With this blond hair, I am literally required to say stupid things all of the time. It's astonishing that anyone listens. But they do, don't they? Usually men of whom we expect more. But what is integrity to an old turtle or a young bronco?"

These women, often disarmed or even humiliated at hearing verbalized some twisted version of what they may have been secretly thinking, would sometimes turn around and rush to her defense. Their presumed camaraderie was not welcome.

Annie would dismiss them with cold majesty, leaving them feeling frivolous and exposed. Then just laugh at their ignorance and naiveté.

But it was the men she really had the fun with.

There were chiefly two types: The puffed-up bulls, and the sensitive lambs. Differences aside, they were all intimidated by her and ended up immobilized and castrated victims of her strength of character and force of will.

The puffed-up bulls by nature assumed that finesse and subtlety was for sissies. It was swagger and bluster that would take this bitch down.

"Tell you what, honey. I've had my fill with beautiful women. But this evening — because I can tell you want me so bad — I'll make an exception."

"Well, aren't I just the lucky girl! And here I thought it was going to be just another lonely night with an aluminum baseball bat and a tube of K-Y jelly. Golly, that is a Louisville slugger between your legs, I hope."

The sensitive lambs she felt some negligible degree of sympathy for.

"I wrote this poem for you. I call it ... *Annie Roberts, Flower of the Hudson Valley.*"

"A poem for me? I'm so flattered."

"Others may not see it. But I know you are a very spiritually aware person."

She bent down to whisper.

"Tonight is the Seventh Moon for the Wretched Sobhan of Jovina. I need for you to bring me the beating heart of a small dog, preferably a miniature Chau. Please! Do this for me. It is my only hope. Tell no one of my leprosy."

Surprisingly, none of her spurned suitors ever spoke ill of her. In fact, none of them never mentioned her again. It saved a lot of explaining.

The resulting self-imposed censorship just added to her evolving legend.

Annie Roberts was presumably rich.

Truth told, she wasn't rich but certainly very comfortable, definitely way beyond worrying about making ends meet.

Her business was for its scale incredibly lucrative. In the multi-tiered hierarchy of the Mary Kay business pyramid, she had more than forty sales ladies reporting directly or indirectly to her. Her annual gross far exceeded similar franchises with two or three times the number of employees. Those who worked for her attributed this to great business instincts and personal charisma, but most of all to her unflinching self-reliance and unassailable autonomy.

She was an impregnable fortress.

Billy summed up Annie Roberts with a stark bluntness.

"She's made of stone."

Pam was quick to jump to her defense.

"She's not, Billy. Not at all."

"That's easy for you to say."

It was. Pam was working for Annie Roberts in the evenings selling Mary Kay products, and presumably had become good friends with her. They were often seen together out and about.

"Only because I know her and you don't."

Tonight was one of the increasingly rare occasions when the three of them — Billy, Natalie and Pam — had gotten together. It was a Saturday evening, late August, and they were waiting for their main courses at Vesuvio's Ristorante, Pam's favorite eatery of late. She used it to wine and dine various clients, and for evenings out with her extensive and growing circle of friends.

Billy couldn't let it go. Something about Annie Roberts really irritated him. Not the things that bothered everyone else. He couldn't put his finger on it.

"I can only go on what I see and hear. Not that I care. What is everybody's preoccupation with her anyway? She's good looking, has a big mouth, but that's hardly unusual anymore. Not enough to set her apart. The modern era teems with self-promoting pseudo-celebrities."

Pam just rolled her eyes.

"Billy Billy Billy."

Natalie piped in.

"She's a role model for a lot of women who don't want to take shit from men anymore but don't know how to put their foot down or don't have the courage."

Billy was put off by Natalie's taking Pam's side.

"Is she a role model for you, Nat?"

"I admire her. But I don't have that problem, do I Billy? The taking-shit problem? Or the putting-my-foot-down problem?"

Pam laughed contemptuously.

"I'd say you're on safe ground there."

Billy looked at her defensively.

"Can you two let me in on what's going on here?"

Pam put on her most sincere face. It wouldn't have fooled a starving cocker spaniel.

"Nothing, Billy. Nothing at all. By the way, you two ..." She shifted her gaze to include Natalie. "... how is the breeding coming? Is there a bun in the oven?"

Of course, Pam already knew the answer to that. She had to. In all likelihood, Natalie had kept her best friend more than well-informed of their lack of progress and dismal failure to make a "bun". It was possible that Natalie had sought some comfort from her, comfort that he was not in a position to offer, since he was part of their defeat, and at least as upset about it as Natalie was.

What the hell was Pam up to? This was hardly the time and place. Natalie's pregnancy — or more to the point, non-pregnancy — didn't exactly strike Billy as material for casual dinner conversation. Anger took over where hurt and indignation left off.

Just as Billy was about to lay into Pam, a stir seemed to suddenly build in the restaurant. Ultimately, everyone glanced toward the front — some tried to be more subtle than others — as she walked in with her characteristic long-legged triumphant stride, planted shoulders, and ass-swinging sashay. She was leading two other extremely attractive young ladies, both tall and dressed for effect, tits bouncing, smiling like they were in the Miss America Pageant. They were clearly apprenticing her show-stopping grand entrance.

Annie Roberts in the flesh.

Annie smiled and as she passed each table, acknowledged the patrons she knew — which included nearly everyone — leading her retinue toward her personally reserved table at the rear. This took them right past the booth occupied by Billy, Natalie and Pam.

As soon as she saw Pam, her face lit up light a billboard on Times Square.

"Pam. What a surprise! Imagine running into you here."

Obviously, she was joking since they probably saw one another here at Vesuvio's no less than three times a week.

"Oh! And the Greens. Natalie. You must be Billy. I feel like I know you."

Annie reached and took Billy's hand, leaned over dramatically and gave it a chivalrous kiss. No-smear lipstick.

Billy pursed his own lips in a grotesquely haughty, unsmiling pucker, and feigned a British accent.

"This feeling has substance. It seems we have met, on one occasion, my lady. Nevertheless, such gallantry pleases the prince indeed."

"And so it should, fair monarch, our being in the company of such delicacies as these."

Annie gestured to the lovely associates who were right behind her, becoming again an urbane, upscale 21st Century entrepreneur.

"These two lovelies have just moved here from Minnesota to help me bring some of the outlying counties into the Annie Roberts fold of extraordinary beauty and other exalting attainments."

Then in mock confidence but still addressing all, she huddled with the two wide-eyed girls, whose smiles seemed epoxied between their powder-dry rouged cheeks.

"Ladies. In these cynical pessimistic times, it is possible to believe that love is impossible. But you are fortunate enough to be witness to one of the great treasures of our contemporary era, more delectable and heartwarming than a Harlequin romance and a bottle of Asti Spumante. Megan and Anyeta, my charm school salutatorians, it's my pleasure to introduce the happiest couple in the world, Natalie and Billy Green."

They all shook hands. No chivalrous kisses this time. Just the standard greetings and gaping grins which dehydrated even the best irrigated gums.

Annie wasn't finished.

"Now Billy. How long have you been married?"

Slightly caught by surprise but always prepared, he answered immediately.

"Two years, two months, three days."

"Isn't that the sweetest thing you've ever heard! Now there's a man who is incurably in love. Natalie, I have to say, you are one very lucky lady."

Was she mocking him? Billy tried to analyze the seductive music which carried her words, to get some idea what the ratio was between sarcasm and sincerity in her encrypted message. Looking into the limestone of her eyes and the rigid marble perfection of her face, gave no clue as to what might be going on in the stony chambers of her heart or the igneous hollows of her twisted mind.

Natalie gave Annie an enigmatic smile.

"Absolutely. One lucky lady. That's for sure."

Annie then shook her index finger at Natalie playfully.

"And if he weren't taken! Well, I just won't go there."

They all laughed. As if they were agreeing on something. Maybe they were. Annie Roberts was such a riot. What a charmer. Queen of the ball. She could have whatever she wanted. Maybe that's what they all seemed to agree on.

"Have a great time! Love you, Pam. I'll call you tomorrow. I have some really great news. Have a mighty fine evening, *Mr. and Mrs. Green.*"

Definitely sarcastic. Billy tried to hide his contempt. What a bitch!

Annie turned to her slave girls.

"Let's go, my goddesses in training. The veal cannelloni here is out of this world. It's my favorite dish to send back to the kitchen and complain. They always return it with a lovely complimentary bottle of Castello di Selvole Chianti."

And away they went.

Eyes overtly and covertly followed them to their table. Only when they were seated and engrossed in their menus did the other customers refocus their attention on themselves and whatever occasion brought them there.

Billy forced himself to glance across the table. Pam looked pleased, almost smug.

"She always has great news."

Billy had missed Annie's remark.

"What are you talking about, Pam?"

"She says that all of the time. 'I have some really great news.' And it always is. It's always great. That's all. So where were we?"

Billy refreshed her memory.

"You were insulting us."

"Oh come on, Billy! I was just asking. No offense intended. It's not like I'm a disinterested party here."

That was all that Billy could handle. He stood up and almost knocked over the waiter who was finally bringing them their meals.

"Pam! It's none of your business! Nat, let's go."

"Go? Let's go? What's going on, Billy? Our food is here. What's gotten into you?"

"I'm not hungry. And if you thought about it, you wouldn't be either."

"I'm not leaving. Billy you are being ... I don't know what you're being. Just—"

"Excuse me. Enjoy your meals. I need some air. I'll walk home."

As he stepped out of the restaurant, he spotted it. How could he miss it? Parked right there.

A pink Cadillac.

It was the one Annie Roberts got for being an empress of a cosmetics empire. This was her reward from Mary Kay Corporate Headquarters all the way down in Addison, Texas, for selling overpriced glop to finger-paint the fantasies of a lot of neurotic and insecure women — pathetic human shells who were desperate to achieve some unattainable ideal.

He stopped in his tracks and stared at the pretentious metal beast.

One single thought crowded out all others.

One indisputable fact.

It sure is pink.

To the Moon Alice

Billy knew all of Natalie's fatal weaknesses. And aside from Ben & Jerry's Ice Cream, orally-induced orgasms, and movies starring Naomi Watts or Sean Penn, she was pathologically addicted to a black-and-white sitcom — one of the first in the history of television — from the mid 50s.

Natalie absolutely adored *The Honeymooners.* Whenever she found them in reruns on late night TV, no matter what time they were on — and now they were typically used only as fillers in the wee hours of the morning — she was there. She would either wait up, or set the alarm. Billy didn't quite get the campy charm of the program, so he would usually roll over and go back to sleep as Natalie tip-toed down the stairs and sat like a delinquent schoolgirl, giggling away as Jackie Gleason's caricature of Ralph Kramden, a bus driving slob, would hold up his fat fist and threaten to send Audrey Meadows, his wife, *"To the moon, Alice."* Naturally, it was Alice who always got the better of Ralph, who despite a lot of street wisdom and help from his daffy neighbor — Art Carney as the lanky, loose-limbed, fast-lip Ed Norton — never could figure women out, much less get the best of them.

This obsession had prompted Billy to go online and find the perfect make-up gift for Natalie. He felt really bad about losing it the other night at Vesuvio's. There had been an uncomfortable détente for three-days running now.

He located a DVD containing all 39 half-hour *Honeymooners* episodes that had run independently in 1955, and even some of the early sketches which had spawned the sitcom, but had only appeared as segments in other variety shows. These "lost" *Honeymooners* skits had originally been broadcast live on *The Cavalcade of Stars* and *The Jackie Gleason Show*, dating back as far as 1952, the pioneering days of network television.

Billy knew that Natalie would absolutely flip out at having all of these programs at her fingertips. No more scouring the TV guides to find the irregular, infrequent broadcast of these dubious gems.

Most importantly, the DVD would allow more regular and healthful sleeping habits for her. She had been for too long paying an unusually high price for her unique and arguably eccentric taste in television comedy.

Not that he felt he had to "make-up" for anything. Without fixing the blame on himself — he genuinely believed he was not that far out of line — he was simply sorry it had happened. The surprise gift would state the unstated, say what needed to be said without him having to say it.

"I have something for you, Natalie. Close your eyes."

He hadn't had time to wrap it. He placed the boxed set on the table in front of her. There was a classic shot on the cover, Ralph and Alice in their sparsely furnished flat, her smirking at him with her arms defiantly folded across her chest, him looking like he was about to blow a gasket.

"Okay, open them."

Natalie went nuts. Dancing around the room, laughing, yelling, repeatedly running over to Billy, hugging him, thanking him over and over, covering his face with ecstatic kisses, then dancing around even more like a crazed school girl.

Finally, she calmed down enough to sit down.

"Oh Billy, you are the best!"

Apparently he had done the right thing.

It seemed all was forgiven.

But he still couldn't entirely get his head around it. Something bothered him. He felt like they had ganged up on him. Annie in particular seemed to thrive on what he judged to be not very subtle antagonism.

He took both of Natalie's hands in his.

"I'm very sorry about the other night. But Annie Roberts really rubs me the wrong way. Pam is starting to as well."

"You've always had a problem with Pam."

"No. I think you have it backwards. She's always had a problem with me."

"Well ... not always. But at the beginning. She was just being protective. That was a long time ago."

"Whose idea was it to go to England and Spain?"

"As much mine as hers. I mean, we just came up with it. What's that got to do with it? You're looking at our little fling in Spain as a personal attack on you by Pam? That's crazy, Billy."

"If she's coming between us, then it is a personal attack."

"Whew! You're really out there, Billy. She's my friend. You're my husband. My lover. My life. It was there I realized how much I wanted to ... you know."

"Say it! Just say it! Have a baby. So here we are. No baby. And Pam is sitting back like some referee. Maybe she is your best friend but there are some things that are just about you and me. No one else."

"Look, Billy. We tried. We're trying. You're right. That's just for us. I know you're — and obviously I am too — you're disappointed. But it doesn't take anything away from us if Pam knows about it. Your mother knows, right?"

"No."

"You never mentioned it at work? To one of your buddies?"

111

"I don't have any buddies. I have you. This is our ... this baby ... it's just us. Nobody else needs to know that we are complete failures at the most basic aspect of male-female interaction. No one else."

There was a long pause. Billy took Natalie's silence as concurrence. He knew this was a great place to move on to some other completely unrelated topic. But he wasn't done.

"Annie Roberts is scary."

"Yes. In a way she is."

"But a ..." Billy poked quotation marks in the air between them. "... 'role model' for you women. Man, I wouldn't want to live in world full of women like her, that's for sure."

"Billy. All I said was—"

"I know what you said. And on some level I agree. She is strong. But she's so totally fucking plastic. It's all about selling makeup. And having the world love Annie Roberts. She's the ultimate — and I never say this about a woman, because it's so typical for men to say it — but she's a total cockteaser if I ever saw one."

Natalie burst out laughing. It soon became apparent she wasn't going to stop anytime soon.

"What's so funny, Nat? It wasn't a joke, you know."

She calmed down enough to talk.

"I don't know. I don't know. Just hearing you say that word. Annie Roberts a cockteaser. It's just funny. I mean, you're right. Yes. You *are* right."

She started laughing again.

"Are you laughing at me?"

"No. No. No. Not *at* you. But calling her that kind of misses the point. It's like saying that Mother Theresa has lousy fashion sense. Or that Adolph Hitler had a bad attitude. It's true but doesn't quite get there. You know what I mean?"

He grinned and held up a fist between them.

"To the moon, Alice!"

"Alright! Now we are getting somewhere. You know how that turns me on."

"To the moon, Alice!"

"Billy. If you don't stop—"

"To the fucking moon, Alice! I really mean it."

"You asked for it!"

She was all over him. He hadn't been tickled since their original negotiations over the baby back in February. But this time Natalie had a slightly different agenda.

"Ha ha ha ... what do you want? ... ha ha ha ... stop it! ... ha ha ha ... you're possessed ... ha ha ha ..."

"I think you need a good teasing."

She reached between his legs.

"Oh yes! I think you're right."

Sure enough. He was ready for a good teasing all right. Immediately she unzipped his pants. Without missing a beat, she was inside his briefs and stroking him with the perfect lightness of touch and certainty of rhythm that three years

112

with someone underwrites with mastery.

"Tease. Tease. Tease. Whoops! Hmm. Teasing seems to be over already."

She was right. His milky semen dripped off her forearm and hand.

"Tease. Tease. Sure to please. What do you think, Billy?"

"I agree to everything. You are very persuasive."

"Then stop worrying. About any of this."

"Worrying is out of the question."

"Tease. Tease. Tease."

Her hands were like jellyfish angels as she continued to caress him, feathering the length of his penis with the soft tips of her fingers. She had brought him to full attention again.

"I think it's time to go upstairs and say our mantra."

"But Billy. I've been saying it all along. A whole new mantra."

"Tease tease tease?"

"What do you think?"

"Nice mantra. Very nice."

It was a Tuesday. This might be their last opportunity for a few nights. Over the next couple days, Billy would be putting the final organizational and logistic touches on a major fundraising event scheduled for Friday. He was facing some very long hours.

They slowly worked their way up the stairs, kissing the whole way. Without either of them quite knowing how it happened, all of their clothes were piece by piece removed, leaving a trail of pants, socks, shirt, blouse, panties, jeans, all of it, from the living room to their bed.

For the next several hours, with no thoughts of their onerous reproductive project hampering the range and depth of their pleasure, they made love. Slowly. Dreamily. Patiently. Passionately.

"I wish it could always be like this."

"It is, Billy. Isn't it? For me it is."

"I didn't mean—"

"I know. We've been trying too hard."

"We shouldn't put all this pressure on ourselves. Look at what we have. I could never have imagined being this happy."

"So when you get through this fundraiser ... we'll just ... we can make every evening just like tonight. Maybe better."

"How could it get any better?"

"It can always be better."

"To the moon, Alice."

But Would It Play in Peoria?

For as long as anyone could remember, the well-healed older families of Orange County had pretty much kept their money for themselves. If they gave in to the rare philanthropic impulse, it was to donate and donate loudly to established national charities — the American Cancer Society, the Special Olympics, the American Red Cross, United Way — but never to any local organization which would directly benefit the local poor. Many of these society families considered the lower income citizens to be pests and wished they would go away. The moneyed class certainly didn't want to do anything to encourage them to stay, assuming their plight was permanent and would always be a drain on the local economy and a blight on their fair community.

Only a couple of these families were fabulously rich — that is, Forbes Magazine rich or Donald Trump rich. But all of them most definitely had enough income and assets to keep over ten generations of Catholic-size families living in relative opulence, a sharp contrast to their struggling neighbors tucked away in the unofficial ghettos of Newburgh.

Billy regularly came in contact with the poor of Newburgh. Natalie with the rich.

They often compared notes and shared their dismay and anger at the way trickle-down economics seemed to be an obtuse euphemism for the trickling upwards — ever upwards — of more and more cash, the incomprehensible and unconscionable accumulation of wealth at the very top. Obscenely rich people using their wealth as some giant Death Star weapon to suck even more money into their already bulging treasuries. Many poor people were barely living at — sometimes living far below — the poverty line, living like Third World refugees in the richest country in the world, watching themselves slip further and further into the black hole of privation and want.

That was what the national statistics reported in no uncertain terms, and Billy and Natalie could personally see it happening right here in Newburgh, New York. Rich people getting richer and poor people being mocked and ridiculed for their hope of claiming even some tiny sliver of the American Dream.

To help close that gap, re-distribute some of the local wealth, put into circulation a teeny fragment of the cash that was sitting stagnant in various bank accounts and low-yield investments, to maybe alleviate a small fraction of the misery spawned by inadequate shelter, Habitat decided to put on a fundraising event, targeting the over-stuffed wallets of as many of the local well-to-dos as they could fit in a banquet hall. This would be an elegant but no-holds-barred courtship of the nearly impregnable social consciences of people who had more money than they knew what to do with, and in some cases more money than they even knew they had.

Natalie, mainly through Pam and her relationships with the politicos and town's upper crust, secured for Billy a Newburgh-area VIP list. Habitat took it from there. From the informal nods and loose verbal commitments obtained face-to-face, then the actual RSVPs that slowly trickled in over the summer — the result of a sustained bombardment of mailers and polite but persistent follow-up phone calls — it looked like they were going to have nearly 300 attending the semi-formal dinner banquet fundraiser, set for Friday August 31st.

They chose to hold it at the Hilton Garden Inn right near the airport. It realistically was the only hotel in town which had the physical capacity to handle a crowd this size in a properly outfitted hall, and provide the kind of food and drink service suitable for the bunch of stuff-shirts and upholstered old hens who would be attending. It was an expensive proposition — frankly somewhat of a gamble — but it was expected to pay off handsomely. Give the people with the bloated pocketbooks the treatment they expected, then relieve them of their cash over the course of the evening. Everyone would go home happy and a little lighter, and Habitat could build more houses.

Billy didn't have much to do until the final week. At that point, he was given the overall responsibility of coordinating the myriad of details surrounding preparations, and then on the actual day of the banquet, not only floor managing things at the Hilton, but from the stage, charming the attendees with fawning introductions, and finally making the keynote plea for them to donate to a worthy cause.

He had actually volunteered for the emcee job. Something about the thought of sucking as much money as possible out of the privileged class of Newburgh stirred his Robin Hood instincts. Billy gleefully jumped headlong into it and heavily leaned on Natalie and Director Blackledge, as he honed the psychology and content of his speech over several weeks. The final address was a masterpiece. It was pleasant and funny, but powerful and focused. Basically, he presented two scenarios and appealed to the self-interest of his jaded, miserly audience.

An artist's drawing, projected dramatically on a screen behind him, depicted two Newburghs ten years out. The first showed the blighted areas of town spread like Kudzu over tracts of once-beautiful neighborhoods, an extended, expanding ghetto threatening to encroach and engulf the more respectable, high-end areas where the very people in the audience now lived. He then showed some graphs, and though they looked like downhill slalom runs, were in fact the projected property values if the cancer of poverty were allowed to spread in the town.

The second artist's drawing depicted the result of carefully formulated but modest investment in selected at-risk neighborhoods, as laid out in Habitat's *10-Year Plan for the Renewal of Hope and Prosperity in Newburgh*. And what a rosy picture it was! The Newburgh in this portrayal had all but eliminated the pockets of poverty, and built on the beauty and integrity of the historic city in ways that enhanced even the currently more prosperous sections.

Planting the seed of hope and growing prosperity gave the attendees the clear message that there was choice to be made, and the choice was theirs. All it would take was some generous but affordable funding.

The clincher was the projected property value charts under the Habitat plan. Property values, which had been fairly flat for the past few years, would ascend rapidly over the ten years, like the trajectory of the Space Shuttle, or happy little souls going to Heaven.

Attractive neighborhoods down the street were a nice thought. Not having peeling house paint, unkempt lawns, dirty children playing in the yard, and low-rider autos in the drive, on adjacent or nearby property, was even better. But having the value of one's house double or triple, now *that* was really great news! Money! More money! That would strike a chord which would resonate like the triumphant end of a Wagnerian opera.

Once the speech was written, Billy spent hours practicing it. Sometimes on his bike ride to the office — which caused some observers en route to suspect he had lost his mind. Sometimes he'd practice in front of the bathroom mirror shaving. Sometimes in bed after he and Natalie had made love, giving him a captive and extremely amenable audience of one.

"Even without the charts, Billy, it's all I can do to keep from writing you a check right now."

"You don't have to pay me for making love to you."

"I think you're ready. It's really good. Really good!"

The speech was as good as it was going to get.

Now it was just a matter of putting everything else together which would guarantee an enjoyable and successful fundraiser, then making sure it all got done correctly and on time.

The week leading up to the banquet was a bitch. It was amazing how many simple things became complicated and how many easy things became difficult.

"So your computer keeps crashing. Just use someone else's. Someone here must have a computer with a copy of PowerPoint that isn't pirated."

"The napkins are supposed to say 'A Renewal of Hope and Prosperity' not 'A Renewal of Hope and Property'. Get it right!"

"Valet parking is supposed to be gratis. These tightwads don't carry cash. Just tell your manager it will be Hilton's contribution to a good cause."

"No, we don't need a coat check girl. This is August. Do you think we're going to get an early winter blizzard?"

"You guys are the ones who suggested candles. Now you're saying they violate fire code restrictions? How about putting a flashlight on every table. Anything but those overhead fluorescents that turn everyone into a cadaver."

Somehow they got through it all. No small thanks to Billy and the vast reservoir of Detroit attitude he brought to the battles, great and small.

The day of the banquet, Billy left the office early. Around 4:30, he arrived at the Hilton and went directly to the ballroom. Things were definitely shaping up. He had printed out a checklist, assembled and modified over the last ten days, and started going through the items one by one. There were a few discrepancies, the result of miscommunication, but by 6:15 all of the fires were put out and he let his own staff know, as well as his three Hilton contact people, that he would be in the lounge getting a bite to eat.

After half-finishing a crab salad and downing three cups of coffee, he called Natalie.

"All systems go."

"Have you eaten? Fainting in the middle of a public address is bad form."

"I fed the butterflies. They seem to have enjoyed the meal."

"Pam should be coming by here around eight. What time will you start the ceremonies?"

"The pigs have to be fed first. So I'd say ... maybe 9:30 at the earliest."

"Good luck, Billy. You'll do fine. In fact, I'm sure it'll be fantastic. See you then."

"Light a candle."

"How about a mantra? Teasing. Teasing. Teasing."

"I'm feeling better already. Love you."

He had his formalwear with him in a garment bag and figured this was as good a time as any to change. Then he would make himself available in the banquet hall in case anyone had any last minute questions or crises. He could use the remaining time to go over his speech.

He slipped into the public restroom and changed. After dealing with such critical issues as the proper placement of the cummerbund — he had only worn a tux once before in his life and couldn't even remember when that might have been — and taming the bow tie, which seemed to have its own agenda for the evening, he looked in the full-length mirror at one end of the restroom. Pretty sharp! — if he did say so himself.

Back in the ballroom, Billy went to the table he had temporarily appropriated for his notes and other personals. He put everything in a pile, ready to take them back out to the car, or at least put them somewhere out of sight.

Now for the speech.

He looked in his briefcase. All of the compartments. Between the dividers. Looked again.

Panic!

Where was it? Where was his speech? He thought he had put it in there before he left work. Wait! He didn't have it at work. It must still be at home.

It was 7:15. The early birds would be arriving in half an hour. But he had no choice. Even if he could fake his way through the fundraising part — he practically knew it cold after practicing it so many times — without his notes, his initial welcoming speech would be a disaster. If nothing else, there was a list of all of the special guests, contributors, organizers and promoters he had to thank. There was no way he could remember all of their names. And if he forgot anyone, it would be a catastrophe.

He could just make it. There and back in less than 30 minutes.

"Hey, Leslie. Hold down the fort. Tell anyone who wants to know that I'll be right back."

"Are you sure? You're not going into hiding, are you?"

"Just need to pick up something at home. Promise."

Billy double-timed it to the car, drove off in a controlled panic, and pulled up to his house in less than ten minutes.

His first shock came when he pulled into the drive. Because it was so far back toward the rear of the house, he couldn't see it until he had himself turned off the street. But there it was in all of its unmistakable inglorious over-the-top luminescence.

A pink Cadillac.

The pink Cadillac — it could be no other — symbol of the big pink ego of Annie Roberts.

What was she doing here?

Billy bolted up the porch steps. The front door was locked. It made no sense. Natalie had to be here. Pam was supposed to pick her up and bring her to the fundraiser.

He peeked in the front window but no one was in sight.

For reasons which seemed to make sense, though he couldn't really say why, he entered quietly as possible. Sneaking into his own house? How weird. At least he wouldn't frighten them. After all, he wasn't supposed to be here. He was supposed to be at the fundraiser.

He slipped his key into the lock and entered silently.

Not a sign of Natalie or the towering cosmetics magnate.

He knew where he had left his speech and notes. In the office upstairs next to the master bedroom. Probably by the printer.

As he slipped up the stairs, he heard something. The bathtub was draining. At the landing, he could see the light from the bathroom was on. Apparently the door was open.

He tip-toed over and with the intuitive stealth of a seasoned voyeur, looked in. There with her back to him was Annie Roberts. The angle of the mirror prevented her from seeing Billy. She had a towel wrapped around her magnificent frame, had another on her head, and was meticulously applying some miracle cream to her forehead and the area around her eyes. She picked up yet another tiny jar, dabbed from it, and spread this concoction onto her eyelids.

What was she doing here? Taking a bath. Making up her face. That was his bath towel on her head, wasn't it? White. Red Cornell University logo.

Bizarre. Really bizarre.

As fascinating as it was to watch a gorgeous, if obnoxious and infinitely vain woman in *his* bathroom transforming herself into an object of desire and wonder, he had no time for it.

He needed to get his notes and be gone.

Billy quickly turned and silently stepped toward the office. It was on the other side of the stairway. Ten or twelve steps just past the master bedroom.

Where was Natalie? What about Pam? Maybe Pam couldn't make it, so Annie Roberts was here to act as surrogate chauffeur.

The bedroom door was closed. Natalie must be getting herself ready in there.

That's when he heard it.

A sound he was more familiar with than any other sound in the world. Even through the solid oak door, it was unmistakable.

It was the unique, high-pitched, gasping, moaning squeal — the laughing cry of utter ecstasy — of Natalie's orgasm.

Then Pam's voice.

"You liked that, eh sweetie? You love this tongue. You love the way I—"

Pam's utterance silenced by what? Natalie's lips? Her cunt?

In that moment, everything became clear to him.

Well ... not everything. There would be more.

Billy tried to catch his breath. He was either suffocating or hyperventilating. His face was on fire, the hot feverish rush of shock. The collective pain of his entire body rebelled against the unreality of it all. He staggered over to the work table and collected the folder he needed.

Somehow he still maintained absolutely quiet. It would be too much to be discovered now. Then he would have to deal with all of this. Inconceivable. Impossible. He'd wait it out. Maybe it was all just a nightmare. He would wake up. For now he had to just keep moving.

As he turned to descend the stairs, he heard humming. It was Annie Roberts in a distracted rendition of some famous aria. Casual and lilting. Billy didn't really know opera. But this was one of those melodies that everyone knew. Infomercials. *You too can own the greatest opera performances of all time ... Callas, Caruso, Pavarotti, Sutherland, Domingo.*

Annie paused. Now he heard soft purrs and light giggling. Better than opera. A love duet.

Natalie and Pam in the bubbly aftermath of their lovemaking.

Also casual and lilting.

How lovely.

Down the stairs. Stealth be damned. He needed to get out of there before his head exploded.

"Is someone there?"

Annie. She must have heard him. He stopped in the middle of the living room.

"Hello? Is someone there?"

He looked back towards the stairs. No one was coming.

When he turned to leave, Billy happened to glance over and notice that there were several pictures strewn about on the coffee table. A photo album sat open. He took a closer look.

There was one photo that caught his eye. There was Natalie — a very young Natalie — in what appeared to be a family portrait. That must be her father. And her sister. And ...

Sitting next to Natalie's father was Pam.

What? Pam. Pam? He didn't get it.

Billy now automatically shifted to autopilot. There was no way he could otherwise function. His brain was so beyond overload, if asked he couldn't have told someone his own name.

He scooped up the scattered photographs, stuffed them into the photo album, closed it and tucked it under his arm.

Next thing he became aware of was pulling back into the parking lot of the Hilton.

Leslie was waiting right inside of the foyer. Looking at her watch.

"Right on time. 7:45 pm. Are you okay? You look ... actually zombie comes to mind."

"Never been better. Maybe once. The whole rest of my life minus tonight."

"Wow! Very conceptual comedy. Save it for them, Billy Crystal." She nodded toward the assemblage of fashionably dressed peacocks and ostriches parading about at the entrance of the ballroom, the real stars of tonight's performance, the very-important-people pretending to relish spending the next three hours being fed quasi-gourmet cuisine, listening to pleas for compassion and magnanimity, and rationalizing why they should open their wallets to help the lazy, undeserving poor of the community.

By 8:15 most of the expected guests were seated. Over the next hour, cocktails and dinners were served, desserts were distributed by a bevy of young waitresses, and finally, additional cocktail orders taken.

Through all of this, Billy sat at one of the three tables at the very rear and in the corner of the hall reserved specially for the Habitat staff, a couple local reporters, and members of other community service organizations that had helped with the fundraiser.

He kept glancing back at the open double doors which served as the main entrance to the banquet hall.

One of his co-workers nudged him.

"Hey Billy. Expecting someone special?"

"You could say that. But maybe not that special."

"Whatever you say."

Then it was time for him to go up.

Some indistinguishable replica of Billy took the stage, one that had been pre-programmed and now was on autopilot. Billy watched his clone perform his requisite duties with exquisite precision and grace. It was like being on the inside of a robot looking out, while at the same time being on the outside of the same robot looking in.

He made the introductions. Basically, he read them off of a list prepared at the office, based on the RSVPs they had gotten, amended at the last minute by the ever-diligent Leslie, as she noted the arrival of a few last-minute notables. These were the same VIPs who always attended these high-society affairs. People who got their validation from other people there to get their validation. Pillars of the community. The people who thought they ran the show. The great and powerful Wizards of Oz.

He then gave his speech. To him it was a lackluster performance. Zombie. Leslie was right. He felt like the walking dead, mechanically going through the motions, distracted by ... what was he distracted by? He couldn't even remember that. Something had happened. Something had shattered his world. What was it? It would come back to him.

Apparently, he didn't come off as badly as he thought. Later, everyone kept congratulating him, complimenting him on the great job he did. His hand and arm were actually sore from so much glad-handing. He felt a sharp ache just below his ears, at the hinge point of his jaw. Yes. Of course. He was suffering an acute attack of a malady common to politicians and other purveyors of bullshit.

Happy face neuralgia.

His address and plea for contributions even got good grades from Henry Blackledge, Director of Operations.

"Looks like we made a killing, Billy."

"A killing?"

"You know. Lots of bucks. Big pledges. As long as we can get these tightwads to pay up, we'll be rolling in cash next budget year. Have any mafia hit men contacts?"

"Mafia hit men?"

Blackledge first looked at Billy quizzically. This was not the smart, energetic, enthusiastic young man he knew from the office.

Or the young man who had just dazzled them from the podium.

He then decided that Billy's near-stupor was just a case of post-game exhaustion. He winked and demonstrated he was no stranger to empathy. He leaned over confidentially.

"Hey. I know it's been a long day. Have a drink, Billy. Have two or three. It's on the house. Thanks for your hard work. You're the best."

Blackledge lightly jabbed Billy in the arm and moved on. He didn't have to move far. Behind him were the Lancasters, part of the "old money" landed gentry. They were both dressed in formal wear, he in an elegant black tuxedo, she in a full-length pearl sequined evening gown, beige with long puffed sleeves. Harold Lancaster pumped the Director's hand vigorously, then Sarah Lancaster gave him a society hug, light on body contact except for the huge flabby breasts she had stuffed into her heavy-lift steel-belted bra, the politically-correct embrace capped with the requisite air kisses on both his cheeks in the manner of the French aristocracy during the Plague.

Billy slipped away, ambling by quartets and sextets of chattering guests — the guests seemed to entirely consist of inseparable couples — all sipping tumblers of scotch, bourbon, and various mixed drinks, most of them three sheets to the wind but well-practiced and steel-disciplined in maintaining the appearances of propriety and control.

He again glanced toward the entrance, and scanned the area around it. No one entering, just two couples managing an early exit, probably to make it home in plenty of time for Jay Leno.

He was glad-handed and back-whapped by a couple more geriatric dignitaries. Not knowing any of them proved to be to his advantage. Even small-talk seemed out of the question. Since he had nothing in common with any of them, it was easy to keep moving along after token courtesies: *"Thanks for coming." "Thanks for your support." "Your contribution is much needed and greatly appreciated."*

Fortunately for Billy, it wasn't entirely an affair of huff-and-harumph pomposity. Interspersed were his colleagues from Habitat, various members of other Orange County NGOs and NPOs, miscellaneous friends and supporters of all causes liberal, who had standing invitations to attend fundraisers of this sort. This included a few people he knew very well, and many he didn't know very well at all but at least recognized.

Several of the people from his office who he rarely spoke to found a new exciting fellowship with him, probably because of his spotlight role at the banquet and the apparent effectiveness of his speech. Several younger staff members amped up with camaraderie, high-fived him (males) or sidled up next to him (females) like TV dating game contestants. A couple more senior members of the service community beamed at him with new or renewed respect — one winked and the other gave him an eyebrow salute.

All of this registered with Billy as in a dream, or as if he were on massive doses of muscle relaxants. He felt like he was moving in his own jello mold.

Then somewhere around 10:45, during the seemingly endless post-dinner, post-ceremonial mixing and milling of the audience, Billy finally saw Natalie, Pam and Annie Roberts.

They were at the other end of the ballroom, not far from the main entrance door — perhaps they had just arrived — talking with Mayor Wayne Brinks. Annie seemed to be doing most of the talking. Maybe she was giving him makeover tips.

Both Natalie and Pam looked as if they were quite intrigued by the exchange. The Mayor and Annie certainly seemed to be yukking it up about something. Brinks talked with big hands. They were up and out and around as he spewed forth his mayoral spew, then they would rest usually somewhere on Annie when he wasn't talking. It was a nauseating display, more for its lack of subtlety than for any cheap feels he may have copped along the way. It would seem that a seasoned politician should have more polish than a truck driver in a strip joint.

Billy briefly saw Natalie glance at him. She quickly averted her eyes back to Annie, who in that moment was again driving the conversation with her usual histrionic fervor.

No wave.

No sign of recognition.

Did she really think he hadn't seen her look?

Then again, what should he expect?

Billy continued to wander. There seemed to be some sort of anti-attractional wave principle operating. Wherever he went, Natalie and company would not be. In fact, they would be on the other side of the ballroom. Not clustered together. But never far apart. The loosely confederated trio continued to circulate and draw more than their share of attention — just having Annie along guaranteed a seemingly endless stream of well-wishers, suitors, flirts, hangers-on, admirers, stalkers, and wanna-bees. It was easy for them to look completely pre-occupied with the business of mingling and affirming their celebrity status.

It was coming up on 11:00 pm and time for the affair to wrap.

Billy had had over the last half-hour or so, a generous share of mixed drinks — mostly vodka and tonic — and now really had to piss. Out of the banquet room and off he went to the nearest men's room, in a hallway off the main reception area of the hotel.

Mission accomplished, he stepped out of the restroom with every intention of immediately heading back to the ballroom, when a hand reached out and grabbed him. A hand with bright red acrylic nails, a fine complement to the red sleeves of her dress.

"Hello, Annie. Your hair looks great. Did you use my conditioner?"

He pulled his arm free of Annie's clutch. Billy had never seen her in public without her Miss America smile.

"Pam wants her fucking photo album back. Now."

"Sure. Let me work on that. You smell good. Did you use Natalie's lavender body spray?"

He turned and walked quickly and decisively back into the ballroom. Annie apparently wasn't following him. In her high heals, she would have had trouble keeping up with his pace anyway. As he shot through the crowd, he looked furtively left and right. Natalie and Pam were not in his immediate proximity anyway. Good enough.

Photo album. He needed to look at the photo album. Immediately.

Billy had at some point, in spite of being in shock and pre-occupied over the past several hours with his duties as emcee and event organizer, noticed the doors to a kitchen service area at the side of the ballroom, though they had been artfully obscured to preserve the splendor of the occasion's decor. He walked directly toward the high floral panels which had been put in place directly in front of them, and ducked into the kitchen, almost knocking over a waiter ferrying a tray of dirty dishes through the swinging double doors.

"Parking lot?"

The waiter nodded toward the rear of the huge kitchen area.

"Right through that back door, sir. Turn left, go around the loading dock and you're there."

"Thanks."

"Have a good evening, sir. Great speech, if you don't mind me saying."

Billy ran straight to his car without hesitating or looking back.

He drove east on I-84 and it wasn't until he reached the Route 9W interchange before his breathing calmed and his heart stopped pounding like a piston pump. He wiped his forehead with his arm, amazed at how much he apparently had been perspiring. His coat sleeve looked like he had spilled a glass of water on it. His shirt was soaked.

He headed north, took the Balmville Road exit and pulled up in front of a small 24-hour diner. Phil's Phast Phood. He ordered a coffee and piece of rhubarb pie from a bored middle-aged waitress sitting on a stool behind the counter — he wasn't hungry but thought he should pay something for the space he would be taking up — and headed to a booth in the very back where he would have some privacy.

The photo album apparently was Pam's personal collection, covering the entirety of her life. In the front were pictures of her as a baby, a toddler, then a little girl. It progressed with the typical shots of her on various holidays, birthdays, at vacations with her family, summer camps, Girl Scouts, with her grandparents, as a cheerleader, and so on.

Billy skipped ahead. It started to get interesting in about the time she was maybe 16 or 17.

Here was Pam at a church, in a choir, with the pastor. The pastor. Wait. He looked familiar.

He pulled out the handful of loose photos and found the family shot with Natalie.

There was Pam. She was sitting next to the pastor — Natalie's father — and he had his arm around her.

No! It couldn't be!

He went back to the photo album. On fourth or fifth to the last page was a wedding picture.

Natalie's father was dressed in an ill-fitting wedding tux, smiling from ear to ear next to his teen bride.

Pam dressed in a chintzy veiled wedding dress was the teen bride.

Behind them with his hands on their shoulders, looking uncannily like Wayne Newton in his declining years, was a bloated tanning-booth bronzed man, in an undersized black pastor's suit. His pompadour — clearly the result of a bad hair transplant and voluminous quantities of hair spray — was dyed ink-jet black. His pelican-like neck hung over and almost completely hid the white collar of his sacred profession.

A crucifix and a *We accept Visa and MasterCard* sign hung on the rear wall, behind a marbled styrofoam altar, draped with a glittery silver and gold-fringed brocade altar cloth.

Both Natalie's father and Pam had the red-eye effect of a bad flash photograph. But the contrast in their expressions was still profound. His was the face of the conquering hero. Hers was that of a frightened slave.

Billy flipped the page.

There were several pictures of some sort of reception party. It appeared to be in the courtesy room of a hotel. Waiters were in the background of a few of the photos.

There were informal shots of people sitting at long tables eating or holding their champagne glasses high in the air in a toast. There was one of the couple dancing — Pam looking especially awkward and self-conscious — in the center of the room. A boom-box sat on a card table against the wall, manned by an adolescent outfitted in baggy powder blue sports jacket. Well-wishers gazed on from the sidelines registering a strange mix of elation, diffidence, indifference, and tacit disapproval.

There was one final posed shot of the immediate family.

Natalie's father and his new bride were of course front and center. Natalie's sister was there. Two older people, maybe a grandfather and grandmother, stood stiff and Christian-stern off to one side. A little boy crouched in the corner, just within the frame of the photo, with an antic smile, displaying several missing front teeth.

Then there was Natalie. She must have only been 16 years old.

Natalie stood next to and slightly behind her father. The lower half of her face was smiling. The upper half — the eyes — looked angry and hurt.

Billy wanted to cry. But he couldn't. He just couldn't.

There were a select few other pictures. Anonymous faces. Happy and sad. Irrelevant faces.

Billy had seen all he needed to see. A numbness spread through his body. As the cold alkaline anesthesia migrated from the center of his chest, out to his limbs, his hands, his fingertips, down through his loins, his legs, his feet, up his neck, across the surface of his face, his scalp, then filled the spongy layers of his mind, seeping finally into the aching center of his consciousness, his entire being shut down.

He could no longer feel anything. No emotion. No sensation. He was an insensate void.

Now it was like watching a movie. Billy Green on the big screen.

He saw his hands continue to turn the few remaining pages of the photo album. Nothing there particularly registered. He spotted Natalie. He felt nothing. There was Pam. Nothing.

After the last page of photos, he saw tucked in the back cover what appeared to be various identification cards and a few documents.

Pam's first driver's license. Name ... Cynthia Scallon.

Pam's Noblesville Community Library card. Name ... Cynthia Scallon.

Pam's updated driver's license. Name ... Cynthia Diamond.

Pam's Blue Cross card. Name ... Cynthia Diamond.

So there it was. In black and white.

Natalie was fucking her step-mother.

"More coffee sir. Let me warm that up for you. Hey, mister. You haven't touched your pie. It's very good, you know. Truckers from all over stop here just for our rhubarb pie."

A different waitress. Where had they been hiding her? This lovely little lass was maybe 17 and unlike the cranky old bitch he had ordered from, actually looked fuckable.

"Thanks. I was just getting to it. It's pretty sweet, eh?"

"Just like me!"

Fuckable.

That's what it all came down to. Fuckable or not fuckable.

Billy had been fuckable to Natalie. At least until tonight. After tonight? Probably not.

But Pam — Cynthia would be more accurate — had been fuckable for a lot longer. And she was probably still fuckable. *Especially* after tonight.

Billy drank his coffee. He even wolfed down the pie. In fact he ate it like he hadn't eaten for several days. Gone in less than 30 seconds from the moment he picked up the fork.

He immediately stood up, scooping up the photo album and loose photos, and headed out of the diner.

Just before he opened the door to the car, he bent over double and vomited.

So that's what undigested rhubarb pie and black coffee looks like.

"Jesus Christ! Are you drunk? That's disgusting!"

It was the cranky old waitress again. Standing with her hands on her hips in the doorway of the diner.

125

"I don't feel well."

"Maybe you'd feel better if you paid your bill."

"Right. Sorry."

Billy fished a twenty out of his wallet and handed it to her.

"Keep it. Split it with the pretty little slut."

She lunged toward him and pulled her arm back to take a swing at Billy.

"That's my daughter, you foul-mouth son-of-a-bitch! Just leave. Or I'll call the goddamn cops. Get out of here!"

Billy jumped into his car and pulled away. In his rear-view mirror, he saw that the young waitress had come out and was next to her mom. They both just stood there watching, probably making sure he was leaving and would cause no further trouble.

Twenty minutes later Billy pulled into his drive. No pink Cadillac this time. In fact nothing. No lights on in the house. No sign of anything or anybody.

This time the front door was unlocked and slightly ajar. Someone had left in a hurry.

Like he had to guess who.

Billy switched on a few lights, walked through the living room, glanced in the kitchen, then went up the stairs, turned on some more lights, and stood at the top of the landing.

"Natalie?"

He knew she wouldn't be there.

He stepped into the master bedroom. At first glance, everything looked pretty normal.

But as he looked around, it was obvious that a few things were missing.

Personal stuff. A few articles of clothing. Her bedroom slippers. A book from the night stand she had been reading. A carry-on bag from the closet.

Was this how the movie ended?

Quite a story. Twisted. Surreal. Sensational!

Boy meets girl. Boy falls in love with girl. Boy marries girl.

Girl has a best friend. Best friend is actually girl's step-mother.

Girl is fucking best friend. Girl is a lesbian. Girl leaves boy.

Quite a story. Probably wouldn't play well in Peoria.

Then again ... who knows? He sure didn't.

Billy had never been to Peoria.

Chapter Four

WHY BRIDGES COLLAPSE
AND TEETH FALL OUT
Late Summer 2007

If Only He Could Cry

Billy hadn't left the house for five days. Or was it four? Six? Twelve?
Had he slept?
Was he awake?
Was there a difference?
He should be hungry. Had he eaten? He couldn't remember.
He stumbled into the bathroom. Someone had forgotten to flush.
There was shit in the toilet.
Was it his shit? Must be.
So there was some shit. It takes food to make shit. Everybody knows that.
Yes. He must have eaten.
Or maybe it was his brains. He had shit out his brains.
Shit for brains.
That somehow really made sense.
He had shit for brains. Now he was getting somewhere.
It explained everything!
Now what?
He sat back down.
He wanted a cigarette. But he didn't smoke.
What was that sound? Was it the phone? It sounded like a phone.
He kept hearing it. Over and over.
That and pounding. Were they building something? It seemed to come from the front of the house. Bang bang bang.
The phone kept ringing.
Over and over. Then it would stop. Then it would ring again. Ring ring ring.
Then there would be the pounding. Bang bang bang.
The door? Why doesn't somebody answer the door?
Oh. He remembered. He was alone.
There was no one else here. To answer. To stop the ringing. To stop the pounding.
Billy wanted to cry.
He had been wanting to cry now for ... how long? Five days? Six? Four? Twelve?
Why?
He didn't know why. Not really.
Top Ten Reasons for Billy Green to Cry.
#10 ...
In the movies, men cried. Maybe when their father or mother died. Or their

buddy got shot on the battlefield and bled to death in their arms. Or their precious little girl lost her battle with cancer. Or their wife ...

But he just couldn't cry.

#9 ...

Oh fuck it. This is stupid. He couldn't think.

He couldn't ... he couldn't ...

Suddenly his head was filled with lightning. Explosions. Screaming. Devastation.

Fuck you! Fuck you! Fuck you! Fuck you, Mr. Harold Green! Sham father of Billy Green. Yes, dear daddy. You motherfucker! Fuck you for teaching me how not to cry!

He froze.

No. Not true! That bastard never taught me anything. He fucking *unlearned* me! That's what *that* asshole did.

I must have known how to cry at one time. Babies always cry. It's their job. But Mr. Harry Fucking Green, factory worker, flatulating, no-good-to-nobody failure, you *unlearned* me. You ... Asshole-Beer-Gut-Tough-Guy-Fuck-No-More. Thanks a lot, sick fuck! Your so-called son, fashioned in your own repulsive, callous, cruel, cold-blooded image, can't squeeze out a tear. That's your legacy. That's your patrimonial endowment. Bravo! Big man. Bad ass motherfucker!

Oh God! What he would give for a good cry.

What would he give?

I'd give my right arm ...

I'd give my left nut ...

I'd give my right eye ...

I'd give your mother's left tit ...

Ha ha ha.

Why was it always left or right?

Oh shit.

He was going crazy. No doubt about it.

How else could you explain this ... this ... what?

What was he trying to figure out?

Goddammit! What the fuck was it?

Billy so wanted to cry.

And the truth was ... not because he had lost his mind.

But because he hadn't.

He had lost everything else but still had his mind intact, right there in the center of everything to remind him of all that he had lost and how none of it was coming back.

It wasn't coming back.

She ... wasn't coming back.

Billy stood up. He looked out the window. It was dark. What time was it?

He needed to get out of there.

That was it. Just leave. Go! Go!

He stepped through the front door. The car was next to the house.

He got in, pulled out into the street. He started to drive.

Billy headed south through town, not entirely sure where he was going, but certain it had to be some place away from … from … things. Somewhere where he knew no one and no one knew him.

Maybe then he could figure it out.

Maybe get something in his stomach.

Maybe even remember how to cry.

And maybe …

Suddenly, lights were flashing. White. Blue. Red. What was happening?

He pulled over, partly out of panic and partly from instinct.

A man appeared beside his car gesturing for him to roll down his window.

"May I have your driver's license and registration, please?"

Billy surprised himself. He seemed to know what to do. Drivers license from the wallet. Automobile registration from the glove compartment.

The man in uniform returned to his vehicle and seemed to be checking on something. Then he came back to Billy, standing a few feet away from Billy's car.

"Please step out of the vehicle, sir."

"I … I …"

"Just step out of the vehicle."

Billy did as he was told.

"Are you coming from some sort of party, Mr. Green?"

"Why no. Why do you ask?"

"Most people don't drive around in this town wearing a tux."

Billy glanced down. Sure enough. It was wrinkled, somewhat soiled, and felt kind of grimy. But he was wearing a tux. The bow tie and the cummerbund were gone.

"Have you been drinking? Your eyes are very bloodshot."

"No … no. I'm just … just … very tired."

The police officer performed a breathalyzer test and confirmed that Billy, indeed, was sober as a judge. Well, as sober as judges are supposed to be, at least while sitting on the bench.

"I'm going to let you go, Mr. Green. But please drive carefully. And try to get some sleep. Have a good evening, sir."

"Excuse me. But why did you stop me?"

"Well. It's unusual this time of night, especially since there is so little traffic, for someone to be driving as slowly as you were. You couldn't have been going more than 10 mph on a major thoroughfare. And you were hunched over the steering wheel. It looked suspicious. Good evening, Mr. Green."

"Thanks."

Billy got back in the car and pulled away. Though it was uncomfortable, he forced himself to drive closer to the speed limit. 30 MPH. That's what the sign said.

It was 11:12 pm according to the digital readout on the radio/CD player.

He kept driving. Through New Windsor, west through Vails Gate, finally stopping at a small local pub in Meadowbrook. He had never been in Meadowbrook before.

This would do.

The place was called Amble Inn and had been designed to cater to a horde of spendy tourists which never arrived. It was chic, in the middle-of-the-road manner of a cocktail bar at the Disney World Holiday Inn. A lot of wood, random pottery and ceramic pieces, pseudo-art on the walls, celebrity head shots, providing a pleasant clutter but arriving at no certain theme. It was the ambience of a highway gift shop.

Billy took a seat in the center of a long wood bar with coins from all over the world embedded in its thick lacquer and epoxy surface.

He ordered a beer from the young bartender on duty and sat quietly, staring at the label.

Eventually he looked up. At first he had no idea who was staring back at him from across the bar. Then it finally dawned on him who the scruffy, bedraggled, unwashed, haggard, pitiable creature was. It was *him*. Even being in a tux didn't help. As wrinkled as the tux was, it still only heightened the contrast between order and chaos, the stylish order of a well-cut piece of menswear, and the anthropomorphic chaos that his current state represented.

Billy immediately averted his gaze. He couldn't look at this pathetic version of himself. It confirmed his worst suspicions.

What a worthless piece of shit.

He opted to again just stare at the label of his Heineken. As boring as it was, it was preferable to looking at himself or trying to take in the soporific scene at the Amble Inn.

He stared and sipped. Stared and sipped. Stared and sipped.

Maybe it was the beer. Maybe it was just getting out of the house. The scrim between Billy and the world gradually started to dissolve. Not completely. But enough to that he didn't feel like he was a prisoner in a gauze cocoon.

He looked around. The bartender was counting the cash in the register.

There was only one other customer. Skinny dude. Dressed in some sort of ill-fitting uniform. Probably a security guard. He was playing solo rounds of pool. He couldn't lose.

The bartender was a decidedly handsome young man, maybe in his mid-20s, athletic build, cropped blond hair, wearing a black Rage Against The Machine t-shirt with the sleeves rolled up to better display his pumped biceps. Apparently done accounting for the evening's meager intake of cash, he walked over in front of Billy, scooped some ice into a tall glass, and poured himself orange juice from a plastic carton.

Billy cleared his throat. The encounter with the cop had only partially loosened his larynx.

"Excuse me. What's your name?"

"Chip."

"Chip is your Christian name?"

"Of course. After St. Chippewa of Ottawa. The patron saint of fried snack foods."

He disgorged a hearty self-satisfied snorting laugh. Chip was clearly quite amused with himself. Then he went on to explain.

"My folks named me Gunther. They always told me, 'Pronounce it *Goontare*.' Like that would be an improvement. So I became Chip. Anyone calls me Gunther or *Goontare* gets their fucking skull bashed in."

"Smart move, Chip. Sometimes you have to put your foot down. So tell me. Do you have a girlfriend?"

"I do. Coming and going. I've got this new chick named Amy. But I haven't told my old girlfriend yet. Twice the action, my man. At least for a while."

"What's your old girlfriend's name?"

"Natalie. She's hot but what a fucking cunt! So sweet when we first got together. But now? Total bitch! She's history, man."

Natalie? Whew! That was a kick in the stomach.

"Give me another beer, will you?"

Chip popped the cap off of another Heineken.

"Sure you don't want a glass?"

"No. This is fine. So. Let's just say you have one official girlfriend."

"Whatever. Where is this going?"

"I just want to ask you something, that's all. Get your opinion. You seem to know your way around women."

"One girl, eh? Okay. Amy. It looks very promising so far. So she's the girlfriend. Shoot."

"So you and Amy have been together for two years and—"

"Whoa! That would be a personal record! But okay. Two years."

"Now you don't know this, but all along, for the entire time you've been together, this Amy girl has been with another girl. She's been *having sex* with this other girl. They're lesbians."

"Bi-sexual. Amy is still fucking me, right? So she's bi."

"Okay. Bi. Anyway, Chip. How would you feel about it?"

"Hmm. That's a tough one, you know? They always say, 'What you don't know won't hurt you.' Right? And in a way, that makes sense here. I mean, it's not like some other dude is sticking his dick in her. It's another chick."

"So it wouldn't bother you."

"I can't say that. Because that's not the whole story. There's a question of honesty here. Keeping something secret that's *that* important."

"Meaning the integrity of your relationship. Being open and deserving trust."

"Wow! That is way out there, dude! Almost biblical. I didn't mean that at all."

"What *did* you mean?"

"Two chicks, man. Making it? It's a major turn-on. Can you imagine fucking two chicks while they are eating one another out? Awesome! For my girlfriend to hold out on me like that, would really piss me off. Have you ever heard of girlfriendslicking.com? It's rad. You can post videos of your girlfriend with another chick. You should check it out. Do you want me to write that down? It's girlfriendslicking.com and it's a free site."

"Uh … no. I can remember that. Thanks, Chip."

"Want another beer?"

Billy hadn't touched the new one he had in front of him.

"I'll just nurse this one. Looks like you've got some customers."

"You're right. Big night here at the Amble Inn. Let me know if you want any more advice. That was fun. Got any stories with three chicks?"

Billy couldn't even manage a polite chuckle. Surrealism seemed to have no antidote. Not these days anyway. It was a wily, unscrupulous pathology bent on destroying Billy's grip on reality — what was left of it.

A couple had walked in — actually, staggered in — and took two stools at the end of the bar. They apparently had already had quite a bit to drink. They were in their early 40s. He was in a three-piece suit but his shirt was open at the collar and his tie was partially hanging out of one of the side pockets. She had on a mini-dress, not the most flattering choice considering the volume of her legs both above and below her knees. The ensemble had a scoop neckline, but since the two top buttons were undone, the center strap of her bra was visible. Two bulbous breasts grotesquely bulged together to form a huge cleavage line. It looked like someone's ass was hanging out the front of her dress.

She smiled at Billy as she leaned heavily into her male companion. The man seemed to be trying to devour the ear closest to him. He had fully cupped a hand over one of her enormous boobs, while the other reached around her tree-trunk torso. She giggled and with no attempt to disguise what she was doing, reached between the man's legs and started to rub him vigorously. She continued to glance over and smile at Billy, presuming he was vicariously enjoying being in on the handjob.

Chip stepped over to their end of the bar, stood directly in front of them and stared. Finally they paused long enough for him to take their drink orders. He then came back in front of Billy to pour and blend.

"It takes all kinds."

"Love is a beautiful thing, Chip."

"Then why sometimes does it make me want to puke?"

Chip sure wasn't much help. If Billy had expected to hear something that made sense or have his death-spiraling spirits raised even slightly, he definitely had come to the wrong place.

He still had half a bottle of beer left. Time to get serious. He finished it in three intent swigs.

Maybe the scrim had dissolved slightly but now a misty fog had rolled in. Two beers and Billy was flying low. His own breathing sounded like the intake duct on the bilge tank for a cruise ship. It took all his energy to just shift from one haunch to the other. His back ached from sitting on the bar stool for the last hour. He needed to piss. He considered just pissing right there. Better judgment got the better of him and he wandered into the men's room. Duties done, he left a ten on the bar, gave a cursory wave to Chip, and left.

The drive home seemed to take forever. He remembered none of it by the time he pulled up to his house. Like the zombie he had several days ago been accused of being, he lumbered into the house, up the stairs, and into the master bedroom. The bed was made, the spread neat and undisturbed. He must not have been up here since Natalie left.

He fell face forward and slept for twelve hours straight, waking in the exact dead-man's pose he had assumed when he keeled over onto the huge waterbed.

A pool of foul-smelling drool, which had spread under his head, greeted him as he fought for consciousness.

Billy tried to upright himself but managed only to slide off the bed onto his back.

He wasn't so much hung over as left over — like a bowl of macaroni and cheese that had sat out all night. Billy felt like his skin was coated with a thick coagulated scum and his insides had melted into a bilious pocket of mucous.

He itched all over and scratched himself with little discernable relief, then got up and sleep-walked through his morning routine.

He peed, splashed water on his face, smeared a fingerful of toothpaste on his gums to break down the thick putrescent slag that had built up in his mouth, then finally made his way down the stairs.

He was now alert enough to feel urgent pangs of hunger, the product of several days of self-imposed fasting.

The fridge was all but empty, as were the cupboards. A wicker bowl in the center of the kitchen table looked like someone had filled it with balls of yarn. There was fruit in the bowl but it was covered in a white fuzz, and liquid was leaking from the bottom of the basket, oozing a sticky pool of slime over much of the table.

Billy opted for coffee. He needed a direct jolt to his nervous system.

After his third cup, the demons woke up. The debate team in his head. The voices which just seemed to want to rant, never coming up with any answers.

What you don't know won't hurt you.

Now ... is that one of those rock solid propositions? Like the Second Law of Thermodynamics? Or Newton's Laws of Motion?

What you don't know won't hurt you.

What if he had never found out? And they had gone on for years and years. Would it have made any difference that Natalie was in an intimate sexual relationship with someone of her own sex?

I mean, it's not like some other dude is sticking his dick in her. It's another chick.

Chip, in his own crude revolting way, maybe had actually hit on something valuable there.

Maybe not.

Let's see.

What if he looked at Natalie's thing with Pam as a whole different game? Like she had some kind of hobby, that Billy had no interest in. What for instance? A chick lit reading group. Or a field hockey team. Or an HIV-AIDS quilting club.

Nope.

Not at all the same.

Reading and field hockey and quilting don't overlap in the least with his interaction with her. Especially the physical interaction. She wouldn't exactly be using her nipples or her clitoris to stitch pieces of cloth together, or knock a ball in a net, or cross-reference literary passages. It would be a real stretch to say there was any overlap between any of those activities and Billy's sexual intimacies with Natalie.

What Natalie had with Pam definitely used the very same physiological components that Billy engaged when he made love to her. A 100% overlap.

Men are accused of being very territorial with women. Possessive. Specifically with certain body parts. Billy had to admit. Yes. It was true. He did feel a degree of ownership. An exclusive ownership. No begging. No borrowing. No trading. No leasing. No stealing. Not on those items.

First and foremost ... her vagina.

And while we're in that region of the body, the butt. Yes, the butt and the butthole.

What about the breasts? Of course, the breasts! They are the second most erogenous zones on a woman.

And wait. The lips, the mouth and the tongue factor in there high on the list. The pleasure goes both ways with the oral orifice — giving and getting. And even putting aside the hard core sex, the thought of Pam or anyone else just kissing Natalie's lips with passion was more than he could handle.

But where does it stop? Would he want some stranger sucking on Natalie's fingertips? Running a feather across her knees? Licking the inside of her elbows? Touching her neck?

Images of Pam doing all of the above popped uninvited into his head. Within moments, he could see the two of them naked on the bed. Upstairs. Just as they had been the night he heard them through the door. The sound of Natalie's orgasm, the giggling and the purring. It all came back. A gigantic torrent of sound, ricocheting in the torture chamber of his mind.

"You liked that, eh sweetie? You love this tongue. You love the way I—"

His whole body burned hot with some combination of anger, lust, hatred, passion, jealousy.

He stood up. Too quickly. He felt dizzy and nearly fainted. He bent over to get blood back in his head.

He stood back up and started to pace.

What you don't know won't hurt you.

The problem was that Billy *knew*. He knew everything now. There was no hiding. There was no pretending.

He continued to pace. Back and forth across the living room. Back into the kitchen.

If only he could cry. If only ...

Somehow he knew it would help.

Suddenly he heard the front door open.

Startled, he turned to see Natalie walking across the living room, heading toward the stairs to the upper level. She had two timid-looking, early 20s, African-American guys in tow.

"It would sure be nice if you answered the phone. JESUS H. CHRIST!! What happened to you? You look terrible."

"Uh ... I was thinking about ... I need to change."

"Take a shower. Shave. Do something, Billy. Have you been to work? Right. Stupid question."

Billy stared at her in disbelief.

"How can you be so casual about this?"

"How can you be so pathetic?" She suddenly realized from the expression on his face how much she was hurting him. "Alright alright. I'm sorry, Billy. Look. We can talk over the weekend. I just need to pick up some things for now. Okay?"

"What day is this?"

"Thursday, Billy. It's Thursday."

She went up the stairs. One of the guys carried several cardboard box flats. He put them down and started configuring them into storage boxes.

Billy followed the other young man up the stairs.

When he stepped into the bedroom, Natalie was already pulling her things out of the closet. All sorts of stuff. Clothes, books, shoes, memorabilia, suitcases.

She spoke without looking at him.

"I'm staying at Pam's."

"What a surprise."

"I don't want you in here. Go take a shower. Join the land of the living again. If it's convenient for you, we can talk on Sunday."

"Sunday."

"Where. Where. We can meet for brunch at Anna's."

"How romantic. Just like the good old days."

"11:00 am is good for me."

"11:00 am. Should I bring my attorney?"

"Billy. Clean yourself up. I'll only be in here for a few minutes. Just what I need for now."

When he got out of the shower, Natalie and her two porters were gone.

In a way, he was relieved. It hurt too much at this point to see her. Maybe by Sunday he'd have it a little more together.

Whatever that meant.

How long does it take for a dream to unravel?

With nightmares, usually the re-entry back to reality is like a gunshot. Blam! You might be left with the horror, fear, anger, sadness. But the screen, movie, projector, actors, everything is instantly gone.

With dreams, it can go one of two ways. Sometimes it's the gunshot effect again. Blam!

Other times the cross-fade is slow. It's more like the feel and flavor of mirrors and clouds, shimmering mirages, bouquets of supernal smoke, a gradual glide on the wings of the subconscious. Images dance and dissolve as reality comes to the fore in its pithy lucidity. The dream lives on through the day as a background melody, a companion to defer the loneliness and humdrum of daily routine.

When dreams become nightmares, it's both.

The gunshot and the slow, gradual cross-fade.

The gunshot inflicts the wound. Then there's the painfully slow cross-fade as the blood, drop by agonizing drop, is siphoned away. As the stuff of dreams drains and paradise oozes into the sweltering anonymous loam of a graveyard.

On that patch of coagulated earth nothing ever grows again.

If only he could cry.

The New Morality

"It's over."

"Stop Natalie. It doesn't have—"

"After what happened the other night? It's over."

"Maybe it is. Maybe it isn't. I don't know what to think."

"You stole Pam's photo album."

"*Cynthia* can have her photo album back whenever she wants it."

"Pam is Pam. She escaped all that. She had to. No one can touch her now."

"She seems to like it when *you* touch her."

"Billy. Don't be crude."

"Crude? I'm not the one sleeping with a … my step-mother."

"Pam is only three years older than me. I don't think of her as my step-mother. She's my—"

"She married your father but is not your biological mother."

"Fuck you, Billy. This is not some twisted Greek tragedy. This is my life. Pam and I were pushed together. She quickly saw what a rotten bastard my father really was. She was afraid. I was afraid. Confused. We leaned on one another."

"That's one way to put it."

Natalie looked around. No one else in the restaurant seemed to be paying attention to them. It didn't seem possible. They were practically yelling. She tried with great difficulty to speak more calmly.

"Your mind works like the typical male. It all comes down to sex. That just happened. When two people are—"

"Typical male? Let me get some perspective on this. You were afraid. Your father was a rotten bastard. Pam was afraid. Your solution to the crisis? Have Pam stick her tongue between your legs. And it's my fault. It's somehow the result of typical male thinking. Christ! If you can untwist that to make some sense out of it, you're a genius."

Natalie just stared at him. Tears were pooling in her eyes. She blinked and they spilled down on her cheeks. She picked up the napkin from her lap and quickly wiped them away.

"I'm sorry, Natalie. This all just hurts too much."

She glared at him. Now she was angry.

"Right. Poor poor Billy. You truly are pathetic. Which is why it's over. I'm divorcing you. Do you understand? Have you got that?"

"Come on, Natalie. It shouldn't have to end this way. Come on. Please try. Please, Natalie."

"You're right. It shouldn't. But that's the way it is, isn't it?"

"Because you say so. Don't I have any say in this?"

"A relationship — a good relationship, that is — is built on trust."

"Trust? Trust? Here we've been married for over two years and you never mentioned something so completely basic, something so defining as the fact that you're a lesbian. And you're lecturing me about trust."

"I'm your wife, Billy. I'm not some category. Not a *lesbian*. Yes, apparently I am bisexual. But I'm your wife. And someone who trusts and can be trusted does not sneak around spying on his wife."

"I wasn't spying. I came back to get my speech. It seemed kind of important at the time, you know? Since everybody there was depending on me. What I didn't bargain for was finding you and Pam in bed together having an orgy."

"It doesn't matter. That never … never should or ever would have effected us. What you and I have — excuse me, what you and I *had* — was perfect."

The waitress was back. Billy quickly grabbed his fork and started pushing the food on his plate around. Natalie just looked out the window onto the street — as if there were something to look at.

"Would either of you like some more coffee?"

"No thanks, miss."

"Is everything okay, sir? It doesn't look like you've touched your meal. I could take that back to the kitchen and have them warm it up for you."

"No. We're fine. Just taking our time."

She walked to the next table with the pot of regular coffee in one hand, decaf in the other.

"Natalie. You say it was perfect. How could it be perfect? This thing has been going on behind my back, what? The entire time? Even before us? Six … seven years?"

"Jesus Christ! I feel like I'm talking to a brick wall. Billy … you can't possibly know everything about me. You don't have to. And I don't need to know everything about you. You're right. There are things that go back. Long before you came along."

"But this is happening now. And has been happening the whole time I've been with you."

"Pam saved me. You weren't around back then. She was. She was there for me when I needed someone. And besides, even now. There are ways you can't be there for me. That's just the way it is. Everybody is more complex than you'd like to believe they are. Including yourself. So I have this other person. What difference does it make? She doesn't replace you. What I have with Pam can't touch what I have — again excuse me, *had* — with you. Is this so difficult?"

"Actually, it is. I can't explain why. But it is. I guess I'm just a typical stupid-fuck male."

"We're still individuals, Billy. As close as we are, we are still individuals. People can't submerge their individuality in a relationship and expect it to survive. If the person disappears, there's no one there to have a relationship. You think you know every little thing about me? When I have to stick in a tampon, do I call you in to share the beauty of the experience? How about you, Billy? You think I don't know what goes on when you take those really long showers, and then when you come out you're not in the mood to make love. Hey, Billy Boy, I touch myself sometimes. So what? Or what about my diary? I'm not allowed to keep a diary without you reading along and making suggestions."

"You keep a diary?"

"Yes. And there are things in there I only share with one person ... that's me. That doesn't take anything away from you and I. Billy, I have shared more with you than any other human being in the world. I opened up to you. I told you about my secret world when I was growing up. But that wasn't enough. I shared my life, my hopes, everything. But that still wasn't enough. You had to spy on me to ... to find out more."

"I'd say that your being a *bisexual* might qualify as something I should know about."

"Yes. You already said that. And why is that, Billy? What difference does it make?"

"Well ... it's you. I want to know everything. I need to know everything. I love you and—"

"What did I call you once? Tragically innocent? Jesus Christ, the writing was on the wall. Frankly, I thought you had figured it out by now. And I gave you enough credit to think that you would put it in proper perspective. It doesn't ... didn't affect us. It was just a part of me that ... well, it's just a part of who I am."

"I never for one moment suspected."

"If you went to Arlington, you wouldn't see the grave markers. You *are* tragically innocent. Or just blind. But I love you, Billy. You will always be that one special man in my life."

"Then don't end it. I'll do what I can. I think ... I think we can still make this work. Please."

"Billy. Don't beg. That's not the Billy I love."

"Then stay."

"No, Billy. It's over."

"No."

"Yes."

"Natalie, please."

"It's over."

And it was over.

The meal was anyway. Even if they hadn't touched their food.

As they walked out of the restaurant, neither speaking, both smarting from things that probably shouldn't have been said, things that certainly didn't help the situation on any level, Billy swore to himself he would go down swinging.

They didn't speak for the next couple days. He started answering the phone again. For the most part, whoever had been trying to call had given up. So the phone only rang a few times, and they were either sales calls or wrong numbers. No Natalie.

Billy finally got it together to go back to work but only stayed for a few short minutes. When he walked in to the Director's office, he was greeted at first by a momentary look of shock, then by the reassuring public relations welcome of someone who would have greeted Benito Mussolini with the same reassuring warmth as Jesus Christ, registering no special wonder that either of them were there.

"Come in. Come in, my boy. How are you? Took a few days off, I guess. I tried calling."

Billy vaguely referred to some personal difficulties that might take a while to sort out. Based on the good will he had stockpiled by being such a solid contributor for over two years, especially his exceptional performance at the fundraiser, Director Blackledge told Billy to take as much time — within, of course, reasonable limits — as he needed. Billy then ducked out before anyone could collar him, giving token waves to a couple of the people who happened to notice him, then picking up his pace so that there was no chance of them catching him before he raced out of the building.

There was no sense trying to explain to anyone else what he could make no sense of himself.

A very empty, silent house greeted his return.

He turned right back around and headed to the grocery store. All the food looked repulsive. He was sure he had lost weight, had no energy or strength, but couldn't bring himself to eat.

Billy finally settled on a king-size bag of kettle corn and two fifth-size bottles of Jack Daniels. He recalled liking kettle corn, and the whiskey would serve other purposes.

He was jarred to consciousness the next day by the telephone. The half-eaten bag of kettle corn had spilled over the edge of the table onto the floor. One of the bottles of Jack Daniels was nearly empty. Billy apparently had slept on the hardwood floor and he felt like he had been broadsided by a city bus. His head throbbed like a clanking anvil and his mouth and throat seemed to have morphed into canvas.

"Ugh ..."

"I'm coming over."

Click.

Natalie.

He waited.

Three hours later she finally showed up.

On one hand, the wait gave him time to clean up a bit, straighten up the place, put the bottles of whisky in the cupboard, and slowly regain cerebral function. On the other, it took so long that casual busywork became anxious pacing became impatient disaffection became anger and exasperation. Why was she taking so long? Why was she fucking up his life?

The hungover brain is not a finely tuned instrument.

He heard a vehicle pull up. A minute later, she tapped on the door, then let herself in.

"Would you like some kettle corn?"

Billy extended the bag from which he had removed a few kernels, which he now forced himself to eat.

"I'm not here for kettle corn. But thanks for the generous offer."

She looked around, seeming to take stock of the contents of the room.

It was a Wednesday afternoon. That struck Billy as a little odd. He hadn't started back to work but he assumed that she should be at her office.

It quickly became evident, Natalie had stopped by the house to get her things. This time with serious intent. She had a van, a driver and another large person with a strong back. Her two power helpers, both Hispanic, stood waiting on the front porch for further instructions.

"So. How are you and the missus doing? Or is she the mister? Isn't that how it works? One is the bull dike and the other plays Holly Homemaker and wears the frilly dresses."

"You are really fucked up."

"I'm fucked up! I'm not the one with a secret life."

"It's not so secret now, is it? I'm getting looks at work. Clever little innuendos in passing from people on the street I don't even know."

"What do you expect? The Good Housekeeping Reader's Choice Award for family values?"

"This is 2007. People are supposed to be beyond this crap."

"As I understand it, ERA doesn't protect the guilty." As if he's quoting a law: *"No person shall face discrimination or abrogation of their rights based on their wanton promiscuity or disregard for the sanctity of their marital vows.* No one likes a slut, Natalie."

"Fuck you, Billy. You don't know what you're talking about. You are looking more and more narrow-minded and ignorant by the moment."

"You can jump in bed with Pam, then jump in bed with me. What exactly do you call that? Musical chairs? Musical beds?"

"You should talk."

"I never so much as—"

"Did you ever happen to notice when you were living with Julianne, Billy, that I never called on Tuesday night?"

Shit. She knew.

"We weren't married then."

"Like a marriage license is the only thing that confers fidelity. It was your choice. And I felt it was none of my business."

"How big-hearted of you."

"Just like Pam is none of your business."

"I guess I should've fucked Katie Burke after all."

Natalie laughed out loud.

"Sure. Why not? I did."

"What?"

"What part of 'I did' did you fail to understand?"

"Katie? The intern from two summers ago?"

"Perky little thing. Tall and slender. Nice flat stomach. I tried to get her to shave her pubic hair but she liked keeping it natural."

"You're lying."

"She probably did it to get to you. Or get back at you. But I couldn't pass up a work of art like that. She was beyond beautiful! What an outstanding lay."

"I don't believe it. You're just trying to poison me."

"Pam tapped into her once too. The night before she went back to her little

Christian hamlet in North Carolina. Pam seems to think lovely Katie will be into girls for the long haul."

"This is pure bullshit. You are just trying to completely mess me up."

"Billy. Believe what you want. None of it means anything anyway. The sooner you learn that, the better off you'll be."

"We meant something."

"Right. Past tense. So get over it. Time to move on. Way past time."

She stuck her head back out of the front door. The two men who had come along to help her move were relaxing. They were getting paid by the hour to listen to two gringos argue. Cushy job this time. One sat on the steps and the other was sprawled on the porch napping.

"Gentlemen, let's go to work."

She was very careful to not touch any of Billy's personal stuff. But she helped herself generously to shared property, clearing with Billy each item before loading it into the truck.

"If I take the bed, will you have something to sleep on?"

Billy's answer was always the same.

"No problem."

"Can I have the bookshelves?

"No problem."

"I'll leave the refrigerator but I want the microwave."

"No problem."

He didn't offer to help but offered no resistance. As far as he was concerned, it wasn't about property. Stuff could be replaced. The important thing that was going out the door — out of his life — couldn't be bought. At the same time, there was no stopping it.

He looked at Natalie. She was sweating pretty hard and had a bandana tied around her head. She blended right in with the two Mexicans she had brought with her to help.

He wondered if either of the two men were married. Neither were wearing wedding bands. Did they know what they were missing?

The waterbed took a long time. They had to drain it. Dissemble it. It was a very expensive piece and Natalie made sure it was treated with ultimate care.

Billy, perched at the kitchen table, getting an early start on the evening's anesthesia by sipping on a tumbler of Jack Daniels on the rocks, couldn't help but make a sneering allusion.

"You are being more careful with that than you ever were with me. I can see what your priorities are."

"Grow up, Billy."

"What I can't get a handle on, sweetheart, is how one moment things are great and the next here you are packing it in. Literally."

The two men were taking the last couple items out to the truck.

"Things were great, eh? Billy and Natalie's little piece of Heaven on Earth."

"Even the night of the fundraiser, I talked to you on the phone and you said—"

"You are so fucking clueless. The writing was on the wall, Billy. These things don't happen overnight. You'll be hearing from me."

She was out the door without even saying good-bye. Apparently, the occasion didn't support even basic niceties.

Billy watched the moving van, stuffed with the household furnishings of a broken dream, pull away from the curb.

He sat and sipped. Slowly sinking into the watery abyss of intoxication. Submerged in a tipsy world of fermented fantasy, where absurdity and reality could sit at the same bar and propose hilarious toasts to the dissolute state of the world, where good and evil were just two more patrons cheering on the home team in the game of life.

Soon it was nightfall. The voices were back.

These things don't happen overnight.

What does that mean?

He knew what it meant. But what did it really mean? That Natalie had been planning this for a long time?

Bottle empty. He broke out another. Who invented the twist cap?

These things don't happen overnight.

As he thought about all that had happened just that year, things started to fall in place. Natalie and Pam plan a wild Mediterranean jaunt without his knowing, Pam assaults him with her fucking know-it-all attitude New Years Eve, then they go away to commune with nature in the raw — he could imagine what went on in the hotel. Or maybe they just sucked each other off right there on the beach.

Then ...

I want a baby.

She really wanted a baby. Really bad.

Billy had to force himself to make the next mental leap. Was it possible? Was he just the brunt of life's cruelest joke? Had he just become a stud animal at that point? A semen donor for the family that Natalie and Pam wanted to build?

What a mind-fuck. What a dream-fuck. What a life-fuck.

After moving her things out of the house, Natalie didn't waste any time. Two days later he had the unique pleasure of being served with divorce papers. All very official. Natalie had hired an attorney and through him had petitioned the court for a divorce. For incompatibility and infidelity.

In an unusual twist which must have baffled her own attorney as well as the judge, she had referenced the infidelity as being hers. And moreover, that the incompatibility was a product of her own infidelity but nonetheless irremediable.

Truth in advertising.

She basically was admitting she had sabotaged their marriage. Her candidness would put her at an extreme disadvantage should Billy choose to be adversarial. He could claim all sorts of pain and suffering, mental anguish, humiliation, damage to his public reputation, his standing in the community — the entire litany of exaggerations and hyperbole used by lawyers to leverage more cash out of the final settlement.

But Natalie knew Billy well. In fact better than anyone else, including himself. She knew his heart and his values wouldn't allow him to use her admission to his advantage.

In the end, her intuition in the matter proved to be absolutely correct. Through his own attorney, one bought on the cheap and on the fly, he signed off on the petition for divorce.

Uncontested. No counterclaim. No objections.

If that's what she wanted, that's what she'd get. A divorce, clean and simple.

Billy just wanted to get it over with.

It wasn't that he was giving up. The divorce decree, like the marriage license, was just paper.

He couldn't give up. Everything depended on it.

Hope burns eternal.

At the bottom of a bottle.

What day was it? What time?

Fuck it.

Billy dialed Natalie's cell phone.

"Natalie."

"Billy."

"Is this a good time?"

"Always a good time for you."

"Are you being sarcastic?"

"Just trying to be civil."

Billy heard Pam's voice in the background. *"Who the fuck is calling in the middle of the night? For fuck's sake!"*

"So, which one of us is better in bed, Natalie?"

"You are so pathetic. How can you ask that?"

"It's easy. I guess I know the answer. Since I'm getting the boot, eh?"

"That is ridiculous. You think I am with Pam just for the fucking."

Pam again. *"Please, please take it into the other room."*

"No. But you must think she's better in bed. Otherwise—"

"And you think I rate each time, maybe from one to ten and add up the columns and take an average and come up with a score? It's not about stats, you know. It's about feeling. Value. Sharing. Commitment."

"Either you like baseball or you like football. Boxing or badminton."

"No. It's not like that. I enjoy baseball. I enjoy football. Not equally or one more than another. I don't ruin that enjoyment by worrying about which one gives me the bigger jolt. When I'm watching football, I don't sit there saying, 'Damn I wish I were at a baseball game right now.' Or, 'This is okay but baseball is better.' It's simple. Can't you understand this?"

"I'm not good enough for you. You're making a choice. Pam over me."

"Pam? You? What is with men? And what's with you? I always thought you were different. Obviously, I was wrong. Everything has to be a competition. Who's best? Who's on top?"

Billy laughed out loud. The forced laugh of a hyena in denial. Or a drunk immersed in self-pity.

"Yeh! Who *is* on top? Who's wears the pants? You or Pam? Who's the stud bull?"

"Who's on top? Like who is the fucker and who is the fuckee? Is that how you

see the world? Is that how you saw us? One person has to be the driver and the other in the passenger seat?"

"It seems to be the way things work out."

"Right. And things have worked out so well. Us. The world. That kind of thinking is why we're in the mess we're in. And always have been. You guys have been running the world. Running it into the ground. Always worrying about who's on top. Who's numero uno. Who's got the most toys, servants, slaves, glitter and gold. Guys don't approach love and war any differently. Who's on top? I'll tell you. The one on top is anyone whose heart beats out of love, not out of fear or envy or anger or lust."

Billy had been rolling his eye through Natalie's angry but heartfelt words. He had had time to gulp down half a tumbler of whiskey and pour himself a refill.

"What are you going on about? I don't need some New Age lecture. I just need to know. For my own sanity. Why you have to go and why you're choosing Pam. What was wrong with what we had?"

"You want an answer to a question that shouldn't have to be asked. Just look at yourself. Right now. There's your answer."

"Alright. I looked. I look absolutely fucking great. So I'm still missing something here. Can't you just give me a simple straight-forward answer to a simple straight-forward question? Is that really asking too much?"

"To the fuck question."

"Yes. That's the one."

Billy didn't really want an answer. Through the haze of his alcohol stupor, he knew that whatever she said at this point would just add to his suffering and humiliation. But it was too late to fold his hand. Pride trumped judgment. Ego eclipsed humility.

There was a long pause before Natalie let out a long deep sigh of exasperation and spoke.

"I enjoyed every single time we made love, Billy. A lot. That should have been very obvious. But more importantly, I enjoyed you. You. I love ... I loved you, Billy. Until you became a petty, meddling, infantile, possessive prick and decided what we had wasn't good enough. You had to have it all."

"I just want what we had. It's *not* all or nothing."

"It is now. Thank yourself for that."

"I don't feel very grateful."

"You shouldn't."

There's No Success Like Failure

Each day was a vast formless void followed by another of the same. The drinking was taking its toll. Billy had switched to Canadian Club hoping the skull crushing hangovers would somehow be mitigated by pricier booze. Alcohol is alcohol. Embalming fluid for the living. The human body does not like being interred alive.

144

He had mulled over his situation from one end to the other, irrational and foolish battling for his patronage, common sense and perspective having been eliminated in the early rounds. When late in the evening exhaustion demanded some peace and quiet, the truculent voices of discord continued their quibbling on into the night, repeating their empty mocking prevarications that the answers to his questions were right around the corner. They never arrived. Nothing was ever resolved. There were no answers. Just more cacophonous shouting. Another whiskey. More questions. More whiskey. More shouting.

His head was an echo chamber full of schizophrenic idiots.

Something had to give.

Something had to change.

Billy had forced himself to started eating again. The bathroom scale said he had lost over seven pounds in only a week. For someone who had very little fat on his body, this was not good. Food was repulsive at best. At first he just upchucked it. Then some of it began to stay down. It was a start.

To eat he had to leave the house. Either go to the grocery store or to a restaurant. After a few days, he felt more comfortable in public.

He decided to really go for broke and make a dramatic leap back into the reality that seemed like the pale memory of a book read long ago. He reported back for work on a Friday. He would then have the weekend to reconsider his decision, if things didn't go well.

It went better than expected. No one asked him any embarrassing questions. Nor were they overly cautious or protective. Probably everyone was keenly aware of what had happened. Newburgh was still a small town in some ways, and there was considerable overlap in Billy's and Natalie's professional communities. Gossip created the same excitement among adults as video games and Barbie dolls did among kids. What would the world look like if Ken and Barbie ever broke up? Hard to imagine.

For the entire day, everyone and everything just seemed to pick up where it had left off. Billy spent over a half-hour with Director Blackledge, much of it receiving yet more praise relative to the fundraiser. Money was already starting to come in, which provided some immediate relief for the cashflow-compromised close of summer. More importantly, it boded well for the next fiscal year. They discussed some long-term projects and Billy walked out of Blackledge's office with a bulleted list that he should get right to work on.

Billy worked quietly all day in his office with a minimum of interruptions. He even went to lunch with three of his co-workers and managed to put down half of a mushroom burger. He pushed the fries around on his plate until one of his companions, whose midsection inner tube of fat did not deter him from overeating, polished them off in the few remaining minutes of the lunch break. The human garbage disposal, as the guy had been nicknamed by his co-workers, conserved time by not bothering to chew. Billy was too awed to gag.

It was regrettable that Billy chose to go back on a Friday. The weekend was a major setback.

Without Habitat and the routine distraction of work, he was plunged back into the pitiful, formless void he was trying to escape. Sixty hours was too much time to have on his hands. Especially in that house.

Everything reminded him of Natalie.

Each piece of furniture, each book in their bookcase, the bed sheets, the towels, what he made for breakfast, the way the light came in the window, the sound of the wind through the eves of the house, *everything* seemed to have some memory attached to it. Everything visited his senses in the company of a knife to his heart.

He stumbled into work on Monday. This time the reactions were not so shrouded by polite concern and respect for his privacy. He looked so bad that no one could mask their alarm. His clothes were fine. It was his eyes. And the flaccid grayness of his skin. It was as if his essential life force had been drained dry, leaving the decaying vessel that had once been a human being.

As he stepped into his office, nothing had a familiarity about it. He sat down, twirled around in his chair, looked out the window, glanced through the door at passing workers, all in an effort to get his bearings. Eventually, he pulled a spread sheet from the drawer of his desk which he had printed just before leaving on Friday. He was determined to get down to business.

Billy couldn't begin to concentrate on his work. He fidgeted, paced, went to the bathroom at least a dozen times, one time sitting in a stall for over twenty minutes in rapt, if frenzied, thought. As lunchtime approached, he slipped past Director Blackledge's office without being noticed, went down the stairs, and hopped on his bicycle for the ten minute ride across town.

Then he stood waiting for Natalie at the entrance to the building where she worked. It was almost noon. Her schedule was somewhat irregular, but he had a feeling — rather he clung to a desperate hope — she would be coming out any minute.

Natalie stepped through the door with several of her Seminole colleagues. She was sharing a laugh with a porcine-shaped girl Billy didn't recognize, who wore her hair like Miss Piggy and giggled like fish-tank oxygenator. Billy came up behind them and fell in step.

Natalie seemed to have eyes in the back of her head under her bobbed hair. She immediately whipped around and did nothing to disguise her displeasure.

"Can't this wait until later?"

"Hey! It's great to see you too. I figured you—"

"Okay, Billy. Let's not get started." She turned to her associate. "Margo, this intruder here is my husband. We'll do this some other time. Tomorrow maybe. Okay? Sorry. Anyway, happy belated birthday."

"Sure sure. Same time same place. Thanks."

Natalie roughly hooked her arm through Billy's and proceeded to steer him away from her co-workers, putting as much distance from them as quickly as she could. Her discomfiture was as thick as coal tar, her disposition as black.

Billy tried to lighten the mood.

"Who was that? The office image consultant?"

"None of your business."

"Are you hungry? We could have lunch and talk."

"I was on my way to lunch with my friend until you unilaterally nixed that. It was her birthday yesterday. Billy, we have nothing to talk about."

"Can you just cool it a bit? I didn't think it would be a problem—"

"Billy, everything is a problem."

"What are you in the mood for? Italian? Chinese?"

"I'm not hungry any more. I'm in the mood for you to grow up. Treat me with some respect. Maybe stop whining like a wounded ferret."

She abruptly turned and pushed them into a Hoagie shop. It was crowded but they found two stools by the storefront window facing the street.

Billy was determined to get things back on track.

"Believe me. I understand! We're totally on the same page. That's why this is so urgent. Why I needed to talk to you right now. I've been doing a lot of thinking. And I think … no … I'm sure now, without any doubt whatsoever, I've got it all worked out."

"I'm sure you do. But as far as I'm concerned, it doesn't change anything. It's settled but for the details. Whatever you say won't make a bit of difference. It's time to move on, Billy. Deal with it."

"No! Please, Natalie! Don't be so hardheaded. Nothing is final until it's final. Hear me out. You are what you are. It wasn't what I had reason to believe. But that's not your problem. It's mine. That's what I've figured out. I love you and I don't need to put qualifiers on that. It's a fact. I mean, yes, I can't deny it. The whole thing, you know, with you and Pam caught me completely off guard. But I don't *per se* have a problem with it. I never have. You have this close friend Pam. A very close friend. So what? Your friendship doesn't have to … to … hurt me. Hurt us. It doesn't take away from what we've had. And will continue to—"

"Billy, what exactly do you want?"

"I want us to be together. Be happy. You and I."

"Jesus, Billy. Even without a dick, Pam is more of a man than you are."

"You asked me what I wanted to do, didn't you? I gave you an answer."

"Yeah, the wrong answer."

"But like I said, I can live with it. It just took me a while to … to … come to terms with it. To get it straight in my head."

"You are a pathetic loser. It's over. And that's that."

"But—"

"I thought maybe you would be at least mature enough to respect me, my time, maybe give me some space. But after today, I can see you're hopeless. Don't ever do this again. Ever! Don't try to contact me. No middle-of-the-night calls. No surprise ambushes. Nothing. You'll hear from me if anything needs to be said. Have you got it?"

"But, can't we—"

"No, we can't."

Natalie almost broke the door of the sandwich shop off of its hinges, she slammed it so hard on her way out. Billy watched her as she crossed the street. She looked like she was crying.

Billy sat stunned. He had completely failed. This turned out to be a bad idea.

Real bad.

One thing he had to admit.

He showed some real talent here.

He was really good at something.

Fucking up, that is.

Two days after his crash and burn at the Hoagie shop, Billy came home and found a letter-size envelope taped to front door.

He sat down at the kitchen table and read.

> Billy,
>
> I was thinking that if you aren't going to live in the house forever, we should put it on the market. We can just split 50/50 whatever we make. I don't want to live there. Way too much responsibility.
>
> Let me know if this is the way you want to go. You can call me at work.
>
> Sorry I can't talk to you in person. I just can't handle it right now.
>
> Love always,
> Natalie
>
> P. S. Don't read into the "Love always", okay? I will always love you as a person, just not as the man for me. We can still be friends?

What bullshit! Friends? How typical. How simplistic. How inane.

It had always grated him when he'd hear some guy or girl talking about their split with someone. How the other person had totally ruined their relationship, messed up their minds, destroyed their desire to ever fall in love again, nearly driven them to suicide, on and on, and then say, 'But we're still friends.' What a crock of shit! Didn't anyone have the honesty and the courage to say what they really felt. 'I hope they ship the motherfucker to Afghanistan and he sits on a land mine.' Or 'I hope she catches herpes from this new guy and dies of starvation when all of the sores seal her lips together.' Or 'I wish I had performed Lorena Bobbitt corrective surgery on him when I had the chance.' Or 'I really hope she finds the kind of man she deserves — Ted Bundy or Jack the Ripper would be perfect.'

Ugly sentiments to be sure. But at least real. Not just more of this empty, hypocritical PC crap that was poisoning the world with smiley faces and repressed homicidal fantasies.

Sell the house?

At first Billy felt immobilized by the thought. A neutral paralysis because, in fact, whatever feeling he had for the place had indeed been neutralized by the events of the recent past.

Yet, it didn't take long for him to acknowledge that, even though this was probably prompted mostly by monetary considerations and Natalie's desire for a total split, selling the house provided him with a significant bonus of sorts — some easing of a good portion of his immediate agony.

The catalyst for most of the suffering and depression he was experiencing was living in that house. Obviously it wasn't the main source. That finger pointed right at Natalie herself. But the house had so much history. They had lived there for the bulk of their marriage. Every pot and pan, every piece of furniture, every picture and throw rug, utensil and appliance, even the tiny crack in the tile next to bathroom sink — Natalie had dropped a large container of bubble bath beads — all of it reminded him of what they had once had, and now was gone.

This wasn't anything intentional on his part. In fact, he made every effort not to think about any of it. Hence, the daily dash for the whiskey almost as soon as he walked in the door. Anything to put a wall between him and the painful truth of Natalie's absence.

But no matter how hard he tried, just being there made it impossible.

Billy couldn't believe how helpless he felt and how far he had sunk. He was becoming a pathetic self-pitying drunk. What a cliché! Man loses wife, drowns his sorrows in gallons of cheap wine or white label whiskey.

Well, at least he could take credit for buying the good stuff. No generic brain embalmers for Billy Green. Canadian Club and his latest preferred poison, Stolichnaya Vodka, both as effective at emptying his wallet as emptying his mind. And destroying his brain cells.

Which reminded him. He went into the kitchen and took the vodka out of the freezer — he could drink it straight up if it was sufficiently chilled — and poured himself a tall glass of what was reputed to be the absolute smoothest vodka available in America. The smoothest? Whether it was or not, it worked for him.

That night he again got blinding, stinking, falling-down, incoherently, unforgivingly drunk.

Approaching midnight, in a near blackout stupor, hanging like a rag doll in a bathtub of now lukewarm water, with an empty bottle of Stolichnaya in his left hand, he made his decision.

There is no way with all of the orphaned objects of a once beautiful relationship staring back at him, turning his home and former seat of marital bliss into an a depressing museum of emptiness and abandonment, there is no way sitting and staring at all this stuff, remaining entombed within the walls that contained it, that he was going to ever get any peace of mind.

He needed to get out of this house.

Yes, Natalie. The answer is YES!! Let's sell the motherfucker! The sooner the better!

He raged on. His alcohol-addled mind was in overdrive, a few neurons still firing away across the vodka-diluted consommé in his cranium.

Regardless of the sale of the property, he wasn't going to spend one more minute in this house than he had to. He would sleep in the park, or camp at the local KOA campground, even remain sitting upright in the drivers seat of his car.

Whatever it took.

He needed out. ASAP.

Billy really had nowhere to go. No real friends. Not the kind who he could ask to stay with. Yes, he had colleagues at work and a vast pool of acquaintances and socializing types. People to drink and hang out with. Do the restaurant thing. Go bowling or to an art exhibition. But not crash on their living room sofa.

So much for that.

What passed for Billy's immediate family lived a thousand miles away. That wouldn't have been an option anyway.

It was late. Too much to think about with a clear head, much less one which was functionally incapacitated until he stopped dowsing it with alcohol and got some rest.

Billy fell asleep. In the bathtub. He would wake up early next morning with a slight shiver, a huge headache, the harsh direct rays of a rising sun screaming through the east-facing window, and his hands and feet pruned like a mummified corpse. He had spent the entire night submerged in the now cold bathwater.

Still inebriated and needing to be somewhat in working order before showing up at Habitat — though he had long suspected several of his co-workers regularly showed up stoned — Billy drank three strong cups of coffee in quick succession.

He walked into his office shortly before 9 am. He wasn't sure exactly how he was going to go about finding a new place to live. But there was certainly one matter he could take care of immediately.

If she was true to form, Natalie would already be at her desk. He dialed her direct line.

"Natalie Green. May I help you?"

"I'm with you. Let's sell it."

"I'll get the ball rolling."

"Thanks, Natalie."

"My pleasure."

Practical Magic

So that's how it all ends.

Billy was sitting in his motel room thinking. Thinking about something Natalie had said way back in college — well, it really wasn't that long ago even if it seemed like an eternity — something she said the first time they got together socially and a few times after.

Kind of a tongue-in-cheek remark. But it stuck with him.

And how will it all end?

Now he knew.

Billy was out of the house. He left most of his belongings there. He only brought along a few changes of clothes, basic toiletries, two novels he had been intending to read for some time, his laptop computer, and his briefcase, which looked quite professional but contained nothing of importance. For sustenance he included three bottles of apricot brandy — he had again switched his drink of choice and this one satisfied as well the raging sweet tooth which had possessed him the last couple nights — and a can of Pringles.

He had no idea how long he would be at his new digs, a modestly priced but clean motel. He didn't care. He was living one day at a time, as they say.

The plan was to look around for a studio apartment of some sort. Something small and cozy. Maybe down in New Hudson close to the Habitat office. Billy Green's little bachelor pad.

Move in. Regroup. Make a fresh start.

It would never happen. But Billy didn't know that at the time.

The Francine Motel wasn't all that bad. He felt like he was on the lam. In a way he was. Running from a reality that had been stalking him like an assassin.

His room was small but sufficient. It had cable TV and room service, even if the food was abysmal. It would do for now.

The finalization of the divorce would take a couple months. All of the details of their finances would not be settled until after the New Year.

Predictably, Natalie wasted no time. She put the house on the market within a couple days of his telephoned nod of assent, using a local Century 21 realtor. The house wouldn't actually sell for almost eight months. They did get an offer two weeks after the house went up for sale. But it dragged on for months, with the prospective buyer having problems getting financing. That deal fell through. Ultimately it would take a while for the big payoff to finally materialize. But there was plainly a lot of interest in a home with so much history and character. Eventually it would happen.

Over the relatively short course of their home ownership, Billy and Natalie had done quite well. They had bought it for a modest $235,000 and with both of them working, not only kept up the regular installments, but made additional payments against the principal of their mortgage. It added up and got the loan down to just over half of the original amount. And of course, they had put $100,000 down on the house in the first place.

While Newburgh was overall not that up-scale — it was no White Plains or Nyack — or in line for significant gentrification, on average the economy was doing fine. The value of their home had steadily increased at over 5% a year since they bought it. The upshot of all of this was that when they would finally sign the closing papers to sell it for $266,500 and pay off the bank, they would have a tidy sum to split between them. After paying off two jointly-held credit cards, a couple other miscellaneous bills, the final utility bills, a dentist bill, then taking care of a few other odds and ends, they would divide what was left right down the middle and each pocket $81,800.

Natalie took care of everything. Billy completely trusted her, and just went along for the ride. Regardless of their breakup and divorce, and a few occasional bitter exchanges of words, right up to the end she proved to be meticulously honest and fair about all of the material aspects of their relationship and its dissolution.

It would all be over and done with by this time next year.

Billy could barely think about tomorrow much less next year. He was living in a parallel universe, its timekeeper working off a completely different standard. In this parallel universe, his concerns were much more immediate and on a much smaller scale — just what he could manage. Taking stock of his situation ...

He was abysmally alone.

He had his room at the Francine.

He had cable TV with two movie channels.

He had two books which he continued to put off reading.

He had his bottles of apricot and peach brandy.

He had his job at Habitat For Humanity.

He did indeed report daily for work, if you could call work: his distracted, seemingly random shuffling of charts and bar graphs on his monitor; his feeble attempts to come up with the required numbers through complicated formulas he must have known, but mostly just stared at as if looking at an anonymous person at a bus stop; and the almost nonsensical summation reports he was mechanically churning out, then hiding from the scrutiny of his boss, consequently producing hollow excuses more effectively than producing solid results.

He just couldn't concentrate and it showed.

One evening, after achieving the distilled clarity of a brandy buzz — which dissolved the jagged rococo of the day and rendered his motel room as a pleasant mescal blur — Billy pondered his professional options. Sometime about halfway through watching *Rambo II* with the sound muted, he knew what he had to do.

Next day Billy quit his job. At the rate he was going, it was only a matter of time before he would get fired anyway. The quality of his work was disgraceful. He could see no prospects of it improving. His heart just wasn't in it anymore. Quitting was a win-win situation. He didn't need them and they probably didn't need him. Not this version of him.

As if to confirm his worse suspicions, they raised no serious objections. Director Blackledge actually looked somewhat relieved.

"I know you've had a lot on your mind. Personal things. This is of course very regrettable. You've made some outstanding contributions here. Effective as of when, Billy?"

"How about the end of the week?"

"Hey, if it makes life easier for you, you can leave right now. No problem. Need a box for your personal stuff?"

That was cold.

Billy didn't need to worry about burning bridges. The bridge was long gone.

Now Billy needed to make some bigger decisions.

Most importantly, he needed to decide if he should stick around Newburgh, or make a fresh start elsewhere. His gut told him he should leave. But the evil whiny voice inside his head — the one that always chatters away to a person when they are at their weakest or most desperate, cajoling, taunting, pleading, whimpering and howling, always opting for the worst possible choice — that little voice kept prodding Billy to stay put. He was sorely tempted. Not because he was partial to Newburgh, but because he was haunted by the completely unfounded and fanciful notion that if he stayed, there might be some chance that he and Natalie would get back together. This was, of course, a pitiable fantasy.

Natalie had already made her decisions and was squarely on the road to implementing them. She made it crystal clear that she was going to stay in Newburgh, and keep her same job. She had even once mentioned going back to her maiden name, and it was self-evident she would continue living with Pam.

Except for brief cut-and-dry phone calls to take care of various sundry items of business — close bank accounts, split household goods, and so on — they didn't talk. Natalie was pleasant enough on the phone, matter-of-fact, helpful, cooperative and efficient. But when the matter at hand had been taken care of, it was good-bye and click. She didn't want any kind of confrontation, nor did she want to chit chat or chum up to Billy. Those days were obviously long gone.

But numbed by his pain and emptiness, Billy still found room to ignore the obvious and continue to believe there had to be *something* which would turn things around with her. Such is dumb desperation. Such is the dysfunction inflicted by torment and self-delusion.

Billy knew where Natalie now lived. Soon after they got married, Pam had invited them over a couple times for an evening of dinner and television. Pleasantries all around. They were such buds back then.

Looking back on that now was humiliating. Infuriating! He was so stupid! Clueless! Why couldn't he see at the time what was going on? Why didn't he even suspect?

Thinking back now, there were many occasions when Natalie would make an impromptu visit to Pam's place by herself. He would sit at home, sipping his beer, reading a book, listening to music, watching the Sports Channel, scratching his balls now that he temporarily was afforded the privacy to do so, just cruising the slow cruise. A couple times he wondered why Pam so rarely came to their house. What were they doing over at her apartment that they couldn't do here?

Now he could easily imagine. Much too easily.

When Natalie returned home, did they ever have sex? Now that he thought about it, he didn't recall that they did. Natalie would never be in the mood, or had a headache, or needed to get her sleep. Of course! She had probably just had three orgasms on the end of Pam's tongue. Why would she need Billy? If he had just plugged Pam three times, he wouldn't feel much like fooling around either.

Yes, it did all make sense. It's so easy to add things up after the fact. Hindsight...20/20.

In the midst of torturing himself with the twisted, maddening reconstruction of events better left buried and forgotten, the light bulb finally came on for Billy.

Actually it was two light bulbs.

First, he accepted that Natalie and Pam were a permanent item. That being the case, he realized that if Natalie continued to see Pam — especially if Billy gave the affair his blessing — Natalie would never need Billy the way he needed her. It's easy to suppose that the love between a man and a woman, and a woman and a woman, are so different from one another that they don't compete. But people — male or female — only have so many orgasms in them. And they can only feel so much love. No matter how you cut it, when someone has two things going on at the same time, one takes away from the other. So the jealousy and frustration he was feeling now, thinking about Natalie and Pam together back then, would be repeated again and again, day after day, night after night. He would always wonder if he was getting his fair share. No! He would always know he *wasn't* getting his fair share. Because he wanted it all. And Pam would always come to the table and be filling her plate. There was no way he would ever be able to convince himself that Natalie was truly and totally committed to him. *That* would royally suck. Considering how much he loved her and consigned every cell in his body to her and her alone, devoted every moment of his waking life thinking about her and trying to find new ways of showing her how much she meant to him — yes indeed, having anyone around who could just saunter in and say, *"Sorry dude, my turn!"* — that would really <u>truly</u> suck.

He toasted this first epiphany by pouring himself more apricot brandy.

Second, people value what they can't have. He was doing it right now, beating himself up over a woman who could find the time to go to the real estate agent with him to sign some papers, but didn't have the time or interest to utter four simple words along the way: *"How are you, Billy?"* No, he couldn't have her. But why should he want to? Why did he so desperately and fatally want someone in his life who valued him so little?

Was it because he couldn't have her?

Probably.

There was corollary to this too. Maybe he had been so available to her, *that* became the reason she didn't appreciate him any more. He sure made it easy! Here I am, babe. Always here. Mr. 24/7/365. You don't have to think about it, be thankful for it, worry about it, work for it. He had made himself as commonplace as a cheap doormat. Nothing special here. Walk all over me.

Two epiphanies in one night! He poured another glass of brandy. This stuff is amazing!

All of which told him what he had to do — had to do immediately before he got cold feet or second thoughts. If he waited, the tiny whiny voice would take over again and muddy his brain and paralyze him against action. The delusional fantasies would start to loop in his head and he'd be right back to ground zero. He couldn't handle any more of it. He just couldn't handle it.

It was time to move on.

Immediately. If not sooner.

Away from Newburgh.

Away from Natalie.

Go! Go! Go! Go!

But ... where?

Irony Is Wasted on the Wicked

Billy packed everything he had with him in a canvas duffel bag and checked out of the motel.

Then he drove the car back to the house and parked it in the drive. As he was leaving, he stopped and looked at one of the fliers the real estate agent had placed in the box mounted to the Century 21 sign in the front yard. Pretty impressive!

Perfect place for a young couple to begin their dream. Good luck with that.

He put the flier back and started walking.

When Billy got to the center of town, he stopped at the ATM machine of his bank. When he referenced his and Natalie's joint savings account, exactly half of the balance he recalled being there two weeks ago remained. He went inside and withdrew $3000 cash. That would hold him for a while.

He continued walking till he reached Broadway. He suddenly felt the urge to get a bite to eat. He really hoped no one would spot him. But at the risk of running into Natalie or anyone else he knew, he slipped into the Capri Restaurant. It wasn't her favorite haunt, but the danger was that it was across the street from Anna's, a place she loved and did frequent.

Billy surveyed the place. Natalie wasn't there. He requested a table in the back. The lunch hour rush was over. There was no problem finding a spot which offered some privacy — a table definitely not visible from the street — where he could plop down to have a luxurious lunch, and think about what came next.

He ordered baked Alaskan salmon in a crème sauce, steamed okra in a buttery lemon-honey gravy, a baked potato with sour cream and chives, all which came with fresh cut fruit salad on the side. He would sip on strawberry lemonade with his meal, have filtered coffee as the final touch.

Just as the waitress thanked him and took his menu, he looked over and saw Annie Roberts come strutting through the door. She scanned the nearly empty restaurant for friendly faces but instead found his.

She arched her eyebrows and smiled her professionally-whitened smile, then started to walk in his direction.

Of all the people he could have run into today, his last day here in Newburgh, during these last few moments when he had to systematically inject some planning and purpose back into his life, critical preparation for running off half-cocked and confused, why did it have to be her? The Amazon army of one.

He hastily steeled himself for her twisted games and subtle manipulation.

"Billy Green. Newburgh's newest eligible bachelor." So much for subtlety. "You don't look very good. Are you getting enough sleep?"

"I sleep till I wake up. But I have to say, it's hard telling the difference these days."

"A ruffled mind makes a restless pillow."

"Is that original?"

Was that a sneer? This was new. He had never seen her drop her lacquered Miss Congeniality act.

"I have to say that Natalie sure looks good these days."

"Are you saying that as a cosmetician or a lesbian?"

"My my. You are cranky. Or maybe homophobic. Not jumping in bed with every man that comes along doesn't make me a lesbian."

"Licking another woman's cunt does."

Annie just smiled a bored smile. The weary disdainful smile of a champion boxer who looks with pity at the pathetic opponent he will in the next few minutes effortlessly proceed to demolish without even breaking a sweat.

She was back to being bulletproof.

She glanced at the duffel bag sitting next to the table.

"Going somewhere?"

"I guess you could say that. Aren't we all? You're not going to stand in that same spot for the rest of your life, are you?"

She smiled. Not at him. But at her own capacity for faking pity.

"So what are your plans, Mr. Green? Seems like your options are rather open these days."

What was her agenda? Was she taunting him? Was she just toying with him? Did she think she was prying some deep dark secrets out of him — grist for the town's gossip mill — information he would gladly volunteer just to end this conversation and be rid of her? Or was she just randomly exercising her shrew prerogative?

"I am thinking about becoming a nun."

"Seems kind of drastic."

"It's been a lifelong dream. It goes all the way back to Catholic school."

"I can see it. Yes. The piety. The asceticism. It's all right there in your eyes."

Why was she so intimidating? He wanted so badly to slap her down. But he couldn't think straight. She was like an anesthetic dart to his brain.

"So Annie. You think it's a good idea? The nun thing. You often use your guiding hand and the altruistic possibilities of your higher calling to help people realize their fullest potential. Selling cosmetics."

That was pretty weak.

"I see. And you're comparing what I do to what? What exactly is it that you do now?"

Did she have some sixth-sense, some uncanny intuition? Or was it on this morning's edition of a local news broadcast that he had quit his job?

"I'm leaving all this behind. I'm becoming an astronaut."

"Is this before or after becoming a nun?"

"Haven't decided. Keeping my options open."

Annie pulled out the vacant chair next to him and slid it close to his own. Then she sat down directly facing him. In an audacious move he seemed incapable of preventing, she took his right hand in both of hers and looked intently into his eyes.

"Billy. You've been through hell. People — probably you too — think I am callous. But I do feel for you. Natalie's a precious human being. Of course you don't want to lose her. Who could blame you? But listen, Billy. You're an intelligent, charming, extremely good looking man. This is not the end for you. I know this is hard to hear and understand right now, but this is a new beginning."

"You're right, Annie. And I'd like to begin immediately. I know exactly what I want to do. Right now, I mean."

"What's that, Billy?"

"I want to fuck you. How about it? Do you want to fuck me?"

"Maybe I do. I don't know. I hadn't thought about it. But you know what?"

"What?"

"It's not going to happen."

"It's not going to happen? Why not, Annie? Why not? I want to really get to know you. But to understand and fully appreciate you, I need to get inside the sticky stench of your birth canal. Deep inside. Let's go someplace right now and fuck. Fuck and fuck hard. Come on. For me. For you. For America."

She stroked his had and stared directly into his eyes.

"No, Billy. It's just not right. And do you know why?"

"No. I have no idea. Why? Tell me why, Annie Roberts."

"It's simple, Billy. I'm just not good enough for you." She let go of his hand and stood up. "Bye bye. You take care."

"But Annie I was—"

"Have a nice day."

She turned around and with her trademark tight-ass-swinging sashay walked away.

She got halfway to the front of the restaurant and suddenly burst into a loud, raucous laugh.

Annie Roberts just laughed and laughed. She laughed going out the door. She laughed going across the street. She laughed walking down the opposite sidewalk. She was still laughing when Billy lost sight of her.

Billy had never felt so stupid in his life. Sure, in the past he had been hurt, frightened, angered, humiliated. But now he felt thoroughly and completely stupid. He knew he was intelligent. But in this very moment he felt like the biggest dumbfuck in the world.

The waitress brought his order. He stared at it and it looked amazing. But he had absolutely no appetite. He asked for his check. It came to $15.87. He left a twenty and walked out.

It was rare to see a taxi in Newburgh. But as luck would have it, Billy spotted one on his side of the street about two blocks away. It was parked and the driver seemed to be in a heated discussion on his cell phone. He was just hanging up and cursing up a storm as Billy approached. Yes, he was available. Yes, he could take Billy to the train station. Yes, get in.

They had to head back north through town, but fortunately the driver took Robinson, several streets west of Billy's and Natalie's house. He had no desire to see it now. Or ever again.

They crossed the Hudson River on the Beacon Bridge. The driver pulled up to leave Billy off at the train station. Billy dropped a twenty onto the front seat — which significantly improved the driver's mood, since the fare was only $8.70 — and got out.

He found a bench with a clear view of the board with train schedule postings and sat down.

On the ride over, and even now as he sat there needing to come up with a plan or at least his next move, he was consumed by self-loathing. Not only had he failed to put the great Annie Roberts in her place, but he had stooped to the lowest of the low in handing her his humiliation and defeat. What was he turning into? Everything that had just come out of his mouth wasn't worthy of the most ignorant scumbag on the planet. You can take the boy out of Detroit, but you can't take the Detroit out of the boy. Is that what it came down to?

Finally, he calmed down enough to bring himself to look at the schedule.

Northbound trains for Poughkeepsie, Kingston, Catskill, Hudson, Albany, Schenectady.

Southbound trains for Peekskill, Croton-Harmon, Hastings-on-Hudson, Yonkers, Riverdale, University Heights, Harlem, Grand Central Station.

What was in Poughkeepsie? Kingston? Or Albany for that matter? Other than a bunch of crooked politicians.

Billy boarded the next southbound train.

The klack-klack, steady metallic hum, gentle rhythmic swaying of the train — a lumbering lullaby of serenading steel — conspired with the overpowering pull of gravity, to weigh down his eyelids, face and head. In twenty minutes or so, he was fast asleep and floating in the loose cracks of realities improperly joined.

So you want to be a millionaire! For the big prize, just answer this question. What is the most exciting, daunting, chaotic, culturally rich, morally bankrupt, unpredictable, sensual, artistic, intense, exhilarating, enervating, materialistic, power mad, sexy, mesmerizing, distracting, inspiring, confusing, ultimately rewarding city in the world?

There's only one place I can think of.

And what place would that be?

It's ... New York City.

You're a winner!

Chapter Five

ESCAPE TO NEW YORK
Early Autumn 2007

The Big Apple

The first thing that happened when Billy arrived in New York City was he got pickpocketed.

He had gotten off the train and was walking through the cavernous lobby of Grand Central Station, when an attractive well-dressed blond bumped into him. She had a distinctively Australian accent.

"Sorry, mate."

The girl had beautiful eyes and an innocent smile. The bump was but a brief encounter. He'd take what he could get. That was the first female human contact he had experienced in quite some time.

"No problem."

He started to continue on his way but she stopped him.

"You might need this."

She was holding out his wallet.

"I ... I don't understand ... did I drop it?"

He took it back and slipped it in the back of his pants. This time he did the button on the pocket flap.

"No, I nicked it. Like to keep up my chops. I never know when I'll need them again."

"You should've kept it. There's over $800 in it. So is this a hobby?"

"Just something to do on my lunch hour. It's kind of a public service. My way of letting frullibles like you — that's fresh and gullible — that you've got to keep on your toes. You're in the Big Apple now. Anything could happen. Say, lad. You've got a really nice face. Too bad I've got a guy. Have a nice day."

That was Billy's welcoming reception to the city he would call home now and ... forever? Who could say? He'd just roll with it and let the cards fall where they may.

He wondered if it was that obvious that he was new here. She had called him a gully or guppy, something like that. Guess he didn't need to ask. He probably had that wide-eyed look of wonder that any Midwestern doofus had impaled on his face when confronted with the ... the *hugeness* of it all. The vast intensity. The pulsing frantic energy. The insomniac intoxication. The mouth-agape awe. The crazed dazzling time-lapse montage of each and every moment. Most of all, the never diminished or depleted numbers of diverse and fascinating people.

Miss Fast Fingers from Australia being a case in point.

The most bland person in New York made the most interesting person in Detroit look like a body that had washed up on the polluted shores of Lake Erie. Or a desiccated corpse left in the trash dumpster of the River Rouge foundry.

Maybe not even that interesting.

A dead person had an excuse for being boring. Midwesterners couldn't come up with one.

But back to the pressing issues of the moment.

Billy needed to find a place to live — an allegedly impossible task, so he'd heard.

This was maybe only his fourth or fifth time here. He had come down for an afternoon and evening a couple times with Natalie. Once with Natalie and his mom. They were all very superficial visits, typically rush-throughs on a weekend. He had a thin grasp of the city. That of a blithe tourist with a disposable camera and a subway map.

He remembered Greenwich Village. It seemed like a good place to start.

Billy spent his first week living in a transient hotel, south of Houston on the edge of the West Village. Not the most glamorous way to begin his honeymoon with the City. He felt like a fugitive.

He kept looking.

He finally signed a lease with a Chinese businessman and slumlord — if you could call a half-page handwritten agreement on the back of an old Cantonese restaurant menu a legally binding document. It was for a 3rd floor studio flat on Henry Street in the Lower East Side.

It turned out that the rats in the area had no problem with heights. They apparently regarded the rickety fire escape scaffolding which ran directly up his outside wall as a jungle gym. That same evening in an attempt to get some fresh air, he left the one window open which wasn't painted shut with layers of dried industrial gray enamel, and woke up to find the place crawling with them — rodents with a lot of survivalist moxie and New York attitude.

They refused to leave. So he would have to.

Cantonese menu lease be damned, he was out the door the next morning.

Luck was with him and he stumbled into what would be his home for many months to come.

Literally stumbled.

He had been beating the pavement for hours. The sun had been beating on him for hours. Now he was wandering the area north of Houston in the sooty East Village. Purely randomly he chose a short step-down to the lower level of an apartment building to get in the shade and take a drink of bottled water. He lost his footing and plunged headfirst to the landing below, rolling with a loud thud against a door. It opened and a very old, extremely fat Italian lady stood there, wearing a bathrobe which left exposed her hairy legs and grimy, leathery feet. An overpowering combination of garlic and fat-lady perspiration exploded from the dwelling. She sounded Sicilian.

"Can I help you?"

"I'm looking for a place to live."

"The basement flat next door maybe you like. It is for rent. Want to see?"

One part exhaustion, one part frustration, created a delirium which rendered the tiny place in Billy's tired, dust-filmed eyes, the answer to his prayers. Prayers he hadn't even prayed. Which was proof that fate must have intervened on his behalf. Things were looking up.

He dropped his backpack on the tattered slipcover of a couch which took up half of the microscopic living room, then dropped the $1100 security deposit and first month's rent into the outstretched hand of Mrs. Rosario Lucchesi, widowed landlady and devout Catholic shut-in.

Billy's new home: 19 Avenue C, Apt A, New York, NY.

Apron Strings

Had Billy retrieved the forty plus messages on the phone back in Newburgh before it was disconnected, he would have discovered four messages — the last sounding panicky and distraught — from his mom. The most recent one said in no uncertain terms that she was worried sick about him, and wondered what could possibly have happened that he hadn't returned her calls. It just wasn't like him.

It wasn't. Indeed, as soon as he got settled into his new place, it finally hit him. He hadn't talked to her in weeks. She knew nothing of what had happened between him and Natalie.

He needed to call her right away. Of course, his apartment had no phone. He was just grateful it had running water and electricity. And no rats.

Now Billy faced a big decision. Not whether or not to call his mom. That was a given.

But whether he should buy a cell phone. Billy hated cell phones.

He had had one in Newburgh but forgot it more often than not. During his recent shuffling around town there, he forgot it for good. If the house hadn't sold yet, it was probably still on the dresser in the bedroom.

Screw it! He refused to join the people's army of cell phone toting grunts, walking the streets, riding the subways, cruising in taxis, eating in restaurants, slogging down martinis at happy hour, taking a dump, grabbing a quickie in a stairwell, making a bet at the off-track, and so on — the sum of activities which pre-occupied *homo erectus modernis* these days — all performed with a piece of electronics stuck to their ears.

He would get a standard, old-fashioned, big-heavy-clunky, sit-on-the-table, wire-to-trip-over, dependable-as-a-clothes-iron, metal-and-plastic, 20th Century, traditional landline telephone.

If there still was such a thing.

Of course, getting a phone could take a while.

Billy needed to call his mom immediately.

He threw on a light jacket — evenings were starting to become cooler — and headed out.

Miracle of miracles, Billy found a payphone that appeared to be in working order, though it showed the scars of many brutal attempts at burglary, desperate goes at pilfering whatever paltry pocket change it might contain.

He tried to get coinage from a nearby news stand but encountered resistance.

"Hey buddy! This ain't no fuckin' bank."

He finally got what he wanted by bribing the guy. He received $5 worth of quarters for a crisp new ten dollar bill.

Billy went back to the payphone, grabbing a city trash basket on the way. He turned it over, took a seat on it, and steadied himself.

This was going to be rough.

"Mom! It's Billy. I'm so sorry I haven't called."

"Billy!! Did you get my messages? I left you messages."

"No, mom. It's a long story. But no."

"Are you alright? Are you okay, Billy?"

"Well ... yes and no. That's part of the long story."

"Just so you're alive. I've been so worried about you. Really worried!"

"I've been worried about me too. I don't know how ... I don't know how to tell you this."

"Natalie! Something happened to Natalie. Is she okay?"

"She's probably fine. Mom. We split up."

"Split up? Oh no! Oh Billy. I'm sorry. But I'm sure it'll work out. People fight. It's all—"

"No, mom. It's over. She's filed for divorce. She won't be coming back."

"Oh Billy! You poor boy."

How could he explain it to her? In many respects, he couldn't explain it to himself.

But he tried.

Billy gave him mom a blow-by-blow account, best that he could, of the events of the past month or so. Not easy. In fact almost impossible. He had been in the center of a vortex of unexpected events which bordered on the surreal. This had rendered him so confused and incapacitated, so disoriented, swallowed by so much pain, it was hard to remember everything, or the order of events. Trying to capture and relate the essential details of his plunge from Heaven to Hell over such a short time, without breaking down and completely losing it, was all he could manage.

As Billy had grown to become an adult himself, his mom had proven to be open-minded, and she had always been a good listener. But Natalie's leaving him for another woman, the fact of her longstanding sexual and romantic relationship with another person who turned out to be her step-mother, her flagrant and unequivocal deception of Billy — essentially leading a double life for the entirety of their courtship and marriage — in the face of Billy's devotion to her, it was all too much for his mom. Even if she were an avid reader of gutter press tabloids like the National Inquirer, Star, and The Globe, even if she were a devotee of the reality-show sleaze that filled TV screens these days, even if she had religiously watched the Jerry Springer Show and similar trash television with its constant fare of deceptions and adultery, incest and pedophilia, fringe pathologies and general weirdness, even if she committed to memory the bizarre directorial efforts of whack movie makers like Jon Waters, Darren Aronofsky, and David Lynch, nothing could have prepared her for what he had just told her.

This was her Billy Boy.

Her favorite son.

Her baby.

"I don't know what to say, Billy."

"There's nothing to say. There's nothing anyone can do."

"You don't deserve this."

"I'm not sure anybody does. It's life. Fucked-up, yes. But it's the way it is."

"Do you want me to come out there? Maybe if I ..."

If she what? She couldn't think of anything. Her sentenced dangled in the electronic hiss of the thousand miles of copper wire between them.

Billy finally filled the silence.

"Listen. I'll be okay, mom. Really. I've got myself set up in New York City. The Big Apple!" He did his best terrible fake accent. "I'm uh Noo Yawker now!"

Billy gave her his new address and promised that as soon as his telephone was installed, he'd call and give her his number. He described his new apartment, embellishing a bit to allay her concerns for his safety and well-being, hoping to create a comfort zone for her protective maternal instincts. She would have been overcome with panic and paranoia if she actually *saw* the place and the neighborhood he lived in.

"Hey. How are you? How's the old man?"

"Fine. Just fine."

It was obvious she didn't want to talk now. She was very quiet.

"I'll call again soon. Love you, mom."

"You're a good boy, Billy."

"Bye, mom."

That was rough. But now she knew.

Even if she needed to know, Billy felt guilty. He knew the news both shocked and hurt her, and now she would be all worried, beating herself up trying to figure out what she could do to help. It just didn't seem fair to dump it on her but he knew he had no choice.

Billy thought about it all evening and came up with an idea that might make things maybe a little easier on her.

The next day Billy shaved, combed his hair, put on his best shirt, and sat in a photo booth he had noticed in front of a convenience market where he sometimes shopped. He smiled variations of his best smile through the flashes of the allotted five different poses.

At home he chose what he thought was the most convincing happy face of the five mug shots, then wrote 'Love, Billy' across his chest, and mailed it to his mom.

The idea was to show her he was healthy and generally happy, in spite of everything.

But moms are smart people. And Billy's mom was particularly sensitive to her Billy Boy. The photo didn't fool her at all. Though she appreciated the gesture — his kind concern for her feelings alone brought tears to her eyes — she could see beyond the superficial smile, the feigned good cheer, the goofy ebullience of his expression.

She just had to look at his eyes.

That told the real story. How much pain he had endured. How much despair had drained him of the joyful optimism of youth. How the scars of betrayal cut into his soul. How the beating heart of trust lumbered now. How the breathing of his love for himself labored like a defeated old man. How afraid he was. How lonely. How sad.

She could see it in those eyes.

It would be a long slow recovery.

Her beautiful boy had reached out. He had embraced the greatest adventure life could offer. To love and be loved. But innocently and blindly he had become a victim. His dream had turned on him. Mocked him. Wounded him. Her Billy Boy. Her favorite son. Her baby.

About ten days later, Billy got his first personal mail at his new apartment. It was from his mom. It said in her handwriting on the envelope, 'Do not fold, spindle or mutilate'.

She had responded in kind. A photograph. How had she talked his father into this?

But there it was. A picture of the two of them, cramped in the tiny photo booth like two overgrown teenagers.

His mom looked pretty darn good. She had obviously put on some weight, much needed after her battle with cancer. Her hair must have been colored. The generous portions of gray from the last time he had seen her were not visible. She looked happy.

But his dad! Oh my God! It was true. Full beard, hair down to his shoulders, thick black leather jacket, smiling like he had just come from a Grateful Dead concert.

Billy laughed so hard he thought he was going to suffocate. He laughed and laughed.

This was way better than a bottle of booze. It was the best he had felt in weeks.

And every time he thought about it?

He laughed some more.

Mom and dad.

His dad was a biker.

Did that make his mom a biker chick?

He laughed all the way to Dobberstein's Liquor Mart.

Bestsellers

Billy had a lot of time on his hands.

Lots and lots of time.

He didn't know anyone. He didn't particularly feel like knowing anyone right now anyway. Probably it was pretty mutual.

He didn't have a job. He didn't particularly feel like having a job. Obviously that would have to change. He had just enough money right now to get by for a while.

So he gave himself time. Time to do a lot of nothing.

This was good and bad.

Good because he had a lot of thinking to do, so much to sort out, priorities to set, a whole new life to create for himself. It was a rare moment in a lifetime —

one that most people would give an eyetooth for — where he had no pressures, schedules, responsibilities, or anything other than a limitless blank slate of possibilities, which he could fill with adventures, discoveries, wonder and magic, at his whim and will. He was a free and unfettered man.

Good ... but bad.

Bad because he hurt so much, was so disoriented he couldn't think, was damaged goods with not a clue as to how to begin the repair job, was restless and unfocused, and no matter what random and planned diversions he pursued, he found that the days often dragged on so slowly, that he kept pushing earlier and earlier the solace of his nightly inebriation. Last night it was barely 6:30 pm when he started his slog through the neighborhood bars, eventually stumbling into a liquor store just before midnight for a chaser pint of peppermint schnapps.

He looked like shit and felt like shit.

The immediate taunting torment of life in Newburgh and images of Natalie had stopped. They weren't right in his face anyway. But they were still in there. A black box of spiders ready to spring open and spread their venomous terror.

As proof, he was being revisited by a demon ailment from the past.

For several nights the sleeping disorder from his high school and freshman college years had come back. He couldn't remain asleep for more than two hours at a time, no matter how drunk he was when he fell unconscious into bed. Several times a night he bolted upright on the wrong end of a nightmare, like he had just been hit with a two-by-four. Some grotesque collage of Natalie, Pam, Annie Roberts would hang on the black wall of darkness, then dissolve, leaving him trembling and sweating, sometimes crying.

Last night had been the worst yet.

When he finally made himself get up after a final terror-filled nightmare of Natalie and Pam conspiring to kill him, no more rested than he had been when he went to bed — probably less — it was approaching noon. Ten hours under the covers but he felt like he had only gotten two hours sleep at best. As quickly as he could move his listless body, he took a shower, slipped on some clothes and made his way out into the streets for his daily ritual of wandering, an empty journey without purpose or plan.

He headed directly north into the heart of the East Village until he got to 8th Street, grabbed a small carton of orange juice from a convenience store, then started walking west.

Just before he got to Astor Place, he came across a new bookstore — at least it looked new compared to the other shops around — called The Book Worm. The front was all windows and displayed a huge selection of the books everybody was or should be reading.

Billy stood in rapt attention as he looked at the titles.

Lady of Grace: The Life and Times of Grace Kelly

Trans Fats, Just Say No!   When The FBI Comes To The Door

Zoned For Immortality   Diary of a Meth Lab Cook   The Orphan Chronicles

Permanent Slavery: The Common Man's History of Capitalism

Inside Swedish Porn   Wishing Stones and Trance Crystals   The Pharaoh's Omelette

Asthma and Anorexia: Symptoms of a Sick and Dying Generation

Vagina Warlords   Female Circumcision as a Modern Metaphor   The Pedo Files

Cosmetic Surgery For Dummies   Leadership Vacuums and Pollster Politics

Dictionary of Text Messaging Symbols and Abbreviations

Who Killed The American Dream?   TTUL *LOL!!*   Spam Your Way To Big Bucks!

BLAM! BLAM! BLAM! - Big Game Hunting in Equatorial Africa

The Hollywood Hills Zucchini Diet   Heartthrobs of Pro Wrestling Picture Book

Why Nobody Likes YOU!   My Life as a Siamese Twin - A True Story (Two Volume Set)

DIY DUI Legal Guide   Dropping Bombs: Eminem Spits the Sh*t Yo!

Bridges to the Pleiades: Utopian Colonies In Space

The Kitchen's On Fire and the Cat's In The Dryer: Life as a Single Mom

The Unauthorized Autobiography of Paris Hilton

As disorienting and unattractive as the window display was, Billy stepped inside. A very gay-looking young man, early to mid 20s, eyed him suspiciously from behind the counter. His concern that Billy was a potential shoplifter or a psychopath trumped any of his predispositions to make Billy feel welcome or to apply the antiquated customer-is-always-right dictum. Billy had to either be the enemy or irrelevant. The clerk was still deciding.

Billy walked the aisles for no better reason than to antagonize the froofy cashier. He wasn't looking for anything in particular and still had the two books beside his bed he had been intending to read now for over a year.

There were several posters around the shop advertising a new novel by some writer he had never heard of.

PETROCELLI

Everything you wanted to know and things you didn't about the trafficking of *young girls* into the sordid, violent world of the **sex trade industry**.

**Violent! Sexy! Tragic!
Gut-wrenching!**

Jesus H. Christ! People just couldn't seem to get their fill of this lurid crap. Sex and violence. Violence and sex. All over the newspapers, magazines, on TV. Everywhere you looked.

America had its national anthem. Its national bird. Its national tree. National emblem. Motto. Seal. Flower. Its national creed and colors.

Maybe it should have a national movie. It would be a no-brainer. The official national movie for the great and powerful United States of America?

American Psycho.

Billy had had enough literary fulfillment and moved on. He gave the cashier his best Downs Syndrome smile and exited the shop.

It was a pleasant enough day and the streets were filled with pedestrians, mostly young. Billy gathered from their dress they were probably mostly NYU students.

He stopped at a small café deli, settled in, and slowly sipped on a tall mug of coffee — their "best organic French Roast" — that set him back $2.00, while he pondered the general state of things. His life in particular.

Billy's head was hurting badly from last night's minimum daily requirement of draft beer and schnapps. Or was it the bookstore? Whatever the cause, it made it impossible to get serious about figuring anything out. Why was he trying anyway? What was there to figure out?

Natalie was history. Here he was in New York City.

Pretty straightforward.

He looked at the girl behind the counter who had served him his coffee. Young. Maybe 18. She had a shiny stud of some kind in her nose, dangly Pokemon character earrings — was she being ironic? — and a single small silver hoop through the piercing in her right eyebrow. Her hair was in long dreadlocks, though he had serious doubts as to whether they were real. She had an angry-sexy scowl on her face, attributable either to menstrual cramps or a real sense that she was completely at odds with the rest of the world. The scowl was endearing. It made him want to turn her long slim body over his knee and give her a spanking.

She noticed him staring.

His faux-angry-young-man charm seemed to have broken through the wall of alienation of a hostess in social quarantine. Smiling, she strolled over and offered to refill his cup — for free! — though the menu specifically listed refills as 90 cents.

"What brings you here so early in the day? You look like you could have used a few more hours of shut-eye."

"It's just my look. I'm perfecting a Dylan Thomas persona, right before he cashed it in. Whaddya mean early in the day? It's after two."

"You've been in here before. Usually late afternoon."

"I have?"

"They say Dylan Thomas had pretty much lost his mind at the end. Looks like you're doing a good job of following in his footsteps. I'm Celeste. And you are?"

"Billy Green."

"That's a pretty stupid name. You should change it. Mine used to be Mary. I always hated it. Way too New Testament. Too virginal."

"You're not a virgin?"

"Believe it or not, I am. But why advertise it?"

She leaned over to warm his coffee. She ended up warming Billy. Actually nearly scalding him. The pot slipped out of her hand and smashed on the table.

"Ohmigod! I'm sorry. Don't move. There's glass everywhere. I'll get something to clean this up. I'm so sorry!"

He was soaked. While the coffee was hot, it had to seep through his shirt and jeans before attacking him. It was uncomfortable but bearable. Billy didn't think his skin would peel off.

Celeste came back with towels, a whisk broom and bucket. Despite being flustered, she proved to be very efficient under pressure and had the mess thoroughly cleaned up in just a few minutes.

"I'm so sorry. You are a mess. What can we do? Do you want to change? But change into what? You could come to my place. It's only a couple blocks away."

Was she coming on to him?

No, Billy. Get a grip!

"No no. I'm fine."

"Really. There's a laundromat right next to my room. I'm so sorry ... uh ... what did you say your name was?"

"Frank."

"Don't hate me, Frank. It just slipped. This is my first day."

"I never would have suspected."

Billy aka Frank, thanked the virgin Celeste and headed back out in the street. There was a decent breeze, meaning his clothes would soon be dry and the coffee stain set indelibly.

A permanent macchiato memory of Celeste.

Formerly Mary. Still a virgin.

He had to admit. New York was a real adventure. The people. The craziness. The unpredictability. The sheer enormity of it.

Could anyone ever know this city in its entirety? Even if they spent their whole life in it?

Would anyone want to? It was such a mixed bag. Mixed and mangled and mulched.

Just like him.

Maybe he belonged here after all.

He was starting to get to know the subways. Great way to get around. Maybe not so clean. But extremely efficient. You could be anywhere in the city in minutes.

There was a subway entrance just ahead. He dropped into the underground and boarded an uptown express. A No. 4 train. Older model. Many layers of graffiti had been removed over the years, but faint ghosts of the street art and tagging could still be seen.

Clack. Clack. Clack.

Long stop at Grand Central Station.

59th Street.

Metropolitan Museum of Art.

86th Street. 125th.

Harlem. Why not?

He got off the train. The Harlem station was littered with copious amounts of trash, most of it snack food wrappers and beverage containers. He headed up the stairs.

Billy walked maybe two blocks along a main boulevard, in both directions. There was every conceivable kind of shop along the way. Barbers, butchers, dry cleaners, pawn shops, stationery shops, laundromats, fruit and vegetable markets, liquor stores, beauty salons, chicken and ribs joints, drugstores, small clothing stores, big second-hand stores. And there was every conceivable kind of person. Fathers with their kids in hand, suited businessmen, drunks with paper bags, moms pushing strollers, children playing, hustlers hustling, pimps pimping, loiterers loitering, old men with canes, young mini-skirted ladies with big asses, delivery men, off-duty guards, on-duty guards, boys and girls coming home from school.

One thing was quite obvious. He was the only white person in sight.

A blue NYPD squad car pulled up along side of him.

"Are you lost or suicidal?"

"A little of both."

"I'd suggest you get your white butt back to wherever you came from."

"Detroit?"

The officer laughed.

"Now there's a fucked-up town! If you survived Detroit, maybe you can handle this after all. But listen, funny guy. I really wouldn't push my luck if I were you. We're low on body bags at the precinct."

"Thanks, officer." To encourage the impression that he really appreciated the assistance, Billy pointed at the very subway entrance he had just exited. "That's the subway right there, right? I guess that's where I should be heading?"

"You're smarter than you look."

"Not everyone can go to college, sir."

Billy turned and walked leisurely to the subway station. So much for Harlem.

He got back on the train, a downtown local. Back to a whiter version of America.

What next? Ground Zero? Statue of Liberty?

He opted to return to the false comfort and forced solitude of his apartment.

Home sweet home.

After a long return trip — local trains stopped at every station — exhaustion was setting in. The boost from the coffee — Celeste you're the best — had long worn off. It suddenly dawned on Billy that he hadn't eaten all day. Proper nutrition was critical to a healthy functioning body. That should be his first priority.

But it wasn't.

He stepped into a liquor store and surveyed the brandy choices, which came in a wide variety of flavors, at a price he could afford. Let's see. Cherry? Apricot? Grape? Peach? Apple?

America. The land of abundant consumer options.

He had been leaning toward peach lately. But maybe to introduce some variation into his diet, he should go for either the cherry or the grape. Wait! Here's a cocoa-flavored brandy and it's only seventy cents more for a fifth. Cocoa it would be. Isn't the cocoa plant supposed to be a good source of vitamin C? And vitamin C is an anti-oxidant. Perfect.

What about food? Drinking on an empty stomach? Bad. Definitely not a good idea. And conveniently, right there was his favorite-of-late solid food.

The cashier handed him his change and Billy carried the bag with the fifth of cocoa brandy and two cans of Pringles — regular and avocado-flavored — back to his Avenue C basement apartment.

There was a letter in his mailbox.

Junk Mail

The letter wasn't addressed to him. It was addressed to Resident. Some sort of mass mailing. Nothing personal. He arbitrarily decided to open it before throwing it in the trash.

It turned out to be an ad for a local spiritual guru with an unusual name … Apocalypso.

We are all neighbors, all part of a cosmic family of animate material,
*all part of the energized plasma of the **Oneness** of*
All That Is and All That Will Be.

But beyond that we are actually neighbors.

*The **Ashram of the Urban Night**, founded to explore and spread the inspired*
*teachings of his Holiness, **Apocalypso Lama Bodhisattva**, is right*
here in the East Village. This flier has gone out selectively to
those of you who are in the proximity of the Ashram.

***Apocalypso** calls this the local community kingdom of*
divine light and perfection of purpose.

You are invited to a very special Open House:

Wednesday October 10th
- 7:30 pm -
635 1st Avenue

To receive Apocalypso's blessings and meet the staff and beatific brothers
of this urban order of enlightened mendicants,
just come as you are.

As the Divine Force created you.

The profundity didn't just end there.

On the back of the flier was a panel with some cryptic bastardized haiku of some sort.

> *"Nothing is sacred."*
> *"Everything is sacred."*
> *"Nothing is permanent."*
> *"This is an eternal truth."*
> *"There are no eternal truths."*

It reminded Billy of a mind-twister he had seen in a magazine one time.

> The below statement is true.
> The above statement is false.

He crumbled the flier into an aerodynamically efficient ball and made his best jump shot in the direction of the waste basket in his kitchenette. It landed on the stove.

He'd have to work on that.

The next day Billy received another letter. This one was addressed to Mr. Daniel Forsythe. He showed it to his landlady and she explained who Mr. Daniel Forsythe was.

"A drug addict. He's dead. That's how you got the place."

Brief and to the point.

"Thanks."

Since Forsythe wouldn't be claiming his mail within the foreseeable future, curiosity got the best of Billy and on the way back down to his apartment he tore the envelope open.

Another invitation. This was turning out to be the week for invites. What a popular guy.

This one actually piqued his interest.

It was for an art exhibition and reception with food and liquid refreshments, apparently a somewhat elegant affair, held in some fancy art space in Chelsea. The invitation was on glossy stock, printed in rich colors, about twice the size of a business card. It looked like the publicity handouts Billy had frequently seen since arriving in New York, promoting special night club events and raves, as well as gentlemen's clubs. The text was in big bold letters, over a white background with a huge pink hog that appeared to be dripping blood from enormous swollen teats on its underside. The exhibit was enigmatically titled ...

Shibboleth: War Crimes and Hog Futures

Catchy.

Billy wondered what it was with these New Yorkers.

First there was the pretentious, rambling invitation from the master prophet 'Apocalypso'. Now this awkward lump of cerebral poop. How about calling it something lucid? Accessible?

New Paintings by . . .

What a concept! Something a person could understand.

But why be so literal? Someone might actually show up.

Regardless, this might be something worth going to. The artist was supposed to be some hotshot contemporary genius. Billy needed to get out and meet people more interesting and better coordinated than virgin Celeste. If nothing else he needed a change of scenery. Harlem didn't work for him. The East Village was filled with shoe-gazers and existentialists. Many were shoe-gazing existentialists. An unfriendly, thoroughly humorless bunch.

Shibboleth was a week from tomorrow. Saturday 8 pm sharp. RSVP. He called and left a message — from his favorite telephone booth, of course, since his phone installation was in a long, impossible-to-predict queue.

Billy felt pretty good by the night of the artsy reception. By then, he had forced himself to cut down on his drinking and actually started eating real food. He had been jarred into a realization of how much he had physically deteriorated, when he stopped at a clothing store and tried on some clothes he thought he could wear to the party. He had lost three inches off his already slim waist, and when he tried on a button-collar shirt the size he had been wearing since college, he looked like a pencil-neck. The mirror didn't lie. If they weren't going to make *Shindler's List II*, he had no reason to go on like this. He bought the shirt and pants in his "healthy" sizes and resolved to fill them out by getting healthy again.

It was easier said than done. Over the coming weeks, it proved almost impossible to quit drinking, because he was still having so much trouble sleeping. Being drunk took some of the edge off of the nightmares. But then again, it killed his appetite, both during the evening binging and most of the next day, resulting in his weight loss.

With an incredible exercise of will power, however, he immediately started limiting himself to only a pint of booze a day, and made himself eat both a lunch and a dinner. He put on weight very slowly, since the sight of both greasy and high-carb food set his already-queasy stomach churning. But forcing himself to eat watery soups and garden salads was a start, and he slowly made progress.

Of course, he was still depressed, prompting him to seek out something to reinforce alcohol's palliative effects. Nearby Washington Square offered some effective options.

Billy wasn't going to jump feet first into needles or snorting. But inhaling and dropping were attractive alternatives.

Despite the presence of undercover cops, buying any of a vast array of psychotropic drugs, especially weed, was easier than getting in on a chess game at one of the numerous public chess boards distributed around the Square. There was always a small army of sleazy characters, usually with stringy unwashed hair. They were typically dressed in tight skanky jeans and denim jackets, regardless of the weather, and walked around with their hands in their pockets and their heads tucked down into their shoulders. They would amble over or veer close in passing, then without making eye contact mumble, *"Wanna buy some weed?"* or *"Hey man, I got some good shit for ya!"*

Good shit, indeed.

Billy was at first a little timid about reopening this door — Billy hadn't smoked marijuana since ... when?

Wow! It had to have been that one time, back in college his freshman year. His surprise birthday party.

In the intervening years, Billy had kept his body cannabis-free, which meant he currently had no tolerance for the drug. Smoking a joint after scoring some 'good shit' and returning to his Avenue C palace was like putting 120 proof vodka in the bottle of a newborn baby. But from what he could recall the next day, it felt pretty damn cool. He slept like that baby — the one sucking down the vodka — and while he had a serious case of brain lint, he had no hangover.

A little toke before dinner — which had the additional medical advantage of significantly increasing his appetite — and one or two later in the evening became his new routine. He often spent the wee hours of the evening, before euphoria segued into oblivion, with a can of Coke Classic at his side, a joint in one hand, and a novel in the other. He noticed that as the effects of the cannabis became more pronounced, it didn't matter whether he held the book upside down or right side up, an unexpected bonus.

The night of the art exhibition, Billy shaved, showered, put on his Sunday best — even if it was Saturday — smoked a little reefer to relax, skipped dinner figuring there would be much more inviting food at the event, checked one last time in the mirror for irregularities, and declared himself ready for his big New York social debut in.

When he marched up the few steps from his subterranean digs, there was a panhandler right there ready to pounce.

Coming up the stairs, Billy must have preemptively been holding his breath. If he had been in the intake phase of his breathing cycle, he most certainly would have been gagging, thus been given some advance warning of the old man's stench-filled lurking presence. Then again, maybe the joint was playing havoc with his olfactory sense.

He could sure smell the guy now. His body reeked, his breath reeked, his clothes reeked, his unwiped butt reeked.

As the pitiful old creature teetered back and forth, it was all the man could do to keep his eyes open, and steady them enough to pull Billy into loose focus.

Billy could certainly see *him* — much too clearly — a mangled human shell in a grotesque tableau of dereliction and decay.

The panhandler was maybe 50 years old but didn't look a day under 70. Even if he weren't stooped over in the unfolding time-lapse of imminent death, he was considerably shorter than Billy, and seemed to be addressing a speaker box in the center of Billy's chest.

"Give me some money for food."

"Please."

"Right."

Billy just wanted to get this over with, so he reached in his pocket and pulled out a bill from the inside of his fold of money. That should be a single. Indeed it was. He handed the old man the buck and started to move around him. The guy shook his head and handed it back. Billy got the message. He turned his back to the old man, pulled out his money and pealed off a five. The guy rolled his eyes and looked at him like he was dealing with Ebenezer Scrooge.

For a pathetic, thoroughly inebriated, brain-damaged, decrepit bum, the old man sure had an attitude.

Billy then handed the old guy a twenty. Finally satisfied, the panhandler walked away.

Billy stood there in disbelief. The old man just shuffled away in silence.

"Have you ever heard the phrase 'thank you', old man?

"I heard of it."

He just kept walking.

Twenty dollars lighter, Billy headed over to First Avenue where his chances of catching a taxi would be better. Competition was stiff but after only a few minutes, he was on his way.

This would be an evening which would ultimately change his life

He had no way of knowing that. He had very limited expertise.

Billy was certainly no expert on art either.

But as they say, he knew what he liked.

There was a lot to like and a lot to loathe.

And so much to choose from.

Yes, both in art and life.

Tonight was typical.

But not really.

Is it ever?

Chapter Six

THE TRAGIC OFTEN HILARIOUS IMPERFECTION OF IT ALL

Autumn 2007

Renoir Albertine Toulouse, Thumb Painter

Peter Toulouse was an expatriate film maker who left a trail of debts and whose departure from the U.S. caused among his friends and acquaintances a wide spectrum of emotions ranging from acrimony to indifference.

Perhaps deluding himself that memories were short and eventually all would be forgiven, meaning he could someday return to the States, he held on to his loft in Chelsea. No one knew exactly how he managed to keep up the exorbitant payments on the place, but the fact that he maintained a presence in Manhattan gave hope to those he owed money to that he had some substantial source of income, and that meant they would eventually be repaid.

The loft was still furnished with the fleeting stylishness of the late 90s — he had made his sudden and surreptitious departure in 1999 — but it held its own. The place was huge even by Chelsea standards, the perfect space for small exhibitions promoting the latest darlings of the New York art world, and parties attended by self-absorbed wannabees promoting themselves.

Peter's brother, Renoir Albertine Toulouse, had the keys to the loft and put it to good use.

Renoir was a pompous, self-important, but increasingly popular post-modern painter who used the cement sidewalks of New York for his extraordinary three-dimensional artworks. He applied paints using no brush, only his thumb. His right hand had in childhood been deformed by a fire — the fingers literally melted together — a life-altering event which paralleled that of Django Rhinehart. It was a handicap which was turned to myth-building advantage by him.

Sidewalk art had the intrinsic downside of being both temporary and averse to being transported to the parlors and business offices of self-proclaimed art connoisseurs, people who had enormous discretionary income to spend. Plus the city had enough on its plate without having to tear up chunks of concrete and ship them to the rich and the ultra rich of New York.

So while his early reputation was launched via the hundreds of twisted but eye-grabbing paintings Renoir had created on the most frequently trafficked walkways of the city, he eventually migrated his work to more traditional — certainly more portable and therefore more marketable — surfaces. Canvasses were the most common but plywood and sheet rock panels bearing his signature artworks became available.

He even expanded into sculpture, bearing his same aberrant but somehow appealingly unique themes and stylistic touches. But the core of his creative output and his commercial success, still remained the idiosyncratic paintings.

Each individual series of these new works was heralded with extravagant and aggressively promoted exhibitions, usually kicked off by throwing a huge — by art world standards — party, where his new masterpieces were displayed, and he played honored host to legions of mesmerized, adoring admirers.

To deflect the megalomaniac overtones of throwing his own parties and receptions, Renoir had at his disposal several sycophants, who were banking on his ultimate Warhol-level of success and assumed that the floodlights of fame and adoration would spill over onto them. This latest party — the launch for *Shibboleth: War Crimes and Hog Futures* — was guided from conception till its fruition this evening by Eleanor Frisson, wife of a highly successful Wall Street brokerage CEO, herself both a patron and dabbler in the arts. Her own preferred artistic medium was glass shards and epoxy, and as payback for putting on tonight's pretentious bash, a handful of her bulky glutinized sculptures stood on pedestals around the perimeter of the room, ready to lacerate anyone who leaned too close or was stupid enough to touch them.

Eleanor buzzed around the room like the excellent Upper East Side hostess she was.

Renoir's only responsibility was to stand conveniently close to the bar, making himself visible and available to anyone who wished to risk trying to break through his impenetrable wall of conceit and self-aggrandizing detachment, such overtures typically marked by heaping asteroid-sized chunks of flattery and unctuous groveling onto the overflowing plate of his bloated ego.

Of course, a big part of being successful in the art world was to create a buzz. And there was no better buzz than a growl. Renoir was as much a master at promoting his own obnoxious, outrageous persona, as he was a master at painting with his thumb. Perhaps more so.

People just loved to talk about what a perfect shit he was. They wore his easy dismissal, his callous perfunctory rejection, like some sort of badge. It was celebrity worship at its worst. Masochism seemed to be the newest sacrament at the altar of the anti-god.

One young man, though it might have only been the side effect of alcohol toxicity, claimed in repeated tellings that Renoir actually spit on him for telling one of his skittishly proffered painter jokes. No one believed that he had the guts to tell the joke. They assumed that Renoir spat on him because he felt like it.

A pair of giddy gay guys had it on good authority that there had been recently circulating a sex tape featuring Renoir in a fornicating bacchanal with two 14-year olds, a boy and a girl, and that a statutory rape case was pending against him, the timing of his arrest being calculated for maximum publicity.

Another attendee, this one a 40ish female whose bloated bosoms told a tale of much cosmetic surgery, bragged about giving Renoir head in the bathroom shortly after arriving at the party. She claimed that Renoir then tried to piss on her face. Everyone just smiled knowingly and shrugged.

It was also worth noting that no one gave more than a cursory glance at Renoir's new masterpieces, over fifty or so, which hung on every available vertical space in the huge loft. The excitement and enthusiasm generated by being there for the evening's events was only matched by the indifference to the art itself.

So why were they here?

It was quite simple. They were here because Renoir was here. This was the place to be.

That Renoir Albertine Toulouse was a man at the center of a vast tide pool of destiny, that he was the next *big thing*, that his time had arrived, that he was a force to be reckoned with, that his artistic vision was becoming woven large into the fabric of contemporary artistic mythos, was the unquestioned verdict of art critics and fans alike. All the gleeful hand-wringing, whispered and shouted buzz, wind-bag hype and hyperbole — warranted or not — was at the core of the mythology that had burgeoned around him during the past eighteen months.

It had now reached critical mass, presumably making Renoir an unstoppable force.

That no one could have accepted all the overblown attention of the media and the gushing adoration of the art world less graciously was equally beyond dispute.

Renoir was the grand master of hauteur. As might be expected, he was in rare form tonight.

His contempt for everyone else in the room was palpable. It was edible. It was breathable. The stench of his ego suffused the entire gathering. It sat like a giant poisoned pig carcass on a medieval serving platter. The apple in its mouth perhaps the disemboweled heart of Henry VIII.

Most approached him with masochistic fear and trembling, doing what was required to pay homage to a ruthless despot.

To the majority he was predictably disdainful. To a few he was randomly merciful. Everyone wished for the best but knew to expect the worst.

There was perhaps only one person present who was not in the least put off or threatened by any of this.

Amethyst Reigns was a hard-core rocker chick with her own ego and agenda. The difference between her ego and Renoir's was that hers was healthy, balanced, nuanced, and flexible. Likewise her agenda was straightforward and revealed with candor. She was a singer and was there to promote herself and the band playing the music she wrote and performed. Self-promotion was hardly an anomaly at events such as these. Probably most of the people milling about tonight were there doing the same thing. Success at the business of the arts was all about making the right connections. The kick-off party for a high-visibility art exhibition would be packed with all sorts of important people.

Amethyst had only arrived twenty minutes ago but decided there was no time like the present to meet the man of the hour himself.

Naïve and unburdened by shyness or anxiety, Amethyst approached him, casually sipping on a slender wineglass of chrysanthemum cider. She was beautiful, in her East Village way, a boldly striking feline temptress, a vessel of dangerously erotic charm not even Renoir could choose to ignore. As he saw her heading toward him, warning bells silently went off but he concealed his disquiet. He took special pains to temper the armor stiffness of his impassive posturing, a defense calculated to deflect whatever wittiness or allure she might be capable of, by chance or intention. His face remained the flinty honor guard to the private workings of his mind. He would hold the element of surprise as his own tactical prerogative.

With the innocence of a lamb ambling down a livestock run toward its slaughter, Amethyst coasted over with casual cool, and halted herself directly in front of Renoir. Her height put her eyeball to eyeball with the great man. She cooed as only an eighteen year old Brookville Long Island girl could coo.

"I've always loved your pictures. I mean … your paintings. Your sidewalk art."

"I do know what you mean. And I'd like to lick your pussy."

The briefest tincture of shock colored the pale planes of her face before her pallor returned to its normal transparent glow. She blinked and smiled butterflies.

"Maybe you could shave first? I chafe."

His leer was rock-steady. He lifted his right hand in front of her face. Three fingers had been fused by the fire into a lumpy phallic melt of skin and flesh.

"I could stick this up your ass. Would that feel good?"

"They told me you were a real charmer. Are you a descendant of Renoir? Auguste Renoir?"

"Was he a real charmer?"

"A little before my time."

"It's my first name. And one by choice at that. More press-friendly than Stanislaw."

"Surprise surprise. Renoir Albertine Toulouse image conscious?"

"Just categorically opposed to design flaws."

He turned and strolled away.

"You can use my Lady Schick. And my Chapstick. Fuckhead!"

Renoir acted as though he didn't hear her and just kept walking, giving superficial waves and hugs along the way.

Amethyst had come to tonight's event with her friend Candy. Candy was one of the few — perhaps the only one — who had no ulterior motive for being there and had tagged along just to tag along. Amethyst spotted her strolling along the walls of the loft space, taking in Renoir's latest offerings, probably trying to figure out what any of it had to do with hog futures. Amethyst headed over to join her, maybe share some girl talk about what assholes some men were — a topic they never tired of, or were short of fresh evidence for.

Renoir himself had headed toward, then settled himself next to a drag queen on a white cream leather love seat. A glaring bowl-shaped chrome light fixture suspended over them at the end of a long arching truss rod, heightened the hollows of their eyes and the shadows of their sunken cheeks. The exaggerated greasepaint of the drag queen and the dull pallor of Renoir's own powdery makeup complemented one another. Dueling phantasmagoria. It looked like the Munsters at a wedding reception for David Lynch.

Renoir again turned on the charm.

"If I reached under that lovely dress, would I get a handful of cock? Or have you got it all safely tucked away in your butt crack?"

Before the drag queen could come back with a witty rejoinder, a commotion at the other end of the room near the entrance pulled their attention. Over the murmuring and hissing of vapid conversations and the trip-hop muzak playing softly in the background, someone could be heard shouting.

"Where is Mr. Melty? Hello! Mr. Melty! I need to speak to the lord and master. The high priest of pedestrian art. Have you seen Mr. Melty? How about you? Have you seen him? What, are you fucking deaf?" She shouted just in case he was. "WHERE IS MR. MELTY?"

At first just curious, but then sensing the potential for trouble — or worse, a blot on his impeccable track record for the most dazzling and rapturous exhibit opening parties in New York — Renoir stood up and looked over the heads of his guests to see what the commotion was about.

No one was going to ruin *his* party.

Then he spotted her.

If anyone could spoil a good time, it was this bitch. She was old and cranky, and though everyone disliked her, sometimes she played the age card to garner smatterings of sympathy.

Miss Francine Ferlinghetti. Bohemian spinster. Trouble maker. Over-the-hill painter clinging to fleeting fame and name recognition from half a century ago.

Renoir started walking to her end of the room.

She was still making a big scene of trying to find Renoir.

"Oh Mr. Melty! Come out come out wherever you are."

Then she spotted him coming. And picked up her pace to meet him halfway. Just as she got within a few feet of him, she looked down and gasped in shock.

"Oh my God! What's this?"

It was a huge dildo she was wearing over her white out-of-fashion capris. She unstrapped it and held it out in Renoir's face.

"Maybe you could use this. It's kind of like a big thumb, wouldn't you say?"

Renoir took it and rotated it between the fingers of his good hand, looking at it curiously. Then he handed it back to her.

"It seems to me you're going to need this more than me. Since nobody's going to stick the real thing in that dried-out, diseased, old cunt of yours."

"Spoken just like the gutter-dweller you are."

Francine Ferlinghetti had been a mainstay of the New York art scene — though now a conspicuously passed-over one — for most of her 68 years. She had scored a huge spike of notoriety as an adolescent prodigy. Unfortunately, like most immature fast-trackers, she never subsequently lived up to the inflated expectations her early meteoric rise had generated. That early success grew out of a resurgence of interest in primitivism during the 50s. She rode the tide as a pubescent superstar, until the neo-primitivist school was shoved aside, becoming irrelevant and largely forgotten by the 60s. Francine subsequently never changed her approach, and art lovers, even her most dedicated fans, fickle as Elizabeth Taylor was to her eight husbands, moved on to the next big thing. Then the next. And the next. Francine was to this day doing her primitive renderings — still not that unlike the Native American art and South American tribal works from which she borrowed heavily — consigning her to the dusty footnotes of art history.

Some revisionists of the history of modern art tried to write her off totally. They claimed that the attention she had gotten early resulted purely from sharing her surname with the beat poet Lawrence Ferlinghetti, who was a fast rising star in literary circles about the same time. There was no truth to this, of course. She was not related to Mr. Ferlinghetti and never claimed any connection with him. In fact, as an isolated young painter barely 17 years old, she had never even heard of him until some article appeared in the Village Voice, derisive of her personally, claiming she was riding on Lawrence Ferlinghetti's merited acclaim, and that her talent for painting equated with Dwight Eisenhower's gifts as a stand up comedian.

The reviewer was wrong then and would be wrong now. It wasn't that Francine lacked talent. She was enormously accomplished, as anyone with an objective eye could see. What she now lacked was youth — America likes its idols to be at their reproductive peak — and currency.

Both kinds of currency.

Her work had not kept up with the times.

And it failed to generate the dimes.

Not only did her stuff not sell, but the angels — rich sponsors who wanted their names mentioned in the same breath as the latest da Vinci, Picasso, or Warhol — had completely abandoned her. They ignored her because her star had long disappeared from the art world heavens. She was irrelevant, hence forgotten. Why promote a declining old fossil like Francine when the action was with fresh, young talents on the rise?

For those artists who were *in* the game, Renoir Albertine Toulouse as a sterling example, the opposite was true. He was literally awash in money from individual and corporate sponsorship.

The intrinsic injustice of this haunted Francine. Lately, this envy had evolved into spiteful vitriol. Thus she had been making a point of sporadically showing up uninvited — actually she was never invited to anything anymore — to wherever Renoir was making a public appearance, and heckling him, as she was doing tonight.

Renoir, who stood a head taller than her, looked down at her like she was a pathetic nobody, which could be argued she effectively was.

"So. What brings you here? No wino parties in the Bowery to crash?"

Deluding herself that she could sway *his* crowd on *his* turf at *his* party, she ignored the insult and turned to address everyone there, who conveniently had closed in a tight circle around her and Renoir. Nothing like a little carnage to inject some fresh energy and excitement into the evening.

"And here, ladies and gentlemen, we have the much heralded Renoir Albertine Toulouse, a self-proclaimed revolutionary. His canvas is the streets. The sidewalks of the proletariat. The battlefield for revolution. Yet look what we see here tonight." She made a grand sweeping gesture with her arms to take in the paintings that filled the walls of the space. "Norman Rockwell meets Doonesbury."

A few people actually laughed at her characterization.

Renoir not only took it in stride but seemed to relish her remarks. He stepped closer to her, still holding the dildo in one hand. He put his free arm around her shoulders, patting her with a patronizing paternalism, despite being half her age.

"Tsk tsk tsk. My petrified piece of ancient history. How could you get it so wrong? Maybe the mind is going, eh?"

She started to say something but he tapped the dildo on her lips to silence her.

"My dear decrepit creature of the past. Look around you. Look at my lovely friends here." He pointed the dildo at the audience, sweeping the enormous rubber phallus around the room, drawing a chorus of laughter. "You are so wrong to call me an advocate of the working class. I am the Messiah of the petty bourgeois. I take MasterCard and Visa. I am, my little sewer troll, the art of the shopping mall. The department stores. The big-box boutiques like Ikea and Costco and Target. You, Miss Francine Ferlinghetti, in stark contrast, are merely a hunter-gatherer. Your fingernails are caked with dried blood and hard clay. You are an antediluvian jester, a primitive buffoon. You are the Golden Calf of antiquation, forgotten myth, and empty ritual. Go back to your teepee or cave or tribal circle. Pass your dream pipe and finger your worry beads someplace else."

The crowd was both fascinated and entertained. The laughter built over the course of his verbal assault. Francine looked both angry and humiliated. She must have a short memory. Tonight was a repeat of every one of their encounters. She now both seemed rattled and still bent on putting Renoir in his place. But there was desperation in her tired old eyes. This had not gone according to her ill-conceived plan.

Renoir continued in a hushed, mocking tone.

"Miss Ferlinghetti. With all due respect, you are in my spotlight right now. And this particular spotlight is reserved for real artists."

He smiled and turned a full circle, making generous eye contact with as many as he could in the room. He wanted to make sure everyone was in his corner. Renoir then comically put his free hand up over his eyes like he was looking for something off in the distance.

"Other than yours truly, do we here see a real artist in the room? An actual working artist who doesn't have to beg people to take her paintings? Someone who is actually respected for their creative work?"

The sheep all bleated dutifully.

"No!"

Renoir started tapping Francine on the top of the head with the dildo.

"There you have it, Grandma Moses. No room for relics here. I think it's time to go."

Francine ducked away from his harmless but humiliating thumping, and with a surprising show of strength, wrenched the dildo out of his hand. She threw it across the room. Then she stuck her withered index finger right in his face, in a last round rally.

"Have the last laugh. For now. But remember, Renoir Toulouse. You are but a pitiable blip. You are history before you are history. You will be sucked into that special place in Hell. With your McDonalds and Microsoft and Pizza Hut and Walmart. Your fast food art will sit beside pallets of Cheetos and gummy bears and Diet Coke. And decompose. It won't have far to go. Shit becoming dirt. And as for this art-for-those-on-the-go tupperware party? It's bye-bye ..." She mockingly twisted her own right hand to look deformed and waved it theatrically in Renoir's face. "... Mr. Melty."

She broke through the circle of gawkers, and headed at a brisk pace toward the door, hoping to be out of there before Renoir got in the last word. Though it was completely unnecessary, since she was obviously leaving anyway, two husky guards, pushed along by Eleanor Frisson, the hostess of the party — anxious to show she had the situation under control — came up behind Francine and grabbed her by the arms. As they started to escort her to the exit, again showing strength and feistiness beyond her age, she broke free.

"I don't need your help. I know the way out."

They still followed her at close quarters, nudging her along.

Renoir stood there gloating, picked up a glass of wine from the tray of a passing server, then silently toasted the departing old lady.

A few people came up to him. The rest dispersed and resumed conversations that had been interrupted by the pissing contest they had just witnessed, not that they didn't enjoy seeing Renoir demolish the old hag, or think that her poor attempt at mockery was anything but the incoherent ramblings of a senile old persona non grata.

Through the altercation, Amethyst and Candy had been standing back from the fray. Neither were particularly impressed or entertained by what had just happened. Candy didn't see any point to it, and Amethyst, fresh off of her own ugly exchange with the artist, felt pangs of sympathy for the poor old lady. Though Francine had brought it on herself, Amethyst felt she had naively walked into a den of lions, and didn't deserve the beating she had taken.

Without saying anything, they converged on a table still full of trendy finger foods and exotic confections. Amethyst bit into a carob treat shaped like a tiny bonsai tree and reflected on the vulgar assault on her by the obnoxious artist. Candy kept dipping her finger into a small heated bowl of melted white chocolate, which was there for adding the final sweet touch to fresh cut strawberries. The strawberries were long gone and Candy no way could let all that white chocolate go to waste — she had a thing for white chocolate.

Amethyst was on her fifth bonsai tree when she finally said something.

"That was lame."

"What?"

"All of it."

"Never a dull moment, eh? How about your one-on-one with Mr. Melty? How was that?"

"Renoir's a dreamboat. Kind of a cross between Charles Manson and Chemical Ali. I want to have his children. By artificial insemination, of course. Just before they drench him with gasoline and put him in an electric chair."

"He's an asshole."

"Like just about everybody else here."

Candy looked across the room and Amethyst followed the line of her gaze. They were looking at Billy.

"What about him?" Candy rarely needed assurances or the approval of anyone else. But at this party they were in enemy territory. A second opinion was welcome.

"Where did *he* come from?"

"The good ship lollipop."

Amethyst nodded.

"He seems pretty okay. I think introductions are in order. Are you up for it?"

"If I'm not back in three months, go for help."

After one more generous dip of her finger in the bowl of white chocolate, Candy eased her way over, trying not to look too obvious or frighten away the vulnerable looking Billy.

"Hi."

Billy looked her up and down — more curious than judgmental — took another drink from the glass he was holding, winced, then looked her over again.

"I'm speechless."

"If you were, we wouldn't be having this conversation."

They say you can't judge a book by its cover. Billy had a strong sense that was the case here. He read on, still in the table of contents.

"What do your friends call you?"

"Candy."

"What about your enemies?"

"Cumbucket."

"Nasty people! Candy it is. Melts in your mouth, not in your hand."

"It's not my birth certificate name. I don't usually tell anyone ... but ... my real name is Susan Kalkin."

Another one. Maybe identity crisis was epidemic around here. First Celeste. Now this enigmatic number. What is it about given names? Maybe he should call himself Cassius.

"Witness protection program?"

"I'm undercover. Society of Mary Magdalene. We're still looking for descendants of Jesus. Right now I'm on the tail of an unemployed pipefitter living at a YMCA in the Bronx."

"My bullshit detector went off on 'undercover'. But I'll hand it to you, that was spectacularly imaginative. Okay. Let's see. Tattoos. Magic Marker make-up. You must be an artist. A performance artist! Snakes. Maybe an acetylene torch. A kiddie pool full of molding cheese. And a Jew's harp."

"No, I'm a service technician on the Goodyear Blimp. Part-time, of course. And I have my own business. I'm an independently contracted fortune-telling mermaid — bar mitzvahs, anniversaries, pre-natal and post-natal parties."

"Ah! A fortune-telling mermaid. See. I was close."

"And you?"

"I'm a loser."

"Does it pay well? Seems like the field is kind of crowded these days. A lot of them showed up here tonight."

"I get by. I've got connections."

"So. What do your friends call you?"

"Billy. Just Billy."

Billy took another drink and winced again.

"You really seem to be enjoying that. What are you drinking?"

"Acetone. Aged in an oak barrel on Rikers Island. But it's the homeopathics I put in it that's makes it really seminal. My cerebral palsy is almost cured."

"Okay, Billy. You're not too boring." She looked at the non-existent watch on her wrist. "My my, how time flies when you're crazy. Before I go back to Bellevue — they're pretty militant about outpatient curfews — come and meet my friend Amethyst. She's a rock star. Sort of."

"Amethyst? Let me guess. Not her birth certificate name."

"I never asked her."

Candy led the way. Amethyst didn't wait for an introduction.

"How do you do? I'm Amethyst."

"I heard. I saw you talking to the big guy. Is he as charming up close?"

"A regular heart throb. But I've always had a soft spot for ax murderers and child molesters."

Billy glanced at Candy. She was smiling at him. Definitely smiling. A truly wonderful smile. Back to the rocker babe.

"So Amethyst. Your friend here says you're a rock star. I'd like to see you rock sometime."

"You will. Candy here is ambassador-at-large for my fan club."

Candy reached inside her back pocket and pulled out a business card. It was clear plastic. There was a rose in one corner and a serpent wound around the edges. She handed it to him.

"Here's my number. Call me day after tomorrow. I want to take you somewhere."

"Somewhere?"

"Trust me. You'll like it."

With that the two girls strolled toward the door and out into a more plausible version of the world. At least one that didn't pretend it was something more consequential than 9 million ants building up and tearing down the anthill. Objectively speaking, that's what New York looked like most of the time. Of course, within the jeweled cocoons that housed the egos and ambitions of many of the ants, it was a different story.

Billy left shortly afterwards. He was going make some token complimentary remark to Renoir on the way out, but couldn't think of anything to say.

Like the expression goes, if you can't think of anything nice ...

Machines of Melanoma

It was Monday, the day after tomorrow. The day Billy was supposed to call Candy. Coincidentally, that very morning, Verizon Bell Atlantic installed his land line phone. His first call was to the number on Candy's business card.

It was a cell phone. It went directly to voice mail. He left a message.

Later that evening, while engineering the tightrope walk between the numbing effects of several Bacardi Breezers and the dreamy bliss of the defoliant-laced weed he had bought from a black guy at Washington Square — and it was a balancing act that required rigorous focus and substance abuse discipline — he tried to call her again with no success. Right to voice mail again. He left another message.

Candy never returned his call. She went one better. A little after 9 pm the following Friday evening, she showed up on his doorstep.

"How did you find me?"

"Are you busy?"

He held up the joint he was smoking.

"I'm medicating. Seriously. How did you know where I live?"

"The miracle of the internet. Pretty amazing what you can find out online. It's called the reverse telephone directory. Plug in a phone number. Up pops an address. So are you ready to go?"

"Go? Are we going somewhere?"

"You and I have a date with music history in the making. I'm sure it'll be an experience you never forget."

Billy put on a clean shirt, one that would be able to fully absorb the cigarette smoke and club stench of a typical underground New York rock bar.

Off they went.

Amethyst's band, Machines of Melanoma, was playing right down the street from his flat. He had told her he wanted to see her rock sometime. She said he would. And he did.

It was not entirely what he expected, though he didn't know what to expect.

Billy loved music. The first time Billy heard music, he cried. How old was he? Maybe two. He could never forget the feeling that spread through him, his whole body gently stiffening like a flower stretching its petals skyward to draw in a warm rain. He was being cradled by his mother, his head sideways across her forearm, his eyes mesmerized by the imagery on the TV. He felt the comforting warmth of her breast on the back of his neck, the nipple like a soft warm mushroom pressed against his ear.

They were watching a VHS of *The Wizard of Oz*. Judy Garland as Dorothy was singing "Somewhere Over The Rainbow". Her eyes were wide and pensive, her lips pouty in the adolescent dreaming of a more perfect world. The utopian reverie of the song bathed him in some unrequited expectation which he could not as a toddler comprehend but felt as both a creamy tenderness and a gnawing pain. It felt good and hurt at the same time.

Little Billy cried. Simple tears of innocence.

Big Billy sure couldn't claim that things were so simple and innocent now. Especially right now. Not in this raucous bar.

What exactly was he supposed to be feeling? He was feeling pain, yes. Agony, yes. Unrequited longing, that was for sure. But this was more like a prisoner-of-war longing. A desperation. He felt caged, battered, tortured by what was apparently supposed to pass for music. Longing to be released or have someone put a gun to his head to put him out of his misery.

Billy and Candy were sandwiched between a very unruly crowd and a musty wall at the Mercury Lounge in the Lower East Side.

Machines of Melanoma were onstage ripping through one of their songs — could these be called songs? Venomous streams of sonic napalm in the guise of throaty chainsaw guitar fuzz, arced fiercely over the heads of the crowd, inciting individual convulsions and communal writhing. Amethyst looked demented and beautiful, and — from what Billy surmised — was in top form. She was in total control and seemed to have the crowd eating out of her hands.

She strutted back and forth on the small stage.

She was certainly playing the sex card. Anyone in front leaning forward could see all the way up her extremely short skirt and catch a nice shot of her closely trimmed pubic hair. There were a lot of guys fighting for the front edge of the stage to savor the view.

She was wearing one of her typically unique and provocative stage outfits. Strips of white tape in the shape of two Xs barely covered her nipples. Black leather suspenders with spikes. A shimmering metallic purple mini-skirt with shiny silver studs and white plastic fringe. Six-inch clear plastic platform shoes. Dayglo green bobby socks. Black fishnet hose. A yellow vinyl nurse hat with a skull-and-crossbones on the front. Make-up so thick it looked like she had applied it with a spatula. Eyes caked with black eyeliner and mascara. Silver glitter on her eyelids.

She looked like a stripper in a bad acid trip version of Alice in Wonderland.

Amethyst suddenly screamed like a PCP-hackled banchee.

"Fuck you and your girly girly habits of submission and cowardice! All of you so-called men are a bunch of pathetic pussy-whipped losers!"

Then she laughed maniacally at her own draconian missive.

The crowd both jeered and cheered.

A young male fan, probably just old enough to get in the club, pressed over the lip of the stage, wagging his tongue as an invitation to lick her. She grabbed her crotch.

"You want some of this? Is this what you want, you pathetic dweeb?"

He nodded and kept wagging his tongue. He leaned toward her as far as he could reach. Amethyst crouched down, grabbed the back of his head with one hand as if to pull him toward her, covered his eyes with the other hand, then spit in his mouth.

She leaped back up and started pumping her fist vertically in front of her, like she had just made a great play at Wimbledon.

"Yes! Yes! Yeah, baby! Oh yeah! Now that's true love! True love! True love, I say!"

The band hit a gigantic opening chord and let it ring on and on, extracting electronic squeals and rumbles of feedback by facing their amps. They were breaking into the next tune. Amethyst gave a proper introduction.

"Ladies and gentlemen. Here's a love song for you. Because you're so ... so ... so *goddamn fucking special!*"

After a huge drum pick-up, the band came in with the subtle grace of an urban assault vehicle. The roar was deafening and anybody who had not had at least nine beers or three Long Island Ice Teas was at a huge disadvantage.

Amethyst launched into a high-pitch wail, which with the wall of guitars in a full-out explosive roar, sounded more like an emergency vehicle siren than a human voice.

Following another cosmic drum pick-up, she came in singing.

The lyrics were barely audible over the sonic storm of the band but from what Billy could tell, they went:

> This is a dance of death
> For war, TV and cancer
> This here is the orchestra
> And baby I'm the dancer
> This is the dance of death
> For giving the wrong answer
> You losers won't stand a chance
> 'Cause I'm the fucking dancer
> We love to see you maimed
> We love to see you writhe
> We love to see your pain
> Die motherfucker die!
> We love to see you burn
> We love to see you fry
> We love to see you squirm
> Die motherfucker die!

This same set of lyrics was repeated several times with no variation in either the words or the musical accompaniment. In spite of the repetitions, the song was at such a fast tempo, they were done playing it in a little less than two minutes.

Several similar tunes — Billy would have said identical, but he took it on faith that they were playing different songs each time — came and went. With each subsequent song the band revved higher and higher, causing his ears more to vibrate and shudder in place, than actually hear. The sonic holocaust usually completely buried what Amethyst was singing. Maybe it was "Somewhere Over The Rainbow".

Toward the end of the set, he gulped down the rest of his beer, and for reasons he himself couldn't explain, made a direct beeline for the stage. Candy just smiled and watched him forge ahead.

"Go Billy! I'll call the ambulance."

Billy shoved aside several moshers, exerting more muscle than he had in years, then made his way to the very front by sandwiching himself between two skinny girls who looked like rock 'n roll vampires, the kind that only came out after sundown every night to prowl psychotic venues like this.

Amethyst slithered to the edge of the stage and spotted Billy. The crowd behind him grunted and pushed, a throbbing mass of explosive but disjointed energy. Suddenly he was smashed right up against the stage. Amethyst reached for him. She crouched down and pulled his face between her legs. She was wearing no panties. He could smell the sweat and secretions of her moist labia.

She bent down further. After licking his ear for the benefit of the crowd, he thought he heard her say, "That's what friends are for." Or maybe it was, "Guess what ends in fur." There was no way to tell in the nuclear din of the music.

Hopefully there wouldn't be a pop quiz.

When the set finished, the crowd in front of the stage dispersed — dispersed as much as it could when there were over 400 people in a 250-capacity club — and Billy headed in the general direction most of them seemed to be going, not that he had much choice in the matter. That general direction turned out to be for the bar, where they could front load enough beer to carry them through the next act.

Machines of Melanoma took about twenty minutes to tear down and get their equipment off stage. Billy noticed that the members, including Amethyst, did all of the work themselves. Obviously, despite their apparent popularity, they had not come far enough down the long road of success to even have a couple of unpaid roadies.

Billy couldn't find Candy. But the place was so crowded, she could have been a few feet away and he wouldn't have seen her.

He did manage to get to the server's station at the end of the bar, screamed his order over the clamorous din, unbearably loud even without a band playing, and was now sipping a nice cold quart of Pabst Blue Ribbon, a beverage brewed specifically for men who had in their entire lives never imbibed a decent beer and thus thought that it should taste like carbonated dishwater.

Suddenly Amethyst was right behind him. He turned just in time to see her whip around to a guy who had been tailgating her.

"Keep your fucking hands to yourself or I'll chew your face off and spit it down your mother's throat!"

Amethyst was obviously still a little crazed on adrenalin from having just performed. The asshole following her would have been safer flicking lit matches into a crate of dynamite.

Tailgating asshole quickly signaled his surrender by raising his hands in the air, then starting to push his way back through the crowd to blend in with other less overtly aggressive rapists.

Amethyst smiled broadly at Billy and to his surprise kissed him full on the lips. Then she pulled away like something had really offended her.

"Eeew! Is that what I smell like?" Then she laughed loud at her own joke and gave him a big rock star hug. "Dude! Thanks for coming. It's Billy, right? Whaddya think? Not that I really care."

Impromptu diplomacy was not Billy's strong suit. Evasive tactics were called for.

"I wish my mom could have seen it. She's a big fan of Barbra Streisand."

"Try again, funny man."

"Well, I'm looking for the right word."

"Irresistible."

"No."

"Incandescent."

"No."

"Indefatigable."

"Too gothic."

"Impassioned."

"Not quite."

"Incendiary."

"Hmmm."

"Iconoclastic."

"Warmer."

"Incomprehensible."

"Maybe. How about 'interesting'."

"You really suck!" She jokingly grabbed him by the throat as if to strangle him. "That is like the biggest insult of all. That's like telling a fat chick she's got nice eyelashes. Interesting? Fuck you!"

She let go of his throat, winked theatrically, grabbed his beer and took a huge swig, then gave him another big hug.

He was flying pretty high both from the two quarts of beer he had had, and the trichlopyr 2,4-D laced weed he'd toked up on before Candy picked him up. Truthfully? Her tits felt really good pressed against him. Sadly she pulled away.

"So what's with the children?" Billy pointed to a small mezzanine which had been cordoned off and was filled with twenty or so kids. All boys. They appeared to be around 12 or 13. They were all wearing identical shirts with the Machines of Melanoma logo on the front. Each one had a different number.

"We sponsor a little league team."

"You're joking!" He studied her face for a sign. "You *are* joking ... right?"

"No, not at all. Our manager thought it would be good PR. We love it."

"Isn't your music a little ... uh ... kinda rough around the edges ... for such young ears?"

"A lot of it is. So that's why we toned it down tonight."

"This was your toned down music?"

"Exactly. We call this our family values set. We don't want to mess them up. They get enough of that in school."

"Whew! I think I'm missing something. Let's be real here. You are way out on the far edge somewhere, left of Chairman Mao. I mean, you make Ralph Nader look like the Shah of Iran. Now you tell me you sponsor a little league baseball team. And you're into family values."

"Billy. I don't know you very well. But already I see you are so clueless. You're missing the point. It's all about irony. This is the fucking Age of Irony. Look around you. America is a country of extremes. That's why we support George W. Bush. He's our ultimate fucking hero!"

"*The* George W. Bush?"

"America. The richest country in the world. The most influential. By far the most powerful. Yet our president is the dumbest guy on the planet. If that isn't irony, then what is?"

"But ... I don't understand. Where does all of this go? What's the point?"

"That's the point. It can only go down. Down the tubes. *That* is where this country is going. *That* is exactly what Machines of Melanoma is all about. We're a celebration of the inevitable descent into chaos. Total anarchy."

"Anarchy. Irony. Down the tubes. Got it." Billy wanted to change the subject. "Amethyst. Would it be ironic enough of me to buy you a drink? Since you were nice enough to invite me tonight."

"You're on. By the way, where's Candy?"

"She's waiting out front for an ambulance. She thought I was in over my head."

"You are, for sure. But really. Where is she? I haven't seen her all night."

"Maybe she's out behind the club sharing beauty tips with the two other chicks here tonight. You seem to have a very male-heavy following."

"I can see getting a straight answer out of you is about the same as getting one out of her. She's a great person, by the way. You be good to her."

"I ... I ... didn't really—"

"Things happen. She likes you. I'm not sure why. We need to work on your political sensibilities a bit. Actually a lot. But she likes you."

"Is she political?"

"She's truthful."

"And she's standing right behind you."

Candy had worked her way over to them. Since Amethyst on her 6" platform shoes towered over everyone, Candy had used the yellow vinyl nurse hat as a buoy in the turbulent sea of bobbing heads to locate her.

They girl-hugged, made some arrangements which Billy couldn't quite hear, probably to get together soon, then Amethyst got ready for a rugby-like battle to make her way through the crowd — hopefully with a minimum of sexual harassment — back to the dressing room by the stage.

Before she left, she reminded Billy.

"You owe me a drink. Dripping with irony. Anarchy on the rocks. Next time, dude."

Using her pointy elbows extended out in front of her as bayonets, Amethyst jabbed and slogged through the crowd. She made great headway. Apparently she had done this before. The band could have been named One-Woman Juggernaut.

Candy took Billy by the arm and dragged him toward the exit.

"Let's get some coffee."

"You want coffee?"

"It's for you. Your eyes look like pimentos."

"They feel like hard boiled eggs. Still in the shell."

They managed their way out of the club.

"Actually, Billy. I think I'll head home."

"That's it?"

"Call me. I want to take you somewhere."

"That's what you said. This wasn't it?"

"Nope. Did you have fun tonight?"

"The jury is still out. But ... yes. I appreciate it."

"Then you'll like me taking you to this other place."

"I'll call you. I will. And leave a message."

"You do that."
They were on Houston Street.
They were headed in different directions.
"Bye."
"Bye."
Music history had been made.
Time for bed.

Speed Sex at Rosario's Kabla Kahn

There were two Billy Greens now, occupying the same body.

It wasn't a struggle for control. No science fiction or paranormal thing going on here.

Just two opposite versions of him, each taking its turn, alternating almost randomly, certainly without anyone at the console flipping switches.

One Billy Green was visited by nightmares, haunted by uninvited visions, hurtled upright on his bed in cold sweats, crying or screaming, doubled over with the cramps and muscular ache of depression, waylaid even in public by fits of sobbing, prostrated by excessive amounts of alcohol, zombied by drugs which now sometimes included tranquilizers and muscle relaxants. At times he was nearly suicidal. This Billy Green was anemic, confused, self-sabotaging, a pathetic pawn on the chessboard of bathos.

The other Billy Green was a young man trying to rebuild his life after an unexpected but manageable set-back. He was gradually releasing himself from his self-imposed exile, meeting new people. His hibernating libido was giving faint signals of a not-too-far-off awakening. This Billy Green refused to give in to self-pity, would not accept defeat, would somehow find strength to meet the challenges and adversity. He saw potential in both the people he met and himself. Sometimes he could even feel hope.

Two Billy Greens. A standoff. An uneasy coexistence.

Behind this troubling intimation of schizophrenia — temporary or permanent remained to be seen — singularly responsible for unleashing the hell he had recently been living, thus triggering this pathological dualism, purely and simply was ... Natalie.

Unfortunately — or maybe not — the tormented could not bring himself to confront the tormentor.

Despite his self-destructive but predictable preoccupation with her, despite the unavoidable fact that she was the femme fatale of both his life and his walking death, Billy had not talked to her — hadn't even dialed her number once — since he moved to New York City.

Often in his moments of madness and despair, he imagined confronting her. He ached to make that call or that face-to-face visit — to charm, cajole, threaten, beg, yell, point the finger of guilt, profane her, slap her, seduce her, court her — do whatever it took to win her back. But he couldn't bring himself to do anything about it. He avoided that moment of truth because he knew what the truth would be. She would coldly and flatly reject him, or even worse patronize him, pushing his disconsolate soul further into the hell of self-loathing and misery.

Finally, more than five weeks after he left Newburgh, he got up the courage to make the call. It was a safe call. Strictly business. One that would avoid setting off the powder kegs of anger and hurt, in the hold of his tormented heart.

Billy had stopped at the bank to replenish his supply of cash. He pulled out $500 from the ATM machine, then checked the account balance. There was an extra $8000 there, maybe a little more.

He went back to his apartment. It was 11:30 am. Probably a good time to catch her at the office. He dialed her direct line from memory.

"Natalie Diamond. How may I help you?"

She was back to her maiden name.

"Billy here. How are you? Can you talk?"

"Sure. Just for a minute. How are you? Someone said you're living in the City."

"Yes. I called to give you my new number and address."

That sounded plausible.

"I put some money in your account. A couple days ago. The house still hasn't sold but some of the stuff has. I thought you might need it."

"Thanks. I never turn away money. But I'm fine."

And so it went. Innocuous. Friendly. Pleasant. Constrained. Lacking any real emotion. Both keeping a cautious distance. Like feuding relatives who had agreed to put their differences aside and now really didn't have much to say to one another. A far cry from the intense emotional clash he had imagined — both hoped and dreaded it would be.

He gave her his new contact information. She said she might need to have him sign some papers related to selling the car. Neither got around to answering the *How are you?* question they had by habit or convention exchanged. For Billy there was no answer. None that would make sense anyway. And if he was being completely honest with himself, he didn't want to know how she was. It would hurt too much. Or totally piss him off.

"You take care."

"I'll take it anyway I can get it."

Lame. It was the best he could do. He was only firing on one cylinder.

Billy hung up the phone and lit a joint. He couldn't think about any of this right now. Natalie. Selling the house. It was all just bullshit. All the love, dreams, plans, laughter, sex, all they did together and shared, now reduced to pulling out a pocket calculator and dividing by two.

What complete and total bullshit.

The grass was starting to take effect.

He remembered he was supposed to call Candy. She had somewhere she wanted to take him. He'd like it. Hmm. He dialed. To his enormous surprise, she answered.

"Billy Green! Such a charmer."

"Why do you say that?"

"I say it to everybody. I have the sarcasm gene. It's usually recessive but both my parents have it."

"I was almost feeling good about your comment."

"You should! I almost meant it ... maybe. Anyway, it's this coming Monday. We have to be mid-town by 8:00 pm. You wouldn't want to miss any of this now, would you?"

"I don't know. Would I?"

"I'll be there around seven. Limo or subway?"

"I don't think I'm ready to be in a closely confined space with you yet. How about separate subway cars. On different days."

He heard the soft bubbling of a laugh.

"We'll see about that. Seven o'clock for an evening that will leave you wondering why you've spent your entire life in a damp cave reading back issues of Rolling Stone."

"You have Albert Einstein's brain, don't you. It's missing from the lab."

"Billy Green! You are a charmer after all!"

Rosario's Kabla Kahn was a new dinner theater restaurant on Park Avenue just south of 53rd. Typically it hosted scaled-down Broadway musicals, comedy roasts, Vegas-style illusion acts, and cameos by big name glitterati. Celine Dion had appeared at the club's grand opening, and Frank Sinatra had through the years promised the owner — they were personal friends from way back — to play the club when it opened, but the Chairman of the Board had the unmitigated gall to go and die several years before, never making good on his promise.

Monday nights at the Kabla Kahn were usually dark, except when the club was rented out for some promotional event or private party.

Tonight was just such a evening.

Candy wouldn't tell Billy where they were going.

"Just what is this?"

"I'm not quite sure. It's a surprise. For both of us."

"I already have life insurance."

"But do you have enough?"

Candy was dressed as only Candy could dress and get away with it. Flamboyant, garish and eye-grabbing, yet somehow still tasteful and very hip. Under a stylish red faux-leather double-breasted full-length coat — it was the last week of October and getting chilly at night — she had on a black silk brocade dudou embroidered with red bamboo leaves, a black velour vest, pipestem blue jeans split and laced up the sides, and white courtney skull print shoes.

Next to her, Billy in his standard civvies felt like a film extra in *Revenge of the Nerds*.

He'd have to work on that.

They exited the subway at 51st Street and walked the two blocks to Rosario's, staring straight ahead, both with their hands in their coat pockets.

Though they were early, the place was packed. They waited in line, paid their "donation" to the not-for-profit Institute for Studies of Modern Sexuality, the Queens-based organization that was sponsoring tonight's lecture and workshop, entered the cavernous main room, then took two seats towards the rear, at a table for eight.

As they waited for everyone to be seated, they looked around, taking in the other attendees.

Candy was the first to say something. Under her breath, of course.

"A mutant strain. I wonder if these people speak Russian."

"Meaning?"

"Chernobyl."

"I don't think so, Candy. This is America's silent minority. People who subscribe to Reader's Digest for the smutty stories."

A young, extremely overweight couple across the table from them couldn't stop smiling. They kept poking one another like school children, then giggling and looking at Billy and Candy, to see if they wanted to join in the fun, though it was not at all apparent how that would happen. Another pair, seated on Billy's right, who looked to be on the crest of their mid-life crisis, completely ignored one another. The lady was wearing a bright red latex hood, dark sunglasses, a black shaggy fake-fur coat, and fingerless purple latex gloves. Her partner was dressed in a seersucker sports jacket Billy assumed he had checked out of the Smithsonian Museum, a white satin shirt open down to his solar plexus, and was decked out in more gold chains than the King of Persia. He stared at a NY Times crossword puzzle through boxy horned-rim glasses and managed for twenty minutes to never once put the pencil he held in his hand to the page. The other two chairs at their table were still empty when the master of ceremonies came to the podium to introduce the speaker and facilitator for tonight's event.

> "Tonight's lecture is titled, 'Speed Sex: What Is It and Why?' Ladies and gentlemen, may I present to you the acclaimed expert on the psychology of human sexuality, Dr. James Hasselworth. Jim?"

Short and sweet.

Nice.

Unfortunately, Dr. Hasselworth would not follow the example set by the anonymous MC. The next hour was the longest Billy could recall in his nearly twenty-five years on the planet.

The erudite but tedious Dr. Hasselworth recounted the entire history of reproduction from its earliest most primitive manifestations among simple protozoans, to the complex procreative mechanisms of the human species, leaving out no evolutionary step along the way. In his discussion of *homo sapiens*, he even managed to make sex less interesting than cleaning wet lint from a shower drain screen.

Finally, in the last ten minutes of the slow crawl through 3 billion years, he got to the point.

No one in the room had been smiling, stirring, fidgeting, or showing any external signs of actually being alive for at least forty-five minutes. The anesthetic effect of Hasselworth's drab voice and monotone delivery would have taken down a charging rhinoceros. But when the phrase 'speed sex' came out over the PA system, it was like the explosion of a howitzer in the hibernating ears of the audience. Instantly everyone came to life.

The gist of the dreary Dr.'s subsequent remarks was this: For 99.99% of the history of animate matter, sex was a quickie. Get in, get it over, get out. Only in the razor-thin slice of time representing the era of contemporary man — and he meant just the last hundred years or so — was the sex act drawn out to great lengths. Excessive lengths! Lengths which embraced extended spans of foreplay, heavy petting and erogenous manipulation delaying orgasm, finally coital or oral stimulation, still often accompanied by a person holding back as long as possible. All of this added up to an unnatural, unnecessary and counter-productive postponement of fulfillment. It even resulted in a gutting or watering down of the desired payoff, the orgasm itself, when it finally arrived.

Speed sex was the answer.

Speed sex got right to the point. Directly and unambiguously.

No fuss.

No worries.

It conserved energy.

It created less perspiration.

It kept boredom from creeping in.

It hormonally generated an endorphin spike.

It freed up valuable time in today's fast-paced world.

It avoided anxiety and suffering associated with prolonged anticipation.

And last and certainly not least — in fact this was probably its greatest selling point...

Speed sex felt good. Real good. Better than good. Better than good has ever felt before!

Dr. Hasselworth compared it to eating candy. He pointed out that eating a candy bar over an hour or two was fine. Putting tiny piece by tiny piece on the tongue, letting it sit there and gradually melt, even keeping the tongue marginally dry so that it wouldn't melt too fast, this certainly was one way to enjoy a bar of chocolate.

> *"But shove the whole damn thing in your mouth at once, attack it, fill every available space with chocolate, have it coat your gums and teeth and tongue and cheeks, letting the flavor expand and explode so that the whole front of your face is screaming with pleasure, then swallow the entire sticky mass within just a couple minutes. Now that's a bar of chocolate!"*

He closed his lecture with what should have been the entire lecture. A simple bit of advice.

> *"Try it. You'll like it."*

Even during the final few minutes of the interminable monologue, which everyone else seemed to find so incredibly fascinating — even titillating judging from the lustful expressions of glee and conspiratorial side-glances he saw all around him — it was frankly all Billy could do to keep his eyes open.

Not that he was tired. It was just so *boring*.

Candy summed it up perfectly. "Hasselworth is not worth the hassle."

They made a break for it long before the "workshop" section of the evening got underway. There was to be an intermission after the initial lecture, providing an opportunity for everyone to take care of the demands of their bladders, then if they wished, to buy overpriced refreshments from a couple portable wet bars that had been set up in the back of the room.

After the break, Dr. Hasselworth would be conducting a Q&A, along the way inviting audience members to share special, unique experiences and difficulties dealing with sexual performance and satisfaction. From these real life examples, he would select one or two volunteers and demonstrate how his philosophy and techniques could be applied.

From what Billy and Candy had heard so far, this only promised to be a complete washout. They made their hasty, poorly concealed retreat out the door and back onto Park Avenue.

As soon as they stepped into the cool October air, Candy went off on Dr. Speed Sex.

"I can't believe people actually pay for that. What a huge pile. A lot of psychological blather. Backfill. Mind grout. Who wants to hear this kind of nonsense?"

"People like us, apparently."

"Exactly. Sucked in again. The article I read made him sound so interesting. Revolutionary. Bleeding-edge. What a joke! I've forgotten more about it than that guy will ever know."

"What's that supposed to mean?"

"What it means."

A few moments passed. Then Billy broke the silence.

"I don't get these ... these public forums on things that are totally private. Marriage and sex, impotence and divorce. Which reminds me. I came because *you* said I would like it."

"I said I wanted to take you somewhere and you'd like it. I didn't say you'd like the somewhere. I meant, you'd enjoy me taking you." She looked at him expectantly. "And?"

They stopped walking. Billy tried his best to throw her attitude. He looked side to side, then cocked his head and stared at her. Despite his best effort to hide it, it wasn't exactly difficult to detect a smile breaking through. Then he broke out laughing.

"You may be the most interesting chick I've met in a long time. Certainly the weirdest."

"And you're not boring. So far anyway. Can we go to your place?"

And they did.

Billy learned a valuable lesson that night.

About putting the whole candy bar in his mouth.

So to speak.

As soon as they walked into his apartment and closed the door, Candy proceeded to use one hand to disrobe him and the other to take off her own clothes. All while giving him the boldest, deepest, most passionate kiss of his entire life.

There was no time to hesitate, question, decide.

It had been quite a while since he had even held a girl, excepting the casual hugs Amethyst had recently given him. He had been numb for so long, his sexual fantasies had pretty much abated, his desire buried under the avalanche of his loss of Natalie.

Like a dam bursting from the tidal wave of a massive and long overdue cloudburst, it all returned in an earth-shattering rush.

Panting so hard he was gasping for air, he pulled his lips away from hers for the briefest moment. In the time it took him to inhale, he found himself on the floor. In the time it took to exhale, he felt his iron-hard penis slip inside her as she mounted him. In the time it took him to reach his hands around her lower back and slide them up along her shoulder blades, he felt her body tighten and arch and heard the beautiful sustained cry, laugh and sigh of her climax. In the time it took her to reach down and put her index fingers on his nipples, then lower her lips to resume the kiss that had started the whole thing, he felt the pleasurable hot rush of his own orgasm build and build and then suddenly, powerfully, and with a final burst of sticky, erotic rapture, fill his entire convulsing body with more pleasure than he thought possible.

From beginning to end — from the closing of the door till his cumshot — less than three minutes had gone by.

The best candy bar of his entire life.

They lay in each others arms for the longest time. There was no hurry now.

Finally, she leaned back up and they looked at one another in the harsh glare of the single bare light bulb that hung down from his ceiling.

"Candy. That was incredible."

"Just the way I imagined it."

"Imagined it? When?"

"The first time I saw you. At the party."

Billy was suddenly slapped by the hand of jealousy. He squirmed and turned his body so that she had to pull off of him.

"Love at first sight then?"

"Not exactly."

"I see. You do this all the time."

"Why are you ... what do you mean?"

"I'm onto you. I get it! I really get it! We got lucky tonight. Lucky you. Lucky me."

Why was he being so harsh? She just stared at him in disbelief. Then she lowered her eyes and fought back her tears.

"Billy. I don't do this all the time. I've only been with three guys in my whole life. Jeez! I'm 23 years old. Gimme a break."

"Three?"

"You're number three. Does that surprise you?"

"Well uh ... I guess—"

"You guess what?"

"Alright. It does. Look at you. You walk around like the tattooed whore of Babylon."

"Since I have no idea who that is, I'll just take that as a compliment."

"Naturally I assumed ..."

"Yes, you assumed. And what did you assume? Ten? Twenty? A thousand?"

"Well, I didn't have a specific number. But certainly more than three. I mean, I bonked more than three girls before I got out of the seventh grade."

"Seventh grade. That is such a bold-face lie."

"Alright. I was exaggerating. But the point is still valid."

"There's a point to this?"

"Uh ... yes? Maybe? What was it? Oh! Sexual experience. Numbers."

"I am sure you were a real Don Juan. In the seventh grade. Do you have the courage to tell me when you actually lost your virginity?

"We were talking about you. Much more interesting."

"You said I was the whore of Barbizon. That's interesting?"

"Babylon ..." Billy was quiet for a moment, lost in thought. "I've just realized something. Ohmigod. I can't believe this!"

"What?"

"I really shouldn't tell you this. I mean, it's ... embarrassing."

"I'm sure you'll turn a pleasant shade of red."

"Okay." Long pause. "You're my third as well. My number three. We're in a dead heat."

"A dead heat. Gotcha. I feel so much better."

"The two of us. We're practically virgins."

"But let me qualify that. The three I mean."

Candy suddenly looked very intense, trying to decide if she should say it. She went ahead.

"That's three, Billy ... not counting my father ..."

Billy was speechless. He started to gulp but realized he couldn't swallow.

"... and obviously, that wasn't *my* choice. To be honest, I can't really remember much about it. I've completely erased it out of my mind."

A huge anechoic silence engulfed them, which seemed to muffle even the boisterous noises of the city.

"That's probably for the best. Forgetting, I mean. Candy ... uh. With your father. Did this happen more than once?"

"It went on for almost two years. That's all I want to say about it. *Ever*."

Candy came over the next four nights in a row. During the day, she had things to do, so she typically left shortly after nine the following morning.

He never asked what she did. It didn't strike him as particularly relevant.

Much to Billy's surprise, he was extremely comfortable being with her. In fact, it felt damn good having someone there with him. He was even more relieved that not once did he wake up in the middle of the night screaming or crying. Without much room to spare in his single bed, they slept in one another's arms, or with Billy's back turned to her and her arms curled around him. Whatever the position, they were a good fit.

By the end of the fourth night, they had made love more than seven times. The sum total of all of the time they spent having sex was just over twenty minutes. Each time it didn't seem possible to Billy it could ever be better. Each time it was. Billy concluded that the candy bar theory — for lack of anything better to call it — was the best best-kept-secret in the Universe.

That last night, Candy told him she wouldn't be around for the next few days.

"What's up?"

"I'm going to visit my family for Halloween."

"Halloween?"

"Next Wednesday. Maybe you should buy a calendar. There's all sorts of things going on."

"Got it. October 31st. Halloween. What gives?"

"They're both atheists. Halloween is a really big deal to them. Bigger than Thanksgiving, Christmas and the 4th of July combined. What can I say? I have weird parents."

"What a shocker."

"It's a hoot! You should see the party they throw. They're in holy-roller country. The local yokels think its Armageddon descending on them."

"And you'll dress up?"

"Absolutely! It's great fun. This year I'm going as the Preamble to the Constitution. That'll definitely scare the bejesus those Bible-belt rednecks."

As they lay beside one another later that night, Candy fell into a deep sleep. Billy was restless, and spent the time recounting their conversation the first night, their confessions about their relative inexperience in the game of random coupling. Just like he had boorishly said, looking at Candy you would think she'd been around a bit. And considering that many guys fucked three different girls on a weekend — if the stories he heard could be believed — he was closer to the monk end of the scale than probably any other male his age in America.

Candy would be gone for several days. So much for their blossoming romance. But if it was built to last, they could pick up where they left off when she got back.

Billy thought about the thing with her father. Not much detail. But two years of some sort of incestuous sexual abuse. It left a lot of room for the imagination. Way too much room. Very dangerous to think about.

What was confusing was the fact that she was going back home to spend time with him. Well, both of her parents. But how does that work? Does she just calmly sit there at the dinner table with the man who took advantage of her, the man who stole her virginity in the defenseless innocence of her youth, and just smile and say, *"Hey dad, can you pass me more mash potatoes?"*

How *does* that work? She said she had completely erased it out of her mind. So all was forgiven? He wondered if her mother ever found out. And how and why had the abuse stopped? Did her father come to his moral senses? Did Candy somehow put a halt to it?

He really wanted to know. He wanted to ask her. She said she didn't want to talk about it. He certainly couldn't blame her. But there were so many unanswered questions.

Billy wondered why he needed to know. What drove his curiosity? He didn't really want to think about this stuff. But it was everywhere. The papers were full of it. Shock TV and even the so-called respectable news programs dwelled on this depressing shit. Especially anything sexual. If it was both violent and sexual, you could bet it would be the centerpiece of television programming for as many nights as the solemn-faced talking heads could milk the story.

He recalled the horrible story that Sister Mary Felicia had related about her father.

How common was this? Was it just a coincidence that a nun he had been close friends with in Detroit, and a lovely girl he was laying next to in New York, had the same incomprehensibly vile thing happen to them?

He thought about his own first-hand experience with abusive men. Though clearly not as calamitous, but certainly as deplorable and disturbing in its own way, he thought about the time when as a boy of twelve, he had been lured by the puppeteering Mr. Rogers. He remembered his father's denigrating and cruel references to his mother's inadequacies in bed, his constant belittling and bullying of her, his macho, relentless, chest-beating intimidation, a form of rape in its own right.

Was all of this normal? Business as usual? Under the spit shine of propriety and family values, honor and Judeo-Christian ethics, was the world actually driven by some sort of carnal madness, sexual mayhem? Were these anomalous moments of sexual pathology or did they point to the true essence and excesses of human nature?

He had never treated women badly. From what other men said — from the way they bragged about their exploits, leaving nothing to the imagination, crassly exposing their true attitude toward women — Billy knew he was the exception to the rule.

But underneath his alleged innocence, was he capable of the kind of brutality that came so easy to most men?

Probably. Given the right circumstances. It was most likely wired into him like everyone else. Could he rape a woman? Men talked rape talk all the time. Mild forms of rape — "date rape" was the most recent incarnation — were apparently very common these days. The interesting thing was that men never said they forced themselves on a woman because they couldn't stop themselves, because they were just so damn horny. No, they blamed it on the woman for tempting them, for being so damn hot and irresistibly provocative. Or more far-fetched, they would claim that they were just "doing the bitch a favor." It was obvious, she actually wanted it and they were there to give it to her.

Billy lay in bed and the minutes ticked away late into the night. He could faintly hear Candy breathing the soft shallow breaths of a deep, contented sleep. Occasionally she would stir slightly and her skin would brush against his, or her arm would readjust itself and her hand would slide gently across his chest.

Romantic love. Now there was another whole can of tomatoes. Was it just a marketing tool? Was it another fairy tale, like Santa Claus or the Easter Bunny or the Tooth Fairy, just there to put a pretty face on the sad reality of life, and make some serious bucks along the way?

Through his screwed-up family life, Catholic school, his father's abuse of his mother, through the mounds of stuff that ran contrary, he still harbored a belief in romantic love. Dutifully and dumbly he had carted it right into his blissful house-of-mirrors marriage, watched it mocked and destroyed by the cunt-licking disloyalty of the woman of his dreams.

He thought about Natalie. If that wasn't love he felt for her, then it was an illusion with more reality than reality itself. An illusion he certainly *preferred* to the reality which eventually cannibalized the illusion. But was it all a dream?

It certainly evaporated with the ease that a dream evaporates, dissolving into the harshness and cruel isolation of real life.

What if it was a dream but he had never woken up? What would it matter? Why should he care about what's real and what isn't?

The questions just kept coming.

Could he ever trust anyone again?

Could he again be close to someone?

Why was he so naive? Why so clueless?

How did he come by his Disney view of life?

Why did this silly naiveté persist into his adult life?

Why was he asking the same questions over and over?

Something was screwed up, that was for sure.

Was it him? Or was it the world?

The questions kept coming. Like a runaway freight train. Only someone had forgotten to attach the boxcar containing the answers.

It seemed he had only been asleep for a few minutes, when he heard Candy's whispering.

"Hey Billy. Billy? Are you in there?"

"Umm ..."

"Listen. I better go. I have to pack."

"What time is it?"

"A little after eight. Bye. See you in a week."

"Umm ..."

Tunnel of Love

Candy was gone. Now what?

Billy lit a joint. The headache stuff.

One thing high on his agenda today would be to score some clean dope, that was for sure.

After he walked around Washington Square, eventually scoring some *"real clean shit, man, clean as Laura Bush's rap sheet!"* — actually from a very well-groomed, smartly-dressed dealer standing quite to himself in front of an apartment building on MacDougal Street — Billy headed into the West Village.

It was Saturday. He had no plans.

As he wandered along 7th Avenue, thinking he might take in a movie, since it had been a while, a bespectacled black dude bearing an uncanny resemblance to Spike Lee, handed him a club invitation. It was for tomorrow night.

TUNNEL OF LOVE
Delicious Debauchery
FETISH ††† FETISH ††† FETISH
Sunday October 28th
10:30 pm - ????
121 West 23rd Street
Flatiron

The invitation didn't pull any punches.
Delicious Debauchery?
That left little to the imagination.
At the same time ... a lot.
Why not?
Billy knew next to nothing about the fetish scene. He knew it existed. He had seen a few posters, been handed fliers for events similar to the Tunnel of Love, seen fetish fashions in some of the storefront windows around town, even recalled seeing fetish art somewhere. It tended to blend in with a lot of the other twisted stuff around town, so had never established itself in his mind as a unique category.

He suspected that some of the clothes he had seen on Amethyst, both onstage and in the photographs and fliers promoting her band, was "fetish wear".

If there was an ideal place to get a quick education in the fetish fashion scene, it was where he happened to be right now — in the West Village. There were numerous related shops on 7th Avenue itself and the streets intersecting it.

Billy accepted the fact that he was going to come off as a real rube going into any of these places, asking for advice, buying his first ensemble.

But what did he have to lose?
His pride? Not much of that left.
He was game.
Much to his surprise and relief, the first shop he went into treated him admirably. Two young sales clerks enthusiastically assisted him, making it not only comfortable trying on various outrageous costumes and gear, but fun.

What Billy didn't realize at the time was that, while a lot of those into the fetish scene were in their normal everyday street attire pretty outrageous — either genuine gothers, openly and outrageously gay, or just advertising their heterosexual availability with shameless immoderation — the truth was that a sizable majority were pretty regular people who used the fetish parties and bars as a 180° escape from their humdrum daily lives, a time-out when they could be as scandalous, brazen and shocking as they desired. Straight people gone wild, at least for a few hours on the weekend.

One of the sales clerks at the fetish shop was a young man, maybe 18 or 19. The other was a girl maybe in her late 20s. It was hard to tell with her. She had so much make-up on, it was like trying to guess the age of a circus clown.

They were not only pleasant and funny, but extremely creative. They took complete control, which Billy ceded without any struggle, basically using him as a big dress-up doll for theirs and his amusement.

"Wait! He's got a great butt. Put him in those yellow latex short-shorts."

"Those are for a girl."

"Who cares? I can see a girl inside there just waiting to bust out."

"Then he's definitely got to shave those legs. Good grief!"

"No no no. Just put these on him."

Edie — that was the salesgirl's name though she said she preferred EatMe — held up a pair of black vinyl thigh-high boots that laced up the front, which incongruously were at their base big bulky military-style shoes. Elegance and battlefield functionality all in one.

"He can shave his thighs and body paint them."

"And check this out!"

Thadeus — the boy sales clerk — came over with a shiny black latex top of such an odd configuration Billy couldn't at first figure out what it was. Thad unbuttoned Billy's regular shirt and helped him out of it, then pulled the new piece over Billy's head. He fastened the collar in back. It was a sleeveless peek-a-boo — meaning it had holes cut out to show his pecs and nipples — also cut in an arc over the navel to tastefully expose the bellybutton.

Now it was time for the headgear.

"Torture straps?"

"Alien hood?"

"Gas mask?"

"Chér wig?"

"Dragonfly antennas?"

"Masochist's menorah?

"How about if we go aviator?"

They finally settled on a taut black latex hood that could be worn under the chin or pulled up over the mouth — it had a white gauze insert for breathing that looked like a cruise ship porthole. Then over the hood, yellow aviator goggles to complement the yellow short-shorts.

One last touch. Edie came up with some vinyl lace-up finger gloves. Also black, of course. They covered the entire forearm up to the elbow, and all of the fingers were gloved, except the middle finger, which was bare almost to the knuckle. It also was elegant and functional, especially if someone maybe wanted to stick their middle finger up somewhere. Hmm. Wonder where that might be.

Edie and Thad stood back and admired the transformation.

"Totally hot!"

"Sick. Really sick!"

"You're a fuck for sore eyes!"

"Everyone is going to want to lick you all over."

"Definitely fit to be tied!"

Which raised an important issue for Billy.

"Um ... most everything has to be laced up on this outfit. How am I going to manage that? I live alone and my mother lives in Detroit. Not that I would think of calling my mom for help on this."

"I see. When are you going? And where?"

"Tomorrow. Tunnel of Love. Over on—"

"Shut up!"

"Massively sick!"

"You are one awesome bitch!"

Billy assumed those were exclamations of approval, irony somehow figuring into the equation.

"We're there every Sunday!"

"Listen. The shop is open until 9 every night. Just come by. We'll take care of you."

They were obviously very excited about initiating a new recruit into their world. Thad especially seemed to relish the idea. He smiled and blinked as he continued to fuss with Billy's outfit.

Okay! They had a plan. Billy would show up around 7:30 or 8 and they'd get him ready, close the shop, then head over to Tunnel of Love together. It promised to be a smashing good time.

Billy got dressed back in his regular clothes, and walked out of the store $224.87 lighter, trying to keep the store logo on the bag hidden against his body. He was committed to going through with this but still didn't feel comfortable walking around advertising that he shopped at Rubber Danish.

RUBBER DANISH

*"Rub it hard and
make it wet!"*

Fetish wear for the disturbed, demented, demonic, diseased, disaffected, degenerate, **warped and wicked**.

On the way home, it occurred to him that he was spending a lot of money. But he decided it was the price of freedom. Of course, he wouldn't be very free if he ran out. He only had forty dollars on him and stopped at an ATM on the way.

He withdrew another $500 and noticed that there was at least a couple thousand more in the account. Natalie must have sold some more stuff.

Alright! Not to worry for now. Not about something as mundane as eating and having a roof over his head, when there were more important things to think about. Like partying at Tunnel of Love and his inauguration in the New York fetish scene.

It's about establishing priorities.

He showed up the next evening at Rubber Danish, and all went as planned. They killed some time, since the doors at the club didn't even open till 10:30 and who wants to arrive early for a party? Finally Billy, Edie, and Thad shared a taxi for the relatively short trip to Flatiron.

The *Delicious Debauchery* reference on the invitation he was handed in the street, turned out to be the name of tonight's theme, not a trademark moniker for the club. Many of the costumes reflected the evening's motif.

One tanned, muscular guy was mostly naked except for a leather thong, tennis shoes and suspenders. He carried a bucket full of heavily frosted cake, which he smeared all over himself. Males and females took turns licking it off.

A girl dressed in practically nothing except plastic flex hosing, which she had wrapped around her hips and torso, allowing revealing glimpses of her reproductive equipment, was laying on the floor either having or giving a convincing re-creation of a grand mal seizure. Two couples standing close by paid no attention to her, while one guy with a vibrator in one hand appeared to be cheering her on. She apparently had a pressurized can between her legs. Periodically whip cream would shoot straight up like a geyser and her one-man cheering section would try to catch it in his mouth.

Another guy appeared to be dripping blood all over himself, squirting it from a plastic bag through an IV tube, the kind seen in hospitals. It turned out to be some sweet red liqueur. He went around squirting it into the mouths of other patrons, or offering girls the appetizing opportunity to lick it off his fat hairy chest. Most declined. Unfortunately, he personally sucked in a little too much of the sweet sticky stuff himself and was down for the count shortly before midnight.

An exquisite girl with intriguingly crooked teeth had on latex lingerie and a long matching silk cape. She had electrical tape on her nipples, leaving most of the front of her torso bare. On it written in henna or some other brown body paint was *'Eat shit and die!'* She went around the club acting like she was defecating chunks of chocolate and offering them to anyone who was not too repulsed to play along. A surprising number ate them.

On and on it went. In keeping with the theme, most everyone there was smearing and licking off various confections or other sugary treats on themselves or others.

As expensive as it was, and as spectacular as it made him look — and he did look spectacular — Billy's outfit was more generic fetish wear, and was not really 'on message'. He wasn't particularly delicious or exceptionally debauched, from what he was seeing.

But neither were Edie, Thad, or probably close to half of the several hundred people there.

It really didn't matter. What mattered was being there.

This was a scene. It was huge. The club had been in the making for a long time.

After paying the $25 cover charge on entering, Billy had walked through the tunnel — there actually was a tunnel, consisting of a long metallic tube eerily illuminated in black light, with random bursts of a strobe going off for any epileptics in the crowd — which led to the cavernous main room. He looked with wonder at the posters lining the walls. Each poster represented a different theme, for the scores of parties that had taken place here over the past several years. Billy couldn't help but wonder how these people could afford this. You'd have to be rich to keep up with it all.

Party themes were varied, sometimes bizarre, always with erotic overtones, if not in name than in execution: neo-primitivism, voodoo, electrical torture, erotic zombies, sex mutants, post-apocalyptics, sports sex, religious sex, future sex, cyber sex, political heresy, religious blasphemy, cyber erotics, cartoons, paranormal, cinema, Michael Jackson, Dolly Parton, James Bond, B&D, S&M,

Ken and Barbie, espionage sex, circus sex, paramilitary sex, sex sex sex. Practically anything that could be mimed, mocked or imitated, anything which lent itself to collective insanity and could be the inspiration for salacious and demented wardrobing, was fair game for a fetish theme party.

There was also a photo board below each poster, showing people in the costumes they wore at each event. It was obvious for a devoted core that this was an obsession, a cult, a veritable religion. They not only had devoted a lot of money to this, they had spent hours and hours coming up with the ideas for their look and presentation, tracking down props, making costumes and accessories, building elaborate mechanisms. This looked like a full-time profession for many of them. Maybe they didn't have real jobs.

In a word, it was overwhelming.

Of course, no one could tell he was overwhelmed or the least impressed, since most of his face was covered with the latex hood, and his eyes obscured behind the aviator goggles.

But Billy sure knew he was in over his head.

He wasn't intimidated. Just very very bewildered.

He recalled learning in high school biology that the human body was 75% water. Lately he had been feeling like his was 75% confusion.

Billy stepped up to the closest of the three bars keeping the party hydrated. The music was extremely loud and he had to yell.

"Rum on the rocks, please. Make it a triple."

"Any particular kind of rum, sir?"

Billy looked at the mirrored wall containing the liquor selection.

"Bacardi. I like their Breezers."

"We have Breezers too."

"Great. Give me a Breezer as well."

"A serious drinker." This coming from a female in a patent leather gas mask next to him. "You're not doing MDMA?"

He heard her say something. Between the mask and the music, he had difficulty understanding what she was saying.

"What?"

"MDMA. Are you high?"

"Do I have a medical degree? Not really."

"A newbie, eh?"

"I did a doobie before coming here. I could roll one if we can find some privacy. Is it okay? You know. To light up? I've never been to this club before."

The bartender gave Billy his drinks.

"Let's go where we can talk. I'm Grace."

She led Billy over to a corner, next to two guys who were dressed as Navy Seals. Surprisingly, in this little nook the volume of the music was less by half. There was a low table and they sat down.

Grace took off her gas mask. She was pretty, with small delicate features. There was a tiny scar over her right eye, but other than that her skin was flawless. Her hair was jet black but was probably dyed for the occasion. How old was she? She looked fairly young but might be in her 30s.

"And you are?"

"Billy. Billy Green, originally from Detroit."

"Where's your chocolate syrup? Marshmallow topping?"

"I'm fasting. It's Ramadan for us Muslims."

"Oh I see. I have a feeling I'm being punk'd."

"But I'm thinking of leaving the religion. Especially after tonight. This is so much better. Do they ever have erotic Islamic terrorist night here?"

"Sort of. They had like a Taliban thing. I can't remember what they called it. It was a couple years ago. I wore a burqa with a strap-on underneath."

"Very creative."

"It got a few laughs. I got a blow job from Osama bin Laden. So Billy. What do you do for a living?"

"I'm an attorney. Mergers. Takeovers. Multi-national corporate cannibalism. And you?"

"Actually I'm a literary agent. Most people don't know what that is."

"I admit it. I don't."

"Someone writes a book. They come to me to find them a publisher. I shop the book around and get them the best deal."

"Sounds interesting."

"It was for a while. But now I hate it."

"What kind of books? Have you represented any I might have heard of?"

"Probably not. I mainly do chick lit. That and women's empowerment stuff. Girly novels and feminist manifestos. Sweet and sour."

"But you hate it."

"It's the fucking egos. The unrealistic expectations. Writers are crazy. Why else would they be writers?"

"You seem to have some issues about this."

"I mean, everyone who comes to me is sure that they're John Steinbeck reincarnated. Except he was a male. So they must be the next Maya Angelou or Naomi Klein. And every one of them thinks *her* book is a bestseller. Like a million people are going to be fascinated with reading about the parallels between the glass ceiling for women in corporate America and female circumcision in some fucked-up tribe in Mali."

"I've been looking for a good book on that very topic. Especially if it has a good map of Mali. Any suggestions?"

"The biggest thing all these pen-to-the-paper types miss is the difference between a good book and a good-selling book. Take *The Da Vinci Code*."

"I have that book! It's right next to my bed. I've been trying to read it for a year now."

"Don't bother. It may be a big seller. Try 35 million copies worldwide. But it's full of holes. All sorts of major inaccuracies and inconsistencies. Still, people loved it. My authors worry so much about dotting their i's and crossing their t's that they don't notice that their books suck. Or at least only appeal to their close friends and their dog, if it happens to be able to read."

"Aren't the i's and t's dotted and crossed automatically by a computer? That's what I heard."

"Then there's all the games I have to play as a female. Publishing, like everything else, is still an old boy's club. These guys are just as big a bunch of pigs as the ones running the tobacco or the pharmaceutical companies. Or the weapons manufacturers or Wall Street."

"So why don't you do something else?"

"Because frankly, these women need to be heard. Whether they make the big numbers like John Grisham or Stephen King or not, what they have to say needs to be out there. Which is another reason I get so pissed off."

"Meaning?"

"I am fighting tooth and nail for my writers. I believe in them. I am fighting the battles they, as wimp-ass spoiled little nerds sitting at a computer all day, could never fight on their own. Yet I get as much grief from them as the thick-headed naysayers who run the publishing houses. I get it from both sides. It hurts. It frustrates me. It really *really* pisses me off."

Suddenly she threw her hands up in the air, signaling a halt.

"Enough! I am here to forget all that. So. What about you? What did you say your line of work was?"

"You know. Corporate legal stuff. Mergers. Like, you know how General Electric gobbled up all of those financial institutions, then started to get into commercial loans, credit cards, the whole financing thing? Well, my firm ..." He stopped talking, took a big gulp of his rum, then stared at it for a bit. "Forget it. Forget everything I just said. All made up. Sorry about that. I just got carried away with the excitement. The truth is that my wife left me and I don't have a job. I'm 100% unemployed. I never was a lawyer."

Grace looked unfazed by his confession. In fact, she was smiling slightly. She took a sip of her drink, some froofy cocktail, then looked at Billy.

Very intently.

"Being unemployed is a lot better than being a fucking lawyer. Just sitting around, you're making more of a contribution to society than a thousand attorneys."

"How's that?"

"You're not contributing to a system that's destroying the justice system, democracy, and everything else America is supposed to stand for. You're not serving the oligarchy."

"I'm not doing shit."

Grace was one of these women who looked good mad. Billy couldn't help but notice how her intensity just increased her sex appeal.

"Billy. How old are you?"

"Twenty-five in December."

"Well I'm thirty-seven. Guys your age tune it all out. But I've seen it happen just in the past ten or fifteen years. Corporations are like a cancer. They just keep spreading. Killing everything in their path. You need to work on your political sensibilities."

"Someone else just said that to me the other day."

"I hope you were listening."

She took all of this very seriously. He had himself never known that kind of passionate commitment. Everything she said made sense. It resonated with Billy intellectually. But he just couldn't get very revved up about it.

"Maybe we can talk about this some other time."

"There won't be a some other time. You apparently don't understand. What happens here stays here. That's kind of the point, isn't it?"

"I can't say I know what the point of any of this is. Why, for example, you are fighting to achieve a voice for your women writers, but sitting here with your tits busting out of a torture bra and your face stuffed into a high-fashion gas mask. I haven't even figured out why I am here."

"Well. I'll tell you what. I'm going to hand you the opportunity of a lifetime. Look around. Walk around." She pointed. "Go lick chocolate syrup off of that guy's crotch." She pointed to a girl who was making out with two other girls. "Go tell those bitches whatever comes to mind at the time and see where it goes. 'Cause that's what it's all about, Billy Green."

Grace stood up, clinked her glass against Billy's tumbler of rum and ice, then walked away.

Had he turned her off? What was that bit about handing him the *opportunity of a lifetime*? By doing what? Walking away?

Billy wasn't quite sure how he felt. Certainly not great. But should he care?

He was starting to really feel the rum. An invisible glassine sanctuary slowly engirdled him, filtering the sensory assault of the club, softening the edges, providing the sense of isolation and clarity he needed to really objectify the situation.

Billy took Grace's advice. He got up and walked around. Just went with it.

A band, the Genitorturers, was now onstage. The raw electronic gothics of their instrumental sound and guttural vocals seduced and bewitched the audience. Everyone in the club moved in tandem, a consensual writhing, shot through with lewd posturing, mimed copulation, mock oral sex. Billy thought that their songs were noticeably more coherent than Machines of Melanoma, lyrically addressing topics which most everyone present seemed to have a pained fascination: masturbation, flesh, cum, bitches, sluts, torture, fucking, lechery, pain, evil, humiliation, bonding with the devil.

It definitely was not their family values set.

Or maybe it was.

Later as the night progressed, there would be more performing acts. The Piltdown Harlots. Dominatrix Mistress Lorraine Fatale, a nihilist performance artist. RAM the Mega Bite Fucking Machine. Burlesque retro by Tits In Tatters. A torch and bondage show by Stacie Savage and Markie de Sade. Ula the Pain Proof Rubber Girl.

Also on the bill was a short video called *Bring It Home To Mommie* by underground directors Caroline Clusterfuck and Natasha Zoom.

Between performances, the DJs took over. There were three on board tonight to provide the manic throbbing pulse which powered the dancing, pseudo-sex, and carnal flirtations — three DJs with stylistic variations to minimize monotony. Tonight's celebrity spinners were DJ Suffer, DJ Quik/E, and DJ Nerv Onna.

Each DJ had his or her — one was female — trademark style, though not surprisingly, escape into erotic abandon was the common theme for most of the music. It was more fun for Billy to watch them perform, than to listen to the music they played. He had never understood or particularly appreciated house, electro, industrial, trance, dub, trip-hop, drum-and-bass, or any of the other sub-genres of techno music which had become the staple for dance clubs.

The entire cavernous club pulsed at the optimum 136-142 beats per minute, the rhythmic pace of a good fleshy genital pounding in the final frenetic gallop toward an orgasm. The costumes were all about sex. The gyrating movement and affected body language was all about sex. The lascivious leering and puckering, tongue wagging and lip licking, were all about sex. From the posters he had seen, this evening's party was slightly anomalous because they hadn't worked the words 'erotic' or 'sex' into the title. Practically all of the other events featured one or the other. Certainly *Delicious Debauchery* referenced it.

It was patently obvious that the celebration of sex, carnal fantasy, and erotic experimentation was what Tunnel of Love — and all the latex, leather, vinyl, PVC, spandex and lingerie — was all about.

What astounded Billy was how *unerotic* the whole thing was.

It just plain wasn't very sexy.

Not from a lack of trying. Everyone definitely got a 'A' for effort.

Nor was it from a shortage of amazing bodies, both male and female, though there was a substantial number — perhaps a third of those attending — of truly unsightly looking people as well. The whole spectrum from breathtakingly beautiful to unbelievably ugly was there.

Another thing that really struck Billy, particularly at the far extremes of this beauty spectrum, was the immodesty of it all. Why some grotesquely fat or some skeletally malnourished individual would want to invite public scrutiny and subject themselves to the likelihood of ridicule, completely astounded him. Likewise, why a person so perfectly gifted that they could command decent modeling fees from any number of fashion or skin magazines, why they would let it all — or most of it — hang out for free, didn't add up either.

Billy could only conclude that the typical Joe and Josephine that came to this place, must be pathological exhibitionists.

Then again, who was he to talk? He wasn't showing his genitals but his nipples — definitely highly erogenous zones — were framed like dollops of caramel begging to be licked, and his hood had a breathing hole that looked like those perfectly round mouths in inflatable sex dolls sold in adult bookstores.

He sure appeared to be fucked in the head, whether he had been or not.

Why else would he be here?

There was only one way he was able to keep all of this in perspective. Simple chemistry. Billy's bar tab for rum and Bacardi Breezers ran to $92 by the end of the night. He would have been completely smashed except for the chemical boost awarded him by some unidentified mood and energy enhancers, generously given to him over the course of the evening, by people he would have no way of identifying the next day on the street. If nothing else, the fetish scene seemed to build a bond of trust between strangers.

Or was it a pact for self-destruction?

Whatever it was, by the end of the evening it was far beyond the reach of analysis or introspection. In fact by the end of the evening, the end of the evening was beyond the reach of Billy's recollection. Somehow at some indeterminate time, he found himself standing and looking down the steps to his flat. There was a horrible odor and he realized yet another bum was curled at his feet, wrapped in a ragged, filthy blanket, caked with dried vomit and drool.

"Fuck a duck."

"Buy low, sell high."

A bum with a keen grasp of the stock market.

Billy entered, set the dead bolt, and slid the four security chains in place.

About twenty minutes after he stumbled into his apartment, the phone rang.

"Hello."

"Are you drunk?"

It was Candy.

"Well ... not ... what time is it?"

"Time for you to get some sleep. Try 4:39. That's in the morning. Listen, Billy. I won't be coming back for a while. I don't want to go into it. But there's some trouble here."

"What kind of trouble? Is your dad raping you again?"

Not the smartest thing to say. The alcohol was doing the talking. There was a long silence.

"I'm fine. Nothing to do with me. I can't talk now."

"It's 4:39 in the morning and there's a crowd standing around you?"

"Billy. Please don't forget about me. I'll see you ... well, I don't know when. But as soon as I get back."

"Right. I can't wait."

"Don't be so bitter. Trust me. Just try. I'm on your side. Bye."

Click.

Nice work. The Billy Green golden tongue of diplomacy strikes again. He felt guilty and at the same time angry.

Billy suspected that Candy was blowing him off.

Hey. Easy come easy go.

Not really.

He crashed. Really crashed. He fell over like a freshly chain-sawed blue spruce, and slept for nine hours on the floor. It saved him having to make his bed — as if he ever made it.

It was early afternoon when he woke up. Perfect time for a fresh start. He didn't, however, feel very fresh. His head felt like it was stuffed with rolled oats. No milk. Just the flakes. Maybe Grace had dropped a Mickey Finn in his rum. He had trouble focusing his eyes and fumbled trying to roll a joint. Once he finally got it right and lit up, he doddered over to the fridge with it dangling from his chapped lips and made himself a cheese and mayonnaise sandwich.

There was a small mirror on the wall at the end of the kitchen area, purely to cover a big hole in the plaster. As he turned, Billy caught a glimpse of himself.

What the fuck!

There he stood, still in the latex costume from the night before.

No doubt about it. This was a very different look for him.

How did he get home? He couldn't remember. There was some hazy recollection of being in a taxi with two strangers who had mountains of pink hair — really really *huge* people. Doing lines of coke on a tiny compact mirror. Were they guys? Or women on steroids. Maybe cross-dressing guys on steroids.

Was he imagining all of this?

Then what?

Right. Candy called.

He undressed and noticed bruises on his arms. Then the black eye. Not all that noticeable. Just some slight discoloration above the right eyeball and redness in the area below.

He must have had quite the evening.

Billy went out for the day. He took *The Da Vinci Code* with him in case he felt like reading. But the pot dampened his literary cravings. Or maybe it was the call from Candy. He had this big hollow feeling inside him, not anxiety so much as a yearning for some undefined thing. Something which he should know about, but for some reason didn't.

When he returned home, he popped open a Bacardi Breezer and dialed his mom.

"Hey! What are you doing?"

"Hello, stranger. I'm making something. A costume."

"This sounds interesting. What kind of costume?"

"I wish I could describe it. But you'd definitely get the wrong idea. It's your father. He has this Halloween party to go to with King Komodo of Detroit. You know. That motorcycle club he belongs to."

"Right. Day after tomorrow. Let me get this straight. He's dressing up too? As what?"

"Billy. He dresses up everyday. You should see him. I'm embarrassed to be seen with him. At least Halloween, he has an excuse to look like that."

"The Hell's Angels thing. He still doing that."

"He says he finally figured out who he is, after all these years. Anyway, all evening I'm supposed to call him Rat, and he's going to call me Barbarella."

"Rat. That works for him. What's the Barbara ... Barbell ...?"

"Barbarella was a Jane Fonda movie. I never saw it. I guess she looked sexy or something."

"Jane who?"

"Jane Fonda. Before your time. She married Ted Turner."

"The baseball player?"

"I can't believe it. Your mother knows something you don't. I would jump up and sing the Hallelujah Chorus except — ouch!! I just stuck myself with a needle. So what about you, Billy? Are you okay? Are you doing something for Halloween?"

"I'm fine mom. I went to a ... uh ... well, it was kind of a costume party last night."

"Have you heard from ... you know ...?"

"No. It's fine. That's the way it goes. She knows my number. Anyway, I should go now. Just wanted to say hi. Tell Rat to stay clear of any big contraptions with a chunk of cheese sitting in the center. Bye, mom. Love you."

"Bye, Billy. Be a good boy."

His dad continued to really amaze him. He must have changed a lot in the past couple years. An awful lot. The guy hardly moved for eighteen years. Now he's going to wild parties.

While Billy had no intention of taking advantage of *Harold V. 2.0* — Billy stored way too much resentment and had no desire to be around him — he was certainly glad for his mom. Finally, his father was paying attention to her and providing some companionship. And some fun. It was the least the old man could do, since she had committed her life to him.

Billy then thought about his mentioning the Tunnel of Love. "… kind of a costume party." Right. That's one way to put it. More like a end-of-the-species ball for terminally-possessed schizophrenics.

He tried to imagine what his mom would think of a scene like that. What she would think about him attending it. She had certainly turned out to be pretty broad-minded. About gay people, about a lot of things. But Tunnel of Love was really pushing the envelope.

Billy finished the Breezer. Popped open another one. Lit a joint.

He started mulling over the entire night. What a completely fucked up, weird experience! Should he go back? Or was it more of a been-there-done-that one-off kind of thing?

Tunnel of love.

What a perfect image.

It was him!

He was stuck in the tunnel of love.

Prisoner of the love train.

Rolling rolling rolling.

Chugga choo chugga choo …

Was there light at the end of the tunnel?

Anybody's guess.

Things weren't looking so good.

Julianne? Natalie? Candy?

Rolling rolling rolling.

Going nowhere fast.

That was him alright.

Chugga choo chugga choo …

Did his life make *any* sense at all?

It sure didn't feel like it.

Gee! What a surprise!

Since he couldn't feel much of anything these days.

Maybe he was expecting too much.

Or too little.

Whatever.

Chugga choo chugga choo …

More Books by John Rachel

The book you just finished is the second of a trilogy. It seems unlikely but in case you somehow missed the first, you might want to see where this all started.

"The Man Who Loved Too Much"
Book 1!

Poor Billy Green! With all of the swell advantages of growing up in beautiful Detroit, Michigan what could possibly go wrong?

Amazon (Kindle): amzn.to/1tyIRiw
Amazon (Print): amzn.to/1z8F8aD
Barnes & Noble: bit.ly/ZDnQVO
Apple iBook: bit.ly/1ycltFD
Smashwords: bit.ly/1w62HOX

• •

"Blinders Keepers"

In this dark comedy, a young man who escapes his hopelessly hayseed home town in Missouri is mistakenly labeled a terrorist and must survive a manhunt by government security agencies, while the President of an America in chaos and collapse perpetrates an end-of-the-world hoax, attempting to reclaim control and get himself re-elected.

Amazon (Kindle): <u>amzn.to/122cnyF</u>
Barnes & Noble: <u>bit.ly/17MtgjE</u>
Apple iBook: <u>bit.ly/11WqJiv</u>
Smashwords: <u>bit.ly/190zmgs</u>
Kobo: <u>bit.ly/18wHki2</u>

• •

"11 - 11 - 11"

Noah was turning 23 and desperate to get out of town. Pulnick, Missouri had always been bland and soporific, but now it was now being invaded by white supremacist meth heads, plagued by an unprecedented crime wave, exploited by spiritualists and local politicos, and driven to hysteria by paranoid rumors that the world would end on November 11th.

Amazon (Kindle): <u>amzn.to/1sEWaf0</u>
Barnes & Noble: <u>bit.ly/1nlgS2Z</u>
Apple iBook: <u>bit.ly/1z8TCKS</u>
Smashwords: <u>bit.ly/1paiJ6j</u>
Kobo: <u>bit.ly/T7181J</u>

• •

"12 - 12 - 12"

Welcome to the parallel universe of "12-12-12". This not what actually happens during 2012. But what unfolds is not more implausible. Nor is it less implausible. It is dark satire, a portrayal of reality with healthy doses of surreality and comedy, spawned by the tragic absurdity of our times. One reviewer calls it "laugh-out-loud brain food for hungry minds."

Amazon (Kindle): amzn.to/1DaFrDL
Barnes & Noble: bit.ly/1w5Yw5D
Apple iBook: bit.ly/1sJasMO
Smashwords: bit.ly/1o9GaSg
Kobo: lnk.ms/c1CWm

. . . .

Coming Soon

"The Man Who Loved Too Much"
Book 3!

About The Author

John Rachel has a B.A. in Philosophy, has traveled extensively, been a songwriter and music producer, is a left-of-left liberal, and has spent his life trying to resolve the intrinsic clash between the metaphysical purity of Buddhism and the overwhelming appeal of narcissism.

In October of 2008, while living in Japan, he completed his first novel, which he prefers to no longer discuss. It fell into a legal black hole, the result of the naïve and trusting Rachel being conned by an unscrupulous publisher.

In November of 2009, he completed his second novel, *The Man Who Loved Too Much*, written over ten months, as he lived in and traveled through Japan, China, Nepal, India Thailand, and Malaysia. It follows the convoluted life of a young man from age 4 to 28, as he tries to find his place in the world. The story is set in Detroit, upstate New York, and New York City. At 800+ pages, it is an epic. This encyclopedia of white trash pulp fiction plotlines has been split into three volumes, the novel you have just read being the second book of the series.

While writing his third and fourth novels in 2010 and 2011 — *11-11-11* and *12-12-12* — which track two years in the life of a young man, a hapless victim born in a hopelessly hayseed town in Bible-belt Missouri, the author hopped around between Japan, Taiwan, Indonesia, South Korea and the Philippines. Those two efforts evolved into the short and snappy adventure, *Blinders Keepers*, both as a novel and a screenplay. Combining plot elements from *11-11-11* and *12-12-12*, *Blinders Keepers* is social-political satire in the tradition of Jonathan Swift, Kurt Vonnegut and Joseph Heller, but revved up and spit-shined to take on the historical new levels of absurdity and dysfunction of the 21st Century. It was published in 2013, after which the author bounced between Japan, South Korea, America, and nine countries in Europe.

He then became somewhat rooted in a small traditional farming village in Japan near Osaka. It was there, immediately after poking himself in the forehead with chopsticks, that he was inspired to plant soybeans and sweet potatoes in his small but promising vegetable garden, and to write *An Unlikely Truth*, published March of 2014. In this political drama, a bright, young, idealistic, Green Party candidate, in his bid for the congressional seat of a very conservative district in Ohio, teams with a beautiful, fiery African-American intern to combat the slick deceptions and ruthless tactics of a sweet-talking right wing incumbent.

After the publication of the entire *The Man Who Loved Too Much* trilogy, he has two more novels in the pipeline: *Love Connection*, a drug-trafficking thriller set in Japan, and *The Last Giraffe*, an anthropological drama involving both the worship and devouring of giraffes. It unfolds in sub-Saharan Africa.

Also in the works is a political manifesto, and a creative non-fiction work, *The Naked American*. It is allegedly an account of his travels since leaving the

U.S. August of 2006, but more likely the product of the voices in his head which have plagued him since puberty. Several publishers have declared that they will do everything in their power to make sure this book never sees the light of day.

The author's last permanent residence in America was Portland, Oregon where he had a state-of-the-art ProTools recording studio, music production house, a radio promotion and music publishing company. He recorded and produced several artists in the Pacific Northwest, releasing and promoting their music on radio across the U.S.

• • •

You can follow John Rachel's adventures
and developing world view at:
jdrachel.com

• • •

Since the open mind recognizes no borders, you are also
invited to join us in the ongoing dialogue about
literature and the writing arts here:
literaryvagabond.com

Legal Notices and Disclaimers:

Seven adapted excerpts from *The Man Who Loved Too Much, Book 2: Entendre* have appeared as short stories in online and print publications: "Dear Ann Landers" was published in the Michigan State University annual anthology, The Offbeat, Autumn 2011; "Make Love Not War" appeared in the American magazine, The Fear of Monkeys, the March 2010 issue; "Baby Fever" was published in the American print magazine, Down In The Dirt, July 2010; "Renoir Albertine Toulouse, Thumb Painter" appeared in The Dirty Napkin, September 2010; "Machines of Melanoma" was published in Paradigm Shift: The New Paradigm, in August 2010; and "Tunnel of Love" and "The Crush" appeared in the Detroit-based online magazine Troubadour 21, in May 2010 and December 2010 respectively.

The Man Who Loved Too Much
Book 3: Oxymoron (Excerpt)

<u>Chapter 1:</u>   THE DAZE OF OUR LIVES

Planet Oblivion

A week had gone by. Halloween had come and gone.

Still no word from Candy.

Maybe she had written him off.

Life in the big city.

Billy was sitting in Planet Hollywood on Broadway, in the heart of the *new* Times Square.

This area at one time had been the unofficial strip mall for all of the depravity, decadence, vice, and almost every commodifiable form of affliction and death, available from the slimy lowlife of New York City. You name it. You could buy it there. Drugs, sex, stolen goods, guns, a gangland assassination.

At night, so concentrated were the bottom-dwelling scum on 42nd Street between Broadway and 8th Avenue, spilling out onto the contiguous streets for several city blocks in every direction, the *selling* public — hookers, hustlers, pimps, fences, hit men, drug dealers, con men, and other illicit entrepreneurs — often outnumbered the *buying* public.

All of that changed in the 90s. Using coercive police sweeps and sanitizing enforcement of zoning laws and business licensing, the area under the direction of then mayor Rudoph Giuliani became a miracle of urban renewal. The massage parlors, peep shows, strip clubs, pawn shops, hooker bars, triple-X movie theaters, adult book stores, and scummy fast food joints were forced out. Planet Hollywood and scores of other multi-national restaurant, tavern and clothing chains moved in and made the Times Square enterprise zone their base for spreading American consumerist homogeneity throughout the Big Apple, eventually turning the entire area into a family-friendly tourist trap — a Universal Studios City Walk with a New York accent.

Billy ordered the Spaghetti Pomodoro, sipped on a glass of ice water with a slice of lemon hanging on the lip, and watched people stroll leisurely by.

They had to be from out of state. They were smiling.

Several booths away and behind him, a boisterous group of six was arguing and causing such a ruckus, Billy's curiosity got the best of him and he turned around to see what was going on. The manager of the restaurant was standing there, partially blocking Billy's view. But it looked like they were members of a rock band, some local act he didn't think he recognized. All musicians wore the same uniform anyway, so it was hard to tell them apart. The manager was trying to keep his cool, but was becoming more animated and appeared to be on the verge of throwing them out.

Then the person directly behind the manager stood up. Billy recognized her at once.

Amethyst Reigns. That must be her band. There was one extra guy with them who stood out only because he didn't. Unlike the other boys, he had on an ordinary button-down shirt over a white cotton undershirt, and a haircut he couldn't have paid more than six bucks for. Maybe he was the band's manager. Amethyst had mentioned something about a manager at the Mercury Lounge gig.

She spotted Billy, winked and gave him a peculiar but not unfriendly smile, then flipped off everyone at her booth and walked over to him.

"Can you help me out?"

"Why me?"

She nodded towards a fat, balding man across the aisle in a three-piece suit with the juice from a BBQ Bacon Cheeseburger running down his chin, trying look up the skirt of a waitress at the next table. She was immodestly bending over to serve another customer.

"Because fat fuck there is busy."

She gave him the address and directions for her studio loft in Soho — an area that had so far been spared being gentrified into million-dollar warehouse spaces and store fronts — and asked him to be there day after tomorrow.

"Say around 6 pm."

"What's the favor?"

Amethyst laid her hand on the table palm up.

"Press the center of my palm with your index finger."

He did.

She held up three fingers.

"How many?"

"Three."

"Perfect. You can handle this. You may be overqualified."

Amethyst then reached down the front of her lowrider pants and pulled out a small medicinal locket. She showed it to him.

"Used to belong to my grandmother."

She took out a tiny pill and handed it to Billy.

"What's this?"

"2Cb."

"What's that?"

"Trust me. Just take it."

Billy spent that evening and the entire night sitting on a bench in a large, popular park near Cooper Union. He wanted to move but at the same time didn't.

On a scrim that seemed to cover the entire range of his vision, projected from the occipital lobe of his brain like smoky filaments onto the shimmering fabric wherever he looked, were images from the last five or so years. If proper billing were to be had, he and Natalie were co-stars of what appeared to be both a comedy and tragedy, though a myriad of other major and minor characters made their appearances.

It was a plotless montage. Or maybe a cinema nouveau experimental piece, ignoring the need for clear exposition and narrative continuity. It was a long dark movie, in the end making obvious that the comedy was only there to mock the tragedy, ultimately pointing to the pointlessness and futility of everything.

The sun came up, as much as it ever came up on the murky eastern horizon over Brooklyn.

He watched as the pace of the city picked up. Never fully asleep, it quickly returned to its normal adrenalin raging tempo, horns blaring, tires squealing, pedestrians hurrying to their daily destinations.

Billy sat motionless but alert.

He had thought with making new acquaintances — Candy and Amethyst featuring prominently — and the change of scene, he would beat the grinning Grim Reaper of the living dead, the orchestrator of his nightmares, choreographer of the ghosts of his past, that demon dervish who with the sinister twirling of his mustache and arrogant flicking of his fingers, played Billy like a puppet slave, jerking and twisting him into impossible and agonizing shapes, torturing him with the worst suffering of all, the self-inflicted pain of his own self-loathing.

Billy stood up, exhausted and drained. He felt foamy and spent. Eviscerated.

Marginally confident now that he could distinguish the navigable elements of reality from the hallucinations, he started making his way back to his apartment.

It was fully light now. The street lamps had all been turned off. He walked across 6th Street, down 2nd Avenue, across 3rd Street, cut through a small park. Behind the only bench in the park was the body of an old man, probably a bum, judging from the state of his clothing, his lack of shoes, and the layer of grime on his feet, hands and face. The old man's head was bashed in and a large pool of blood spread out around him. He was obviously dead.

Billy stared at the corpse for some time, intrigued by the amoeba-shaped hematological puddle that in slow motion was pooling on the cement walkway. His emotional stasis felt curious. He was not in the least concerned about the loss of the man's life, or even what his own role as an innocent bystander might entail. He felt nothing.

Finally he exited the park.

He continued along 2nd Avenue and spotted some graffiti on an abandoned building. Primitive and spartan. Nothing to distract from the message.

Art imitates life.
Life imitates art.

Okay. But what if there was no art?

Would that be the end of life?

Ah! That's what happened.

Art disappeared. Everyone died.

Metaphorically speaking, of course.

He stopped at a liquor store. How could you not love a town where the liquor stores open for business at eight in the morning?

Finally back to the dismal torpor, the sheer ugliness of what he called home.

In less time than it would have taken him to eat the bowl of cereal he should have had, Billy finished two bottles of pre-mixed margaritas.

He slept for 14 hours straight. Then he smoked a joint. Slept 9 more hours.

When he finally woke up, he saw that someone had thrown a brick through his window. There was no note attached, so it wasn't a secret admirer.

He carefully picked up the large shards of glass, whisk-broomed the splinters into a dustpan.

Maybe he should read a book. He still had those same two staring back at him bedside.

Naw! Too much work. He might learn something. Or worse, find out things he didn't want to know. He had already had too much of that.

Billy lay down. Not that much different than sitting up. Except he had a better view of the water-stained, yellowed, peeling paint on his ceiling.

He wished he lived by a beach.

That way he could stick his head in the sand.

Up his ass would have to do for now.